# THE HAWKSBRIDGE ANGELS

*By Julian Smart*

The Hawksbridge Angels

The Train to Hawksbridge

The Ramsburgh Variations

The Hawksbridge Worm

Emma Vernon's Northminster Ghost Stories (with Harriet Smart)

# THE HAWKSBRIDGE ANGELS

## A THOMAS RUFFORD MYSTERY

by

**Julian Smart**

Published by Anthemion



First Edition



ISBN 978-1-907873-70-6

Made with Jutoh

# PREFACE

IT is a question that confronts every scribbler of memoirs – do the events of his life merit a literary treatment? It is a bold thing, to be the narrator of one's own story – how can one be sure that what is extraordinary to the writer, is not commonplace to the reader? – who might perhaps have had even more outlandish experiences, and might scoff at one's own.

It is well known how the brain tends to fashion a story out of the sequence of events known as the human life. Therefore, is not every life a story? How, then, should we determine which should be written down and offered up, and which should not?

I am glad to say that my life as a philosopher is behind me, and therefore I shall answer the question purely from the perspective of the markets, which regulate so much of our lives. A story is worth telling when the readers deem it so. And I therefore submit my tale to the whims of the market, happy to let my readers decide my literary fate, and if the mood takes them, to commend it to others.

Now I have justified the arrogance of publication to myself in a general sort of way – by reducing it to the standing of a commodity such as soap or marmalade – I will add some remarks about the book itself, that might save the reader from needing to consume a large portion of the book before taking its measure as worthy of his time. After all, the content of a book is less manifest than a bar of soap or a jar of marmalade.

My story concerns a young man who tires of a rarefied academic existence and whose life is upended when fate, and a delinquent father, bequeath him a gift that takes him to an obscure town in northern England. He becomes entangled in a deadly mystery that concerns both outsiders – including two artists that may be well known to you – and the townsfolk. While the outcome of this case may also be known to you from the national press, the intimate story of this young man and his own troubles will not. It may amuse you to compare what you have read in the press, with the perspective of one who lived through each tormenting episode. And I present the further strange puzzles and secrets that our hero encountered, and of course the people he befriended, and the enemies he made, for you to love or hate, as you see fit.

As I pen this, it occurs to me that I may damn myself with my writing, especially where pride lurks behind the narration of my adventures. In that I may still be as naive as that man of nine-and-twenty stepping onto the train to Newcastle in search of a new life, all those years ago. Well, be that as it may – the facts are as unembellished as I can manage, and if I present a picture of a flawed man, then I have no regrets for recording the truth. Judge – and enjoy – as you will!

— Thomas Rufford, June 1862

*Where the heart leads, the head surely follows.*

— Iona Tavistock

# CHAPTER ONE

## July, 1848

MR Richard Fenwick, of Fenwick & Tripp, gestured elegantly towards a chair, and I sat down, surveying the sparsely-furnished office. Pictures of long-dead solicitors and old scenes of Blackheath decorated its walls. I wondered what motivated a man to pursue an airless life of arcane language and the mostly tedious intricacies of strangers' lives. A good income, I supposed, and the less tangible benefit of respectability.

"How is life in Oxford, Mr Rufford?" said Mr Fenwick. "I gather you are a Fellow at Queen Mary College now – that must be satisfying."

I shrugged and uneasily pushed my hand through my hair. It was not a topic I liked to discuss. "I fear I'm losing faith in academia," I said. "I don't like what I'm becoming – rarefied, and inward looking."

"Oh dear!" said Mr Fenwick, evidently at a loss for a reaction to this. His solution was to change the subject. "I'm sorry about your father, Mr Rufford. Dr Rufford was much loved, and will be missed. I have experience of his care, and his skill and authority were most impressive."

"Thank you," I said. Mr Fenwick seemed genuine in his regret.

"It was heartbreaking to hear of his admittance to Greenwich Asylum last year. Fortunately, as you know from my letter, he made a will when he was still of sound mind. I thought it best to discuss the contents with you in person – thank you for making the journey."

"It was little trouble, as I had to attend the funeral yesterday," I said. This had been a perfunctory affair, with few attendees as my father had alienated most of his friends and relatives in the latter part of his life, with his drinking and womanising. My mother had died a few years ago – perhaps of a broken heart. It had been a love match, from what she had told me; but she had been sorely disappointed from almost the first day of their marriage. My father was quite incapable of fidelity.

"Now, if we may consider the will," said Mr Fenwick. "Things are simpler for me to administer as you have no siblings."

He gave a nervous laugh, and I could see he immediately regretted the remark. As Mr Fenwick winced and coughed at his own insensitivity, I said, "I never craved a brother or a sister, but that is my weakness for wishing away any competition!"

Mr Fenwick cast a grateful glance at me before continuing.

"Well, you are the main beneficiary. However, there are also debts, and I'm afraid they amount to not much less than the value of your father's house. So I suggest that the house be sold."

"Not to worry," I said. "I haven't been living off my expectations!" I laughed at the thought. "I said my goodbyes to the house last night." With only the housekeeper for company, I had spent a melancholy evening among the familiar surroundings of my childhood home in Blackheath.

"I don't have room for any of the furniture," I continued, "and I never cared for my parents' taste in art, so I would be grateful if you could arrange for its dispersal." I started to rise from my chair.

"Please be seated, Mr Rufford. There is more, and it may come as a slight shock."

"Oh?" I said, lowering myself back into my chair.

"There are also some investments, totalling some £10,000 – railways, sugar, that kind of thing."

"Goodness," I said. "That is surprising."

"Certainly a gratifying amount. However, that is not what I meant to warn you about. I don't know if your father – or mother – ever mentioned a Mrs Margaret Kington?"

I strained my memory. "No – I can't say that name means anything to me. How is she relevant?"

Mr Fenwick adopted an expression one might pull when chewing a piece of gristle. "How can I put this delicately? Your father had a relationship with Mrs Kington – now deceased – for a number of years. She was a patient of his. I'm sorry to have to bring this up."

"Ah. Well, my father was imperfect, but I was seldom aware of the details. My poor mother did her best to protect me."

"She was indeed a saint!" said Mr Fenwick. "But I don't think she knew that Mrs Kington had left your father her house."

"Her house?" I repeated, incredulously. "Why on earth would she...?"

"She had no male heirs – having sadly had a number of miscarriages – and she was clearly in love with your father. Your father confided in me about her twelve years ago, and the affair lasted until she died a couple of years ago. I wonder if her death hastened the sickness of his mind. It is really very sad."

I was silent for a minute while I took in Mr Fenwick's information. It meant that my father had been preoccupied with this woman since I was around thirteen years old. What mental tortures had my mother silently suffered, all this time?

Mr Fenwick gave me a few moments before continuing. "So your father has owned the property – near Hawksbridge, in Northumberland – for two years. And now it is yours."

"Good God," I said. "What kind of house is it?"

"It's called Ramsburgh, and I gather from the deeds – and your father's allusions to it – that it is generously proportioned. Mrs Kington's husband was a businessman with many interests, and quite wealthy, and he predeceased her. I believe she bequeathed most of her money to good causes, but the house had sentimental value to them – that is, Mrs Kington and your father."

"How extraordinary," I said. "So that's where my father went on those long trips." I sighed. "I didn't expect to learn so much about my father today."

"The house is occupied by a caretaker, but I don't have an up-to-date report on the house's condition. So it may end up costing you a fair amount, unfortunately. It's a mixed blessing, shall we say! But if you wish, it can be sold."

"I will go and inspect the place," I said. "I would like to revel in my ownership for a little, while I consider what to do."

"Of course," said Mr Fenwick, placing a large bunch of keys on the desk. "Best of luck with it. But Mr Rufford – please don't get up just yet."

I smiled and settled in my seat again. "What now, Mr Fenwick? Not another house? Or have I inherited some lawsuits from the neighbours?"

Mr Fenwick got up and with some effort, took hold of a tea chest that had been sitting next to his desk, incongruous in its roughness next to the well-crafted and highly polished furniture around it. He placed it next to my chair.

"This is yours. Please take a look, and I will explain."

Frowning, I dipped my hand into the sawdust, pulling out a patterned plate adorned with Chinese dragons and a gold rim. I then extracted a small coffee cup, similarly decorated. I looked at Mr Fenwick, eyebrows raised.

"It's a box of samples that Mrs Kington sent to your father."

"I see. They are quite pleasing, I suppose. Do they have any significance?" I said.

"Yes, Mr Rufford. You now own the factory that made them."

~

The Great Western Railway train back to Oxford was busy, and even the First Class carriage felt cramped. I stared through the open door in a reverie, recapitulating my conversation with Mr Fenwick, until I was startled by the door slamming shut. On my knees I held a small wooden box, which I had requested be filled with some of the smaller items from the crate for me to take home.

My head was full of questions and vague images – a house that shifted in my mind between various sizes, designs and ages, and a brick factory with huge chimneys and rows of enslaved workers. And a small town in the north of England – remote from the society I was used to, and no doubt remote too from the pontifications and intellectual sparring that characterised my Oxford life. What a relief it would be, to sweep that all away and live a more practical life – and yet might my brain atrophy? Might this accelerate a tendency to mental infirmity that was, even now, in my bloodstream, a distinctly unwelcome inheritance?

It was true that my current existence was becoming uncomfortable. A short-lived love affair had introduced awkwardness between her father – a colleague – and myself. My research on the philosophy of sexual relations had met with a frosty reception, and one of my best friends had left the town – and the academic life – to work in the family business. Although I should be proud of my Fellowship, and privileged to call the beautiful city of Oxford my home, there was something missing.

Keen to distract myself and return to the physical world, I

opened the box and took out a coffee cup, unfolding its linen wrapper carefully and turning the object in my hand. I looked intensely at the pattern, as if it held the answer to my future.

"I always think it looks more like a lion than a dragon."

I looked up, and found that the speaker was a handsome woman some fifteen or twenty years my senior, wearing a flamboyant hat and an embroidered burgundy cloak over a green and white striped dress. In the depth of my contemplations, I had not registered anything about my opposite companion beyond a blur of material and skin.

"Yes," I said. "I have to say, it does resemble a lion, now you mention it. I imagine the lion was a more compliant model."

She smiled, and her penetrating and approving look heated my cheeks. The intensity of her female energy was extraordinary.

"Hawksbridge Dragon," she said. "I have some myself. A gift for a lady, perhaps?"

"Well, no," I said, wondering how much to explain. "It's a gift to me, in a manner of speaking. An inheritance."

"I see. Just enough for an intimate coffee party?" Then she slyly added, leaning forward in a conspiratorial manner: "For example, you, me, and an interesting person of our mutual choosing? I look forward to it."

Embarrassed, I looked around. Some of the others in the carriage were determinedly pretending not to hear, while others were staring in a disapproving manner. A middle-aged businessman next to me, sporting a large, white moustache, looked up from his book and said, "Really! Have you no shame, madam?"

My companion turned slowly and deliberately to face him and stared at him for a few painful seconds. The man started to flush and sniff.

"More than you have manners, sir," she said, and turning back to me, she smiled as though entirely unperturbed. It was a fine example of self-control and I was tempted to applaud. The man muttered under his breath and went back to his book, and the other disapprovers were rattled enough to look away. My companion was clearly the dominant animal in this pack.

"Now, where were we? Ah yes – we were arranging a little coffee party. In which case, I should introduce myself. My name is Francesca Campbell." She leant forward to shake my hand.

"Thomas Rufford," I said, transferring the cup to my left hand in order to free the other.

At that moment, the train moved off with a judder, and the cup flew from my hand, landing in several pieces at Mrs Campbell's feet.

"Oh, bad luck," she said, picking up the pieces and handing them to me. "We may have to disinvite our distinguished guest."

"Not necessarily," I said, putting the pieces in the box. "It seems I may have access to unlimited supplies."

"Interesting," said Mrs Campbell. "Aha! Your inheritance. Let me see... you are agonising over giving up your present life, and moving to an obscure northern town – Hawksbridge."

My look of amazement encouraged her further.

"I could see it in your face when I got into the carriage. I flatter myself – forgive me, I am too young to eschew vanity, but too old to care who knows it – when I say that most young men are distracted by my presence. You, on the other hand, were distracted by something momentous happening in your life. You have supplied the remaining clues."

"You astonish me, Mrs Campbell," I said. "I have barely begun to decide what to do about this" – I tapped the box – "but a complete change does have its appeal."

"Precisely my attitude, and indeed, my conundrum! I am on my way to visit an old friend, who is tolerant of my foibles – but she is the exception. My dead husband's friends bore me to death, and my family are cold fish. So I have been thinking of sticking a pin in a map, and finding a new place to amuse me."

"As casually as that?" I said. "You wouldn't fear ending up on a mountainside with only goats for company?"

"Oh, I am used to old goats. But perhaps you are right; a more orderly method might be better. I could pick a town name from the conversation I overhear on the train. For example, the first town mentioned by a presentable young fellow on a train. That's as good a method as any, would you not say?"

~

By the time Mrs Campbell and I had stretched our aching limbs and alit from the train into the gloom of the station, I had acquired a vivid picture of my companion's interests. These were many and varied, and included horse-riding, opera, and European travel; but I suspected that the most intriguing aspects of her life could not be discussed in a public carriage. It was a shame, I reflected, as I placed my box of china on the platform, that I would never unlock those mysteries.

"Well, goodbye, Mr Rufford!" she said, extending a hand. "I have enjoyed our conversations immensely. It would have been fearfully tedious otherwise. Perhaps we shall meet in Hawksbridge, and we will have coffee in dragon cups, and remember our journey like old friends!"

"I should like that, Mrs Campbell," I said, enjoying the strength of her grasp, "though I think our futures may be too uncertain. It has been a real pleasure – and unexpected."

Mrs Campbell gave me her most devastating and enigmatic smile. "My carriage awaits. Good luck in Hawksbridge!"

For a minute I stood and watched her walk down the platform with her bag. It was hard to know which part of the day was more fantastical. I felt a pang of regret as I realised that I would probably never see Mrs Campbell again; and if I should seek her out, the magic would be lost, and she might be a stranger to me, having moved on to other things, other people, and the new horizons she was searching for. I wondered if she might be the kind of person who never found the elusive life that only existed in her imagination. How could reality ever live up to her energy and expectations? Did that make contentment impossible?

"Oi! Watch yourself!" a voice said, and I realised I was an obstacle in the flow of disembarking passengers. I picked up my box and set off for the college.

It was a pleasant walk in the failing evening light, and when I arrived, my aching arms forced me to set the box down for a few minutes. I had stopped outside the college chapel, and the choir was practising. The heavenly chords and cadences, and the beauty of all the ancient buildings that made up Queen Mary College, seemed to be telling me to stay. This was an embodiment of civilisation that would surely not be found in a small market town in the north of England. And yet, I was suspicious of the privilege that was currently granted to me. I did not wish to grow fat and complacent and arrogant, and gradually ossify into one of the busts that lined the niches of the college's Great Hall. The thought of being further suffocated by the formality and strictures – of which there were many – was quite unbearable.

"I am not my own man here," I said aloud. "You are beautiful, but I will not be captured." In that moment my mind was made up, and picking up the little, fragile box that contained a part of my destiny, I strode back to my panelled and gilded cage. The bars would be dismantled tomorrow, and I would prepare to face all the new challenges of a place called Hawksbridge.

# CHAPTER TWO

THE excitement of my momentous decision was tempered by a sense of loss, not only of the familiarity and charm of Oxford, but of a dazzling light that had shone on me for a few hours, before being extinguished. A tangible darkness remained: the absence of Mrs Campbell. No doubt she had this effect on all the men she met – and some of the women – and she knew it. It was a combination of grace, beauty, intelligence and energy – in other words, the life-force; the essence of what it meant to be a human being.

But I forced myself to push Mrs Campbell to a corner of my mind, and concentrate on the task in hand: to give notice, to write to warn the caretaker at Hawksbridge of my imminent arrival, and to make travel arrangements for myself, and – to be sent separately – my possessions. The Oxford term had ended, so there would be little trouble from the Dean. And there were precious few people to mourn my absence.

It took only a fortnight for me to find myself travelling again, this time a tortuous journey northwards to Newcastle, with nights also spent in London, Nottingham and Leeds. Now there was no interesting female to distract me from a sense of foreboding – a visceral sensation that I had made entirely the wrong decision and was about to make a great fool of myself in a crumbling ruin in a town that did not need me. I had not yet made contact with the Hawksbridge Pottery Company Limited – I had spent an hour drafting a letter, but had torn it up after deeming it pompous and priggish. I was sure any interference from me would be most unwelcome. But I would pay them a visit when I was settled into my house, or rather (if I was honest with myself) when I had found the courage.

The changing accents at each inn reminded me of how far from familiarity I was straying. Even with the newly-laid train lines, spreading ever more rapidly across the country, the going seemed slow and tedious. When my train finally pulled noisily into Newcastle, I was sick of the taste of coal smoke and the constant chatter of my fellow travellers. My bones ached, and I longed for a bath.

From the station, I could see a huge new hotel being constructed, with an elaborately-decorated stone façade: long rows of windows were stacked six or seven high, with alternating curved and triangular pediments that were designed to mesmerise and lure visitors with classical excess.

The promise of luxury was tantalising, but I had to trudge a little farther to an ancient inn near the centre of the city. The stationmaster at Oxford had recommended it and given me directions: "My choice would be The Old George, sir – it's humble, but quite adequate for a night, and you can walk from the station. There are more costly and glossy places, but they can be busy and you don't want to be wandering around the city all tired and famished, sir!"

I was grateful for the man's consideration – at this point, any berth would have done. However, it was a longer walk than I had anticipated, and darkness began to clothe the jumble of buildings in a sinister shroud. As I turned into Old George Yard with the hotel in sight, I nearly collided with a thin-faced girl who was leaning against a wall. My heart gave a lurch and my tired brain was thrown into confusion. "Hazel! what... how...?" But my beloved, wronged, Hazel was long gone, and as I looked closer, I could see that the similarity was superficial.

"I could be Hazel! Yes, that's a pretty name. Would you like to buy Hazel a drink, sir? You look like you need one yourself."

I felt a mix of pity for the young girl, who was trying her

best to be beguiling – despite her conspicuous lack of nourishment and her patched coat – and utter embarrassment at my mistake.

"I'm sorry, I mistook you for someone else. But she's dead..."

"Bloody hell, what a gent you are!" she said. "I look like your dead doxy, do I? Well, you can go to blazes." She spat on the cobbles, and sidled away, seeing no prospect of business here.

~

Standing listlessly at the windows of my room, on the top floor of the inn, I stared out through the lumpy glass panes at the collage of walls and roofs that the gas lamps of Newcastle were struggling to illuminate. I had entered the inn in a foul mood, which had diminished a little after a welcome if fatty meal of mutton.

I opened a window, and music floated up to me from the tap room, where guests were having an uproarious time – contrasting all the more woefully with my own state. Someone was performing a popular song, and his audience was joining in lustily for the chorus, which was all I could make out:

So pity me, pity me, maiden am I
No lover to kiss me, nor with me to lie
A maiden I'll stay, unkissed will I be
Till the waves and the wind bring my true love to me.

She was certainly no maiden, the poor girl I had encountered. Somewhere in the gloom, she was probably still plying her trade. At least Hazel had never needed to do that. And then I remembered, as I did too many times to count, that without me, Hazel would still be alive and busying herself in a lavish house – carrying the coal, dusting the statues, curtseying to her betters. Or she might have found a better love than mine, and be a solicitous mother to several adorable children, in a ramshackle but cheerfully painted cottage.

I shut the window to blot out the incongruous cheer below. My tears added to the distortions of the glass, until I could make out only meaningless shapes, and I closed the shutters and started to remove my dusty clothes. The room had a low ceiling, supported by crude, unpainted beams that were riddled with beetle tunnels, and they reminded me of the reason I was here. Was Ramsburgh a little like this place – sprawling, ravaged and worn out? Was it even habitable? I hoped that in the morning, my energy would return and I would feel the spirit of adventure flow through my veins once more, rather than the spectre of melancholy and defeat that now clung to me. I blew out the candle, drew a grey, greasy blanket over myself, and fell almost immediately into a deep sleep.

~

The bustle of the awakening city stirred me into consciousness an hour after dawn. I was refreshed, but I felt a twinge of nerves when I remembered that this was the day when I would don the mantle of a different life: that of a landowner and – how strange this sounded to my Oxford persona – a businessman. It was as if I had been offered a position, and this was the first day at the office, perhaps to be given the benefit of the doubt for a short while before being judged by those around me. But this was a position I could not easily resign or be ejected from.

The hotel manager found me a four-wheeler that would take me all the way to Hawksbridge – at considerable cost. I did not want to put up with a stagecoach's lack of privacy, with the added bother of finding a carriage to cover the last leg of the journey.

I watched Newcastle's streets become less showy as they approached the outskirts; huge, many-chimneyed factories were spreading in the cheaper districts. Who knew what toil and misery lay behind the blank brick façades: a thousand life stories made of hope and despair; human life forever renewing and stumbling on, despite everything that a relentlessly changing world conspired to throw in its path. As I looked out, I met the gaze of a man leaning his exhausted frame against a factory wall. With his lined, saggy features and dirty clothes, he had the look of a man who was ready to give up, but could not afford to, and he held my gaze steadfastly and accusingly as the carriage passed. I looked away and knew – at least for that instant – that I had no grounds for complaint.

At last the air cleared and I was in the country. For several hours, I watched the hedges and trees sail slowly past me; my book lay unread on my lap and I fell into uneasy contemplation of my past and future.

We stopped for lunch at a village inn, which was full of pipe smoke and strange vowel sounds, and I downed a welcome ale before my driver signalled the resumption of the journey. Another two hours passed before the heat and the rhythm of the four-wheeler lulled me to sleep.

I was in a railway carriage. Opposite me, Francesca was bestowing a devastating smile on me, one that told me of her desire for me. She spoke: "We will have coffee, my dear, and I will tell you all. You will have everything from me." She held out her clenched hand, but blood was dripping from it. She opened her hand to reveal a fragment of a broken cup, piercing her skin. Still she smiled.

I looked down at my knees and realised I was naked. At that moment, a familiar girl sat down next to Francesca. "Don't you have anything to do with him!" she said to

Francesca. "He's poison!" It was Hazel – or was it the prostitute? "Poison!" she repeated.

"But..." I found myself stammering. "I didn't mean to hurt anyone!"

"Go to blazes!" said whore-Hazel, opening the door and jumping out of the moving train with a shriek like a locomotive whistle.

Francesca's smile had vanished, replaced with a look of reproach and disdain that stabbed at me. "You have killed her," she said. "How could you?"

I tried to say "You are wrong about me," but the words made no sound. Francesca had become the man from the factory, staring and staring, accusing me as the representative of the well-born and comfortable.

The train stopped its jerky progress. "Ramsburgh!" the man suddenly said. I felt myself being shaken, and realised it was my driver. "We're at Ramsburgh, sir. I'll get your luggage."

~

Still dazed with sleep and disturbed by the lingering memory of my dream, I stood in the gravel driveway in the evening sunshine and looked up at the mass of sandstone blocks and windows that constituted Ramsburgh. A squat tower of four storeys seemed to be the most ancient part, adjoining a taller, slimmer sibling on its left. Then came other, more recent – and I supposed, more practical – additions, including a three-storey tower over an arched entrance. The overall effect was a pleasing jumble of misaligned frontages and varying roof levels, with crenellations that helped unify this accretion of parts.

"Damp and draughty, no doubt," said the driver. "Are you staying long? Maybe they'll put you in the big tower!" He chuckled to himself, presumably at the thought of my discomfort.

"Yes," I said. "I believe I'll be staying a while." I thanked and paid the driver, and was left alone with my bags on the gravel. It seemed that I had inherited a castle of moderate proportions: one that was mercifully fit for a family, not an entire garrison. At first glance, it did not seem in danger of falling down, but what lay within might tell a different story.

"Extraordinary," I said under my breath. Set in a cradle of mature, majestic trees, with distant hills visible beyond, the scene would not have disgraced the easel of a distinguished landscape painter.

I became aware of being watched; on the first floor of the old tower, I could see the face of a young woman at the window. From what I could make out of her, ill-lit and criss-crossed by astragals, she did not have the appearance of a servant. I smiled, and the woman returned a polite smile before withdrawing into the depths of her tower. "My tower," I mentally corrected myself.

There was the sound of a metal latch being opened, and a man of about thirty-five years strode from the Gothic entrance towards me. "Mr Rufford? I'm Matthew Shipley, the butler. Welcome to Ramsburgh, sir. I've been looking after the place for the last few years."

Unlike the woman in the window, Mr Shipley was not about to waste a smile on Ramsburgh's new master. His words were ostensibly welcoming, but I judged him to be less than pleased about sharing the house with a new male. He had probably enjoyed ruling the roost.

"Thank you, Mr Shipley – I appreciate you taking care of it, although I confess that until three weeks ago, I had no knowledge of the house's existence."

"So I understand from your letter," Mr Shipley said. "Mrs Kington liked to have her intrigues and secrets. But she trusted me, and you'll have no complaints about my service."

"I'm sure that's the case," I said, while not being very sure at all. I could not immediately judge if I liked Shipley: but then, perhaps we did not have to get on beyond the formalities and necessities of our relationship.

"I'll give you a tour of the house, sir," said Shipley, picking up my bags. I followed him into the hall. The room was whitewashed and a wide stone staircase wrapped around three sides; family portraits had been densely hung, accentuating my feeling of being a mere visitor. A large window high above the stairs gave a decent light, and the hall was a far cry from the bare stone, gloom and rusting suits of armour that I had imagined as I had approached the house.

Shipley ushered me into the drawing room, which was on the corner of the eighteenth-century part of the building. It was some thirty feet long with large windows on two sides, and comfortably furnished. For the first time, I had a sense that this could be home, combined with the peculiar feeling that it was far more than I deserved. I had not worked for it – it had simply fallen into my lap, complete with servants and faux ancestors. How was this right? The image of the reproachful factory man flickered into my mind. Somehow, I would have to prove myself worthy of it all.

A succession of rooms, stairs and corridors followed – a big dining room with a bay window, the kitchen in the old tower, and a rabbit warren of service rooms, including Shipley's room at another corner of the building. My bedroom was above the drawing room, also with huge windows on two sides, and above the dining room was a magnificent library with an oak desk that I could easily imagine myself behind, working on the book I always promised myself I would write.

There was an unobtrusive door at the end of the corridor by the library, that Shipley seemed intent on avoiding.

"Where does this lead?" I asked.

"That's to the stair servicing the old tower," said Shipley. "Beyond is Miss Davison's quarters, above the kitchen. I'll not intrude on her, and you can speak to yourself when you're ready."

"Miss Davison?"

"Mrs Kington's niece. She has permission to live here, ever since her parents died. She has this floor of the tower, and her old housekeeper, Mrs Northcutt – she was her nanny – has the floor above. Not good for her arthritis, those steps, but she turned her nose up at the East Cottage – mind you, it's cold and damp, so I don't blame her. The tower gets some of the heat from the kitchen, and the walls are three feet thick."

"I see," I said, taking this news in. "I hadn't realised I would be sharing the house." This would explain the woman in the window.

"Aye, I dare say it's a lot to swallow." Shipley laughed. "But it would be a shame to keep Ramsburgh all to yourself, wouldn't it? At least until you get yourself a wife. Miss Davison is a sour and contrary sort, or I'd suggest a marriage that would kill two birds with one stone! But you may find differently, sir."

"Yes, well – thank you, Shipley," I said, not appreciating this reference to my personal affairs, nor the unkind appraisal of my new neighbour. "I have no plans of that sort. Shall we look at the next floor?"

"Just some bedrooms, sir – nothing much to explain, so I'll leave it to you now. I'll go and find Mrs Felton, the housekeeper, and make sure the supper's in order. But we'll need to find a proper cook, sir."

"Yes, of course."

"Oh, and the maids are Alice and Pearl, sir."

"Thank you. I will be down before long."

I could not resist a peek behind the forbidden door. It opened onto a spiral stone staircase, and this was, I realised, the purpose of the slender tower. Opposite me, an ancient-looking door was set into the massive old tower wall, leading to Miss Davison's suite of rooms. I would pay her a call in the morning, when I was feeling fresher and, I hoped, a little more confident in my role of master of the house.

I felt the rigours of the journey begin to catch up with me, and I decided to postpone exploration of the remaining rooms and go straight to my bedroom, where Shipley had left my bags.

I surveyed my bedroom. The walls were decorated in a turquoise floral paper – perhaps a little feminine for my tastes, but not offensive. The bed was generous and fortunately not too frothy in its carvings, and there were two large mahogany chests of drawers, and an upholstered armchair. A few landscape paintings of indifferent quality hung on the walls, while a large ornate mirror had been placed over the fireplace. Whilst the furnishings would need to be changed in time, it was already a comfortable and calming room.

A bowl of water had been left for me on one of the chests, and stripping naked, I splashed it on myself, relishing the coldness and air upon my skin.

Drying myself, I went to the window that looked out westward, to the side of the house. The view over the hills was glorious, and the trees cast long shadows in the sinking sun. It might be a little inconvenient to be outside Hawksbridge, but the distance was not great, and Ramsburgh's situation did have the advantages of privacy and natural splendour.

Still naked, I went to the bed and lay down to test it – it was a little lumpy, but after the discomfort of the journey, it was heaven. I closed my eyes, and the power of my exhaustion overwhelmed me.

~

When I opened my eyes again, it was dark, save for a candle that had been left for me on a tray, together with some bread, cheese and fruit and a mug of what turned out to be weak beer. I realised with horror that some poor maid – or Shipley himself, or maybe Mrs Felton – had come in to find me asleep and unclad. This was not the ideal introduction to my staff: they would think me some kind of libertine. I hoped to God that I had not been having indecent dreams – of Francesca, perhaps – with embarrassing consequences. I would need to be more careful in future.

# CHAPTER THREE

MY waking consciousness struggled to find a sense of place. For a moment, before I opened me eyes, I was suspended in an alien world I could not grasp. Then I realised what was absent: the bustle of an Oxford college as its occupants prepared for the day, and the noise of carriages and tradesmen beyond the college gates.

Instead, there was birdsong, occasional distant footsteps and little else. It was at once frightening and exhilarating. The motivations and patterns of my old life were gone; a blank canvas had been laid out for me, and now I must learn to paint the colours of my future.

After throwing on some fresh clothes, I took my supper tray down to the kitchen. A heady aroma of bacon greeted me – the housekeeper was at the range, and she turned towards me with a welcoming smile.

"Ah! Mr Rufford! I'm very pleased to meet you, sir. Did you sleep well in your new house? It will take a while to be used to it, I expect. It's nice to see a proper master at Ramsburgh again, and I do hope you will be happy here. Let me take that for you, my dear. I'm Norah – Norah Felton."

Mrs Felton was in her fifties, with a friendly and motherly demeanour. Her natural beauty was still evident despite the burdens of age and duty.

I handed her the tray. "Glad to make your acquaintance, Mrs Felton. Do I have you to thank for bringing me my supper?"

"It was no bother, my dear," she said, composing her face and betraying only the briefest flash of an amused smile. "You were out cold, but I thought you might need something in case you woke in the night."

I coughed and broke her gaze, looking down at the cast iron hulk of the range and the spluttering bacon. "I'm sorry if – if I was not entirely – decent. I was tired and so I didn't..."

"Of course you were, my dear!" Mrs Felton touched my arm reassuringly. "I don't mind at all. You're a healthy young man, and these things happen! Don't you worry about it."

"Thank you," I said, relieved at her tolerance, although her words rather confirmed my mortifying state last night.

"Now then – if you go to the dining room, I'll bring you your breakfast."

I obeyed, and took up my place in the dining room, feeling distinctly awkward in solitary splendour at the head of such a large table. Perhaps, I thought, I could make a breakfast room out of my study, or some other smaller room.

I considered my new housekeeper and temporary cook. I had immediately felt at home with her, and what might have been an overly forward manner to some had seemed quite touching to me: and indeed, exactly what I needed to help steady me in this unfamiliar environment.

I had time to examine the room in more detail. Unlike the drawing room, which was adorned with oil portraits of a high quality, this room was cheaply hung with engravings – European and oriental scenes, which were pleasant enough, but hardly set the pulse racing. There was, however, one small portrait, in delicate pastels mounted in an oval frame: the serene face of a young woman confidently looked out at me. She wore a low-cut, blue dress, the diaphanous folds of which were economically suggested by smudges of white chalk, and there was the suggestion of a smile on her lips. Perhaps this was Mrs Kington, or her sister, Flora Davison's mother. It had often struck me that the more lifelike and beautiful an old portrait was, the more tragic it was for the beholder, knowing that the subject would in all probability be long gone. And this woman was indeed attractive.

Despite this morbid thought, I was just contemplating moving her to my bedroom to keep me company when Mrs Felton arrived with my breakfast.

"I hope this is all right, Mr Rufford. I'm not as good at making coffee as Mr Shipley, but it should be drinkable."

"This looks wonderful, Mrs Felton," I said. "And I wasn't expecting coffee. Thank you!"

Mrs Felton smiled, and as she turned to go, I said, "Mrs Felton – I'm thinking of calling on Miss Davison this morning. Is there anything I need to know, so I don't make a fool of myself?"

Mrs Felton stopped and thought, fiddling with a lock of hair that had become detached from her bun. "Well, her parents died when she was sixteen, of typhoid, God rest their souls. She has a housekeeper, Mrs Northcutt – Meg – who was her nanny, and is a bit severe – more serious than me, like! Protective of her mistress. But she will get used to you, and I dare say you will charm her soon enough. Miss Flora can seem frosty, but I think that's mostly shyness. She's used to being on her own. Though she will be glad of your company, and I do think she needs to see more of the world. She has made herself too comfortable in that tower!"

"Thank you," I said. "I will exercise caution."

"Good luck, sir! She won't bite. Meg, on the other hand..." She winked, and left me to my breakfast.

~

On my way out of the dining room, I encountered Mr Shipley in the hall. "Good morning, sir," Mr Shipley said. "I hope you had a pleasant night."

"Certainly, Shipley. Thank you." I examined Shipley's features for any sign that he knew what the housekeeper had seen, but Shipley had a butler's ability to adopt a blank expression when required. Was one eyebrow slightly raised? I would have to check for this potential signal in future, should any similar situation arose.

"Oh, Mr Rufford – we need to discuss a few administrative items," Shipley said. "We have some repairs to do, and I've taken the liberty of getting cost estimates from a number of builders. I just need to go through a few things."

I sighed. Since my meeting at the solicitor, the inevitability of facing building work lurked at the back of my mind – indeed, there might be a never-ending stream of it.

"Yes, of course. Shall we say this afternoon, at three? In my study?"

"Very good, sir."

Shipley went about his business, and I headed upstairs to seek out Flora. How very grand that sounded: 'My study.' It was next to the drawing room, and I had only poked my head in once. It was as much a sitting room as a study, with its comfortable armchairs and elegant tables, and a glorious view to the west gardens. Perhaps it had been an escape from the ladies for Mr Kington; somewhere to smoke and avoid conversations about flower arranging and the health of old relatives. But the ominous pile of paperwork that I had noticed on the desk meant that a desire to escape *from* the study would be more likely.

I opened the door to the staircase tower, feeling a little giddy at the sight of the stone stairs winding down to the ground floor. I approached the door to Miss Davison's suite and knocked. I heard nothing, so knocked again, more loudly.

After a few seconds, I heard footsteps, and the door opened. In the doorway stood a young woman with an uncanny resemblance to the woman in the portrait.

"Oh! Mr Rufford, is it?" she said.

"How do you do, Miss Davison! Yes, Thomas Rufford – I do hope I'm not disturbing you, but I wanted to come and pay my respects. Shall I return another time?"

"No, now is fine," she said. "Do come through."

I followed her into a narrow hallway, passing a door to what I assumed was her bedroom. Also off the hall was another spiral staircase, which presumably led up to her housekeeper's rooms. Her sitting room was at the back of the tower above the main kitchen. The only window was small and overlooked a courtyard to the rear of the house; but Miss Davison – or whoever had decorated these rooms – had made the most of the scant light with bright yellow wallpaper and a large mirror opposite the window.

My hostess sat down on a small sofa, and indicated an austere-looking elbow chair, whose hard seat thankfully bore a faded tapestry cushion.

I heard slow footsteps descending the internal stairs, and an unsmiling, thin woman in her sixties appeared in the sitting room doorway. "Who is your visitor, Flora?" she demanded, standing with her hands on her hips.

"It's Mr Rufford, Meg. This is my housekeeper Mrs Northcutt, Mr Rufford."

I got up and extended a hand. Mrs Northcutt did not take it, but instead peered at me suspiciously. "I see," she said. "I thought you looked familiar. About time there was a captain of this ship, but I'm jiggered if I can understand why it should be you. Your father was –"

"All right, Meg, thank you – we can manage."

Mrs Northcutt muttered something under her breath, and slowly and deliberately stomped back up her narrow staircase to her quarters, sighing with rheumatic pain. There was something comical about this performance that made me forgive her rudeness.

"So, Mr Rufford – how are you enjoying Ramsburgh?" Miss Davison said, fixing me with piercing eyes.

She had probably not meant it that way, but to me, her enquiry seemed proprietorial, as if I were merely staying at a genteel hotel, and she were its manageress. It must be difficult for her, I reflected, to have her private domain invaded, when she had been queen of the castle for the last few years.

"It's splendid," I said. "I had not expected it to be quite like this. I haven't taken it all in yet."

"Ah. You did not expect a lodger, did you, Mr Rufford? I'm sorry to take up valuable space in your house."

There it was – the bitterness of the niece who was disappointed in her expectations, aware of the indignity of being there on sufferance as a poor relation instead of being handed the glory and status of ownership.

I stroked the arms of my chair, rendered smooth from many years of similarly absent-minded handling. "Miss Davison, that is a little unfair – naturally, I have no objection to your staying! I realise how difficult it must be for you."

Miss Davison remained silent for a moment, her jaw clenched defiantly, still observing me. "Oh, it can't be helped," she said eventually. "My aunt must have fallen deeply in love with your father, scandalous though it was at the time."

I was curious. "Did you meet my father? What did you make of him?"

A ginger cat was nosing around, sniffing at my shoes, and it jumped onto Miss Davison's lap. "Yes, he was here as a guest," she said, "both before Mr Kington died, and after. He was... affable, I suppose most people would have said. He was often making jokes and telling anecdotes, about patients or his travels. I could tell that my aunt admired him a little too much from the first time he visited. My uncle was ill, and was mostly confined to his bed, so thank goodness he could not see the way she looked at your father – at least, I hope not. It was cruel. I'm sorry, Mr Rufford, but it was." Her irritation was reflected in the way she dumped the cat onto the ground, and it ran out of the room in disgust.

"Indeed," I said. "I would not defend my father in any way. I had only an inkling of his behaviour; my mother must have suffered greatly. I gather they met when he treated your aunt's heart condition in London."

Miss Davison snorted. "How appropriate," she said, pursing her lips and staring at her knotted hands.

I stood up and walked to the window, feeling suddenly breathless and confined. Then I turned and said, "I apologise for my father, Miss Davison. He has disrupted this house, and your family. I can only try to do the best I can here in Ramsburgh, and in Hawksbridge. And I shall be very glad of any advice you can give me – you must be very familiar with how Hawksbridge society works."

Miss Davison nodded her head almost imperceptibly in acknowledgement of my apology, and said, "I lead a quiet life here, so I don't follow all that goes on, but I will be as helpful as I can. Perhaps I can start with a little warning about Mr Shipley."

"Oh?" I said. I did not particularly want to hear gossip that would complicate my relationship with my staff, but there was nothing to be done except to hear her out.

"He has taken a few liberties with the house, I'm afraid. He is far too partial to drink, and has entertained women in the house. I do not get on with Mr Shipley, and he does not care for me."

"I'm sorry to hear that," I said. "I will bear it in mind. So far he has not stepped out of line with me. I hope you will not dispel my favourable impression of Mrs Felton: she seems a reliable sort, and she has been kind to me this morning."

Miss Davison smiled. "I like Mrs Felton – she doesn't wear any nonsense. She did not take to your father, so it is admirable that she is not prejudiced against you."

I felt a strong desire to terminate this encounter, that if prolonged, would only further expose the strangeness of my position and the paternal misconduct that lay behind it.

"Thank you for seeing me, Miss Davison," I said. "It was a pleasure to meet you. Perhaps you will dine with me now and again."

"Of course," said Miss Davison, leading me back into the small hall. "Oh – I nearly forgot. The Rector – Mr Neville – was here yesterday wanting to speak to you. He strongly disagrees with your choice of artists for the Market Hall murals, and wishes to dissuade you from employing them."

My blank expression elicited a look of pity mixed with impatience.

"You don't know about...?"

At that moment, there was a shriek from the floor above. "Flora!" came the stern voice of Mrs Northcutt. "Your wretched cat has dug its claws into me again!"

"I'm sorry, Mr Rufford, I must go and attend to Titian. He becomes impossible if his routine is interrupted. Mr Neville will doubtless call again soon and will explain about the murals. Goodbye!"

The door closed on me, and I could hear the muffled complaints of Mrs Northcutt and Flora's apologies. I lingered for a moment in the dark limbo of the staircase tower, pressing my hands to its cool walls in an attempt to distract my senses. I contemplated this first meeting: the more I considered it, the more unsatisfactory it was. As I suspected that she might, Miss Davison still bore feelings of injustice; my father had been an embarrassment and a source of conflict and misery in the house, and that he – and then his son – should inherit it was a horrible travesty.

And yet, I reminded myself, Shipley recognised my authority, and Mrs Felton had betrayed no sign of her antipathy to my father.

I opened the door to my landing, momentarily flooding the tower with light, and felt relief as I went through and closed it behind me.

It was mildly annoying that Miss Davison had not explained about the murals and the agitated Rector. There seemed to have been a case of mistaken identity. But it would be interesting to meet the Rector anyway, as an emissary of Hawksbridge society – he might suggest ways in which I could make myself useful to the town, and begin to atone for my father's sins.

# CHAPTER FOUR

MY second awakening in Ramsburgh was more satisfactory than the first, with no sense of embarrassment and – despite Flora – less guilt at being an interloper in my own property. I was now master of Ramsburgh, come what may, and I was determined that whatever this afternoon's revelations about the condition of the house, I would not be intimidated.

Mrs Felton was as cheerful and accommodating as she had been yesterday. I had just speared the last rasher of bacon with my fork when I heard the doorbell ring, followed by the sound of male voices, and after a moment Shipley entered the dining room.

"Excuse me, sir – it's the Rector, Mr Neville. I've asked him to wait in the hall – will you receive him?"

I was intrigued. It seemed Flora's mystery might be solved sooner than I had expected. "Please show him into the drawing room, Shipley, and I'll be there directly," I said, finishing the last dregs of my coffee. "Oh, and if you could provide him with some tea or coffee?"

"Very good, sir."

I would have preferred a little more preparation for this encounter with a representative of the Hawksbridge establishment. But I straightened my back and reminded myself that I was myself now a man of consequence. I strode into the drawing room with such assumed confidence that I wondered whether I was overplaying it, and slowed my pace.

"Mr Neville, good morning! I'm very glad to meet you," I said. "Thomas Rufford. Miss Davison said that you might visit again soon." I held my hand out.

Mr Horace Neville rose from his chair to shake my hand. In his late forties, with greying hair, strong cheekbones and sunken eyes, Mr Neville had an air of benign solemnity shaped by the demands and rituals of his religion. It flashed through my mind that Mr Neville had the advantage of many years' practice for his role in this scene, whereas I was a novice at mine.

"Mr Rufford, I am pleased to meet you too. Let me welcome you warmly to Hawksbridge. I hope to see you at St Ninian's on Sunday." His handshake was firm, and his demeanour wary, I thought. "But I must confess that I am preoccupied with the matter of the mural – please forgive me if I cannot indulge in the pleasant conversation that our first meeting deserves." He sat down again and pursed his lips.

"I'm sorry to hear that, Mr Neville," I said. "If I can help, I will. Would you be so kind as to explain the situation to me? I have much to discover about Hawksbridge."

"Very well. You are aware of the imminent decision by the Mural Committee?"

"Alas," I said, "I am barely aware of a mural, except of its existence, as Miss Davison mentioned."

"It does not exist, yet, and if it goes ahead as most of the Committee seem to want – it will be a stain upon Hawksbridge. I do not exaggerate, sir."

I was baffled, and a little amused that Mr Neville was getting himself so exercised about a painting. "Surely," I said, "it cannot be as harmful as that, can it?"

The Rector sighed. "I see that I will need to explain it from the beginning."

Mrs Felton brought in a tray and began to serve tea. "I didn't know if you wanted tea so soon after your coffee, my dear," she said to me, "but I brought in a cup for you anyway."

"Thank you, Mrs Felton," I said, cringing at her familiarity in front of the Rector, and yet a little gratified by her warmth. I had evidently drawn out Mrs Felton's maternal instincts. "Yes, please."

The Rector waited for Mrs Felton to leave before taking a sip of tea and launching into his explanation.

"I have to go back fifty years. This was when the Town Hall was built – given to the town by Sir Horatio Tantallon, whose son perished with a dozen or so townsfolk in a terrible fire. It was at his textile mill, in Roman Street, and he blamed himself – he was a broken man thereafter, and the new Town Hall was his penance. Sir Horatio died of grief before the building was completed, and although he spoke of religious decoration inside the hall to remember the victims of the fire – proposing the idea of angels rescuing the souls of the victims from the factory – it was never done. There was simply no money left."

I nodded. "And now there are moves afoot to complete Tantallon's project?"

"Exactly," said Mr Neville, raising his cup to his lips. "There is the Mural Committee, and you are represented on it, sir."

"I am?"

"Well, to be precise, the Hawksbridge Pottery Company, which I understand you own."

"Ah, I see," I said. "Yes, I was surprised to find myself in this position. However, I have not yet involved myself in its workings. I intend to visit in the next day or two."

"You may not know that your company is built on the site of Tantallon's factory. And so Mr McPhee – one of the directors – has made it his business to mark the fiftieth anniversary of the tragedy by commissioning a mural for the Town Hall, and many of us in Hawksbridge have gladly supported this laudable aim. After all, it is an opportunity to bring godliness to civic life, and help us remember our mortality and the glory that awaits us all. Most of us, anyway."

He frowned, and I supposed he had someone in mind for the torments of Hell.

Mr Neville continued. "The pity of it is, sir, is that two artists of the basest possible morals are likely to be chosen – making this not so much as an act of praise and respect as a monument to sacrilege and debauchery! It is intolerable!"

The Rector's cup shook a little in its saucer as he reached for it. It was clear that this was a subject of considerable pain for him. I adopted as sympathetic an expression as I could muster.

"It will make the town a laughing stock," said Mr Neville, putting the teacup down again lest it spill its contents. "It will be a vulgar display that everyone will know as the work of two disgusting reprobates who should be cast from these isles, not rewarded with riches and bovine adulation as they are currently."

"Good Lord," I said. "Can I ask who these sinful artists are?"

"Henry Shaw and Edward Walker." The Rector almost spat the names out.

"Really? You cannot be in earnest!" I said. These were not just any jobbing painters; Shaw and Walker were amongst the most respected artists of the day. Inseparable, highly talented, and with a string of successful exhibitions to their name, they based their subjects and technique on fifteenth-century Italian old masters, using religious and mythological themes. I had been to one of their exhibitions in London only last year, and had been exhilarated by the vibrancy of the colour, the detail, and the voluptuous figures, invariably showing more flesh than was strictly necessary. Their reputation for artistic genius was unfortunately accompanied by a certain notoriety – mainly the breaking of female hearts, with many tales of excess and cruelty. And yet, the beauty of their work quietened any public misgivings about their moral life. Indeed, for some, it only confirmed that they were not like normal men in their abilities and desires, and should not be judged as such.

"Perfectly, I assure you," said Mr Neville. "They may be much admired, but that does not excuse their utter wickedness. It will catch up with them in the end, mark my words, and it will tarnish everyone who has had the lack of wisdom to employ them."

"That is a blow," I said. "I'm a great aficionado of their work myself. Must I forgo the pleasure of their art?"

"That is up to you and your conscience," said the Rector. "But there is no reason to bring them and their immorality into Hawksbridge. I trust I have your support in this, Mr Rufford?"

"I can certainly pledge to find out all I can – but I don't feel I know enough to sit in judgement just yet. After all, it would bring a lot of prestige to the town, which is presumably why Shaw and Walker are in the running. I will talk to Mr McPhee."

Mr Neville did not look pleased at this. "Prestige, and perhaps commercial gain for your company by association. I'm sorry, but I do have to call into question the motives for choosing these men above more suitable candidates, such as our own Mr Falkirk. Although he is scarcely a moral paragon either, I regret to say; but he is at least contrite, I think."

"Forgive me – who is Mr Falkirk?"

"Johnny Falkirk is a competent artist living in Hawksbridge. He paints both landscapes and portraits, and I'm sure he would be quite adequate to the task."

"I see. I suppose the Committee is looking beyond 'adequate'."

"Hubris, sir! Hubris!"

The Rector seemed to check himself, and he adopted a more conciliatory tone.

"All I am asking, Mr Rufford, is for you to use the position in which you unexpectedly find yourself to persuade members of the Committee of the folly of commissioning such a controversial and worldly pair of artists. Such a course would be against the spirit of the endeavour, and that is the politest way I can describe it. I trust you to do the right and proper thing for the benefit of your newly adopted town."

I was aware I was being manipulated, especially by the reference to my undeserved inheritance. I nodded, and said, "I will look into it, Mr Neville, armed with this knowledge. But I am afraid I cannot guarantee I can persuade anyone of anything, being – as you rightly point out – a newcomer, and having yet earned no one's trust or respect."

Mr Neville rose from his chair. "You do not entirely reassure me, sir, but then my expectations were low. You must find your bearings, of course. Please do what you can. Thank you for receiving me – and send my regards to Miss Davison."

We shook hands, and I showed the Rector out.

I closed the door and returned to the sitting room, so lost in thought about this strange skirmish that I forgot myself and picked up the tea tray to return it to the kitchen. Mrs Felton appeared, and whisked it away from me.

"I'll take care of that, sir! How did you find our Rector, then? He sounded more gruff than usual."

"I seem to have ruffled more feathers, Mrs Felton," I said. "He disagrees with a commission, and I am supposed to interfere. He was not happy when I hesitated."

"Oh, I wouldn't worry about Mr Neville, my dear! He thinks highly of himself, but there are plenty who would take your side over his, any day, whatever it was about. My late husband used to say that Mr Neville could give up preaching and make a good living selling sanctimony by the bottle. He had a good turn of phrase, did my Charles." She sighed, and fell silent for a moment.

"I'm sorry, Mrs Felton," I said. "I didn't know about your husband."

She turned, smiled, and said, "Thank you, my dear. Ah well, he's in a better place now, assuming he's been forgiven for disrespecting the clergy. And I keep myself busy. Speaking of which, is there anything else I can get you? More tea?"

"No, I don't need anything else," I said. "I think I'll get some fresh air and walk into town."

"It's a lovely day for it – it won't take you long, perhaps half an hour at the most. I believe you can get a good coffee at The Duke's Head."

~

It was still early enough for me to do a little exploration of Hawksbridge before my appointment with Shipley. It had not rained for a few days, which made the roads easier to navigate, but I was still grateful for a pair of sturdy boots. As I came down the hill from Ramsburgh towards the town, the signs of activity grew gradually more numerous, though hardly on a par with Oxford. A small wave of panic gripped me momentarily as a voice in my head said, "You don't belong here. You are an imposter. Everyone knows what your father did. Run back home!"

I shook my head as if to cast off an imp, and concentrated on observing my surroundings. An impressive sandstone arch remained from ancient fortifications, once a bulwark against restless Scots and other raiders. As I passed through it, I made a mental note to explore the town walls, if there was much left of them. I retained a boy's fascination with the residue of the country's dangerous past, to which I was now connected by virtue of my own crenellated home.

Beyond the gate, I passed The Duke's Head, which would do for refreshments later. I stopped at the window of a bookseller, my eye caught by the sight of writhing bodies. In a startling lithograph, a voluptuous woman in a falling robe was being stolen away by a lustful god, chased by distressed female onlookers in similar states of undress. The sense of movement and drama was compelling, and no doubt the original painting must have been extraordinary. It was entitled 'THE RAPE OF PROSERPINA', and a card under the print proclaimed in large letters, 'AFTER THE FAMOUS ARTISTS SHAW AND WALKER'. I recalled that the myth of Proserpina told of her abduction and rape by the god Pluto, with Venus and Minerva vainly attempting to stop him. A popular renaissance subject, it was typical of Shaw and Walker to revive it.

So, I thought, the bookshop was taking advantage of rumours, before the final decision had been made – a foregone conclusion, it would appear. I stared at the picture for a while, inflamed by the immodest aesthetics of the scene whilst ashamed at my own response to such violence. The artists would no doubt have delighted in my confusion.

Finally, aware of how my gawping would look, I dragged myself away and walked past. But then I overcame my cowardice, went back to the shop, and stepped inside. The proprietor of Hunter's Booksellers looked up from the account book he was examining and smiled at me.

"Good morning, sir!" he said. "Isn't it a lovely one? Is there anything you are looking for in particular?"

"Good morning! Well – no, but I was interested to see you have a lithograph of a Shaw and Walker. It's striking."

"Oh yes, I have sold a lot of these in the last few days. I will have to order some more. The prospect of those lads coming to town has everyone agog, so I cater to demand, even though this sort of thing" – he waved in the direction of the picture – "is not very Hawksbridge, if you know what I mean, sir."

"I can imagine, yes. It's certainly a frank piece – a little disturbing. But I'm an admirer of the artists." I made a quick decision, anxious not to get too deep into a discussion of naked women with a stranger. "I would like the print, please."

"Certainly, sir. It's the last one, so bear with me while I retrieve it from the window." Mr Hunter proceeded to pick his way carefully through the window display, pushing aside several attractive little piles of leather-bound books.

As I did so, I was aware that one of the customers – a pleasant-looking young woman in a rust-coloured dress – had turned around from a book stack and was regarding me with some amusement.

"It's rather uncompromising, isn't it?" she said. "I hope your wife will approve."

I was taken aback. She had seen through me, that was obvious; I had only been in the town a few minutes, and already I had exposed a weakness for risqué prints.

"Ah – it's – a kind of research," I floundered. "I have been asked my opinion about the commission of the new mural, so this is... helpful."

She smiled again at me charmingly, but with a narrowing of the eyes that spoke of a playful disbelief.

"Of course, of course. Research that is no hardship – the best kind."

"Fortunately, I do not have a wife to contradict me on this purchase," I said.

The young woman's eyes widened again. "Fortunate to have no wife? That is much more shocking than the picture."

"Sorry – no, of course not, I meant –"

"I am teasing you: I perfectly understand. Forgive my rudeness – Phyllis Drummond." Miss Drummond inclined her head and held out her hand.

"Thomas Rufford," I said, shaking her hand.

She seemed surprised. "Rufford?" she said. "Goodness."

"Shall I create an account for you, Mr Rufford?" said the bookseller.

"Yes, yes – please do, thank you. And can I leave this with you for a while?"

"Of course, sir. I'll have it wrapped for when you return."

"What has caught your eye, then, Miss Drummond?" I asked, indicating the book in her left hand.

She looked down at it as if she had forgotten she was holding it, and immediately put it back on a shelf. "Oh, nothing, just a curiosity. Nothing I would read myself, but I was amused to see it here." Seeing that I was still wearing a quizzical expression, she was forced to explain further. "It's a copy of that awful book, 'The Predilections of Reverend Malamor'. Full of scandal and bad writing."

"You intrigue me," I said, stepping forward and reaching for the volume. I read from the title page. "'The Predilections of Reverend Malamor, or The Hypocrite of Eaglesville, by John Bland.' Now I think of it, I remember a colleague mentioning it as an offensive bit of nonsense – one of those passing fads – but I haven't read it. Since you've brought it to my attention, I'm tempted to buy a copy."

To my surprise, Miss Drummond snatched the book from my hands and stuffed it back on the shelf. "I beg you not to, Mr Rufford – it will not repay your time. The only reason I picked it up – but you will think me strange."

"I assure you I won't," I said. "Please continue."

"Very well. It amuses me to find inscriptions in books and imagine the former owners. In particular, if it's a gift. It's only a silly whim, not a serious study, of course. I am already making too much of it!"

"And did you learn anything from this one?"

"Yes – a gentleman has given it to a female," said Miss Drummond, "and I suspect he wishes to indicate a wild side of himself – that he is not tied to convention, and regards society with a cynical eye. It is a daring gift, and one might deduce that a passionate love affair was in progress. But then I am a writer myself, and full of fancy, I am afraid."

I smiled. "Fascinating. I would never have thought to conclude that, but I'm sure you're right. Alternatively, the reason the book is now here instead of on the recipient's shelves is that she was outraged by it, and rejected both the gift and her suitor's advances." She nodded to concede this possibility. "I prefer your happier interpretation, though," I added. "Are you published, may I ask?"

A customer had come into the shop, and Miss Drummond looked around self-consciously.

"A little, but I won't bore you with the details. I do hate talking about myself in public. I'm sure our paths will cross again, and then you may quiz me. Please excuse me – I will just find my father something to read, and then I must hurry home. It was nice to meet you, Mr Rufford."

~

On the street, I glanced back through the bookshop window. Miss Drummond had adopted a scholarly pose again, absorbed in a book. I had dismissed the half-formed notion of inviting her for tea at Ramsburgh. Now I regretted my timidity, for she was exactly the sort of articulate and presentable female I imagined myself dining with, dancing with – perhaps more. In my mind's eye, I could already see Mrs Felton fussing over her. But then again, such forwardness, particularly after my questionable art acquisition, would doubtless have made irresistible gossip for Mr Hunter.

I contented myself with the thought that the town was small, and the opportunity for fraternisation would surely come again. I walked past a butcher hung with carcasses, and then I came to a road leading to a church. Thinking that some calming ecclesiastical architecture would help quieten my churning mind, I turned off the main street. I was surprised to see the Rector striding towards the church porch from the opposite direction. It was too late for me to change my own direction without seeming rude, so I smiled and continued, until I could see that Mr Neville was in a foul temper. As our paths met at the porch, the Rector stopped and glared at me.

"Well, Mr Rufford. I'm sure you will be happy to know that your intervention will be unnecessary. I have just had word that the Committee has chosen" – he was unwilling to say their names out loud – "*those* artists. The Devil has prevailed, and the town will regret it, just you see!"

With that, he marched inside, slamming the heavy, ancient church door in my face.

# CHAPTER FIVE

TWO weeks had passed since I had met Phyllis, whom Mrs Felton had informed me was the daughter of Dr Anthony Drummond. He was apparently a doctor with a fine reputation and a possible means, I thought, for another meeting with Phyllis. I could not muster the courage to have 'The Rape Of Proserpina' in a public room, so it was banished to a bedroom on the second floor where it hung impertinently next to a respectable watercolour of Jerusalem.

The meeting with Shipley about defects in the castle stonework and roof had resulted in the commission of a builder, and scaffolding soon appeared at the front, slightly marring my enjoyment of my domain. But there was plenty to distract me. I had written to Mr McPhee, and he had enthusiastically given me a tour of the factory and a litany of statistics about the consumption of raw materials, firing temperatures and a steady increase in sales.

After I had admired the new designs for a forthcoming range of dinnerware, McPhee – a lively man with a walrus moustache as impressive as his command of facts and figures – had poured us each a sherry in his office and expressed his delight at the imminent arrival of the artists, Shaw and Walker.

He had roared with laughter – a little unkindly, I thought – at my description of the Rector's discomfort. "Mr Neville's proper work is the saving of souls, not the adjudication of art," he had said. "He'll get over it; or he'll enjoy being crotchety about it."

This afternoon, I was in my study, eyeing with displeasure a pile of papers that my new Hawksbridge solicitor had sent me to look over: a miscellany of investments I had inherited from my father, and which I was supposed to examine with a view to retention or disposal and reinvestment. Sighing, I opened a copy of Walter Scott's 'Rob Roy' that I had found on the shelves. Like Scott's hero Frank, I had met a fair lady while in pursuit of my Northumberland manor – but I could not be destined for such an adventurous life as Frank's. I was certainly not constitutionally suited to a life of running around with excitable Jacobites.

Thinking of Francesca, I wondered what had become of her. A wandering, rebellious spirit, she would certainly have caught Scott's attention and his imagination. And then there was Phyllis – equally intriguing, but seemingly content with her quiet existence, attending to her father's literary needs, while writing... writing what? I might have to feign a mild illness or anxiety to contrive another meeting, supposing Phyllis still lived in the same house as her father. Or perhaps I would invite her and her father to Ramsburgh.

As my mind skipped from one pleasant speculation to another, I became aware of the doorbell ringing, and muffled voices. Shipley's now-familiar footsteps approached, and he knocked on the door.

"A lady to see you, sir," he said. "She didn't give a name – wanted to surprise you. Said you would know her."

"Really?" I said, getting up. "How mysterious." Phyllis? But she didn't strike me as one to play such a trick. For a moment, the darker recesses of my mind conjured up the ghost of Hazel, and a shiver ran down my spine.

When I turned into the hall, an elegant woman had her back to me, examining a painting. She was dressed in a green riding habit and a feathered riding hat. She turned, and to my astonishment, I saw it was Francesca – if anything, more appealing than in our previous encounter, and smiling broadly at me. "Thomas!" she said, and walked towards me with outstretched hands. "How wonderful to see you! I have come to claim that coffee. Are you surprised?"

"I am... amazed!" I said as I clasped her hand. She put her other hand over mine, and kept tight hold of me.

"I feel as if we are old friends," she said. "I hope that doesn't sound too silly."

"Not at all," I said. "I was thinking about you just now, as it happens. I thought I would never see you again."

"Well, here I am," said Francesca. "I will tell all, in return for a coffee."

"Of course!" I said, finally able to withdraw my captured hand.

Shipley had been hovering, presumably to ensure that my guest was respectable, and correctly interpreted my enquiring glance. "Of course, sir – I will serve coffee in the drawing room. And I will get your horse stabled, ma'am."

With Shipley out of the room, Francesca leant forward and to my surprise, gave me a brief kiss on the cheek.

"I am so excited!" she said. "I have been looking forward to this moment for weeks." I indicated the way to the sitting room, and as we left the hall, Francesca said, "What a gorgeous house, Thomas! You don't mind me calling you Thomas, do you?" I smiled and shook my head. "And you must call me Francesca. Old friends cannot be stuffy about these things."

She went to look out of the west-facing window. "And views to die for, too! You lucky chap. Shall we sit here?"

There was a small table and two chairs by the window, for the purpose of taking refreshments while admiring the hills. I took my seat and was amused that Francesca was acting the hostess. Perhaps she would soon be giving orders to my staff.

"You can't keep me in suspense like this," I said. "How are you here? Are you visiting someone? What are your plans?"

Francesca smiled wickedly. "Oh, I do enjoy a little mystery. Forgive me. The truth is, I was bored of society, of my husband's friends and relations, and of London. I have a little money, and no obligations; and your Hawksbridge sounded so appealing. A charming market town, with a leisurely pace of life, full – potentially – of friendly faces. And one friendly face in particular. I know it's a little capricious of me, but so what? There is no law against caprice that I know of."

I considered this. "It's splendid to be able to choose one's home based on what would be pleasant, rather than what's necessary," I said. "But are you sure you don't need a more urban life? Is Hawksbridge going to be exciting enough for you? Aren't you used to boisterous parties and people of consequence?"

At this point, Mrs Felton came in with the coffee, and I introduced Francesca.

"I'm very pleased to meet you, ma'am," Mrs Felton said. "I was thinking Mr Rufford was in need of a little female company." Turning to me, she added, "Begging your pardon, my dear!"

"Not at all, Mrs Felton – you are quite right," I said. "To be honest, I was getting heartily sick of my own company. I'm almost inclined to think I just conjured you up, Mrs Campbell!"

"I assure you, I am quite real," said Francesca. "I am here and in the flesh. You may pinch me if you wish." She looked at me with an intensity that suggested she would quite welcome this test of her corporeal reality.

Mrs Felton smiled and left, and Francesca continued: "What were we saying? Ah yes, boisterous parties, and so forth. I have thought a lot about that, and have concluded that I want to try a different, more reflective life. Besides, I can arrange my own parties that I will fill with interesting people, such as Mr Thomas Rufford."

"So you possess a house in which to arrange these parties?" I said.

"I do, I'm delighted to say. I engaged a very diligent agent who found me a cottage. It needs a lot of work, but parts of it are quite habitable."

"A cottage? Somehow I don't see you..."

Francesca shrugged. "Well, not quite a cottage. It's a brick farmhouse – Elizabethan. I was tremendously lucky to get it, and at a good price because of the condition of the roof. Will you come and see it? I'm going to have such fun bending it to my will."

"I would be delighted to visit," I said. "You do seem to be well organised. And I hadn't imagined you galloping around the countryside on horseback. I should like to see that!"

"Certainly, if it amuses you. Do you not ride?" I shook my head. "Then you must learn, and we can ride together. In exchange for instruction, you may help me choose wallpapers. And I will need new furniture! I sold most of mine – my husband had poor taste in these things."

"But he obviously had good taste in women," I said.

"Flatterer! When it came to me, perhaps, but in mistresses – emphatically not." She took a sip of coffee and her face reflected the bitterness of her memories, the drink, or both.

"But enough of me!" she said, brightening. "What of you? Are you happy here? Have you had adventures? Are you accepted by the natives?"

~

"Extraordinary!" said Francesca, transfixed by the engraving of the fleshy, unfortunate Proserpina. "What a brave purchase."

In the drawing room, I had explained what had transpired since our first meeting – omitting, of course, the embarrassment of my first night at the house. While she would no doubt be amused, it would need to wait for better acquaintance, perhaps to be traded for a salacious confidence of her own. Francesca had then insisted on a tour of the house, during which she had made gratifying noises of approval and admiration in each room, in the manner of an excited prospective purchaser.

"A little impulsive, perhaps," I said. "But I thought it might help me deliberate about the mural."

Francesca gave me an amused look, much in the way Phyllis had after my original bluster. "Naturally, you're an admirer of women – with natural figures. That's nothing to be ashamed of."

I coughed and tried to change the subject. "This is a modest room, but the views to the west are fabulous."

"Indeed they are," said Francesca, brushing past me to go and stand in the window. "If you invite me for the weekend, I would like to stay in this one. Not that I wish to presume!"

"You would be very welcome," I said.

Francesca suddenly put her hand to her head, taking off her hat and pressing her temple.

"Are you all right?" I said, alarmed.

"Just one of my headaches," she said. "Sorry – they are a nuisance. I think the sunshine has set it off."

"Here, sit down," I said, indicating an elbow chair that had been placed against a wall, and closing the shutters to leave a small chink of light. "Can I bring you some water?"

She sat down and smiled up at me, still pressing her hand to her head. "No, I'll be fine. Actually – there is something that might help. But I should not trouble you."

"No, say, and I shall be happy to do it," I said.

"Well – it helps a great deal when my maid massages my head. But it would be wrong of me to ask you."

"Nonsense," I said, though I was nervous at the prospect. "I will try my best."

"Thank you," said Francesca, getting up and turning the chair a little. "If you stand behind me, that would be best." She sat down in the chair again and freed her hair, so that it flowed over her riding habit.

I took up my position and tentatively ran my now trembling hands over her head. "I don't know what I'm doing, I'm afraid," I said, with as much nonchalance as I could manage, while realising that the husk in my voice indicated otherwise. "You might need to tell me..."

"No, that's fine," said Francesca. "That's helping."

I looked up and noticed that I could see Francesca in a mirror on the dressing table on the other side of the room. Her eyes were closed and a faint smile indicated that the massage was having an effect.

I grew more confident and moved my hands slowly from the back of her head to her temples, where I had seen her put her hands, and I applied a little pressure with my fingertips. This elicited a small sigh. "Very good," she said.

Moving my hands back across her head, I accidentally brushed the top of her ears, and I heard her breathe in deeply, before exhaling slowly. "Good," she repeated faintly. She appeared to be in a trance-like state, and I wondered if she would fall asleep.

Eventually she opened her eyes, and said, "Goodness! You should have been a doctor like your father, Thomas. My headache is almost gone." She stood up and deftly arranged her hair. "Thank you! But I should be on my way – you surely have better things to do than attend to my silly ailments. And my horse will be getting restless."

The spell was broken, but I knew that I would savour this moment. It had been months since I had touched a woman, and – typically – that had ended in near-disaster. Last summer, I had had an affair with Penny Stevens, the attractive daughter of a fellow don. Although she was too young for me and we shared few interests, I had yet imagined myself madly in love with her, and not merely mesmerised by her alluring curves. For a short while, Penny had thought herself with child, and although thankfully she was not, it sobered us sufficiently to terminate the affair. Not for the first time, it made me question my own judgement.

"Oh! I nearly forgot," she said, donning her hat. "Shaw and Walker are looking for models. They're already lodging at The Dog and Hare, and the ladies of Hawksbridge are all of a flutter with the notion that they could be immortalised by such distinguished young men – and of course, fascinated by their good looks and bad reputations. I think I will go and try my luck – do you think I should, Thomas? Or perhaps they won't want a wrinkled old hag in their masterpiece!"

I hesitated. I immediately detested the idea of those rogues pawing at her. "Hardly wrinkled or old. I'm sure you would be a marvellous subject, but... I'm not sure they would respect you. I could not advise it."

"Oh, Thomas!" she said, tilting her head and smiling at me. "I do believe you're jealous. How sweet!"

"Nonsense!" I said, kicking at a loose floorboard. "I just think they may be – dangerous, that's all."

"Perhaps that's the attraction," she said, and gestured towards the door. "Shall we?"

~

Francesca mounted her horse with admirable precision and energy, and as I waved goodbye from the gravel path, she touched her temple with her crop and said, "Thank you for my medicine! So much better! I shall see you soon. Let's arrange a feast!"

Aware of Flora's face in the tower window above me observing the scene, I watched Francesca disappear down the driveway, and tried to comprehend what had just happened. A woman I had met once on a train had, on a second encounter, successfully inserted herself into my life with the force of a gas explosion; had made me care about her, even be protective about her, and had put enough trust in me to allow my touch. It genuinely seemed that we were firm friends already. It was not as though any of this were disagreeable. It was simply that I did not know if I should be capitulating so thoroughly, so quickly. And was it worrying that she had followed me to Hawksbridge? Or was it simply a wonderful expression of her impulsive personality? Despite all these doubts, I knew that in the end I would follow my instincts, however much they had led me into trouble in the past.

And yet it was not Francesca that I dreamed of that night; not even Phyllis. It was Hazel who again visited me in my fitful sleep: her face, streaked with tears, appeared behind bars that she gripped and pulled in vain. "Help me!" she cried, before a dark figure loomed up behind her, struck her, and dragged her away. I woke up, gasping for breath, my heart pounding. I pulled up a sash and breathed in the fresh night air. Why could my past life not leave me alone? It seemed that the more I embraced my new existence, the more Hazel would stretch out her bony fingers from the grave and clutch at my guilty soul.

# CHAPTER SIX

ON Sunday, when I got to St Ninian's – with the hope of seeing Phyllis – it was a minute to eleven o'clock. As I walked down the aisle glancing about for a familiar face, McPhee caught my eye and smiled, and so I had no choice but to share his pew.

"Good morning!" whispered McPhee. "Neville looks to be in a foul mood. This should be interesting." I nodded with a grimace, and then scanned the pews – on the opposite side near the colonnade, Phyllis was sitting with a respectable-looking man who might be her father. There was no sign of a mother, however.

The organ music stopped and Mr Neville announced the opening hymn from the pulpit. We stood, and as we did so, Phyllis turned and recognised me, favouring me with a faint smile and nod of the head. McPhee saw it and appeared amused, but thankfully the hymn had started and he did not pass comment.

When it came time for the sermon, Mr Neville planted his hands heavily on the edge of the pulpit and exhaled, as if weary of the unending sins of the human race. He adopted an expression familiar to me before a beating from my headmaster.

"Today I want to talk about *hubris*," the Rector boomed. As his words reverberated, he paused to look around the congregation. What he saw did not seem to please him.

"Hubris is a kind of pride," he continued. "Pride and the confidence of a fool who does not understand or care about the consequences of his actions, but acts to gratify himself, in defiance of our Lord. We have all been guilty of it, but some more than others. In everyday life, hubris might be the adoption of a position that he is not worthy of or born to."

At this point the Rector glared at me, and although smarting at the implication, I decided to look impassively back at the Rector until he chose a new victim.

"Or it might be casually neglecting one's prayers," Neville went on, "thereby imperilling one's immortal soul. This is a small but significant sin. Naturally, more prodigious forms of hubris have been displayed by dictators over the centuries. These are easy to discern. But it may be happening in front of you, and you are blind to see it. You may be part of it, as you are carried along in a tide of misguided enthusiasm." Again, the Rector let these words sink in and the echo die around the walls and columns of the austere stone building. I could see puzzled faces as their owners tried to work out where they might have gone wrong.

"You may witness a *monstrous* example of hubris *today*," said Mr Neville, punctuating words by striking the pulpit with his fist, "and *here* in this very town. Members of this very congregation have enabled it! I speak, of course, of the employment of two *reprobates* to commit sacrilege in our town hall. Ah yes, famous reprobates – well-regarded reprobates – but reprobates nonetheless."

At this point, I noticed that the scruffy-looking man in the pew in front of me was nodding his head, and muttering "hear, hear" and other less audible phrases. Judging by the colour of his cheeks and listless demeanour, he was probably drunk.

"I speak of Mr Henry Shaw and Mr Edward Walker, who should not so much be given a hero's welcome and our hallowed walls as a canvas for their blasphemous scrawls, as asked politely to leave so that we may honour our dead ourselves, using the talents of our own people."

"Yes!" shouted the drunk. "Our own people! Chase the swine out."

The Rector looked uncomfortable, found the source of the interjection, and evidently hoped that a short stare would be sufficient to silence him. He then continued with his condemnation.

"I have heard enough about the women they have wronged, and seen enough of their outrageous so-called religious paintings – that are nothing of the sort – to know that we need neither the pollution of our town by their very presence, nor their artistic efforts that are plainly thin disguises for degenerate displays of flesh. And yet, for many in Hawksbridge, the lure of the famous – or notorious – is enough for these concerns to be dismissed. *This* is hubris, *this* is unacceptable, and *this will not stand!*"

The Rector had reddened and his eyes were wide as he glared at the embarrassed congregation with self-righteous fury. The drunk got unsteadily to his feet, and clapped. "Bravo, Reverend!" he said huskily. "You tell 'em! Drum 'em out of town, I say. I'll lead the charge. Damn the arrogant buggers!"

McPhee darted out of his pew and took the drunk by the arm. "Now, Mr Falkirk, we mustn't say such things in church. Let me take you into the fresh air, and then you can say whatever you wish about these men."

Under protest, Falkirk let himself be led out of the church. The congregation stopped staring, and turned again to face the angry cleric in the pulpit. He was evidently struggling to contain his emotions, and he cut short any final words he was going to say. Singing the next hymn was a relief to all.

When the service was over, Mr Neville was in no mood to greet us all as we filed out, and a curate was assigned to this duty. Outside in the bright sunshine, I found Phyllis alone – her father had gone to check on the drunken Falkirk who was slouched over a gravestone.

"Miss Drummond!" I said. "How are you? Did you find a suitable book for your father?"

"Oh, hello, Mr Rufford," said Phyllis, adjusting her hat to

avoid the sun's rays. "I am well, thank you – and yes, I got something to amuse him. A strange novel by Edgar Poe, with a long title I can't remember. Something about Nantucket. He says it's complete nonsense, but he carries on reading it."

"Sometimes nonsense can be very agreeable," I said. "You have yet to tell me what you yourself write. I'm sure it can't be nonsense, or if it is, it will be ingenious nonsense."

Phyllis smiled. "Let me think how to characterise my writing: let's say, moderately intelligent hogwash. Just bright enough for enjoyment, but not so intense it becomes a chore for my audience. By necessity, of course, because we women are not allowed to be too precocious, and erudite I am not. In the end, all most of us want in a novel is a decent story, some characters we can admire or despise, and the company of prose that is not too dull – would you not say?"

"Ha! Possibly," I said, "although I suspect you have greater ambitions than that. Anyway, I should like to read one of your stories. I take it you are represented in Hunter's?"

"I am. But not under my real name."

At this point, McPhee appeared. "The unfortunate Falkirk has shambled off," he said. "He will live. Miss Drummond, good morning! Your father told me to tell you that he has a patient to see. So, Thomas – you have previously met the daughter of my favourite doctor?"

"He was buying an improper print," said Phyllis. "I was scandalised. Smelling salts were nearly in order."

"That I don't believe," said McPhee. "After all, you are a novelist. Scandal is your raw material."

"As I explained," I said, now a little tired of justifying myself, "the print was a Shaw and Walker, whom the Rector obliged me to consider because of –"

Phyllis giggled and momentarily touched my arm by way of apology. "Of course. According to Hunter, a good proportion of the town had the same idea. And now the cats are among the pigeons. Poor Falkirk! He really thought he had a good chance. I don't blame him for being so cross. But someone should get him off the drink – it won't improve his work."

"I believe his misfortune is not limited to his art," said McPhee. "Forbidden love, I heard."

"Oh, poor man," said Phyllis. "I wish there was something we could do. He really does have potential."

"Yes, he needs a commission," said McPhee. "Something to keep him out of trouble. Well, I'll ask around. Now, Thomas – how would you like to meet Shaw and Walker? They have a kind of cattle market going on today, to find models for the mural. That's probably part of Neville's anger – young women, and even some of the more self-regarding young men, absent from church to attend Shaw and Walker's den of iniquity! Anyway, I'm curious, and I have a business proposition for them, which will do as an excuse."

"Really?" I said, astonished. "Well..."

"Go on!" said Phyllis. "You can't miss an opportunity to speak to your heroes."

After a moment's thought, I said, "Very well. You can tell me about your business proposition on the way. Miss Drummond, I had wanted to speak more about –"

"All in good time," she said. "Enjoy your trip to the studio. Good to see you both, Mr Rufford, Mr McPhee!"

~

As McPhee explained on their walk, the artists were staying in a cottage behind The Duke's Head. For them, it had the advantage of privacy, compared with rooms in the main inn building, while still being serviced by the inn's staff. The proprietor, Mr Minto, had offered them very favourable rates in exchange for the prestige of their presence: The Duke's

Head would be able to boast of the association for many years to come.

"I wouldn't be surprised," said McPhee, "if they changed the inn name to The Artist's Rest, or some such."

"Assuming they don't totally disgrace themselves at some point," I said.

"That would be a risk, yes," agreed McPhee. "Or perhaps an advantage, so long as they stop short of actually ravishing an archbishop's wife."

As they walked, it occurred to me that I might find Francesca there. If so, I must not act the prig, I told myself. The idea of the artists disrespecting her in any way was hard to bear; but Francesca valued her freedom, and I had learnt from Hazel – this, if nothing else – that interference in a woman's independence was a losing stratagem.

The cottage was accessed via a narrow lane, and in front, a group of women were chatting excitedly, evidently awaiting their turn. As the two men approached, a young woman ran out of the house with her hand over her mouth and tears running down her cheeks. Before I could decide whether I should offer assistance, she had disappeared down the lane. I exchanged a glance with McPhee.

"Rejected?" said McPhee. "I hope no worse than that."

A man appeared in the doorway. "All right, ladies," he said. "Thank you – we have all we need." Was that Shaw or Walker? He was not conventionally handsome – his angular cheekbones giving him an underfed look – and he wore a stained tunic. Yet his face had appealing character; it was easy to see how such a man, embellished with fame, might hold the attention of impressionable young women who yearned for something different from the usual parade of respectable, well-turned-out, bland young suitors.

The waiting hopefuls, whose giddy eagerness seemed to have only increased with the sight of the fleeing woman, expressed their disappointment with tuts and sighs, and set off down the lane. The artist looked on with a frown as McPhee and I remained.

"Yes?"

"Good afternoon!" said McPhee. "Mr Walker? Or Mr Shaw? I am Frederick McPhee, a director of the Hawksbridge Pottery Company, and this is my colleague Mr Thomas Rufford. We have a small business proposition for you."

I felt a jolt of pride at this description of my role, feeling it to be a promotion from mere owner of the business. I would have to work harder to justify it.

"Ah yes," said the artist. "I believe you were on our side on the Committee. Thank you. Henry Shaw, sir." He extended his hand to McPhee and myself. "Why don't you come in? We have beer, if you're partial."

I ducked my head as I entered the low cottage door. It led directly to a sitting room, where Mr Walker was reading a newspaper with a mug in his hand.

"Ned, we have visitors. Mr Rufford and Mr McPhee, from the Pottery."

Edward Walker grunted and stood up. He was taller than Shaw, and I thought he must be finding the dimensions of the cottage a trial. However, neither could complain about comfort here: Mr Munro had obviously pulled out all the stops for them. The chairs all had immaculate cushions, the walls were recently whitewashed, and floor was clean and covered in a large rug.

"Not trying out as models, are you, gentlemen? We have all the men we need, but still..." He peered at me, and then McPhee. "We might be able to make archangels out of you."

I smiled and shook Mr Walker's hand. "No, sir," I said, "we just came to pay our respects. I am a great admirer of your work, and in fact I have just bought a print of your Proserpina."

Mr Walker chuckled. "We have sold well in Hawksbridge on the mere chance of our arrival. We should try that trick elsewhere, eh, Henry? Put about a rumour." His laugh became a loud cough, and he stepped outside to avoid inflicting it on the rest of us.

"Unfortunately, our publisher and engraver get most of the profits," said Shaw. "Hardly worth the trouble."

"Most unfair," said McPhee, as Shaw poured a tankard of beer for him and myself. "Have you always worked together, if you don't mind my asking?"

"Since we were eighteen," said Walker, who had returned and was wiping his mouth with his handkerchief. "Just seemed the best way to do it. Cheaper, too."

"We occasionally work on our own paintings, of course," said Shaw. "But they're not as well-known as our large works."

"Interesting," I said. "Do you sell your individual paintings?"

"Not yet," said Walker. "Perhaps one day. After so many years of working together, it seems queer to present ourselves any other way. And we don't like the idea of competing with each other and spoiling what we have. But we shall see."

I was aware that this was sensitive ground, and was anxious to move on to another topic. "Did you find all the women you need?" I said, and then cursed myself for my choice of words.

Shaw laughed. "Oh yes. We have recruited some very fair damsels who will make creditable angels, gathering up the poor souls from the burned factory. And others to model as the victims."

"Quite a throng, wasn't it?" said Walker. "Yesterday, we even had a fine lady turn up on horseback and demand to be seen."

I nearly choked on my beer. I knew exactly who this would have been.

Shaw whistled in an exaggerated manner. "Good Lord, she was quite something. I felt we were the ones being interviewed! A more mature woman, of the kind Ned likes."

He turned to the two guests. "Poor Ned lost his mother at a tender age, and he's been searching for a replacement every since."

"Get lost, Henry," said Walker. "Just because you wouldn't have a hope with a fancy lady like her –"

"Sorry, gentlemen," interrupted Shaw. "You didn't come here to watch us bicker. Did you say you had a business proposal?"

"Ah yes," said McPhee. "We are thinking of producing mugs and plates to remember the Roman Street disaster, illustrated with your finished mural. There would be a modest royalty associated with this. Would it be of interest?"

"Don't see why not, for the right price," said Shaw. "Ned?"

"If they're of sufficient quality. We would need to see a proof."

"Excellent – thank you, gentlemen. I will be in touch about it in due course. We will let you get on with your important work!"

I hesitated on the threshold, my head scraping on the door frame. "I'm curious – are you going to employ this older woman in your mural?"

"Might do," said Walker. "We'll think of a use for her, won't we, Henry? After all, she was so insistent."

"My notion for her is an angelic matriarch, guiding the neophytes," said Shaw. "But our ideas are still in flux. We shall see."

"Thank you for your time, Mr Shaw, Mr Walker," said McPhee. "I'm glad to see you have been made comfortable here."

"Yes, indeed," said Shaw. "We even had a little present from one of our followers." He leant down and pulled an object out of a bucket near the door. It was a dead rat, which Shaw held by the tail, making me recoil. "Left on the doorstep last night, with this charming note." He retrieved a piece of paper from a pocket in his tunic and held it up. I took the paper and read out the words 'WE DONT NEED MORE RATS' before handing it back to Shaw.

McPhee shook his head in disgust.

"I'm sorry," I said. "What a wicked thing. I assure you very few people here share this sentiment."

"Well, we know what your Rector thinks," said Walker, "and no doubt he has persuaded some of his flock to think likewise. But don't worry. We've got thick skins. Seen worse. Now, gentlemen, I have an appointment with a mug of beer and a cheroot." And he disappeared back into the cottage.

Shaw dropped the dead animal back in the bucket with a thud. "Good day, gentlemen!" he said, following his friend into the house, and gave us a grin before closing the door behind him.

"Shocking," said McPhee as they retreated down the lane. "But given their history, a little understandable."

"I don't think that can have been the Rector's hand," I said. "I'm sure he would have used an apostrophe."

"In which case," said McPhee, "the field is still wide open for the identity of our rat man. I'll put money on a jealous husband or lover, who has spent the last few days hearing far too much about our celebrated visitors."

"Or perhaps a miserable, under-appreciated artist," I said.

~

I was weary as I trudged back up the path to Ramsburgh, but the low afternoon light was painting a fine picture with the shadows of the trees and towers. Flora was sitting on a chair on the front lawn, sketching the house, and I came up to her.

I stood and got my breath back after climbing the slope of the drive. "Miss Davison! Hello! May I take a look?"

"Good afternoon, Mr Rufford," she said, with a smile. The sunshine seemed to have put her in a better mood than I was used to. "Of course! It's not my usual medium, so please don't judge me too harshly."

I looked over her shoulder at the drawing, which was confident and detailed.

"It's exquisite!" I declared. "I like it very much."

Flora inclined her head. "Thank you. I think it's better than the one I did yesterday from the north side of the house, with a view of the lake. But that's never been as interesting since the swans... since they left."

"We had swans?" I said. She nodded. "What happened to them?"

Flora frowned. "It's a bit of a mystery – at least, the 'why', not the 'what'. Mrs Kington marched out of the house one day with a fouling piece, and blasted the poor things to death – four of them. Then she just marched back into the house without saying a word. I think she had to pay a fine, as they officially belong to the Queen."

"Good God!" I said. "And no one knows why? Was she mad?"

"She seemed sane enough in other respects," she said. "Perhaps the swans sometimes made a mess around the lake, but they never harmed her. They were beautiful creatures – when they flew in formation, it was extraordinary. I miss them. None ever came back."

"That is awful," I said, and tried to change the topic from this melancholy theme. "So – what is your usual medium?"

"Embroidery. I know – not everyone sees it as an art form, but I take it seriously."

"Goodness! I should like to see some, if I may."

"Certainly," said Flora. "I'll look out some presentable examples."

"Capital. By the way, I have come across a novelist in Hawksbridge, but she's reluctant to inform me of her pseudonym and the titles of her books. Perhaps you'll know."

A cloud passed over Flora's face, and she sighed. "I suppose you're speaking of Miss Drummond."

"Yes – that's her! Do you know her?"

"I used to, very well, when we were young girls."

"Ah," I said. "I suppose it's easy to drift apart when adulthood beckons."

"Quite," she said. I wondered if there was more to it than she was letting on, and I regretted being the cause of her troubled expression.

"I'm sorry," I said. "It's painful to you – I should not have said..."

"It's all right, Mr Rufford. It's all in the past. Her pseudonym is Iona Tavistock. They're not really your kind of book, I wouldn't think – more for romantically-minded females. But you may find them amusing."

She closed her sketchbook and started to pack up her things.

"Thank you," I said. "But I didn't mean to spoil your afternoon – must you go? You looked so elegant and at ease; and now I've lumbered in and disturbed you. I am a fool – please forget I was even here."

Flora stopped what she was doing, sighed, and then fixed her eyes on me. "You weren't to know. How were you to know anything about this place? Good afternoon, Mr Rufford. I hope you enjoy Miss Drummond's books."

With that, she grabbed her things and set off for the house, leaving me wondering what hornet's nest I would stumble into next.

# CHAPTER SEVEN

THE next morning, I was obliged to inspect the Ramsburgh building work with the contractor and give my assent to further stone repair. But I was impatient to get this task over with and read the novel that I had borrowed from Mrs Felton.

I had asked Mrs Felton if the name Iona Tavistock meant anything to her, and she had said, "Miss Drummond? Of course – I have several of her books. Shall I fetch one for you? I'm not sure it's a style a young man would care for –"

"So I have been told," I had said. "But indulge me! I'm curious to know what makes Miss Drummond tick. Perhaps her writing will give me some idea."

Mrs Felton had returned with 'Lady Harlington's Estate', which would have been a handsome volume had its red cloth cover not been disfigured by a brown mark.

"Excuse the tea stain, my dear. I think you will like this one. It's a bit different from her usual. It's not my favourite, mind – it's a bit sad. But I won't spoil it by saying anything more."

"Thank you, Mrs Felton!" I had said. "I shall let you know what I make of it."

The builder, Mr Laughton, was a pleasant and diligent man, but his complaints about the difficulty of obtaining the correct quality of sandstone were lengthy and I struggled to maintain the interest I knew I should take in the improvement of my property. At last I was freed of my duties, and since the weather was clement, I took a chair into the west part of the garden – out of sight of Flora's tower – to read Phyllis' book.

The heroine of this tale, I found, was one Rose Forrester, daughter of a merchant who has fallen on hard times. In despair, she relinquishes her impecunious true love in order to marry rich but tyrannical Sir Langley Harlington and save her family from penury. Despite a torrid time at the hands of her husband, she shows a flair for estate management, and her charitable works make her a beloved figure in her village. But her power grows, and with it, her ambition. Sir Langley's trust in her becomes absolute, and as infirmity sets in, he begins to repent of his former selfishness. Ultimately, Rose becomes corrupted by her improved circumstances, taunting him with her admirers, while her penitent husband forgives her misdeeds. She neglects her family, and it is Sir Langley who is left to send them money. Finally, she lets him die in miserable circumstances, and she consolidates her position as the richest, toughest and most influential landowner in the country.

The afternoon light was fading as I read the last page, containing the devastating poem of love, regret and forgiveness that Sir Langley writes to his wife before expiring. I had to wipe tears from my eyes, and sat for a while in contemplation.

It was evident to me that Phyllis was trying to overturn the conventions of her genre: here, the heroine became a self-centred villain, and the villain transformed into a kind of hero in his new-found tolerance, generosity and self-deprecation. The switch was gradual, almost imperceptible, and I could well understand why Mrs Felton had chosen the book for me, and also why it was not her best-loved Tavistock. It made for uncomfortable reading in the light of the simplistic judgements of character that everyone – myself included – made every day, and it presented the terrifying possibility of one's own moral fall.

But more importantly, it cemented a respect for Phyllis that had been growing since we had first met. She had surpassed her own yardstick for a satisfying novel, while demonstrating a deep pity for frail humanity. In her guise as Iona, she had moved me greatly, and it disturbed me.

~

My reverie was interrupted by a whimpering noise. I span around trying to locate the source: limping towards me from the trees that bounded the garden was a creature. As it came closer, it became clear that it was a sandy-coloured, rough-coated dog with the eyes of a spaniel, of indeterminate lineage and in a poor condition. Its hair was matted with dirt, it seemed malnourished, and there were sores and cuts on its legs and abdomen.

The dog stopped in front of me, looking up at me with apparent desperation. It yapped a few times, and then collapsed at my feet, breathing heavily with an alarming wheeze. The animal did not seem to have much life left.

"Lord!" I said, kneeling down to gently touch the creature's head. "Who do you belong to? What happened?"

The dog seemed to trust me, or had no energy to do otherwise. "Shipley! Come quickly!" I shouted. I had no great experience of dogs, and was not especially an admirer of them, but the plight of this animal touched me, and I felt a responsibility to try to save its life if at all possible.

Shipley and Mrs Felton, alerted by Pearl – one of the maids – who had been shaking dusters in the doorway, both emerged from the house and approached with as much speed as each could manage.

"What's wrong, sir?" said Shipley, and then he saw the dog. "What in God's name...?"

Mrs Shipley put her hand over her mouth at the sight. "My goodness! Let's get him inside and deal with his wounds. Oh!" she added as she peered closer. "It's the Irish pedlar's dog, isn't it?"

"You could be right, Mrs Felton," said Shipley. "I heard they found him dead in a ditch a fortnight ago. His dog was by him, but it ran off after they took his body away."

I gathered the dog up, and we took him into the kitchen. Mrs Felton spread a blanket and then a cloth on the table and I carefully lowered him down. The dog's eyes were half-open, and he passively let us tend to him.

"I think he knows he's going to be looked after," said Mrs Felton, as she cleaned the dog's wounds. "I'll give him a little bit of meat in a minute."

The dog started to whimper in pain, but when I stroked his head, he calmed down again. "I wonder what his name is," I said.

Shipley sank into a chair to watch the proceedings. "Seems to like you, sir. If he's the pedlar's dog, I think I can recall it. The pedlar was quite a regular here, sir, as Mrs Shipley and Mrs Northcutt couldn't resist his trinkets and silk shawls."

"That's not entirely fair, Mr Shipley. It was very convenient to get some necessities for the house just when we needed them – pots and needles, that kind of thing."

Shipley grunted. "Not the best quality. Anyway, your father made quite a fuss of the pedlar's pup, sir. I'll not be surprised if he recognises your smell."

"I hadn't thought of my father as a dog-lover," I said. "Strange. You said you remembered the dog's name?"

Shipley stood up and leaned over the dog. "Fox!" he said.

The dog opened his eyes wide and raised his head off the table, his tail trembling. Shipley chuckled and sat down again, "That's it. Daft name for a dog."

"But he does look a little foxy," said Mrs Felton.

Mrs Northcutt appeared at the door. "Goodness me, Mrs Felton! What do you have there?"

"The pedlar's dog, Meg. Half-dead, he was, but I think he'll mend."

"What a state it's in. Is it staying? That's a lot of work, keeping a dog happy. And the expense. And the noise! I'll not have it disturbing Miss Davison's sleep."

"She has a point," said Shipley, looking at me. "Are you

looking to become a dog-owner, sir? It's not really the animal for a gentleman – a cast-off mongrel like that."

I sighed and stroked the dog's muzzle. "I don't know. For now, we'll look after him until he's better. Then we can make a decision." But I already felt a connection to this lost soul.

Now Flora was at the door, having heard the commotion outside and voices in the kitchen. "Oh! Goodness, is it alive?"

"He is," I said. "He's called Fox."

"Really?" said Flora. "Fox! How odd." The dog had opened his eyes at the sound of his name, and looked around nervously at the newcomers.

"Pedlar's dog," said Mrs Northcutt. "Probably ungovernable. Best to put it out of its misery."

"Margaret!" said Flora. "Hush! That's a terrible thing to say." Mrs Felton pursed her lips and shook her head. "He looks so starved. I believe boiled chicken is a good thing to give a sick dog."

Mrs Felton straightened her back. "For pity's sake! Where's your blessed cat, Miss Davison? He's about the only creature in the house not to have given us the benefit of his wisdom."

"Doubtless his advice would be the same as Mrs Northcutt's," said Shipley. "Well, there's one thing we can be grateful to our pedlar for. At least he didn't have a donkey."

~

A crate was found to act as the dog's bed, and over the next few days, Fox's strength grew. He graduated from a hesitant walk around the garden to accompanying me on short country walks. Mrs Felton doted on the animal, and even Mrs Northcutt had been caught casting admiring glances at him, despite herself. Fox seemed to bring a better humour to

Ramsburgh, and I was surprised at my own affection for the animal. But the dog made it easy: for there was no doubt who his new master was, and Fox was never happier than when with me.

A little over a week later, I resolved to walk into Hawksbridge and call on Phyllis. I could both congratulate her on her novel, and invite her and her father for supper at Ramsburgh (Mrs Felton had informed me that her mother was no longer living). It was high time to be bold, I thought, and besides, Fox was an excellent way to disarm Phyllis. Who could resist those eyes?

A few days before, Flora had offered to sew a sling for me to carry him with in case Fox grew tired on a long walk.

"A wonderful idea, Miss Davison," I had said, "but are you sure this isn't trivialising your sewing skills?"

"Of course not, and I'm not offering to embroider it," she had said. "It won't take long."

I had stood still while Flora measured me, holding the dog. A couple of hours later, and Fox and I were trying out the latest thing in canine transport.

"Very comfortable," I had said. "I just hope this regal conveyance doesn't go to his head."

Setting off for town, I was pleased to see that Fox had sufficient energy to trot alongside me. Instead of going all the way to the end of Ramsburgh's drive, I decided to turn into a lane that cut a corner off the walk, but was often too muddy to be a sensible alternative to the gravel drive. Today, however, it was quite dry, and the woodland on either side was pleasant and full of birdsong. A couple of hundred yards along the lane stood a group of three estate workers' cottages, now looking sadly run down and empty pending renovation. I made a mental note to discuss them with Shipley. My butler had briefly mentioned the cottages, but had not conveyed to me any urgency with respect to their repair.

But were they all empty? I thought I saw something move

inside the middle cottage. An animal, perhaps? But looking more closely, the encroaching vegetation by the front door was less overgrown than in front of the other cottages. I stopped for a minute, and strained my eyes, looking for signs of occupation. But I could see nothing more, and I did not feel inclined to confront anyone – or anything – that might be inside. Shipley could investigate later. I moved on, with an uneasy feeling that I was not yet entirely in control of my estate.

Fox was starting to tire as we walked under the medieval gate of Hawksbridge, and I had to scoop him up into his sling.

As I approached The Duke's Head, I saw a gaggle of people outside, near the lane leading to the artist's cottage. For a moment I thought they must be hopeful models, but it became obvious as I approached that they were subdued – indeed, in shock, from their demeanours.

I found Phyllis amongst them, wearing a grim expression.

"Good morning, Mr Rufford," she said when she caught sight of me. "Have you heard the terrible news?"

"Good morning, Miss Drummond," I said. "No, I haven't – what's happened?"

"Something dreadful has happened to one of the artists. My father is in there talking to the police."

"Oh my God," I said. "You mean – dead? Surely not!"

"I'm afraid so. I don't really want to stand and gawp like this, but I want to check that my father is all right when he comes out. He may be somewhat distressed."

"Of course," I said. "Let me keep you company until he does. I was going to ask you and your father over for dinner, but that seems of no consequence now."

Phyllis looked at me and smiled. "That is very kind of you. When we can think about it properly, I would be delighted, and my father would be too. He knew your father. I'm sure he would be interested to meet you."

"Extraordinary," I said. "My father seemed to know

everyone in Hawksbridge – even Fox here." And I patted the dog's head.

"I was about to ask what, or who, you had strapped to your body. He is delightful. I'm just sorry I'm a little distracted at the moment, or I would give him more attention."

"Naturally." I now felt it was in poor taste to bring a dog into this alarming scene. "I suppose I ought to offer a statement to the police, since I saw both of them last week."

"Oh dear – and I encouraged you," said Phyllis. "Did they seem on bad terms?"

"You mean foul play is a possibility?" I said. "I doubt that. No, they seemed very happy with each other's company. There was just some silly, friendly banter. I must say, they were like brothers – they had, as far as I could tell from my brief visit, an enviable relationship."

"I expect it was an accident," said Phyllis. "I don't know why I should have thought otherwise. How macabre of me."

"Well, it is your job to dramatise," I said, putting Fox down to give my back a rest and allow the dog to stretch his legs. "I read one of your books..." I trailed off, struggling to find the words to describe my reaction to it that were not either gushing or trite.

After an awkward pause, Phyllis said, "You hated it. Of course you did! But don't worry, I'm well aware that I can't please everyone. It wouldn't be your kind of book anyway." She turned away and scrutinised the lane to watch for signs of her father.

"Phyllis, no!" I forgot myself and grabbed her shoulder in my horror that she had misunderstood me. "I mean, Miss Drummond!"

She spun round to face me, with a look of puzzlement and irritation.

I removed my hand. "I'm sorry. But I loved it. 'Lady Harlington's Estate' – I was entranced. It was all so very vivid to me. I confess" – I hesitated – "I shed a tear at the end."

Her expression softened. "Really? I'm not sure whether to believe you. But you look sincere."

"I am, I assure you. I would not insult you with a dishonest appraisal. What would be the point? Except to spare your feelings..."

Phyllis smiled. "I'm so glad you would not consider my feelings, Mr Rufford."

"In this matter only, of course," I said, aware I had walked into a trap.

"Well – thank you. I'm pleased you enjoyed it. I'm quite proud of that one. And yet..." She sighed and gestured towards the cottage. "Everything seems absurd and trivial in the face of death."

"Isn't that partly why we need literature?" I said. "To prepare us for the difficult things – and to celebrate life and the world. You give people catharsis and comfort."

"What a lot of responsibility that is!" said Phyllis. "But you are very sweet. I am encouraged."

We had to step aside to avoid a horse and cart that was turning in to the lane. The cart bore a coffin, and we exchanged glances.

"The poor man," said Phyllis. "Perhaps the Rector was right all along – they should never have come to Hawksbridge."

In a few minutes, the cart emerged from the lane again, and disappeared in the direction of the undertakers. Shortly after, Dr Drummond walked towards us with a solemn expression.

"That's all I can do," he said. "I have conveyed my findings to the police; there will not be an autopsy. In my opinion, it was a tragic accident." He sighed. "Mr Shaw is distraught. They are interviewing him in the inn."

"It's too awful," said Phyllis, squeezing her father's arm. "Father, this is Mr Thomas Rufford. I told you about him – he lives in Ramsburgh now."

Dr Drummond's mood was lifted a little. "Ah, Mr Rufford! How nice to meet you, despite..." He gestured towards the cottage. "Your father was an interesting man. I had some stimulating discussions with him."

"Thank you, sir," I said. "I had hoped to introduce myself before. I have been reading one of your daughter's books – she is extremely talented."

"Ah, well, yes – it's an unexpected turn of events, but Phyllis does seem to have a way with words."

"I've been writing for over ten years, Father!" Phyllis said.

"Of course, of course," said Dr Drummond, a little absently. "I can't get used to you being so grown up. Now, I'm a little worn out by this incident, so forgive me for retiring for some rest. It was good to meet you, Mr Rufford. Please call on us, and I'll look out our best sherry. Goodbye, my dear." He squeezed his daughter's hand and made his way down the street.

"I must go and speak to the police," I said, although I would far rather have taken a stroll with Phyllis around the town walls. It seemed that such a pleasure would have to wait.

"Why don't I stay and look after Fox for you?" said Phyllis. "It might make it easier for you."

"That would be very kind," I said. "Are you sure? He's still a bit of an invalid after losing his old master, but I'm sure he would appreciate a gentle stroll."

"Certainly! Hand me his lead, and we'll see how we get on. Come on, Fox, how about a little walk?"

Having rested, Fox looked amenable to taking my place on a perambulation through Hawksbridge.

"You see!" said Phyllis. "I am favoured. Good luck, Mr Rufford!"

"Thank you! Be good, Fox," I said, and walked down the lane with trepidation. At least the body had been taken away, but God only knew what remained inside the cottage. It had been so neat and cheerful, and now it would always be remembered as a place of tragedy.

I explained myself to a constable stationed outside the cottage, and was directed to the back door of the inn to await the Inspector in the innkeeper's parlour. As I approached the parlour, I could see Mr Minto talking quietly to Henry Shaw at the foot of the stairs; his hand was on Shaw's shoulder as the artist choked back tears. I supposed that Shaw had been given a room in the inn. If Minto had been disappointed at the destruction of his dreams of glory, he had the humanity not to show it.

I did not have long to wait for the Inspector, a middle-aged man with more the look of a bank manager than a detective.

"Mr Rufford? Thank you for coming forward. My name is Inspector Simmons. I gather you saw Mr Shaw and Mr Walker two Sundays ago. Is that correct?"

"Yes, Inspector. Mr Frederick McPhee – a director of the Hawksbridge Pottery – suggested I come along with him to see the artists."

"I see," said the Inspector, scribbling in his notebook. "And what is your relationship with Mr McPhee, and with Shaw and Walker?"

"Mr McPhee is my colleague – that is, I am the owner of the Pottery."

The Inspector's eyebrows went up. "Indeed? Forgive me – you seem a little young."

"I suppose I am. It was an accident of inheritance," I said.

"A felicitous accident, to be sure. And the reason for visiting Shaw and Walker?"

"Mr McPhee wished to discuss a business proposition – commemorative mugs and plates bearing their work. And he was just curious about them, having recommended their employment for the Town Hall mural."

"Uh-huh," murmured the Inspector, scribbling quickly. "And were you curious, too?"

"I confess I was," I said. "I admire their work."

"This was your first meeting with them?"

"Yes, first and only meeting. I found them polite and content. Apart from having received a kind of threat –"

"Ah yes, the rat and the note. Mr Minto mentioned it."

"Do you think they are significant?" I said.

The Inspector grunted. "I don't see a need to jump to any conclusions about that. Mr Walker's death has all the hallmarks of an unfortunate accident, perhaps assisted by the intake of an unwise quantity of alcohol. Anything else you think might be relevant, sir?"

I ran over the events of that day in my mind. "No, I can't think of anything, but if I do, I will let you know."

"Thank you, Mr Rufford. I appreciate your cooperation. That's all I'm needing for now." With the closing snap of his notebook, the interview was over.

~

There was no sign of Phyllis and Fox when I got to the street, and I had some time to examine the buildings around me in more detail than previously. The pleasant, solid appearance of the inn, with its bright white walls and black window surrounds, was at odds with the knowledge that an inconsolably distraught artist lay within. The town walls, and the massive earth mound on which they were built, loomed behind the streetscape. Beyond that, the tops of a windmill could be seen, hard at work grinding corn. The purposeful spire of St Ninian's pierced the urban horizon; and all seemed ordered. Sudden death struck a jarring note here. But an equable mantle of stone, tile and paint would always hide the unending human drama within. For a gloomy moment, civilization seemed to me to be nothing but a confidence trick.

An excited yapping interrupted my thoughts, and I saw Phyllis and Fox coming towards me.

"Hello!" said Phyllis. "You were in a dream. How did it go? We had a nice little walk, didn't we, Fox? Nothing too strenuous."

The dog was pleased to be back with his master, and I made a fuss of him. "It was very straightforward," I said. "It seems to have been an accident. The landlord was trying to comfort poor Mr Shaw – I wonder if we should try to help him in some way."

"I think we need to leave him alone to grieve for a while," said Phyllis. "But yes, we must see what can be done, in due course. I don't suppose he will want to paint for a long time, which will be a double loss for him."

"Speaking of which," I said, "I wonder how far they got with the mural."

"Shall we go and see?" said Phyllis. "Is that ghoulish?"

"I don't think so," I said, although a little unsure.

"I'd like to see what was completed – if anything – before it gets whitewashed, as it surely will be," said Phyllis.

The Town Hall was open, and with some trepidation we ascended the stone stairs that led to the elaborately pedimented door. Scattered in the grand atrium lay cloths, trestle tables, ladders; and a handful of other people, having had the same thought as Phyllis and myself, were staring at the walls in silence.

The artists had not been idle: they had sketched out the outlines of their composition, and the mostly uncoloured ghosts of angels were leaning down to pluck up unfortunate mortal souls, just as Shaw had said.

But two angels had been coloured, if incompletely: both showed a good deal of heavenly flesh. One had no head, other than a faint black contour that the model's mother might have struggled to recognise, but her body was lovingly portrayed, including a naked breast. The other angel was more complete:

she was mature and voluptuous, but no more modest in her attire; she was casting her sad, dignified eyes down upon the scene and raising her arms as if to conduct the movements of the others.

"How beautiful she is!" said Phyllis.

"Yes – she is – ravishing," I said, unable to take my eyes off her. For this angel, in her revealing, diaphanous robes, held aloft by a pair of powerful wings, was none other than Francesca.

# CHAPTER EIGHT

TWO days later, I stood in front of the Hawksbridge Pottery Company in Roman Street, rain dripping off my wide-brimmed hat. McPhee had picked a fine day for a meeting, and the inconvenient distance between Ramsburgh and Hawksbridge compared with the compactness of Oxford was becoming irksome. However, I acknowledged to myself that this was one of the penalties of privilege, and one I would need to get used to.

"Very glad to see you, Mr Rufford!" said McPhee, ushering me into his office. "Sorry you had to get soaked, but it'll be worth it. We have some interesting matters to discuss. Walton, can you get Mr Rufford a cloth to dry himself with?"

Mr Walton came back with a clean cotton square, and McPhee waited patiently for me to get dry. "I had the police call on me yesterday," McPhee said. "I told them what I could, which isn't much. What did you make of the Inspector? Not the most zestful of men, perhaps."

"No, but quietly competent, I should think," I said. "They don't seem to believe there was anything suspicious about Walker's death."

"I hope they are keeping an open mind," said McPhee. "After the rat... it's all most unfortunate. And we spent so long on this project, and championed them despite opposition. Ah well, that's nothing compared with the loss of a brilliant artist. The country is indeed deprived of a bright star. Just imagine what he – they – could have accomplished! They were so young."

"We still have Shaw," I said, "and I hope he can be encouraged to continue, when he's ready. Perhaps he could be persuaded to finish the mural?"

"Do you think so? That would be wonderful. Let's try to encourage him."

I nodded. "So what surprises do you have for me? You have been a little mysterious."

"Of necessity," said McPhee. "You never know who may be a spy. I half-jest, but the competition is becoming heated. I speak, of course, of biscuit ware. As I'm sure you know, biscuit ware is unglazed pottery, which we can use for decorative items, such as plaques and small statues."

"Indeed," I said, having only the vaguest knowledge of such things.

"Well, our competitors have developed some interesting techniques. Minton has their 'Parian ware', and Copeland has their more prosaically named 'statuary porcelain'. Both replicate very closely the smooth texture of classical marble sculpture, which enables the manufacture of huge numbers of small statues for very little money. Almost everyone will be able to buy this art, not just the rich."

"Impressive," I said. "And are we working on a similar thing?"

"You may be assured that we are," said McPhee. "It is a great opportunity, and we cannot afford to let it go. Think of the market for lithographs that emulate distinguished works of art – we know that the public will go out and buy these reproductions in great numbers."

I nodded, thinking of my own recent purchase.

"And now we can do the same thing for sculpture: duplicating famous works, but also creating entirely new ones. I'm tremendously excited about it. We're thinking of calling it 'Marbleware'. But we must move quickly. I hope you will concur that we need to spend some money in furthering our own process, which is at an advanced stage."

"Definitely, Mr McPhee," I said. "I agree that this is a substantial opportunity. How much more should we be spending?"

"I estimate a couple of thousand pounds to perfect the porcelain and set up the manufactory. Plus a hundred for each mould. These are up-front costs, naturally, and then there are materials and labour at the usual rates."

"And we have this to spare?"

"We have, I'm happy to say," said McPhee, looking a little smug. "No need to trouble the bank. Hawksbridge Dragon has been selling exceptionally well: an increasing public interest in Asia seems to have helped us."

"Then I'm all for it. Do you have any prototypes?"

"That was my next point," said McPhee. "Please follow me, Mr Rufford."

The director took me out of the office and down a corridor, and opened a door into an airy, well-lit office.

"I think you met Mr Joseph in your last visit."

"Yes, I had that honour," I said, and Mr Joseph bowed his head respectfully.

"Please show Mr Rufford what we have so far," said McPhee.

"Certainly," said Mr Joseph, and he deftly removed cloths that were covering several objects on his bench.

I was astonished. "They're just like miniature stone statues!" I said as I inspected the white, artfully-draped men and women frozen in elegant poses. I reached out my hand. "May I?" McPhee and Mr Joseph nodded, and I ran my fingers over a female arm. It had the exact feel of polished marble – cold and smooth, but not glossy like the gaudy, glazed porcelain figures I was used to seeing on mantelpieces. I was particularly enamoured of the female bather who was seated on a rock, bending over to dry her legs, almost entirely naked.

"We have some more work to do on the quality of the porcelain," said McPhee, "in particular by adjusting the proportion of felspar, but we're nearly there. And Mr Joseph here is a master at what he does, and he will help to make us all a tremendous amount of money!"

I congratulated Mr Joseph, and we returned to McPhee's office. But the triumphant mood was immediately quelled by finding the office occupied by Inspector Simmons, who was being kept company by Mr Walton.

"Inspector! What can I do for you?" said McPhee.

"Good morning, Mr McPhee – Mr Rufford. Sorry to disturb you again, but I wondered if you might help me with the whereabouts of Mr Johnny Falkirk. I believe you know him?"

"Ah – only very slightly, Mr Simmons," said McPhee. "I last saw him in church, two Sundays ago, before Mr Rufford and I went to visit Mr Shaw and Mr Walker. I helped him out of the church, then he sat on a bench for a while, and after Dr Drummond had made sure he was sufficiently well, he wandered off. That was the last time I saw him."

"I'm afraid I've never spoken to him, Inspector, and the last time I saw him was outside St Ninian's," I said. "He's not at his home, then?"

"No, nothing so convenient," said Mr Simmons. "His mother says she's not seen anything of him since Friday, and he is proving elusive. Well, thank you, gentlemen – if you do see or hear anything about him, please be so good as to come along to the police office. I'd be much obliged. We don't wish to arrest the man, only to have a word. Good day!"

~

By the time I had tramped back to Ramsburgh, the sun had come out and my clothes had dried off. The meeting with McPhee and the buoyant discussions of the company's bright future had put me in a good mood, despite Simmons' reminder of darker circumstances. I had been struggling to maintain an interest in plates and teapots, but it was far easier now that the company was engaged on producing egalitarian 'art' – accessible to the middle classes, at least – and the designers and directors were pleasingly liberal in the pieces they were prepared to manufacture.

There was a paradox, I had to admit. On one hand, the colourless figures were austere, pale and pure: redolent of nobler, classical times. On the other, the most appealing and sought-after examples would undoubtedly be beautiful women in a state of undress, in elegant poses that showed their pale flesh to best advantage. But this was nothing new for art. And while society had turned its back on some of the excesses of the previous century, it was not yet prepared to censure the sensuous when it came to public and private art.

I moved these thoughts to a mental compartment for deployment in a social setting, should the occasion and company warrant it. It was more important to seek out Mrs Felton and lunch.

I was greeted at the kitchen door by a solicitous Fox, who was getting more energetic by the day. "I'll take you for a walk after my lunch," I said, fobbing him off with an ear scratch. "Ah! Mrs Felton. Any chance of a bowl of soup and some bread?"

"Of course, dear," said Mrs Felton. "I've made some nice chicken and leek broth. Any news from town about...?"

"Good. No, I've not heard anything, except that the police want to ask some questions of Mr Falkirk. He seems to have disappeared."

"Lord!" said Mrs Felton, preparing a tray for my lunch. "Could he have something to do with it? The butcher came this morning, and he says that there are some shocking rumours about what those two artists got up to. The womenfolk have been going mad over them, and there are some aggrieved husbands – whether with reason, or not, I don't know. Anyway, it seems there are plenty of people who would be glad to see the back of them."

I sighed. "I hate to say it," I said, "but the Rector's intuition may have been correct. But these rumours could be completely scurrilous, and unless verified, we shouldn't countenance them, for the sake of Henry Shaw. He must be in a terrible state, poor man. He's lost his best friend, his business partner, and perhaps his motivation to work. Let's not add character assassination to his woes!"

"Well said, my dear," said Mrs Felton. "You are quite right. We should not judge too quickly. Goodness, what a stir all this is. You have come to us at a strange time indeed!"

"I'm starting to think I'm a harbinger of doom, Mrs Felton," I said, crouching down and stroking Fox's head.

"Stuff and nonsense! A breath of fresh air, more like. Now you get settled in the dining room, and I'll bring you your lunch."

~

As I drank my soup, my mind wandered onto the pleasant memory of Francesca, immortalised as an erotic supervising angel, beating her strong wings and holding sway among the lesser celestial beings. Somehow, that epitomized what I knew of Mrs Campbell: a natural authority over others, palpable dignity, and yet also a highly sensual animal quality. It was an intoxicating combination.

What would it be like, I mused, if she were to be modelled in the Hawksbridge Pottery Company's new biscuit ware? Although the original might ultimately prove elusive, I could have a reproduction Francesca in my study for ever; I could adjust her position to my heart's content, to get the best view of her profile, her face, the pleasing curves of her hips...

My daydreams were interrupted by Shipley at the door.

"Letters for you, sir," he said, and handed me two sealed envelopes.

I looked at the handwriting. One was clearly female, the other I judged to be the messy scrawl of an infirm or possibly inebriated male. The latter was unlikely to give any enjoyment, I thought. But the first could be from Francesca or Phyllis, as I was unfamiliar with either hand.

I decided against deferring gratification, and opened the neater missive. To my surprise, it was from neither Francesca nor Phyllis.

> Bewick House, Eglingham Road, Hawksbridge
>
> Dear Mr Rufford,
>
> Forgive me for writing to you directly, but please let me welcome you warmly, if belatedly, to Hawksbridge! I am Olivia Harris, a friend of Miss Davison, who has told us of your move to Ramsburgh. I do hope you are settling in well and find the house and town to your liking.
>
> My husband – David – and I would very much enjoy meeting you: to which end, we are holding an evening party this Saturday at around 8pm which I hope you and Miss Davison can attend.
>
> Faithfully,
>
> Olivia Harris

After a moment of disappointment that the letter was from a stranger, I realised I should be grateful for this kind gesture. I hoped I could repay Mrs Harris' curiosity in me. Perhaps she had a daughter she wanted to introduce to me. In any event, it would be interesting to meet some Hawksbridge natives.

Thoughts of pleasant introductions to potential brides were quickly wiped from my mind after I had ripped open the second letter. The hand was as wild inside as it was outside, and full of angry crossings and underlinings. It read as follows.

Mr Thomas Rufford,

We have met, a long time ago now, in better times when my beautiful sister Hazel was still alive. That she is not, I say is your fault, and your fault only. You set off the mischief that led there, and though no one will recognise you as her murderer, you may yet be hung for another death: that of Mr John Oliphant.

Letters have come to me that put me in a damn powerful spot. Yes, more powerful than a rich man sitting pretty in his castle, pretending innocence. These letters, then, you sought to steal, and the upshot of that was the deaths of two righteous people, mourned awfully by their folk. The letters, and the knowing of where I got them from, would send you to the gallows, easy as snapping my fingers. What do you think of that, Mr Rufford?

But I am a fair man and I will give you a chance. You get me 500 pounds in new sovereigns, and I will get you the letters for you to burn. This is compensation for the loss of my sister, that a judge will never give me – the judges don't look after the wronged ones, do they?

I could not find your friends, but no matter, if you get me what I ask for. Then I will not seek for them. Then it will be over. But not until you pay me what you owe me for my loss.

You set about getting this from the bank now, Mr Thomas Rufford – new sovereigns, mind – because I am coming for you, and I want you to have it ready. If you go to the law about this, the letters will be with the police in no time. And then you are a dead man. BE WISE!

Alan Sharpe

# CHAPTER NINE

I FELT a shock akin to being struck on the head with a cricket bat. I seemed to be choking, and stood up to take a deep breath, but the room was swaying and I had to sit down again abruptly. Terror racked me, and I held the letter tightly, scanning it several times to be sure I had read it correctly.

There was no doubt: I had failed to shake off the demons of my youth that were haunting my dreams. Hazel's brother had found out my address, and at any moment could appear – no, *would* appear – to exact his revenge.

Mrs Felton came in to collect the tray, and stopped halfway across the room. "Mr Rufford! Are you all right? You look as pale as death."

I quickly folded up both letters and tried to pull myself together. "I am fine, thank you, Mrs Felton. I was just thinking of the past, and the things that should be left there. But I have had good news, in that Miss Davison and I have been invited to a party on Saturday."

"If you're sure you're all right – but that is nice for you. And it will do Miss Flora a power of good. I've said it before and I'll say it again: she spends far too much time cooped up in her tower. You can take the pony trap – Miss Flora uses it occasionally, and she can help you master it."

I nodded, and beckoned to Fox, who was waiting more-or-less patiently by my chair. A walk was exactly what I needed, and the dog's cheerful innocence and appetite for life might help give me perspective.

Out on the hill, I took gulps of the wind that chilled my face. For a few seconds, I managed to push the letter from my mind and enjoy the pure, physical sensations of being outdoors. But my fears came rushing back soon enough, and I wondered if I would have been better talking affable nonsense with the reassuring Mrs Felton – or even confessing my sins to her. Throwing sticks for the eager Fox did not ease the dread that the letter had instilled in me. For I *was* complicit in those two deaths. If I had taken different decisions, disaster might have been averted. And yet, I reflected bitterly, how easy it is to march towards a catastrophe whose origin can be traced to one seemingly innocuous decision or twist of fate, and whose inevitability is cemented by each misjudgement along the way.

It would be necessary, I thought, to sell some investments and raise the money, in case I could not persuade Alan Sharpe to leave empty-handed. It would be a blow to my wealth, but not a fatal one. The most severe problem was how to do this without arousing suspicion. Perhaps I could feign a gambling habit.

I knocked on Flora's door to discuss the party invitation.

"Ah, yes," she said, "I received mine this morning."

"I shall try to be good company," I said. "What are the Harrises like?"

"They are kind people," said Flora. "Mr Harris is – or was – a banker, in London, but he wasn't enjoying it, so he retired early and they moved here where they both have family connections. You will like their house. Olivia and I occasionally meet for tea, and I've been teaching her embroidery."

"I'm intrigued," I said. "It's good of them to ask me. Oh, and Mrs Felton said we might use the opportunity for you to show me how to drive the pony trap."

"Of course, Mr Rufford. There's nothing to it, and Jenny has a fine temperament."

"Good! Shall we convene around half-past seven on Saturday? I'll have Howard bring the trap around then." Howard was the ageing but still-capable Ramsburgh factotum for whom groom was one of many titles.

This arranged, I cast around for another task to take my mind off the unwanted letter. My thoughts turned to poor Henry Shaw. It was remarkable how the man had quickly gone from glamorous art idol to object of pity since coming to Hawksbridge. I felt it my duty to see that Shaw was as comfortable as it was possible to be in his present state of misery, and to offer congenial words of comfort, however futile. It was unlikely that he had friends here.

~

My second journey into town that day was drier than the first. But I would far rather have been transported back to the earlier outing, free of the weight that now hung around my neck – around which the feral Alan Sharpe could put a noose.

At The Duke's Head, I got directions to Shaw's room, and knocked on the door. After a moment, Shaw opened it, and recognition slowly dawned. "The pottery factory man, isn't it?"

"Yes – Thomas Rufford," I said. "I hope I'm not intruding, but I wanted to offer my utmost condolences, and also to ask if there is anything I could assist you with. This is a most wretched state of affairs."

"Ah," he said. "Yes. Kind of you. Can't think of anything I need, but you can take a drink with me, if you like. Some company wouldn't be disagreeable."

Shaw closed the door after I had entered, fetched a mug and poured beer for us both from a jug that I imagined was replenished frequently, judging by Shaw's ruddy cheeks. Then the artist removed some clothes from a side chair, dragged it to a Pembroke table, and gestured for me to sit.

"Still can't believe it," he said, staring past me at a stain on the wall after taking his own seat. "Known him over twenty years. One minute you're laughing together, the next..."

He shook his head and swigged from his mug.

"I've written to his mother," he said. "Newcastle. They'll be wanting to take him back for his..." He frowned and swore under his breath.

"Do you know how it happened?" I asked.

"Yes and no. The Inspector says he was drunk and simply stumbled and fell, smashing his head on the grate. So yes, he may have hit his head. But Ned was no clumsy oaf. I don't believe he just fell. It's absurd."

"I see," I said. "Do you have any reason to think someone was there, and maybe pushed him?"

"Way I look at it," said Shaw, "is this. He never had any trouble standing up before, and we've got outside of our fair share of liquor in our time. But we've never lost the use of our legs. And then we come to a place where the Rector rants against us like a loon, and we get dead rats dumped at our door. Then Edward..." He evidently could not bear to complete this sentence. "And I'm expected to believe this was just an accident? Do I look like a total *fool?*"

A flash of anger made him say the last word so loudly and vehemently that I jumped a little.

"Did you discover him?" I said, hoping that it was not insensitive to probe.

"Aye," said Shaw, the mug in his hand trembling a little. "I was out all night – I hate myself about that – and when I came back in the morning, there he was, stretched out with his head in the fireplace. Blood everywhere."

He took another draught of beer and sighed.

"Raised the alarm at the inn. Police came. Doctor came. Can hardly remember it, I was in such a daze."

"It must have been heartbreaking," I said. "I think the Inspector is considering all possibilities, since he was looking for... Well, I'd better not say."

"I know the bastard he's looking for. Mr Falkirk, isn't it!

Might be him. Might not be him. But someone in this godforsaken town knows something, and it's mighty rum that the talentless little runt has suddenly disappeared."

He tried to pour more beer but the jug was empty. He grunted and slammed it down on the table, making a dent on the polished table surface.

"The police aren't taking it seriously. Of course not – they wouldn't want the town sullied by scandal! They'll just ignore it, get rid of me, and then they'll get on with their lives, while mine is ruined. But I'm not going to let that happen, because I'm not leaving this bloody place until I know who killed Ned! He'll bloody haunt me otherwise, one way or another."

He suddenly looked intensely at me. "Perhaps there is something you can do. I've heard you haven't been here long. Maybe you're not tainted yet."

I realised that I would inevitably be the subject of gossip, but it made me uncomfortable nevertheless. In its domain at the edge of the town, Ramsburgh had promised privacy, but that was probably an illusion.

"How could I help, Mr Shaw? The police are the best people to investigate –"

"Damn the police," said Shaw. "They aren't interested in the truth, only what's convenient for them and those pulling their strings. If they were in any way competent, they'd have found Falkirk by now. And it won't make a difference if they do – they've made their minds up already. Accidental, they'll say, and then Ned's legacy will be to be remembered as the fool who fell over in his cups and killed himself. And I don't mind saying, it will reflect badly on me too."

The artist got up and started pacing the room. "You did offer to help, Mr Rufford. And you seem to me a decent fellow, not one to let a wrong stand."

I conceded that I had indeed put myself in a position of obligation, both by my offer and by my association with the company that had solicited the artists.

"Very well, I'll try asking around: as I'm a newcomer, there will be a limit to what information will be forthcoming. But I suppose there's no harm in trying."

"That's the spirit! Thank you," said Shaw, slapping me on the back. I had immediately regretted my promise – there was scant hope of me finding out more than the police already knew. However, it occurred to me that my enquiries could start here in this room.

"Mr Shaw, if you don't mind me asking: why were you away the night Mr Walker died?"

Shaw stopped pacing and turned away from me, towards the window. "I'm ashamed to say it, Mr Rufford. I was with a woman who came to offer as a model. Me and Ned never could keep away from women. They are our inspiration – maybe our downfall too. I was with a widow on the other side of town, all night. I had spent a long day in the Town Hall, and my muscles ached. This woman made it all better: poured me a bath, made me a meal, and everything pleasant you can imagine." He laughed. "And some things you shouldn't."

I smiled to hide my embarrassment at this revelation. "I see," I said. "And you told the police this?"

"Not in so many words. But yes, I had to explain my whereabouts. I could see their contempt when I told them, and now her reputation is ruined." He shook his head.

"So you got back in the early morning?" I said.

"Not so early. About half-past eight. I'd left him at about seven o'clock the previous evening."

"And the name of the woman in question?"

Shaw frowned. "Not sure the relevance. But the police know, so you may as well. Bess Shannon. I haven't troubled her again. Don't think she'd be so keen."

"Thank you for the beer, Mr Shaw," I said, getting up. "I'll ask around and find what I can, but I can't guarantee anything. I'll come back and see you in a few days anyway."

Shaw shook my hand warmly. "Can't ask anything more.

Thank you, Mr Rufford. You may be the only friend I have in Hawksbridge."

~

I stood in the street wondering what on earth I had just agreed to. The townsfolk would not appreciate a relative stranger poking his nose into their businesses and trying to outsmart the police. And would I not simply be encouraging the delusions of a troubled man?

On the other hand, I thought, in their haste to find a solution, the police were often waylaid by a particularly appealing but incorrect theory. The unfair incarceration of Hazel was testament to that, with its horrible consequences.

Also, a convenient trait of humanity was the powerful impulse to talk, and besides, my detachment from Hawksbridge life might be an advantage, putting people off their guard. There was a fighting chance of picking up gossip that might shed light on Walker's death, one way or another. Perhaps someone saw him inebriated and unsteady. Or someone other than Walker might have been seen entering the cottage. And it would be a welcome distraction from my own worries.

Next, I had the unpleasant job of raising some money. I called on my solicitor and told him that I needed to raise cash for paying some Oxford debts. My solicitor suggested shares to sell, and since this would take some time, also offered to find a moneylender to advance the cash. This meant that I could call on the bank to pick up the five hundred sovereigns within a week. I resolved to be an expert in using the pony trap by then.

I rewarded myself with a trip to the bookshop. Phyllis was not there this time, but scanning the shelves, I encountered the copy of the scurrilous novel that she had been examining. 'The Predilections of Reverend Malamor, or The Hypocrite of Eaglesville, by John Bland.' I smiled at the title, and took it to the desk.

"Good morning, sir," said Mr Hunter. "It's turned out fine now, hasn't it? Let's see what you've found." Putting his spectacles on, he examined the book, and his cheerful expression evaporated. "Mr Rufford, isn't it?" he said, peering up intensely at me and back at the book. "Are you sure, sir? I don't think this is the quality of thing you're after. I'm sure I could find something more suitable, if you can just –"

"I'm quite sure, thank you," I said with some irritation. First Phyllis, and now Mr Hunter – they made unlikely censors, seeming to fear some kind of adverse chemical reaction between myself and this vulgar novel. But if I wanted to read a vulgar novel, then no one was going to divert me to more worthy tomes.

Mr Hunter paused for a few seconds as if evaluating the consequences of setting fire to the book to render it unavailable. Then he said, "Certainly, sir, as you wish," adopted a studiedly neutral expression, and wrapped the book up carefully. "That will be a shilling, please, Mr Rufford."

# CHAPTER TEN

FLORA was a good teacher. I soon discovered that I enjoyed driving the pony trap – the first time I had tried to control any animal larger than a dog. This was going to make travelling into Hawksbridge much more pleasant in future.

"Excellent, Mr Rufford," said Flora. "Jenny is getting used to you."

After a moment, I said, "Miss Davison – should we perhaps address each other by our Christian names? I really would prefer it if you called me Thomas."

"Very well, Mr – Thomas," said Flora. "You may call me Flora if you wish."

"Splendid. Let me practise. Thank you, Flora, for my very pleasant driving lesson," I said, and she responded with a faint, forbearing smile. I felt this to be progress in the thawing of our relations, that had started with such a chill.

Bewick House was a handsome sandstone villa built to a generous plan at the end of the last century: it had a timeless classical style, with its symmetrical grid of windows and refined decorative flourishes. It was entirely the kind of house, I thought, for a retired banker with a moderate sense of his own status and an appetite for hospitality. But I found that I had grown fond of the accretion of different styles that characterised Ramsburgh, and the perfection of Bewick House seemed almost stark.

As we alit from the trap in front of the house, a groom appeared and took Jenny around to the stables. The door opened, and a woman in early middle age strode towards us.

"Flora!" she said. "How lovely to see you. Mr Rufford – I

am so very pleased you could come. I hope it wasn't terribly forward of me, but we are all so curious about you!"

"Thank you, Mrs Harris," I said. "I was honoured to be asked."

"Now then, Olivia," said a voice behind her. "He'll think we've been gossiping about him."

Good living had compensated David Harris for a slight limitation in height, although not to a grotesque extent. He held his hand out to me, and gave mine a firm and friendly shake. "Welcome, Mr Rufford! I am very much looking forward to hearing your impressions of Hawksbridge."

"Come, let us introduce you to the other guests," said Mrs Harris, palpably excited by the thought of the social transactions she was about to facilitate.

She led us through a blue-painted hall to a large drawing room with tall French windows, chinoiserie wallpaper, and armchairs in an ornate French style that were not at all to my taste.

"Mr Rufford, Flora, this is Mrs Edith Craven, and Mr Nicholas Craven. Nicholas is a teacher at St Saviour's School."

After the introductions, they all sat, and I said, "Can I ask your subject, Mr Craven?"

"I am the art master," said Mr Craven, "although I have plenty of other duties. I find it a rewarding occupation, especially when a student of real talent emerges."

The Harrises' butler, Marshall, proffered a tray with glasses of wine to Flora and myself, which we took.

"Did you teach Mr Falkirk, Nicholas?" Mrs Harris said, in an innocent tone that belied the unhappy associations of the name.

"Ha!" said Mr Craven. "Little Johnny Falkirk. Yes, I taught him. He has great promise, although perhaps not as much as he would give himself credit for. I hope he has come to no harm."

"Or done anyone else any harm," said Mrs Craven. "It is

all too disturbing. First this terrible death, and then Johnny goes missing."

"What is your professional opinion, Mr Craven," I said, "of Shaw and Walker? Their paintings, I mean, not their reputations."

"Which leave a lot to be desired," said Mrs Craven primly.

"Maybe so," said Mr Harris, "but Mr Walker did not deserve this."

"Oh, of course not," said Mrs Craven in a horrified tone. "I do hope I haven't been misunderstood!"

"Be that as it may," said Mr Craven, "I do think the pair of them are geniuses of our time. Or is it a single genius, because they create as one? Created, I should say. Who knows what this has done to Mr Shaw."

"I went to see him a few days ago," I said.

"Really?" exclaimed Mrs Harris. "How exciting! Do tell all. How was he?"

I now felt a little uncomfortable about having put my cards so freely on the table. The Inspector would surely not have done that. On the other hand, this was hardly an interview room and it was unlikely that I would gain much information from those present.

"He was subdued and unhappy, as you would expect," I said. "But mostly angry, with – as he sees it – a lackadaisical attitude from the police. He believes it was no accident, unlike, it seems, the Inspector, who didn't seem in a great hurry to apprehend Falkirk."

"Good Lord," said Mr Harris. "He really thinks it was a murder. But what if it was indeed a murder, and likely to be uncovered as such in due course? Then wouldn't Shaw himself be a suspect? He may be protesting too much, and actually has something to hide."

"My dear!" said Mrs Harris. "What an extraordinary notion. Why on earth would Mr Shaw kill his own friend, and ruin their wonderful business partnership?"

"Why does anyone commit murder? Money or women, usually," said Mr Harris, waving his empty glass at the butler to be refilled.

"Well," said Mrs Craven, "I have heard some quite unpleasant things on that score – their womanising, that is."

"Goodness! Do not spare us anything you know, Edith," said Mrs Harris, her eyes wide with curiosity.

"I heard Mr Shaw was with a woman the night Mr Walker died," Mrs Craven continued. "A widow – I won't say her name, it wouldn't be right."

"She's referring to Bess Shannon," said Mr Craven, helpfully.

"Nicholas! I wasn't going to say," said Mrs Craven. "But yes. What a carry-on!"

"Doesn't that give him an alibi?" said Flora. "Presumably she can testify that Mr Shaw was with her."

"Ah, but will she?" said Mr Harris. "It is terrible for her reputation. And besides, he may not have been there for the whole night."

I had to concede that this was a possibility. Shaw could be lying, and he could have returned to the cottage earlier.

"That still doesn't provide a motive for murder," said Mr Craven. "Unless they had both been courting the same woman. But those two don't sound like the type to be so devoted to a woman – more the kind to get their pleasure and move on. And Bess Shannon is – forgive me, I mean no disrespect – surely too ordinary for bohemians like Shaw and Walker."

"Perhaps," said Mrs Craven, "it wasn't Mrs Shannon at all. Perhaps there was another woman they were both after. I heard..."

At that moment, Mrs Harris got up from her chair with a smile to greet someone who had appeared in the doorway. I had my back to the door, and so I stood up and turned around in preparation for an introduction.

"Francesca!" said Mrs Harris. "You look so beautiful. How do you do it? But first – introductions. Everyone, meet Mrs Francesca Campbell. We met only a few weeks ago, but we are already firm friends. We have Mr Nicholas Craven, Mrs Edith Craven, my husband David, Miss Flora Davison, and I gather you already know Mr Thomas Rufford."

Francesca smiled and bowed, her eyes lingering on me for a moment. "Thank you for inviting me, Mrs Harris, Mr Harris – your house is sensational. Perhaps you will give me some decorating advice? I have some rooms I just can't make my mind up about."

"It would be my pleasure," said Mrs Harris. "Marshall, please fetch Mrs Campbell a drink."

Francesca sat on a chair near to me, and beamed at me. "This is a nice surprise, Thomas," she said.

"Yes indeed," I said, "but not nearly as surprising as what I saw in the Town Hall."

Francesca laughed heartily. "I suppose I should be embarrassed about that. But I refuse to be. It's not the first time I have been a model, and I hope it won't be the last."

I could see recognition dawn on Mrs Craven's face, and she nearly spilt her drink. "Goodness!" she said. "You are...?"

"The heavenly angel," said Mr Harris, who, judging by his inability to take his eyes off her, was clearly much taken with Francesca.

Mrs Craven's face reddened – I imagined she was trying to reconcile the semi-naked image of Francesca with the person in front of her.

"Oh, you've all seen it?" Francesca said, and covered her face with her hands in a gesture of self-consciousness that was not altogether authentic.

"The mural – or the fragment of it – is very well executed," said Mr Craven. "I have to say that Johnny Falkirk could never have achieved it."

"Johnny would have been lucky to get such a model!" said Mr Harris.

"So what have you all been talking about?" said Francesca. "I feel in need of some gossip that isn't about me."

"Yes, you were saying, Edith?" said Mrs Harris.

Mrs Craven looked alarmed. "Oh, nothing, really," she said. "I really can't remember."

"We were speculating about whether Shaw might have murdered Walker," said Mr Harris.

"Oh! David, I think we should change the subject," said Mrs Harris. "Remember, Francesca knew them. It is too ghoulish of us."

"It's quite all right," said Francesca. "I barely knew them. It is tragic, of course, but I had not formed a friendship with either of them. However, I don't think they were the murdering sort, whatever that might be. They were joined at the hip – they even finished each other's sentences."

"Women and money, though," said Mr Harris. "They can both do strange things to a man. I promised not to say anything... but I have an idea about the money side of things."

There was a hush in the room: all eyes were on Mr Harris.

"I play cards every week with a man in the insurance business," continued Mr Harris. "And he told me that something odd had happened. He said that a colleague of his had sold Mr Shaw an insurance policy, not three weeks ago. Quite a large one. It was to pay out in the event of Mr Walker's death. Shouldn't generally go blabbing about a man's personal affairs, but in this case, it's peculiarly interesting, don't you think?"

"Good Lord," said Mr Craven. "Have you told the police about this?"

"Not yet," said Mr Harris. "It's not my place. The insurance man will, I believe, and he probably already has."

"I've heard they don't like to been seen as fools," said Mr Craven, "and wash their dirty linen in public. They might be able to withhold their money without the police being involved."

"Still, it's not my place," repeated Mr Harris. "I'm a great admirer of Shaw's work, and I don't want to get him into trouble needlessly. He could be innocent, but I could still hang him with a few words. I don't want that on my conscience. No, I'm staying out of it. And please – do not repeat what I just said. For all I know, it could be a fabrication. Yes, it's probably a boast from a stupid clerk trying to puff himself up."

My thoughts were in confusion. If this allegation were true, it would put Shaw in a very different light. I would have some awkward questions for Shaw on my next visit.

~

When Mrs Harris announced the entertainments part of the evening, I had a moment of dread. I did not have anything to contribute. It brought to mind the dreams I often had when I was suddenly on stage without any lines or indeed any acting talent. But Flora rescued me, by suggesting that I read a favourite poem. I obliged, with Keats' 'Bright star, would I were steadfast as thou art' – a short poem but a passionate and tragic one, to the extent that both Mrs Craven and Mrs Harris were soon dabbing their eyes.

There followed Mr Harris' demonstration of the Northumbrian smallpipes, which squeaked and droned a tune that was just discernible as a well-known folk song. Mrs Harris looked apologetic throughout, but the little assembly was generous in its applause.

Mr Harris was pleased with the reception of his efforts. "Thank you! I've been learning for six months now," he said, and I thought I heard Mrs Harris mutter, "Seems like six years."

Flora proved very competent on the piano, accompanying Mrs Harris' strong soprano.

"You've been practising!" said Mr Craven. "I rather think that's cheating!"

"Quite possibly," said Mrs Harris. "Now, Nicholas. What have you got for us?"

"Bring me paper and a pencil, and I'll show you," he said.

Mr Craven sketched some creditable caricatures of each of them, which created great amusement.

"As good as a Punch cartoon!" declared Mr Harris on examining his. "Very clever."

Rather reluctantly, Mrs Craven took to the piano and played a slow rendition of Handel's 'Harmonious Blacksmith', a tune that always disagreeably reminded me of piano practice and endless scales.

"Do help yourself to a syllabub!" said Mrs Craven, encouraging everyone to pick up a cup of the creamy dessert. "And then – only Francesca is left to perform! What will you surprise us with, my dear?"

Francesca took her dessert and with the deliberate movements of a stage magician, settled herself in front of a small table. Glancing up to ensure she had an audience, she began to eat.

I met Flora's puzzled gaze. Was eating a syllabub an entertainment?

Francesca carefully scooped more syllabub and ate it, each time with a little flourish. It was a rather sensual performance, at odds with the tone of the party.

Finally, she put her spoon down on a napkin and pushed the remainder of the dessert towards her audience.

"I present: a syllabub tongue."

As I and the others looked into the cup, mystified, Francesca jiggled the cup, and to my combined horror and amusement, there it was: a tongue, wagging backward and forward, the syllabub's consistency lending a horribly realistic, visceral quality to the sculpture.

Mr Harris burst into immediate laughter. "Brilliant!" he said. "That is... utterly disgusting." Mrs Craven was wearing a frown and pursing her lips, but the others followed Mr Harris' example.

"Lord!" said Mrs Harris when she had finished laughing. "I didn't expect that."

"You are an artist," said Mr Craven. "Where did you learn such a thing?"

"An unserious acquaintance, a long time ago," said Francesca. "I'm sorry, that was very silly. I will do penance now, and play you something." She quickly consumed the quivering tongue and went to the piano, where she did justice to a sweet Chopin nocturne.

~

Presently, Mr Craven and Mr Harris started a game of cards, and Mrs Harris, Flora and Mrs Craven were deep in a conversation about a forthcoming charity bazaar. Francesca and I were left on our own on a sofa.

"That was very naughty of you," I said. "But it was certainly original."

"Who wants to be predictable?" said Francesca, sipping a glass of port. "Anyway, Thomas – how are you? What have you been up to? Have you bought yourself a good horse yet?"

"Alas no," I said, "but I have just learned how to drive a pony trap. I know, it's not the same."

"It's a start," said Francesca. "You'll be able to come and see me in my solitary splendour."

"That doesn't really fit you," I said. "You will always find a way to be at the centre of things! How did you get to know the Harrises?"

"Oh – Olivia and I were walking on the town walls, and we got talking about the weather, as you do. But I immediately realised she was a superior kind of person, and I insisted we have tea."

I smiled. "I wish I found it as easy as that."

"But you will always have people coming to you and making friends!" said Francesca, pressing his arm. "You are irresistible."

"You are very kind," I said.

"Oh, I can be," she said mischievously, lowering her voice almost to a whisper. "I can be so, so kind."

# CHAPTER ELEVEN

THE guests were enjoying the evening too much to notice darkness encroaching. As Flora and I said our goodbyes after the party and found Jenny waiting for us outside, a wind was getting up and it had started raining hard. Mrs Harris had insisted that Francesca sleep at Bewick House: it was no night for a woman to ride home alone.

We held on to our hats and were grateful for some moonlight to guide us. By the time we reached Ramsburgh, a full-blown storm had developed, and several large tree limbs had fallen near the house. Howard rushed out to take Jenny to safety, and as Flora and I approached the front door there was a loud crash of glass from the direction of the tower, followed by a shriek. I could not see what caused these noises from the front, so I ran into the house and up the tower staircase, followed by Flora. Titian, Flora's cat, shot down the stairs past me, and then Mrs Northcutt appeared. She was in a distressed state.

"The sitting room window!" she said, trying to catch her breath. "Something came through it. Such a shock." She sat down on the stair. "Oh, goodness. I shouldn't have run like that. But it scared me half to death."

Flora had caught up with me, and was about to speak when there was a huge peal of thunder.

"Oh!" said Flora. "That awful storm. Meg, are you all right?"

Mrs Northcutt nodded. "Yes, I will be in a moment."

"I'll try to find Titian," I said. "And I'll get Shipley to board up the window. Meanwhile, feel free to use the sitting room, or any other room you need. You can choose a bedroom each."

"Thank you," said Flora. "Titian's an indoor cat – Lord knows what would happen to him if he got outside. He has no common sense at the best of times."

"I'll see what I can do," I said.

Before I reached the bottom of the staircase again, Shipley appeared. "Can I help, sir? Sounds like there's a window staved in."

"Yes, Shipley – it's in Miss Davison's quarters. Can you try to board it up, for now?"

"Certainly, sir," said Shipley. "I'll go and fetch some things. I'm afraid I opened the kitchen door for a moment and the cat ran out."

"Damn," I said. "Well, can't be helped. Thank you, Shipley."

In the kitchen, Fox was whimpering, distressed by the storm. Mrs Felton and I made a fuss of him, and then, when the dog was calm, I said, "Right, Mrs Felton, time to find that blasted cat. Wish me luck!"

"Are you sure, my dear?" said Mrs Felton, putting her hand over her mouth in a worried gesture. "It's diabolical out there. A tree could fall on you! Better a dead cat than a dead Thomas."

"I'll be fine, Mrs Felton," I said, amused and a little touched by her use of my Christian name. I smiled reassuringly at her; but going back out into the storm was the last thing I wanted to do.

I wrapped my coat tightly about myself and opened the door, sending a gust of wind into the kitchen that rattled the pots and pans on the wall. I slipped out and closed the door behind me as quickly as possible.

A break in the clouds gave me just enough moonlight to have a decent chance of seeing the cat. There was no sign of Titian in the grounds to the front of the house, so I ran down the drive and stood at the junction where the track went into the woods. I could just make out a light: was that the cottage where I had sensed movement previously? Still, there was no time to investigate that now. I scanned the edge of the woods and went a little way in, but decided against venturing further in as it became too dark and hazardous.

Starting to return to the house, I caught sight of the dilapidated summer house. It was on my list to have it restored, or replaced if it was too far gone. Perhaps the cat had found shelter there? As I walked towards it, the wind suddenly intensified, hurling rain into my eyes so that I struggled to see. But as I approached, I could hear a howl. My instinct had been right: the sound was coming from inside the summer house. A broken pane in the glass door indicated how the cat had entered.

I grasped the handle and tried to open the door, only to find that it was locked. I shook it more violently, and the rotten structure gave way, showering broken glass onto me: a shard pierced my neck, and a rusty nail ripped a tear in my coat and shirt. I could not tell if it had penetrated my skin. It was pointless trying to find out now, so I stepped inside, where I could just make out Titian cowering in the corner. I slowly advanced, calling his name, and then made a quick lunge and managed to grab hold of him.

As I made my way back over the broken wood and glass, I tripped, but managed to keep a firm grip of the struggling, terrified cat as I fell painfully on my side, banging my head slightly on the paving slabs in front of the summer house. I struggled to my feet, half-blinded by the sheets of rain, and so buffeted by the wind I could barely stand. But I set course for the blurred mass that was – I hoped – the house, and as I approached the kitchen I could see and hear Flora and Mrs Felton calling my name. I was now starting to feel the pain from various parts of my body in earnest; I staggered towards Flora, dumped the cat in her arms, and then sensed a growing blackness as the ground rapidly advanced towards me.

~

I was standing on the lawn outside my Oxford college. A crowd of people were arranged in a circle around me, staring. I could recognise some of them: Hazel, naturally, was in the middle, her accusing eyes blazing at me. My former colleagues looked mockingly on, while Francesca clung to Henry Shaw, giving me a cold, contemptuous smile before kissing the artist on the lips.

"I've done nothing wrong!" I pleaded. "Leave me alone!"

"He's diabolical," said Mrs Northcutt. "Put him out of his misery."

The college building changed into Ramsburgh, which started to crumble. Flora's tower disintegrated into dust, and the rest followed suit.

"See that," remarked Shipley, "that's your doing. Should never have come."

Hazel opened her mouth and started talking, but her words were soundless.

There was a peal of thunder, and a ginger cat jumped out of the crowd and ran towards me with fangs bared. At the last moment, as it leapt, it turned into Sharpe, wielding a large shard of glass. "I told you, murderer – new sovereigns!" he said as he plunged the glass into my stomach.

"Sharpe! Get away from me!" I cried, trying to run, but unable to move.

"Thomas, dear, what is it?" said a gentle voice.

"Sharpe – he tried to..." I said, and then found that I was waking up. "Oh..." Pain suddenly assaulted me from all sides.

"Everything's all right, my dear," said Mrs Felton. "You've just had a bad dream."

"What's happened?" I said. "I feel..."

"You've had a terrible time," said Mrs Felton, "but you're getting better now. You were out in the storm, remember?

You got so many cuts from the summer house, and the cat, and you got a lump on your head too. Now, don't say I didn't warn you! But what's done is done."

I tried to move my limbs, and found that my right arm was heavily bandaged up.

"Dr Drummond said you have been lucky with that arm. He had to cut away some flesh, I'm afraid – you had a nasty wound from a rusty nail, and it became infected."

I groaned and tried to relax again. "If that's good luck, I definitely don't want any of the bad sort," I said.

Mrs Felton smiled. "Dr Drummond has given me instructions about changing the dressing. I'm your nurse now."

I looked up at Mrs Felton's reassuring face. "I couldn't ask for a better one," I said. "Thank you."

"It's no trouble, my dear," she said. "I enjoy it. Now, do drink some water. You must be parched!" She held up a mug, and I obliged.

"My God – my head! All this for a cat. It definitely wasn't worth it."

"Don't let Miss Davison hear that!" said Mrs Felton. "She feels awful about it. But she does dote on that daft animal."

"How long has it been since the storm?" I said.

"It's Monday today. The storm was the day before yesterday," said Mrs Felton. "You've been feverish – muttering all sorts of nonsense, you have!"

"Really?" I said. "I hope I didn't embarrass myself."

"Not really, dear," said Mrs Felton. "Just the kind of gibberish to be expected, considering. But you did seem worried about going to prison!"

I felt a prickle of sweat and horror that I may have bared my soul unwittingly. "Oh," I said. "I can't imagine..."

"My poor husband once stole a pie at Christmas, when he was about eight," said Mrs Felton, getting up from the bed and smoothing the bedclothes. "He was still having nightmares about the police coming for him, at the age of forty! I expect you did something you can't even remember now. The tricks the mind plays on us! Would you like a bite to eat? Some beef soup and bread, perhaps?"

"I would love some, Mrs Felton," I said, glad that the topic had changed. "Thank you."

~

Mrs Felton's soup gratefully consumed, I fell asleep, and was later awoken by a knock on the door.

"Thomas, you poor thing!" said a familiar, sensuous voice. "Or should I say, St Francis!" I opened his eyes to see Francesca standing by my bed.

"I have been worried about you," she said. "I heard from the Harrises about you, and the summer house. You look wretched. But you are now a hero to Miss Davison, and, I hope, to her cat. You will no doubt be getting presents of dead mice."

"None yet, or they've been removed, fortunately," I said. "Thank you for coming. I must say, you're a sight for sore eyes. This bedroom is becoming extremely dull, and so am I."

"You? Dull? Impossible!" said Francesca. "I wouldn't stand for it. Are you in much pain?"

"A little," I said. "Actually, more than a little. Both the summer house and the cat got their claws into me, and I slipped and hit my head, like the clumsy fool I am."

Francesca tutted and shook her head. "Ghastly. But it could have been worse. Are you feeling any better?"

"I think so. By the way, I dreamt of you," I said. "You were kissing Henry Shaw."

"Goodness!" said Francesca, and she giggled. "What fun I must have had."

"Well, I certainly didn't," I said. "It's been torment lying here having nightmares."

"Then I must give you something to look forward to. How about tea on the afternoon of Saturday the fifteenth, at my house? Just the two of us: Francesca and St Francis. I promise no party games, unless you want some, of course."

"That sounds most irregular, and most enjoyable," I said. "I would love to come. I'll try to be fit by then."

"Good," said Francesca. Her eye was caught by a book on my bedside table. "Ah! You have a copy of the notorious 'Predilections'. Mrs Harris told me about it."

"I haven't read it yet," I said, "but Miss Drummond – the doctor's daughter –"

Francesca laughed.

"What?" I asked, puzzled.

"You make her sound like a card out of 'Happy Families.' Sorry, do carry on."

"Miss Phyllis Drummond," I continued, "discouraged me from buying it, and so did the bookseller, so it must be interesting. What have you heard about it?"

"That it is a malicious and cynical attempt to smear the clergy, and indeed the great and the good of society in general. And it is very... indelicate. There was even a move to ban it, apparently."

"In that case," I said, "I will procrastinate no further." I started to reach for the book, but I could barely move my right arm, and groaned.

"I have an idea," said Francesca. "If you tell me who this mysterious Miss Drummond is, I will read you some of the book. Then we shall both be enlightened about the evil ways of the Reverend Malamor."

I smiled. Could Francesca's nose be a little out of joint at the notion of me consorting with other females? It was an intriguing thought.

"That would be charming. I imagine you to be an marvellous reader. Miss Drummond is a writer, whom I met in

Hunter's. She was looking at this very book, before being dismissive of it. She writes fiction. In fact, I've read one of hers, called 'Lady Harlington's Estate'."

"Well?" said Francesca. "Was it any good?"

I paused, examining Francesca's expression. It would be unfair, I thought, to describe the novel in glowing terms, because it was obvious that Francesca was disquieted by the competition.

"It was quite accomplished," I said. "I enjoyed it."

"Goodness!" Francesca said, attempting breeziness and magnanimity. "What a lot of interesting people there are in this town. I'm not sure I can keep up."

"Francesca," I said, "there is no need. You are already the most fascinating and delightful person in Hawksbridge."

Francesca smiled. "I should hope so," she said. "I do work so hard at being fascinating and delightful. Now, let's have a look at this wicked thing. 'The Predilections of Reverend Malamor, or The Hypocrite of Eaglesville, by John Bland.' Chapter One: Malamor's Arrival. The arrival of the Reverend Tobias Malamor in Eaglesville was anticipated with only a little less fervour and curiosity than the second coming of Christ..."

~

When I woke again, the light was starting to fail, and I was alone. For a moment I wondered if I had dreamt Francesca's visit, before remembering how much I had enjoyed her reading voice – it was rich and full of expression. I wished I had not fallen asleep, but I was, after all, still a convalescent, and so it could not be held against me.

I got up and found I felt a little better than in the morning, though slightly dizzy and in possession of an unpleasant headache. I walked around the room a few times, and moved my right arm to free it a little, trying not to think about what was under the bandage.

Putting on my dressing gown, I decided to walk up the stairs to the two upper bedrooms, to exercise my joints. In the room where I had hung the Shaw and Walker print, I stopped to admire the curves of Proserpina, and savoured the memory of assisting with Francesca's headache. I wondered if Francesca would have been able to help with mine, if she were here now. It would certainly have been a welcome distraction.

Leaving the room, I turned along the corridor towards the second bedroom, and as I did so I noticed a small movement at the end of the corridor. The large tapestry that covered the end wall was flapping, as if in a breeze; perhaps a draught was coming up the stairs. I went over to the tapestry and pulled it back at one side. To my surprise, I found a door. I turned the knob and tried opening the door, but it was locked. How odd to cover up a useful cupboard, I thought. Unless the door was a dummy that once led to a part of the house that had been pulled down – or had fallen down. I shuddered, hoping that this did not signify an intrinsic weakness in the building.

I descended the tight twist of stairs, and I was about to go back into my bedroom when I heard the door to Flora's tower open behind me. I turned to see Flora emerging. She looked a little embarrassed to see me in my dressing gown, which had become untied and revealed my night shirt.

"Good evening, Thomas!" she said. "I'm sorry to disturb you, but I just wanted to come and say thank you for Saturday night. I have been to see you a few times before, but you have been asleep. We have all been worried about you. I should not have asked you to go after Titian in that weather."

"But you didn't ask me to be a clumsy fool and do this to myself!" I said, tying my gown. "That is entirely on me. But thank you, and I'm glad to have found Titian. Is he recovered from his excitement?"

"Yes, yes – he is perfectly all right, if a little subdued. Are you still in pain?"

"A little, but I'm improving," I said. "I just walked upstairs to get my blood circulating, after being supine for so long. I found a door behind the tapestry at the end of the corridor. Have you any idea what that is? A cupboard, I assume?"

"Oh!" said Flora. "Goodness. Yes – I mean I do know what it is, but it isn't a cupboard. It's what they called the master's closet."

"You mean there's a whole extra room, and I didn't know? I should have noticed from the windows from the west garden – assuming it has a window."

"Yes, there's a window," said Flora. "It's not a large room, though. I've only been in a few times – it was out of bounds, but when I was young, my friends and I would occasionally steal the key and sneak in, when the Kingtons were away. It's where my uncle would retreat and write letters, read books – and sometimes entertain friends. I suppose it was a private escape from everything and everyone else. Quite sensible, really."

"How extraordinary," I said. "But why should the room be hidden away like that?"

Flora shrugged. "I would imagine that when my uncle died, my aunt didn't like to be reminded of him. The room was so personal to him, you see. And she must have had terrible feelings of guilt. Or at least I hope so! Sorry, I shouldn't say that."

"And I presume it was too delicate a matter for anyone to mention to me," I said, "since my father was the cause of this state of affairs!"

Flora nodded. "But that's water under the bridge. There's a chance she didn't even clear out her husband's things."

I shuddered. "That's a chilling thought. I feel I would be

intruding – but on the other hand, I'm very curious about the room."

"Would you like me to fetch the key?" she said. "Then we could open it up together – if you don't mind, that is."

"I would like that very much. If you don't mind me being in this state..." I indicated my gown.

She smiled, and said, "Of course not. I'll get the key. There's just enough light."

# CHAPTER TWELVE

FLORA had fetched the key, and stood poised at the door, looking amused at my expression of anticipation. "Shall I?" she said.

I nodded, and she turned the key in the lock. She stood back and let me push open the door.

I ventured in, followed by Flora. My first impression was of a small, calm, private space where a man could retire to think, write, read, and perhaps smoke. Papers still lay on the walnut bureau – probably the very ones Mr Kington was looking at shortly before his death. Against the opposite wall was a red velvet-covered sofa, and above it hung two pictures: a beautiful portrait of a woman, gazing dreamily to one side with one breast exposed, and the other a scene of happy debauchery featuring a faun and several naked, well-nourished maidens. My lithograph, I thought, would be quite at home here.

I glanced at Flora, who shrugged. "It's a man's room," she said. "I fear my uncle got more solace from these pictures than from my aunt."

By the little window – which was missing a piece of glass, presumably a result of the storm – was a small tilt-top table and a mismatched pair of fruitwood chairs from the last century. It was not hard to imagine Mr Kington sitting here, staring moodily out of the window, glass of port in one hand and a cigar in another, brooding over the quirks of fate that brought a rival into his house.

I brushed the dust off a chair, and took a seat. Flora did the same. We both looked out at the hills that were fading behind the curtain of evening, and we sat in silence for a while.

"What I don't understand," I eventually said, "is why your uncle didn't just kick my father out. He had every right."

"He was becoming increasingly ill," Flora said, "and he was also still desperately in love with my aunt. My aunt still looked after him: so that situation was, I think, better than the alternative. He was never a one for drama. He was not the strongest man, but I liked him very much."

"It's tragic," I said. "Do you think this room could ever be somewhere to be happy in again?"

Flora stood up. "It's just a room," she said, breaking the gloomy spell. "If you decide to be happy in it, then my uncle's ghost will surely not stop you."

"Then I have your blessing to use it?" I said.

My tone of sincerity made Flora laugh. "Am I such a monster?" she said. "Of course you do, but you don't need it. And after all, you saved Titian. Once again, I am in your debt."

"Once again?" I said.

"After not tossing me out onto the doorstep with my housekeeper and my cat when you arrived," Flora said. "You might have wanted the tower to yourself. You might still do."

I smiled. "It wouldn't be the same without you. Where would I find a sense of purpose, without cats to rescue?"

~

In the morning, as I waited for a visit from Dr Drummond to check on my dressing and general progress, I contemplated with some pleasure last night's discovery. I had not stayed for long in the master's – my – closet after Flora had left. Today I would see it with fresh eyes – when the light of day would, I hoped, purge any ghosts – and decide what to do about the furniture, decor, and Mr Kington's abandoned things. I felt strangely enlivened by the prospect of the room. My study on the ground floor was all very well, but it was public and a little formal. This little place, tucked away on the top floor, seemed the perfect retreat to be at ease, think, and plan.

But plan what, exactly? As I had implied to Flora last night, my raison d'être was a little unclear, aside from maintaining the house and its estate, and receiving occasional bulletins from Mr McPhee. However, there was something important that demanded my attention: Henry Shaw, and his plea for help in getting to the truth behind his friend's death. Perhaps my new hideaway would help concentrate my mind.

I was both relieved and anxious when Drummond arrived: I wanted his expertise, but I was not looking forward to seeing my wound when the doctor changed the dressing.

"Good morning, Dr Drummond!" I said. "I'm sorry to make you come out all this way."

"That's quite all right, Mr Rufford," said Drummond, taking his pulse. "I like visiting the place. It reminds me of old times. As I think I mentioned, I knew your father. We had some fascinating exchanges on medical matters. He spoke fondly of you."

He gently removed the bandage, and expressed approval at the way the wound was healing. I gave it a quick sideways glance – it was not as bad as I had feared. I plucked up courage to quiz the doctor.

"Dr Drummond," I said, "might I ask you a question? It's about the Walker case."

"Oh, yes? Certainly," he said. "What a dreadful thing. I feel for his friend, Mr – Shaw, isn't it?"

"Yes, Henry Shaw," I said. "In fact, it was Shaw who prompted my question. He wasn't sure that it was an accident. But you must have been convinced it was."

Drummond started to replace the dressing. "On the balance of probabilities, I believe it was accidental. Walker's head injury was consistent with hitting the grate. There was a mug of beer and a nearly empty jug near him, indicating inebriation and therefore a probable loss of faculty. There were no signs of intrusion or a conflict, and there were no bruises on him apart from around the wound."

"But it's just possible that someone might have caused it?" I persisted.

"Well, yes – but it's not likely. And there was no evidence of anyone else, so there would be little point in pursuing any other line."

"But evidence other than at the scene of Walker's death could, theoretically, point to another person, could it not?" I said. "I mean, if someone confessed, for example."

"Again, yes – but I'm not aware of any such evidence. Are you, Mr Rufford?"

"No," I admitted.

"Of course, the irony is," said Drummond, "that the poor fellow would have been dead in a few months anyway."

"I beg your pardon?" I said, astonished.

"Oh, yes – he came to me with his lungs in a very poor state. Tuberculosis, I'm afraid. He was quite brave about it. His friend must have known, as he was coughing most dreadfully. The mural he was painting would have had a special significance: he might have hoped for angels to guide him to Heaven, too."

I was lost for words for a moment. "Perhaps it's almost a comfort to Shaw," I said, "that this event only put forward the inevitable by a few months, and avoided a drawn-out and painful death."

"I have to say, Mr Rufford, that I heartily agree with you," said the doctor. "After all I've seen – such a death is preferable to many others. Although," he added, "it wasn't instantaneous. He bled to death over several hours, but he would have been unconscious throughout, most likely."

"Good Lord," I said. "Does that mean he might have been saved, had someone found him immediately?"

"Possibly," said Drummond. "Without a post-mortem,

it's not possible to say with any certainty how much trauma was inflicted on his brain. But it may have been survivable. The blood loss was ultimately the cause of his death."

I nodded, feeling nauseous.

"Now then," said Drummond briskly. "Your wounds are healing nicely, but we need to worry about your own head. You said you felt dizzy?"

"Yes, a little," I said.

"You have suffered a mild concussion. I advise that you rest for a few days at least. And when you are better, you may follow this prescription, if you wish." The doctor handed me a letter.

I opened it. It was an invitation from Phyllis to take tea with her father and herself, when I was better; and she also expressed her alarm at my accident and wished me a speedy recovery.

Drummond smiled. "We both hope to see you when you are fully well – but not before! My daughter is a strange wee thing, Mr Rufford. She is critical of almost everyone and everything. She tolerates very little, I regret to say. But she spoke of you with respect, so I anticipate that a tea party will be a pleasant occasion for all of us."

"I am very honoured, Dr Drummond. It would definitely be a pleasure to come. I will let you and Miss Drummond know when I am feeling strong again."

"Strong enough to face the Drummonds!" he said, chuckling. "Aye, you will need to make sure of that."

~

When the doctor had gone, I could wait no longer. I got dressed and started to run up the narrow staircase, but quickly slowed to a walk when my head started thumping again. The master's closet appeared in a very different aspect today. Light seemed to disinfect it, banishing yesterday's gloomy mein and revealing the potential of the room as a comfortable haven. The simple beauty of the bureau's grain and craftsmanship, the anticipation of intimacy implied by the little assemblage of table and chairs, the elegant curves of the sofa: I could not have chosen better myself. The furnishings were neither pretentious nor puritanical, and the walls were painted in an intense blue – a fitting background for art.

I was even inclined to keep the pictures, adding, of course, a few of my own choosing. I could imagine a silhouette portrait of Francesca hanging over the bureau. Or perhaps Phyllis? Or both, one facing the other, in matching frames.

Today was not the day, I decided, to spoil my good humour by poring through Mr Kington's papers. I tore a blank page from the notebook lying on the bureau, found a pencil in one of the pigeon holes, and started to write down what I knew of the Walker case.

*Times*

*Sunday, August 20th - Rector rails against Shaw and Walker, Falkirk is rowdy and aggressive. I meet Shaw and Walker. Dead rat and note.*

*Monday, August 28th - Shaw visits the widow.*

*Tuesday, August 29th - Walker dies overnight with head injury and is discovered by Shaw. Drummond and police believe it to be death by accidental fall. FALKIRK GOES MISSING!*

*Wednesday, August 30th - Shaw asks me for help.*

Doesn't believe it was an accident.

Saturday, September 2nd - Harris tells us hearsay about Shaw's insurance policy. IS THIS TRUE?

Tuesday, September 5th - Drummond tells me about Walker's illness. Did Shaw know about it?

## What else do we know?

Rector was against them. May have raised indignation in others, including Falkirk.

Who else was badly disposed to Walker? HUSBANDS or LOVERS of models. MODELS themselves if treated badly? Unknown former lover of Walker? Something from his past life!

What about Shaw? The promise of insurance money, or jealousy between them? Is he violent? Saw a flash of anger.

FRANCESCA! Did they both admire her?

## What next

Look at the artists' cottage. Could there be any evidence left?

Ask Shaw about the insurance policy. Also about any enemies from outside Hawksbridge.

Talk to the widow Shannon about when Shaw

*arrived and left.*

*Talk to Francesca.*

*WHO IS THE OTHER MODEL? Shaw must know.*

*Find any associate of Falkirk who might report on his character and perhaps locate him.*

I put down the pencil and stood up to stretch. I did not know whether I had clarified or muddied the waters. After all, a suspicious mind can cast doubt on the most innocent actions and people. So many scenarios were possible, even if most were improbable. But known suspects could be eliminated: Shaw himself, if he had a cast-iron alibi, which was by no means certain; ditto Falkirk. But it was the unknown potential suspects that particularly bothered me. Someone as controversial as Walker might have accrued a number of people wanting to see him squashed. But dead? That would take a man or woman with a disturbed mind or an overwhelming grievance.

I decided that a walk around my estate to check for storm damage might help me think. Despite the headache, I was feeling much stronger, and desperately needed some exercise. But thinking about the grounds reminded me of the cottage in the woods. I needed to go and investigate, but if someone were squatting there, it might be hazardous. What if – heaven forbid – Alan Sharpe was hiding out there, biding his time? Then I would be walking straight into a trap. I would need a lieutenant, preferably armed. I went downstairs, put on my boots and overcoat, and went to find Shipley. He was in the kitchen, loafing in a Windsor chair and reading The Hawksbridge Herald.

"Good morning, Shipley," I said. "Anything about the Walker death?" I gestured at the newspaper.

"Good morning, sir," said Shipley. "Nothing new, no."

"What do you think?" I said. "Have you heard anything? Do you think Falkirk might have had anything to do with it?"

Shipley laughed. "Johnny? Impossible. Anyway, I thought it was an accident, sir."

"Yes, probably it was, but some people seem to think that Falkirk disappearing is too much of a coincidence."

"If I were Johnny, I would probably make myself scarce," said Shipley. "After all he said about those artists. It's bad luck. But he's not the type – all bluster, he is."

"Interesting. Anyway, the reason I came down was to ask if you could accompany me. I was going to look around the estate for storm damage, and there's also something I've been meaning to ask you."

"Being taken care of, sir. Lots of firewood being collected, and some trees will have to come down. Oh, and some slates missing, and that window of Miss Davison's to repair. But nothing we've not seen before. That scaffolding on the front held, which is a miracle – must have been the stones the builder weighed it down with. What did you want to ask?"

"The cottages in the woods – I've been past them a couple of times, and I could have sworn I saw movement in the middle cottage. And I thought I saw a lamp during the storm. So I wondered if you would accompany me there, in case some rogue has taken up residence. I don't want to knock on the door on my own."

Shipley put the newspaper down, and looked uncomfortable.

"Oh, you don't need to bother yourself with that, sir," he said, in an exaggeratedly relaxed drawl. "I'll go and look at it presently."

"Thank you, Shipley, but I would rather see for myself, and I need some protection."

Shipley frowned. "But you are still recuperating, sir. It would be on my conscience if something were to happen to you."

"Thank you," I said again. "I appreciate that. But I think the two of us should be able to manage the situation. Do you have a weapon?"

The colour had drained from Shipley's face. "Of course, sir," he said, getting out of his chair. "I have something suitable in my parlour."

As I waited for him to return, I wondered at this strange attitude of Shipley's. Was he terrified of confronting a possible ne'er-do-well? Or was there another cause?

Shipley reappeared carrying a truncheon, a grimly heavy piece of wood with a grip formed from turned ridges. "A retired constable gave it to me," he said, retrieving a set of keys from the hook board. "Should make most villains think twice."

"That looks ideal," I said, opening the kitchen door. "Shall we?"

# CHAPTER THIRTEEN

SHIPLEY'S jaw was set rigid as we walked to the wood, and it made me more nervous of what we might find.

When we reached the cottage, Shipley opened the gate and then clumsily banged it shut. Any occupant would certainly know we were coming. All the shutters were closed – I remembered at least one being open previously. I went up to the door and knocked. We waited, and there was no answer, so Shipley unlocked the door and went in. The door opened directly into the sitting room, beyond which there was a door to a small kitchen.

"Hello!" I said. "Anyone here?" I went to open the shutters, and the light revealed unambiguous evidence of occupation. Although the walls and ceilings were streaked with mould and in need of replastering, the place seemed just about fit for human life, with some basic furnishings, including a round table which bore an unlit candle, a mug, and a couple of dirty plates.

"Someone was here a while ago," said Shipley. "Probably long gone."

As he spoke, there was the creaking of a floorboard upstairs, and they exchanged glances. With trepidation, I ascended the stairs, and paused at the top.

"Hello!" I said. "Whoever is here, please show yourself. We mean you no harm. We just want to have a word. We're just going to wait on the landing." I did not want to startle the person, or persons, into lashing out.

After a moment, a head appeared cautiously around the bedroom door. It was a young woman, with untidy brown hair and a nervous expression.

"Oh! Hello, Matthew," she said, and she came out of the room. "Is there something wrong?"

Shipley was silent, but shifted uncomfortably from one foot to the other, producing more creaking from the floorboards.

"You know each other?" I said, looking from Shipley to the young woman, trying to gauge what relationship there might be between them.

"Who are you, if you don't mind me asking?" said the young woman.

"Thomas Rufford, ma'am. I own this cottage, and I am a little perplexed to find someone in it, since it's awaiting renovation. May I ask your name?"

"Oh. Mary Barker, sir. Matthew, please tell him, won't you? Have we done something wrong?"

Shipley looked both ashamed and furious. "Quite the little innocent, aren't you, Mary? You know perfectly well you are trespassing. Where is Johnny?"

"Trespassing?" she said. "Oh, no, Matthew, that's not right. We paid you fair and square."

"Paid you?" I echoed. "What's going on, Shipley?"

Shipley ignored this and asked again, "Where is he, Mary?"

Mary shrugged and said, "He went out. Probably to get rid of some beer!" She continued to stand in the doorway.

Shipley elbowed her out of the way, and I followed. There was no sign of Falkirk, until Shipley wielded the truncheon under the bed and provoked an "Ow!"

The missing artist reluctantly emerged from his hiding place, dusted off the grime, and sighed, while Shipley stood in the doorway to stop him bolting.

"I told you to make yourself scarce a week ago, Johnny," Shipley said. "You should have gone."

"Couldn't think where to go," Falkirk said, and he sat down on the bed looking defeated.

"Shipley, please explain what's going on," I said. "What are these people doing here?"

"Very well, sir. I'm afraid I took pity on Johnny and Miss Barker, and let them use the cottage when they had no place to go. Johnny hasn't done anything wrong, but the police might have come to the wrong conclusion. But they were supposed to be out of here by now."

Mary barged past Shipley and sat on the bed next to Falkirk, putting her arm around him.

"Well, that's a nice tale, Matthew! Not the whole story, though, is it? We've been coming here for months, on and off. He's been charging us for it," she said, looking at me and pointing to Shipley. "Not just us neither. He's been providing a 'lodging for the affectionate,' he called it. What a pretty name! Regular cupid, aren't you?"

I looked at Shipley and he nodded. "I'm afraid it's true, sir," said Shipley, with what seemed like genuine remorse. "I have been making a little on the side, after I lost at cards to a devil in The Duke's Head. I will give you back every penny, you can be sure of it. I'm very sorry, sir. I'm afraid I've let you down."

"Yes. I'm disappointed. I thought you were much better than this. But we'll discuss it later," I said, suppressing a considerable urge to berate him. "What's important is: have we been harbouring a possible criminal?"

"Criminal?" exclaimed Falkirk. "That is not true! I've done nothing wrong. Ever since the blasted mural was proposed, my life has been a misery. God must hate me, but for what reason?"

"If you have an alibi, Mr Falkirk," I said, "then you should have nothing to fear from the police. Can you vouch for him, Miss Barker?"

"You mean was he with me when that man died? Yes, he was. He was right here with me, doing what he likes to do. All ruddy night."

"No need to be crude, Mary," said Falkirk. "But yes, sir, I was. I love my Mary, and she loves me, but her parents despise me, so what else were we supposed to do?"

I nodded. "Unfortunately Mary might not be regarded as a totally impartial witness, but it's a start. Shipley, did you see them on that night? This was Monday, August the twenty-eighth, or early on Tuesday the twenty-ninth."

"Indeed I did, sir. I went to get payment on the Monday night – God forgive me – and they were both here. About ten o'clock, after I'd finished my duties at the house. It was dark, with little moonlight, so I had to take a lamp. It seems unlikely to me that Johnny here would walk into town after that, especially with a pretty girl to keep him warm."

Mary smiled at the compliment.

"He was already quite drunk. Not only that, sir, I had offered to bring them some breakfast for sixpence more. So I went around at seven o'clock in the morning, and Johnny was in a deep slumber. Could barely rouse him. It had been raining in the night, but nothing was wet in the house: there were no muddy footprints. I remember that because I was making a bit of a mess with my boots, and it had been quite clean inside. Mary was annoyed about it."

"I was that!" she said. "We hadn't been outside so much as to take out the chamberpot."

I was impressed with Shipley's powers of observation. It certainly seemed a clear-cut alibi to me – would it to the police? It was a risk that Falkirk would need to take.

"You need to talk to Inspector Simmons," I said. "The more you hide, the more they will think you have something to hide."

Falkirk had his head in his hands. "How can I? I don't want to go to prison. Or hang!"

"I don't see that you have any alternative," I said. "You can't be a fugitive for the rest of your life, especially if you're innocent. We will come with you, and Miss Barker and Mr

Shipley will vouch for you. The fact that you stayed here gives you a far better chance than if you had simply been at home in your own bed."

"He's right, Johnny," said Shipley. "I just fear," he said looking at me, "that I may have got us both into trouble. I am such a fool."

"For harbouring a possible criminal?" I said. "Perhaps, but on the other hand, when you invited Mr Falkirk here, it was before Walker's death, and you already asked him to leave. True, you didn't report Falkirk's whereabouts. They may want to make a song and dance about that, but they may well not want to bother, if we are honest and present them with all the information they need."

I remembered another confession that might be required.

"Mr Falkirk," I said. "The rat...?"

"It was me," he said, slamming his fist onto his knee repeatedly. "I was in a rage. And I was drunk. It was pure jealousy. Why should incomers get the work? Why not give me a chance? My grandfather died in that fire, so who better to work on the mural? Well, it wasn't fair, and I still believe it, but I should not have done what I did. That's why I scarpered. It will look too bad for me."

"I think they will understand," I said, hoping that this would be the case. "It's just an unfortunate coincidence. But you have a very strong alibi."

Mary massaged Falkirk's shoulders and said, "Will you do it? I think you should. I shall tell them everything, even though they may punish me for not letting on where you were. I think that's all we can do, Johnny. It will work out. And I will always love you, you know that."

Johnny nodded, and leaned his head against Mary's. Shipley and I withdrew downstairs to give them both time.

"Well, this has been instructive," I said. "I had no idea the estate had been of such service to the town."

Shipley cringed. "I'm very sorry, sir. It will never, ever

happen again. I was in a bit of a tight spot, you see..."

I waved my hand dismissively. "We'll discuss it later. The main thing now is to get through the next few hours without incurring the wrath of the police. Can you get the pony trap ready? I suggest I drive Miss Barker, and you and Falkirk can walk."

~

The four of us made a curious procession into town. Falkirk attracted the stares of several passers-by, and I feared my association with Falkirk would not improve my nascent standing in Hawksbridge. But I hoped that by talking to the police, I might help someone so much less fortunate that myself.

Inspector Simmons was at the police office, and was visibly confounded by the unexpected arrival of the man he was seeking, accompanied by a strange posse.

I received the courtesy of being interviewed first. Simmons ushered me into a small, stark room and indicated for me to take a seat at the table, and a constable was brought in as witness.

Simmons cleared his throat and turned to a blank page in his notebook. "It's good to see you again, Mr Rufford. Goodness – I ask you to tell me if you hear anything about Mr Falkirk's whereabouts, and then you bring him here yourself! Very obliging. So I'm grateful to you for that."

I nodded warily, wondering if this was some kind of tactic, or to be taken at face value.

"Now, you said when you came in that Falkirk and his... friend Mary Barker were living in a cottage in your estate. Did you know about this?"

"No, Inspector, I did not. It was an arrangement with my

estate manager, Mr Shipley, that I was not aware of. Falkirk was in residence before the murder, as he will tell you."

"I see," said Inspector Simmons. "So Mr Shipley knew of his whereabouts when Mr Walker died, but failed to mention it."

"Yes – he knows that was wrong now, but to be fair to him, no one came to ask him about Falkirk. Also, after Walker's death, he insisted that Falkirk leave. This didn't happen, because Falkirk was frightened of being wrongly accused."

"And Falkirk's alibi – not that he necessarily needs one, mind – is that he was in the cottage on that Monday night?"

"Yes, Inspector, and both Mary Barker and Mr Shipley can back this up in some detail."

"Interesting. It would have been useful to have talked to Mr Falkirk before, but we are where we are. Thank you, Mr Rufford. I do hope we won't have to discuss this matter again."

When each of the four of us had been interviewed, Inspector Simmons politely thanked us and told us we were free to go.

"But I would be grateful if none of you made any trips in the next couple of weeks," the Inspector added. "Just in case we need to question you further."

When they stood on the road again, Falkirk looked as though he were about to faint, both with relief at not immediately being arrested, and a lack of sustenance. Mary took him back to his house, where he lived with his mother, and Shipley and I were left to make our way back to Ramsburgh in the pony trap.

"I think Simmons accepted most of that, sir," said Shipley as Jenny plodded up the hill. "Wouldn't you say?"

"It's a little hard to read Inspector Simmons," I said, "but yes – the fact that Falkirk wasn't detained is a good sign. Assuming he confessed to the rat, I think Inspector Simmons has been very fair about it. What did he say about you not informing them about Falkirk's whereabouts?"

"He quizzed me about it, and I apologised. He said it was a serious matter, but also that I'd been very cooperative today. Does that mean he'll overlook it?"

"There's a good prospect of it," I said. "Your position at Ramsburgh must have helped a little. And perhaps also your friendship with the constable who gave you the truncheon!"

Shipley nodded, and cleared his throat. "I would understand if you asked me to find new employment, sir. I just ask that you give me a decent reference, if you could find..." He could not bring himself to finish his sentence.

I considered. For Shipley to have taken advantage of his position and derive an illicit income from the estate – it was foolish and a betrayal of trust, there was no doubt about that. And yet his remorse seemed genuine, and he had handled the day's events well. Plus, he was adept at managing the estate, and he was efficient and generally unobtrusive in the house. His loss would be a blow.

"If Inspector Simmons can give you a second chance, then I certainly can," I said. "If you let me know how much you gathered from this enterprise, I will deduct it from your pay at a mutually agreed rate. Then, let us consider the matter closed."

"Thank you, sir," said Shipley, wiping a tear of relief from his eye with his knuckle. "I won't let you down again, sir, I promise."

We drove on for a few minutes in silence, and then I remembered something I had been meaning to ask Shipley for a while.

"Shipley, are you aware of an incident at Ramsburgh involving swans?"

"Aware, sir?" he said. "I had to clean up the damned mess. I won't say anything against Mrs Kington, as she was a fine mistress and if she was led astray, it couldn't have been all her fault. Begging your pardon, sir."

I nodded and said, "Go on."

"Well, whether it were the peculiar state of things in the house at the time, or something else, I couldn't say, but I heard a couple of shots and ran out of the kitchen door to the back of the house. I could see Mrs Kington at the lake, and when I drew closer, two swans were dead and one injured. A fourth came back later, and she went out to shoot that too. Both times, she just went back in without saying anything to me, but her face showed she was in a fury. I had to wring the neck of the injured bird – I've never had to despatch such a graceful creature, and I didn't like doing it, but I had no choice. I buried them at the edge of the woods. One might say if she didn't want the creatures on her land, it's her choice; but in this case, she was wrong, and it cost her. It's a rum thing."

"Rum indeed," I said. "I might occasionally throw a book across the room in anger – but to take it out on a living creature! Though my Oxford colleagues would think my crime the greater. Anyway, I suppose someone like Mrs Kington must have been used to shooting game."

"You would think so, sir, but that's the strange thing – she didn't, any more. She'd given up shooting a few years earlier, because of her Christian principles, she said."

~

After lunch, I asked Mrs Felton for a jug of coffee, and took it up to my closet to order my thoughts, beginning by putting the business of the unfortunate swans out of my head. This was a mystery that was unlikely to be solved so long after the event. Fox trotted after me, and after begging to be fussed for a few minutes, eventually settled happily on the sofa while I took a chair by the window.

Falkirk's alibi was convincing. Shaw would be disappointed – that is, if Shaw himself were blameless. Or, if Shaw had been involved, he might simply be disappointed that the police were not diverting their attention to Falkirk.

There was the matter of widow Shannon. Would she give a sufficient alibi to Shaw, just as Mary Barker had for Falkirk? I would need to talk to her.

I wondered if I had made the right decision to be lenient with Shipley. Now I understood Flora's comments about him when we had first met. Was this Shipley's only infraction? I would need to assume so, for there were more pressing matters. A fear was pulling unpleasantly at my stomach – the prospect of an angry Alan Sharpe appearing at the house and demanding payment. I did not know if my fragile reputation would survive that, even if I managed to silence Sharpe with the bag of sovereigns. The money! I had not yet called in on the bank to fetch it. It was too late today, so I resolved to go into town first thing in the morning, interview Bess Shannon if she permitted it, and check if the money was ready.

I realised that I had been thinking only of myself – what if others in the household were in danger from Sharpe? From what I could remember of a brief meeting some years ago – when Sharpe had come to the servant's parlour asking for money from Hazel – he was a sullen and crude man, for whom criminal acts probably came easily. Hazel had been short with him, and clearly there was not much love lost between them. His claim of tragic bereavement rang hollow.

It did not bear thinking about that this man could be stalking the house at any moment, threatening its oblivious occupants. The right thing to do would be to warn everyone – or at least Shipley. But I could not countenance the thought of explaining myself here, of sullying my honour so soon. And besides, if queried by the police, they would then be obliged to either tell the truth or lie, each of which would have its own egregious consequences.

But I longed desperately to unburden myself to someone. Would Flora understand? No, she would be disappointed and alarmed that I should have such a history. But Francesca – yes, perhaps she would be able to sympathise with the reverberations of love. Her animal nature was barely kept in check, and she was experienced enough to appreciate the imperfections of the human heart. I judged that she would be the least shocked of anyone I knew, and would probably lie for me if need be.

I would tell her everything, and damn the consequences.

# CHAPTER FOURTEEN

BESS Shannon opened the door cautiously. "Yes?"

The widow Shannon was in her early forties, with an appealing, slightly plump face and brown locks that belied her years. She wore an apron and was wiping flour off her hands.

"I'm sorry to disturb you, Mrs Shannon," I said. "My name is Thomas Rufford." Her frown softened as she recognised the name. "I'm coming on behalf of Henry Shaw – I don't want to pry at all, but I need some information that may help him." This was a half-truth – she might equally have information that could hang him – but he had to satisfy himself that Shaw was blameless, and it was possible that she would be able to shed light on other of the artists' associates.

"Oh," she said, taking in this information. "Nice to meet you, Mr Rufford, but I don't know if I can help."

"I think you can," I said. "I would be very grateful, Mrs Shannon."

"Very well!" she said, letting me into the house. "I'll try."

The smell of baking bread grew stronger as we walked down the narrow hall. She showed me into her sitting room, plainly but not shabbily decorated, with whitewashed walls on which hung a few old prints. A small harp sat in the corner, next to a music stand.

"There you go, Mr Rufford – do sit here, it's quite comfy."

I sat down in an upholstered armchair, which had frays and scratches indicating the attentions of an animal.

She sat down on the sofa opposite, and images flashed into my head of Mrs Shannon and Shaw becoming intimate on it. It was perfectly understandable: Mrs Shannon was a fine creature, buxom and rounded without being stout, and she spoke with a soft voice that seemed refined for a shopkeeper's wife.

"Oh!" she said, standing up again. "I am forgetting myself. Would you like a cup of tea?"

"That would be delightful, if I'm not putting you to too much trouble," I said.

"No trouble at all," she said, and walked to the door.

I could not resist admiring the curves of her retreating figure. I felt a pang of jealousy, thinking of how Henry Shaw must have easily won her over with his fame and rough charm, and how much enjoyment he must have had of her. It was so long since I had known the pleasures of the flesh, and I ached to press myself against an obliging female.

I felt ashamed as she came back with the tea, putting the tray down with a smile. "There we go. I made some biscuits earlier – I hope you like them."

"Thank you, Mrs Shannon," I said, reaching for my teacup. "This is really so good of you, especially when I come here asking to talk about... personal matters. I will try to be as brief as I can."

"Let's get it over quickly, then, and perhaps we can talk of other things," Mrs Shannon said. "I'll start: Henry and I were enamoured of each other, and he stayed one night in this house: the night that poor man died. I have not seen him since. I expect he is embarrassed to talk to me, and also full of grief for his friend."

"Thank you for being so candid with me," I said. "I'm sorry he hasn't had the manners to talk to you since."

She shrugged. "I have learnt that the less you expect, the less you are hurt. I miss him a little, but he has his own affairs to get in order. Are you friends, Mr Rufford? He told me he didn't have any in Hawksbridge."

"Acquaintances, at present," I said. "But I felt the town owed him more courtesy than it has hitherto shown him, and offered to make some enquiries. Henry suspects that Mr Walker's death may not have been an accident."

"Really?" she said. "He thinks that? I know there were rumours about Johnny Falkirk, but I never believed them, and anyway he hasn't been arrested, as far as I know."

"Mr Falkirk has a very good alibi," I said. "I did just want to check that Henry had one, too."

"I see," said Mrs Shannon, taking an elegant sip of her tea. "Well, he came to me at about... I think just after seven o'clock that Monday evening."

"And he stayed all night?"

Mrs Shaw blushed and put her hand briefly over her mouth. "I'm afraid so, Mr Rufford. Are you very scandalised?"

"Not really," I said. "You are both attractive people. It seems quite natural."

"Natural, maybe – moral, no," said Mrs Shannon with a sigh. "What has happened to me? But my attitude is, you don't know when you're going to meet your maker. You might as well live a little before that. And when a handsome artist gives you outrageous compliments, and tells you you're uncommonly pretty..."

She found a handkerchief, dabbed her eyes, and smiled. "Silly old thing, I am. Sorry. What were you saying?"

"I was wondering if he stayed all night, and you said he did. So you were awake when he left?"

She stared at him, her mouth open. "Oh! Mr Rufford, I tell a lie. Now I think about it, I don't know when he left, because I was so deeply asleep. On account of... er..." She covered her face with her hands and rocked a little. "Oh..."

I smiled. "Of course. So we don't know exactly when he left?"

She frowned. "I did wake once. I heard a cockerel crow, and he woke too, and then he... paid me more attentions, but then I slept until at least eight o'clock, and he was gone."

"That must leave a very small gap in time," I said. "Do

you know when the cockerel usually crows?"

"About four o'clock, maybe five o'clock, I think. I'm sure he didn't get out of bed then."

I cleared my throat. "Sorry to ask this, Mrs Shannon, but do you have any idea how long it might have been before you got back to sleep? This would narrow down the possibilities further."

"Goodness me, Mr Rufford," said Mrs Shannon. "Am I to have no secrets? Let me think. It was quite a long time. Henry had a great appetite, which was a fine compliment to me, I suppose, but I do remember it being a little tiring. So I would think it was about an hour before I got to sleep. And he was snoring a bit, so he had already fallen asleep."

Mrs Shannon drained her teacup and poured us both some more.

"Well. I cannot believe I have just told you these things. I have only just met you! I would scarcely tell this to my doctor!"

"My apologies, Mrs Shannon," I said. "It's just bad luck that Shaw should need to rely on such information. Or perhaps good luck, since it tells me of his innocence. I will of course say nothing of this to anyone."

"Thank you, Mr Rufford. But I thought you were supposed to be Shaw's champion, and yet...?"

"I know – but I had to convince myself first that I wasn't being used in some way. And I wanted to ask if you had heard anything else that might be relevant – anyone threatening him and Walker, for example? He might have let something slip to you."

"I'll try to think," said Mrs Shannon. "But first I need something stronger than tea. I need to calm my nerves a little! I'm that flustered! Would you like some port?"

"Thank you, Mrs Shannon – it's a bit early, but... oh, yes please. After putting you through this inquisition..."

"Good," said Mrs Shannon. "I wouldn't want to drink on

my own. Oh – you don't have a horse getting impatient outside, do you?"

"No," I said. "It was such a nice day, I decided to walk. And I can't ride a horse."

"Really?" said Mrs Shannon, opening a cabinet. "I'm shocked. A country gentleman like you, in his castle on the hill, not being able to ride?"

"I do have a pony trap. As you probably know from local gossip, I've been more of a city person. I never learnt. But I will. I have a friend who has promised to teach me."

Mrs Shannon put the port and glasses down on the tea-table and sat down. She filled the glasses, and said, "He did mention one curious thing."

"Yes?" I said.

"I was joking with him, asking whether he could afford to keep me as his mistress. He said the payment for the work at the Town Hall was good, so he could buy me furs and jewellery. Of course, I have no use for them, and he was only being silly. Then he looked a little serious, and said that he would be coming into a lot of money in a few months. He said it as though he didn't want it. Does that make any sense?"

"Ah," I said. "I think I might know what that is. I need to ask Mr Shaw about it. Thank you. So – Mr Shaw wasn't worried about anything – or anyone – else?"

"He was annoyed about the Rector being so against the pair of them, and some idiot put a rat on his doorstep – I suppose that was Johnny, as he was so aggrieved about it all." I nodded. "But apart from that, he didn't mention anything. Most of the time he was telling me how much he loved me, which must be a fib – we only met the day before! But he knows how to lead a woman astray. He's a master at it."

She looked at me intensely with piercing blue eyes, the port apparently giving her confidence. "Now, you, Mr Rufford. I don't see you telling nice fibs to corrupt a poor woman! I think you're a man of honour."

"I hope so," I said. "But I'm not perfect."

"I've remembered something else," she said. "I should have been more put out at this than I was. Henry was telling me that they were squabbling over one of their models – a rare, magnificent beauty, he said. They were both beguiled by her, but Mr Walker was the winner as he got to paint her. And you can see her in the Town Hall – very lovely she is too."

I nodded. "I have seen it – indeed, I know her. And I have to admit, I can be counted as one of Mrs Campbell's admirers."

"Fine thing for a man to talk of when he's making love to another woman," said Mrs Shannon, taking another sip of port. "But Henry is the sort of man who is far too easy to forgive."

At that moment, there was a loud bang from the kitchen, which I quickly identified as the familiar noise of a window sash whose ill-balanced weights had failed it. There were plenty of defective windows like that in Ramsburgh that closed as if by an unseen hand. However, the shock caused Mrs Shannon to jump and lose her grip on her port glass, which went tumbling to the floor, but not before acquiring a spin on the edge of the tea-table. It shattered into tiny pieces across the wooden floor.

"Oh! Clumsy me," she said, pushing the table aside and kneeling on the floor.

"Let me help," I said, and knelt to retrieve some glass fragments.

"Thank you – you can put them on this saucer," she said, "but be careful, I don't want you leaving all bandaged up."

For a while we both concentrated on finding the shards. I was aware of Mrs Shannon close by me; I could hear her slightly laboured breathing, and smell the fragrance of bread from her apron and the scent of rosewater. Her hips made brief contact with my leg, which sent an intoxicating wave of desire through me.

Eventually, there seemed to be no glass left to pick up, and we knelt on the floor looking around us. I stole a look at her, and she smiled at me, as if acknowledging the strange intimacy that we had strayed into.

Reluctantly, I got up from the floor, ignoring the pains from my storm injuries. I held my hands out to her, and she accepted the help. "Thank you!" she said, heaving herself up with a sigh of exertion. When she had straightened her back, she held on to my hands for a moment longer, and I felt a stab of excitement again.

"Well," she said, letting go of my hands, "that was fun. The next time you come, I'll find an ugly ashette to break, unless you would like to play cards instead."

"Thank you," I said. "After all my awful questions, I'm surprised that you would open your door to me again."

"But I'm being presumptuous," she said. "Silly me. Why would you want to visit me again? You have the information you wanted."

"Because I enjoyed your company? Do I need to bring a list of further questions, then?"

Mrs Shannon smiled and accompanied me to the front door. "You are very welcome to visit me again, questions or no questions. I don't suppose your reputation would be improved by it: but if you wanted to come, I would be glad of it."

I took her hand and kissed it. "So would I. Thank you, Mrs Shannon. Goodbye!"

~

As I walked away, the fresh air felt good on my red cheeks, flushed as they were with port and exhilaration. I had flirted outrageously with this woman, and she had not minded;

indeed, if I was not misreading the signals, she had encouraged me. What pleasures beckoned in future liaisons?

It was good, I thought, that I had imbibed alcohol before visiting the bank: it would give me courage to appear confident. So I marched in, and endured the manager looking over his spectacles in a quizzical and mildly disapproving fashion. The money was ready, but I realised that it would be too heavy and conspicuous to carry on foot. I would need to pick it up later in the pony trap.

My next port of call was Shaw. I hoped that my head was clear enough to ask everything I needed to ask.

When I entered the room in the inn, Shaw was sprawled in his bed, half of the bed linen on the floor. He had drunk a great deal more than I had. "Mr Rufford! Thomas! Tom!" he said. "What've you got for me? Eh?"

I pulled up a chair by the bed. "Some questions, mostly."

"Damn you," he said, clutching his forehead. "Damn you and damn the devil drink. Spit it out, then."

"I've been talking to Mrs Shannon..."

"That bitch!" said Shaw. "What's she been saying about me? Going to lie about me, because I've had no time to sweet-talk her? Does she want me in Hell for seducing her?"

He sat up and leered into my face. "What did you want with her, anyway? Wanted her for yourself, did you? Did you covet those big titties of hers? Ha! I knew she was a floozy."

"Mr Shaw!" I said, feeling all too well that Shaw had hit his mark about my desires. "She is not a floozy, she is a good woman, and I only wanted to see if she knew anything that would help you."

"Good woman – very funny, Tom. She was a very wicked woman for me. So? What did she say?"

"She mentioned that you said you were going to come into some money in a few months."

"None of your bloody business!" shouted Shaw, standing up unsteadily and starting to pace up and down. "That's not what I asked you to do – poke around my private affairs. What are you up to? Are you working for Inspector Simmons? If you are, then..." He raised his fist.

"Please calm down, Mr Shaw. No, I just want to be in possession of all the facts. This can only help you – I need to know everything, just as the police do, and then maybe I have a chance of discovering what happened. And refuting anything people accuse you of."

Shaw lowered his fist and sighed, giving me the impression of a deflating balloon. "Perhaps. Oh, my head. I'm a fool. I'm never drinking again." He sat down on the edge of the bed and twisted the sheet around his hand. "I took insurance out on poor Ned. I knew he was ill, though we barely discussed it. I was afraid I would lose my inspiration, my very talent, if Ned died. So I took out insurance. I know how bloody evil that looks. But I did not – do I even have to say this? – I did not kill him! I needed him. We needed each other."

I nodded. "I know. I don't believe you did it – Mrs Shannon gave you a pretty good alibi. So, thank God for your physical wants. However – surely the insurance company are going to query it now? The police will want to investigate."

"No, they won't," said Shaw, "because I wrote to cancel the policy after Ned died. I realised that they would, at the very least, tear it up because I didn't declare his illness. Fraud, I suppose they'd call it: fair enough. So, as long as they don't make a fuss, I should be all right. You're not going to squeal about it, are you?"

"Of course not," I said. "You wouldn't cancel a policy that was motivation enough for murder. I just want to ask one more question of a personal nature –"

"Oh, go on, man," Shaw said, with his head in his hands. "I can't imagine what's left, but go on."

"Mrs Shannon said you and Ned quarrelled over Francesca – Mrs Campbell. I assume you didn't come to blows over her?"

"Oh, for God's sake! Her? Of course not. She's comely, but I wouldn't fight anyone over her. I admit I did want to paint her. We did argue a little. But Ned was passionate about it – about her – and I let it go. Well, he was a dying man. I may be selfish, but a dying man deserves a few pleasures before he goes."

I frowned. "Pleasures?"

Shaw waved his hands. "Figuratively! He may have had his way with her, I don't know. I don't care. What's the bloody difference?"

Quite a lot of difference to me, I thought. "Anyway, I was wondering if anything occurred to you about the cottage that was different. I assume there was no sign of anyone else there, or the police would have noticed."

"Well, what about this? I went into the cottage yesterday. I'm thinking of moving back in. Ned bought a bottle of port the day before he died. Said it was in case he had any smart company. Women, I suppose he meant. Neither of us touch the stuff."

"Yes?" I said.

"I didn't notice it before, but I went to the dresser, and the port had been opened, and some of it drunk."

"Interesting," I said. "And you can't account for who it might have been?"

"No. Ned wouldn't have had it. And Minto has always had beer when I've been with him. Don't know who else would have been in the cottage."

"That could be significant," I said. "Have you told the police?"

"No, those fools wouldn't believe me anyway. They'd say I'd drunk it myself! I haven't made myself popular with them, the last few days."

"Oh – how so?"

He shrugged. "May have had a few too many and lost my

temper a bit. One of the guests here must have complained. Whining prigs."

I thought for a moment. "Could someone have opened the port after Ned died?"

"Unlikely," said Shaw, "because Ned had locked it away out of the reach of the servants, and put the key on a high shelf out of sight. We've had our stuff pinched before, so he was careful. It was lucky the dresser still had a key to it."

"That's a useful piece of evidence," I said. "On another topic, I suppose you heard that Falkirk has been questioned and released by the police. He has a good alibi: he was on my estate on the night in question."

"I heard," Shaw said. "But I'm not letting him off so easily. Someone who is scoundrel enough to leave a dead rat might be capable of more."

"I'm afraid I'm convinced he had nothing to do with it," I said. "He was too drunk to make it from Ramsburgh to here, certainly in the time available."

This enraged Shaw. He leapt up from the bed. "Whose side are you on?" he shouted, advancing on me.

I thought it best to withdraw, but Shaw kept following me downstairs, still shouting. On the street, Shaw bellowed, "You pigeon-livered dog! You're in it with the lot of them – all the damnable, sneaking, cowardly, snivelling rats of this cesspool of a town! God piss on you all!" He drew breath, eyes shining with anger and teeth bared. "Where are you, Rector? This is your doing! You killed him, you high and mighty goat's testicle! Is this your work, or your idiot god's? Come on, Horace Neville! Come on, Johnny Falkirk! I'll take you on, and Ned will look down and laugh as I smash your brains into the mud!"

Windows had opened, and a small crowd had gathered. A couple of youths were cheering him on.

I was at a loss. Shaw was physically stronger than me, made stronger by his rage. "Mr Shaw – please," I said, "let's go back inside, and then we can discuss –"

"Go back and discuss what?" Shaw shouted. "Whether you fucked my woman? Or Ned fucked that –"

Fortunately, at this point the gesticulating Shaw slipped and fell, and was temporarily stunned into silence. I tried to help him up, but Shaw landed me a blow on the jaw that sent me sprawling into the street.

"Whoa! Whoa!"

I looked up and saw a pony trap looming over me. At the reins was Dr Drummond, and Phyllis was next to him; they had nearly run me over. Phyllis quickly alit from the trap and helped me in, before taking the rear seat. Dr Drummond set off again, and I looked around to see several men manoeuvring Shaw back into the inn.

Dr Drummond put a steadying hand on my shoulder. "Let's have that tea party, shall we, Mr Rufford?" he said with a smile.

# CHAPTER FIFTEEN

Dr Drummond examined my jaw as Phyllis brought in a tray.

"Some bruising," he said, "but I don't think it's broken. Try opening and closing your mouth as wide as you can. Is it painful?"

"A little," I said.

"It could have been much worse," said Dr Drummond. "A glancing blow, I would say. What was the cause of this altercation, if I may ask?"

"Foolishly, I offered to help Mr Shaw," I said. "He didn't think Mr Walker's death was an accident, so I said I'd make some enquiries, as I felt Hawksbridge had treated him badly. I don't know what I was thinking, because the police will have done as much as they can. Anyway, he objected to my conviction that Falkirk was innocent, and turned nasty."

"An amateur detective, eh?" said Dr Drummond. "Ramsburgh obviously isn't keeping you busy enough."

"I think it was very considerate of you to try to help," said Phyllis. "The poor man must have been driven mad by Mr Shaw's death."

"Aye, that and the drink," said Dr Drummond. "Getting into affrays isn't advisable after your recent tussle with a storm, Mr Rufford."

"I know – it hasn't been much good for my head," I said, massaging my temples.

"Have some tea," said Phyllis. "It makes most things better."

I wondered what she would think if she had known about my earlier tea engagement. It had been an altogether peculiar day: the company of delightful females one minute, and vicious battery the next.

"Thank you for rescuing me," I said. "God knows what might have happened otherwise."

"I shudder to think," said Phyllis. "You must try to stay out of trouble – we might not be around to whisk you away next time!"

"I will try," I said.

"But tell me," she said, "did you find out anything about Mr Walker's death?"

"My dear!" said Dr Drummond. "Please don't encourage the man. And as I said, it was purely an accident. There's no use in leading Mr Shaw into thinking otherwise. He needs to face the unfortunate but inescapable fact that no one else was to blame."

"I feel I have been chasing my tail somewhat," I said. "I've established that it couldn't have been Falkirk, and it couldn't have been Shaw himself. As you say, the most likely explanation is that Walker got drunk and tripped. But there was something that Shaw said today that bothers me."

"Yes?" said Phyllis, her curiosity clearly piqued.

"He said that a bottle of port had been opened, when he didn't expect it."

"Goodness!" said Phyllis. "A clue. How fascinating."

"Could have been anyone," said Dr Drummond. "You would have a hard time using that in a court of law."

"True," I said, "but it might tell us that it's worth investigating further. Neither of the men drank port, and Shaw had no idea who else might have had it. The bottle had only been purchased the day before, and it had been locked in a dresser."

"My feeling, Mr Rufford, is that you should leave all this to the police. So far it has only got you into trouble. And," he said, turning to Phyllis, "we wouldn't want you to come to more harm, would we, my dear?"

"Certainly not," Phyllis said. "I think you are generally an asset to Hawksbridge, Mr Rufford. It would be a shame to see you chased back to the safety of Oxford."

I smiled in acknowledgement. "I have no wish to return. I confess I like it much more here than I could have imagined. But as you see, I do need to find more to occupy myself."

"Tell me, Mr Rufford," said Dr Drummond, "what was your occupation in Oxford?"

"I was a tutor of philosophy," I said. "But I was growing uneasy with it. Sometimes when I watched a colleague lecturing on this esoteric theory or that, I would find myself wondering how much good it really did. And so much time was spent on arguing over specious or trivial claims: I became suspicious of the whole circus. It seemed more a court where wide-eyed students pay homage to wise old wizards, and then themselves become puffed up with this so-called knowledge. A racket, in fact, and a massive waste of human endeavour."

Phyllis looked amused. "My," she said. "And where does religion figure in your estimation, given its close proximity to philosophy?"

At this point Dr Drummond held up his hand. "Enough! I wish I had not asked. It is better that we do not discuss religion, nor politics. It always ends in raised voices in this household. Let me try a more innocuous question. How are you finding Ramsburgh? I must say I was delighted to see it again the other day. It is magnificent, in such a splendid setting."

"Thank you – it has surpassed my expectations. I am very comfortable there, and I have just discovered a secret room that I can hide away in."

"Of course – the master's closet," said Phyllis.

I looked at her in surprise. "How did you know?"

"I used to come and play at Ramsburgh," she said. "I was great friends with Flora. And we took special delight in going into rooms that were forbidden to us."

"Come to think of it, she mentioned she knew you," I said. "I'm sorry you're not still friends."

"And I," said Phyllis. "It broke my heart – and hers."

"Might I ask what happened?"

Phyllis sighed. "It's difficult to explain. I did something she disapproved of. She was quite right: it was unforgivable."

"My dear," said Dr Drummond, "I have never been able to fathom it. You were such wonderful friends, and I enjoyed having her here. Was it really too hard to mend?"

"Yes: I don't blame her. There is nothing to be done about it. Let me pour you some more tea, Mr Rufford, and we shall find something that we can all discuss with no discomfort to anyone present."

"I know," I said. "Your books. I was very taken with 'Lady Harlington's Estate', as I mentioned already – but this was when Mr Walker had just been discovered, so I didn't get time to properly discuss it with you. The progression of the characters totally convinced me. What made you think of the story, or is it a procedure too mysterious to be spoken of?"

Phyllis laughed. "I was in a contrary mood, I suppose. I wanted to tip everything upside down. Good turns to bad, bad turns to good – a simple enough theme, and hardly original, but it amused me to do it on my terms."

"The book captures my daughter's essence," said Dr Drummond, standing up. "Always contrary."

"Am I so very impossible?" said Phyllis, putting on her sweetest tone and looking innocently up at her father.

"Unendurable," said Dr Drummond, kissing the top of her head. "But I know you're just trying your best to be outrageous, so I don't take anything you say too seriously."

Phyllis pouted in mock annoyance.

Dr Drummond pulled out a pocket-watch and looked at it. "I must visit a patient now, I'm afraid," he said. "He's a hypochondriac, but the poor fellow has worried himself into being ill in earnest. Mr Rufford, you're welcome to stay until my daughter wants rid of you. I'm glad we met today, if strangely. Good day!"

I thought Dr Drummond to be a fine old fellow, but I was happy to be alone with Phyllis.

"So, Mr Rufford," she said. "Having rejected philosophy, what interests you? Besides distressed artists and animals."

"I suppose art and music – the usual things. And I am learning an appreciation of ancient houses and their upkeep, and also a little of the pottery business. Besides, I don't entirely reject philosophy. It's just the obsession with it I can't stand. The ideas may be intriguing, but they are done to death."

"I tend to agree," said Phyllis. "But what should we be spending our time on instead?"

"The improvement of man, perhaps, in practical ways."

"And woman, do you not think?" she said.

"Of course; I was using 'man' to include your kind. I mean..."

Phyllis nearly fell off her sofa laughing. "'Your kind'? Are we a different species?"

I flushed red at this slip of the tongue. "Sorry. I think you know what I mean."

Phyllis tried to keep a straight face, with limited success. "Oh dear," she said. "How ill-mannered of me. You know, you are quite sweet when you are flustered."

This reduced my pang of embarrassment, even if I felt a little patronised. "You do not see me at my best," I said. "It has been an odd day."

"Poor Thomas!" she said. "May I call you Thomas? I think after today we are sufficiently acquainted."

"Please do, Miss Drummond."

She raised her finger like a schoolmistress chiding a student.

"Phyllis," I corrected myself.

"That's better," she said. "And anyway, you may be right. We might as well be a different species. It makes life more interesting in some respects, and intolerable in others. Our inconsequential differences gives bigots an excuse to keep us in check."

"I know this prejudice exists," I said, "but I suppose I haven't been sufficiently aware of it. If I had had a sister, I would have been more informed – and angry, no doubt."

"I should hope you would," said Phyllis. "You would have seen what a poor excuse of an education she was entitled to. But I can get too tedious on this subject, as my father would readily acknowledge." She stood up and smoothed her dress. "I feel in need of a walk. Will you join me?"

"Yes, I would like that," I said. "But after all this tea... I just need to..."

"Of course," said Phyllis. "Let me show you the way." She led me to a privy in the rear garden. "I'll meet you at the front door."

On my own for a few minutes, I turned over the day's events in my mind. I could not quite believe that my friendship with Phyllis had progressed so quickly. And I had, it seemed, made another and quite unexpected friend. My social life was in danger of becoming interesting. Not forgetting Francesca... but then, no one who met Francesca was likely to do that.

~

"Where would you like to walk?" said Phyllis when I had joined her at the front door.

"Ah – that's easy," I said. "After I first met you in the bookshop, I had a sudden compulsion to ask if you would be my guide around the town walls. But of course, that would have been very forward of me, and besides, you would have had better things to do."

Phyllis laughed. "I'm touched you thought of me as an

oracle on the subject. But you shall have your wish. I shall try to remember what I can of our history. This way!"

I followed Phyllis down a road of old houses of differing heights and styles, lending a chaotic beauty to the street, and then up a steep flight of stairs.

"Mind the mud," said Phyllis, and she strode up a bank of grass. Out of breath, we now stood on a high section of the fortifications. "Isn't it glorious?" said Phyllis. "Knight's Mount."

"Wonderful," I said. We could see over the lower portions of wall and for miles beyond Hawksbridge: cultivated fields, forests, the odd village, and distant hills, unfurling to the horizon like a tilted map and artistically lit by the late afternoon sun.

"Medieval, I presume?" I said.

"Originally, yes, when the Scots were less reasonable than they are now. The better-preserved parts were built by Queen Elizabeth. It transpired that they were an expensive folly, since they were never needed."

We continued to follow the wall, and I marvelled at the amount of earth and stone that went into its construction.

"We have Elizabeth to thank for this beautiful walk, then," I said. "How strange that something with such grim purpose can become so peaceful."

"It is a perfect contrast, yes," said Phyllis. "Speaking of peace, I wonder if poor Mr Shaw will find any, and begin his painting again. I hope he finishes the mural."

"He didn't look to me to be capable of anything so refined," I said. "But perhaps in a few weeks."

Phyllis stopped and turned to me. "Will you continue your investigation? I must say I am intrigued. If you have evidence, you must surely follow it up. But it's not much, is it? There must be a thousand port-drinkers in Hawksbridge, to say nothing of visitors to the town."

"It is tantalising," I said. "There's a good chance someone

else was there that night. That still doesn't mean it was that person's fault, but it would be a great coincidence."

"If someone was there, they could not be innocent," said Phyllis. "At the very least, they should have talked to the police. And my father has been assured by Mr Simmons that no one else is suspected of being there that night. My father was quite upset about Mr Walker's death, and spoke of it at length."

"It's a good point," I said. "Either that person has something to hide, or they were afraid of being wrongly accused. Perhaps they have a reputation to consider. But still: they have effectively obstructed the police."

"Will you inform Mr Simmons?"

"Yes, I will," I said, "even though he is likely to dismiss it."

"You should consider women," said Phyllis. "That is, if Mr Shaw and Mr Walker were the libertines that rumour leads us to believe, then might not a woman be involved? One of his models, perhaps."

"Yes, it's possible," I said. "They interviewed a lot of models, so perhaps one of them was unhappy about being rejected for the mural."

"What about the models that weren't rejected? The two angels we see in the town hall, for example. You said you knew one of them. But I would imagine the police have interviewed them."

"I don't know if they did – but yes, I know Mrs Campbell, slightly. I'm pretty sure she wouldn't be capable of such a crime. She said she didn't have any kind of relationship with either Shaw or Walker."

Phyllis shrugged. "Perhaps she's not the angel you think she is," she said. "And the other one – the outline? You need to find out who that is, Inspector Rufford."

"You're quite right. Thank you. I should have asked Shaw about her."

We walked on, and came to a mound with a path running around its base, the path being sheltered by an earth wall – presumably once a defensive ditch to hide in and take pot shots at the enemy.

"People call it Lover's Bastion now," said Phyllis. "I can't remember the original name. You can walk along here and be hidden from view. I find it very useful when I don't want to talk to anyone."

We made our way along the path, which did indeed feel improperly secluded. "I love to just listen," Phyllis said, stopping. We could hear the sound of birdsong, muffled chatter in the town below, and the far-off peal of bell-ringers practising. A faint breeze flicked loose wisps of Phyllis' hair as she stood motionless.

I suppressed a sudden impulse to kiss my companion – but it would have destroyed so much in an instant. Yet this place implied an intimacy that Phyllis must surely have been aware of. It flashed through my mind that Dr Drummond would be happy to see his daughter married off to the new proprietor of Ramsburgh, and it was easy for me to imagine myself and Phyllis walking through our grounds in a state of marital bliss, dogs and small children playing at our feet. That would be in no way disagreeable.

I punished myself for these foolish thoughts by breaking the spell. "We had better be getting back. Your father will think I have led you into further trouble."

"Yes," she said sighing. "Well, I haven't been much of a guide, but I don't think walks should be too worthy. If we carry on around here, we'll get back to where we started."

"It has been wonderful," I said. "I hadn't realised how beautiful all this would be. I'm lucky that fate guided me here, of all places."

"It's our gain," said Phyllis. "You will come and see us again soon, I hope?"

"Most certainly. And you must come to Ramsburgh."

"Yes, please! Although it will be awkward if I see Flora..."

"We will think of something. But it's my house, and I shall see whom I please."

We had reached the steep steps. "Beware of these in winter, Thomas," she said. "They have been responsible for many broken bones. My father calls these steps his pension."

I smiled. "I like his sense of humour," I said. "And yours."

"Good," said Phyllis. "Now, enough flattery – you must go home and rest. I fear you have exerted yourself too much after earlier."

Not as much as I would have liked, I thought.

"Will you be all right on foot?" she added. "Shall we find a carriage?"

"I'll be fine," I said. "It's not an onerous walk back to Ramsburgh."

~

The evening light cast a charming glow on the landscape as I walked up the hill to Ramsburgh. Stopping to rest, I turned around and looked at the stony curtain around the town, now rendered golden in the sunset; the sky was adorned with streaks of pinks, greys and blues in slowly changing patterns. I wished I had been an artist and able to capture such a paradisical vision.

If I possessed such a skill, I pondered, I would also be able to capture the vitality and corporeal delights of the women I had lately met, as Walker had with Francesca. Walker and Francesca – I had not yet allowed myself to think about them in the way that Shaw had implied. She had denied any relationship, but was this the truth? Was it any business of his? Or did she have some connection, however tenuous, to

Walker's demise? She was a port-drinker – I remembered it from the Harris' party. But that she should be involved was unthinkable.

I would have to go back to Shaw to ask him about the mysterious, unfinished angel. Even if Shaw was a violent ingrate, this investigation was not something that I could simply drop. It would be like casting aside a gripping story halfway through.

I sighed, and trudged back up the hill, my head a confusion of thoughts that were at one moment concupiscent, and at another, disquieting.

# CHAPTER SIXTEEN

THE next morning, I wrote to Inspector Simmons to let him know about the port bottle. I felt it unnecessary to mention the insurance policy, since Shaw had cancelled it: no purpose would be served by having Shaw charged with attempted fraud. If the insurance company wanted to take the matter up with the police, then that was their concern.

Yesterday was catching up with me, and my head and jaw were aching; so I decided to delay my visit to the bank, and instead rest.

I fetched 'The Predilections of Reverend Malamor' from my bedroom and walked up to my private lair. Francesca's reading voice had been so soothing that I had scant recollection of the book – I must have fallen asleep almost immediately. I settled myself on the sofa, and began reading.

## CHAPTER I: MALAMOR'S ARRIVAL

THE ARRIVAL of the Reverend Tobias Malamor in Eaglesville was anticipated with only a little less fervour and curiosity than the second coming of Christ. The death of the previous Rector had left the post unoccupied for some months, and the announcement of his successor was the cause of much talk: for Malamor was already a noted figure in London society, to the extent of an occasional appearance as a newspaper cartoon along with political worthies of the time. An attractive fellow of unnatural height, with piercing green eyes that were more often than not burning with enthusiasm, his tireless ambition to improve the nation's morals – including several pamphlets that had strayed dangerously close to Puritanism – led him into the public spotlight.

So the people of Eaglesville – with a few exceptions amongst the most staid of them – considered themselves fortunate to be

> singled out for the pastoral care of this distinguished holy man. The precise reasons for his relocation from the intellectual centre of the country to a small northern town were unexplained, but were credited to a wish to rediscover a modest and simple life. It was a great compliment to the people of the town; and so the Reverend Malamor was enthusiastically welcomed into its bosom.

The first few chapters established Malamor as a figure of admiration, not least amongst the single females of the town. The townsfolk were not treated so positively. The gluttonous Mayor drooled over the new Rector, at one point literally, and the medical profession were portrayed as charlatans who were charmed into giving the Rector access to their patients for the application of 'healing ministry' of a dubious nature. Malamor went where he pleased in the institutions of the town, and devised numerous worthy schemes which attracted generous contributions. As he put it in his sermons, he had the privilege of being guided by the Lord to awaken the latent virtues and energy of the good residents of Eaglesville. And then he got to work on Mrs Raine.

> Mrs Raine's party was exceeding her expectations. Tobias Malamor had lent a consequence to the event that the merchant friends of her husband could never hope to match. She had been congratulated on the party by several important people already, including the Mayor. And now the Reverend himself had disentangled himself from the knot of his admirers and was approaching! She dabbed at her hair to make sure it was in place.
>
> "Mrs Raine!" said Malamor. "How wonderful this evening is. You are the most accomplished of hostesses. And the most beautiful."
>
> Mrs Raine simpered. "Oh, you flatter me – but thank you! I hope you have had some good conversation – I fear you may not find your intellectual equal here."
>
> "I am perfectly satisfied on that account, Mrs Raine. But it was you I particularly wished to speak to. I wanted to ask if you

have given any thought to the Missionary Society that I mentioned on Sunday. I feel Eaglesville is brimming with good Christians who may feel their destiny is not being entirely fulfilled, and might wish to contribute to – or even partake in – the Church's important work in less fortunate countries."

Mrs Raine almost squeaked in her eagerness to cooperate. "But of course, Mr Malamor! I would be honoured if Mr Raine and I could be founding members of the Society. You will find us quite generous in causes we truly believe in."

I read on. Mrs Raine and her husband, who lived in a fine old house on the edge of town, were easily separated from a substantial portion of their money, and Malamor became a frequent visitor to the house. Indeed, Mrs Raine was cast in a spell that left her husband increasingly disaffected and distraught. But there was worse to come for Mrs Raine's fifteen-year-old daughter, Rose.

Rose had hoped that the little room in the attic would have kept her from Mr Malamor's reach. No one outside of the household knew of it. But to her terror, she could hear heavy footsteps on the narrow staircase. They were unmistakeably those of the Reverend. It was too late to take the key out of the lock on the outside and secure herself inside, and so she crawled under the sofa. She could hear him enter each adjoining room in turn. And then the door to her haven opened, and she could see the Reverend's long legs. She closed her eyes, frozen in fear.

"Ah, Rose! Are you playing hide-and-seek with me? How sweet. But I'm afraid I have won this little game."

She heard him walk back to the door, take the key out of the lock, and replace it on the inside, before turning it. She was trapped.

I closed the book. It was becoming very uncomfortable reading. The horror of the last scene aside, there were strange correspondences here with Ramsburgh. Rose's hideaway could be this very room, and as for the seduction of Mrs Raine...

I was getting hungry, so I went downstairs where lunch

was being prepared, and took Fox for a short walk before eating.

I returned to the top of the house and opened the book again, struggling to overcome my repulsion, but needing to know what came next. Young Rose's seduction was handled obliquely, but her subsequent state of mind was distressingly documented.

I read further; the Missionary Society was flourishing.

> Mr Malamor had assembled thirty or so of the residents, of varying ages but all infected by the same earnestness and keenness to do good – to suffer penance for the relative ease of their own lives. With a series of rousing speeches, the Reverend had inspired them and quieted any misgivings.
>
> "By your deeds you will be known!" he said to his disciples, who wore expressions of yearning for spiritual guidance. "Some of you may be roused, I hope, to put aside your present comfortable condition and go to Africa, to India, to wherever you are needed, and teach God's word. The natives will be grateful to be educated in the ways of our superior beliefs, and will gladly endure the white man's diseases as a worthwhile sacrifice. Smallpox, tuberculosis, dysentery, even venereal disease: all are Heaven-sent tests for them that will be accepted as a necessary accompaniment to the civilising influence of our proud missionaries. If populations are sometimes diminished, it is nothing – they will swell again, but now bearing the standard of Christ."
>
> An "Amen!" was heard from the assembly. And so it transpired, just as Malamor had wished: a dozen of the Missionary Society had set out from their congenial homes to suffer the unknown deprivations of exotic lands and to familiarise the natives with Christianity and novel diseases. Seven missionaries died, and only two returned. Of the remainder, there was no record. It had been prescient of the Rector to obtain further contributions before their departure.
>
> Another cause was dear to Malamor's heart: a grand new Asylum for the Poor that could accommodate unfortunates from this parish and beyond. Another committee, another drive to raise funds: all was grist to Malamor's never-ceasing mill. The

> Asylum had facilities for the poor to know the dignity of labour, and thus help fund the running of the institution; it was a regrettable fact that this had been extended to the construction of the building, a stiff task for the weaker workers, especially the children, and resulted in a natural trimming of the workforce. However, this made for more space for the remaining residents, and allowed an expansion in the offices and reception rooms for the staff. Malamor was chairman of the Asylum board, and was kindly attentive of many of the poor unfortunates, in particular the young women who doubtless appreciated that such a busy, distinguished man would give them his valuable time.

Fox came and bothered me for another walk, but I was now too deep in this grim tale to stop. Mr Raine died of grief, leaving Malamor to marry his widow. From this position of wealth – now amplified with funds of mysterious origin – he continued to exert his will over the town, and became Mayor. The Rector's desires became ever more sordid, and various worthies – including the Archbishop of Canterbury and several members of Parliament – were drawn into his web of depravity. Eventually, he contrived to pit all the factions and societies of the town – many of which had been created by himself – against each other, and the ensuing unrest resulted in the burning and destruction of much of the town. Malamor disappeared, to spread – as the author told it – more Christian values in other parts of the world.

When I finally closed the book, Fox had long since deserted me in search of more promising company. I felt exhausted by this preposterous book, and a little sullied. But more than that, I was disturbed by the reminders of the scandal that had once enveloped Ramsburgh. Were these similarities pure coincidence? It was eerie, as though the author were reaching through the pages of the book to torment me.

I wondered what kind of a man the author, John Bland, must be to have written such a book. Angry at his own circumstances, disillusioned with society in general, perhaps even a Chartist; or was it written with controversy in mind, for the simple purpose of earning a living? For it must surely have made Mr Bland wealthy, if it had caused such a stink that it was nearly banned. If it had been an act of revenge, it would have been a satisfyingly lucrative one.

Could he be a local man, writing about people, events and places he knew, and then adding his own fantastical twists? I considered the points of similarity.

Eaglesville – clearly that could be a play on Hawksbridge.

The attic room – perhaps it was silly to associate it with my prized closet. After all, many large houses would have similar rooms. But the description still fitted to a strange degree.

Mrs Raine – an anagram of some kind? Nothing came of that, but then I thought of the French word 'reine' – or 'queen' in English. Mrs Kington! That was either far-fetched, or too close for comfort. Mr Raine – his cuckoldry and death paralleled Mr Kington's. Reverend Malamor – he bore little resemblance to my father, of course, but the role of interloper was familiar. And could Malamor have been modelled after Reverend Neville? Both were painfully pious, but this was hardly unique for a minister of the Church. Malamor was a grotesque caricature that I could not imagine having any basis in reality.

And what about Rose? I threw down the book in disgust, and leapt from the sofa. I felt I was going to be sick, and lifted the window sash to get some air.

Rose could be Flora. Rose was a daughter rather than a niece, to be sure: but she bore a name with a similarly horticultural origin.

~

As I walked downstairs, lost in disagreeable thought, I became aware of a commotion in the hall.

"He was asking to see him, miss. He's in a terrible state. Thinks he's going to die, though the doctor doesn't reckon so."

I found Flora talking to Minto, the proprietor of The Duke's Head, and Shipley was also present. Minto was fiddling with a riding crop in a slightly agitated way.

"Oh, sir, I'm glad to see you. Mr Shaw is ill with a fever, and says he's wronged you and would like to see you before he dies. Which I doubt he'll do, sir, because according to Dr Drummond –"

"Thank you, Mr Minto," I said with a sigh. "I suppose I shall have to come. Mr Shaw is about the last person I want to see at present" – I ran a hand over my aching jaw – "but there's nothing for it. I'm just so dog-tired."

"I'll drive," said Flora. "Perhaps I can help."

"Are you sure?" I said, feeling a wave of relief that I might not have to face Shaw alone. "He's a brute of a man, and I shouldn't ask you to –"

"No, it's quite all right, Thomas," Flora said. "I often feel I should be making myself more useful, so this is the perfect opportunity."

"In that case, I would be incredibly grateful. Shipley – can you get the pony trap around?"

Shipley nodded and scurried off to find the groom.

"Thank you, Mr Minto," I said. "We'll come as quickly as we can."

"Good," said Minto. "I think it will calm him. I don't suppose Mr Shaw has any other friends here. And given what's happened to him..."

"Quite," I said.

On the way into town, I was sorely tempted to ask Flora about the book, but had a strong notion that this would only cause hurt and trouble. Instead, I described to Flora the aspects of my investigations that were fit for repetition.

"So you think there might be some significance to this port bottle evidence?" said Flora.

"It's more a case of whether the police think so," I said. "But I do find it a little disturbing. Or I might simply be too much influenced by Shaw's diseased imagination. After all, he's grief-stricken and addled by drink. I might be given to paranoia in a similar situation – God forbid I should ever be so unfortunate."

We left the pony trap with the inn's groom, and I knocked firmly on the door of the cottage.

"Come in!" said a female voice. We entered, and in the bedroom we found a woman I recognised as one of the barmaids, sitting by Shaw.

"Thank heaven!" she said. "I'm needed inside. He's been making precious little sense all afternoon. Here's a towel for mopping his face – it seems to help."

She left, and I brought an extra chair from the sitting room. Shaw was sweating and muttering something unintelligible, and tossing his head from side to side. Presently he opened his eyes and collected his thoughts.

"Ah! Thomas, my good friend. I am glad to see you. I've been wanting to say sorry, you know, for... for striking you like that. Totally uncalled for. I was out of my mind. I'm a fool: you were trying to help."

"That's quite all right," I said. "You didn't break anything, and Dr Drummond has looked it over."

"A good doctor, Drummond. A good doctor. He says I'll make it! I don't know. Why should I make it? Why not both of us? The port... who drank it?" He stared at Flora. "Was it you?" he said. "Did you drink it? No, no, no, you're not Ned's whore..." And he closed his eyes and fell to muttering again.

Flora and I looked at each other.

"Henry," I said, "this is Miss Flora Davison. She's a neighbour of mine." It seemed best to simplify matters. "She's going to help look after you, just while you're in this fever."

Shaw raised his head. "Oh – thank you," he managed to say. "Very kind. I would like water, please. So thirsty."

Flora fetched him a mug of water from the jug that had been left for them, and also wet the cloth. She helped him drink, and then dabbed at his face with the cloth. Shaw heaved a sigh of relief and his movements became less agitated. He soon fell asleep, snoring occasionally.

"Thomas," Flora said after a minute, "I can manage on my own. You look so tired. If you want to take Jenny back, I'll have Minto drive me home later."

"I don't know if I should leave you with this man," I said. "He's a little unpredictable."

"I shall be fine," said Flora. "The inn is close by if I have any trouble with him. And besides, he's too weak to get up to much mischief."

"Thank you," I said. "But I don't like –"

"Off you go!" ordered Flora. "I will report back to you this evening or tomorrow morning."

I was not entirely happy about the arrangement, but Flora seemed determined to do her bit, and my fondest desire at that moment was a hot bath followed by a strong cup of coffee. So I capitulated, and stopped first at the bank. Happily it was still open, and I was able to retrieve my heavy bag of guineas, to be lodged in Ramsburgh's safe. With all that was going on, I had nearly – but not quite – forgotten about the threat that still faced me: malevolent reverberations from my impulsive past.

# CHAPTER SEVENTEEN

I WAS curious to know how Flora had got on with Shaw, so after breakfast I went to Flora's tower door and knocked. My bath last night had been so relaxing, and my need for sleep so great, that I had been oblivious to Flora's return. I now felt apprehensive, and regretted leaving her alone to cope with Shaw.

She opened the door, and to my relief, she seemed unflustered. "Good morning!" I said. "I just wanted to check you didn't have any difficulties with your patient."

"Oh, thank you," said Flora. "No – he slept for a while, and when he awoke, the fever had abated and he was much more lucid. He was very grateful, and still apologetic about hitting you."

"Perhaps that has brought him to his senses," I said. "Did he talk about anything significant?"

"Not about Walker, no – in fact we ended up talking about art, and I told him about my embroidery. He asked me to bring a piece to show him next time I go."

"Next time? That's very good of you," I said.

"Not really," said Flora. "He's quite an interesting man, and I might even learn something from him."

"That really is a weight off my mind," I said. "Thank you. Please let me know if he says anything more about Walker."

"I will! Oh – and he said he was going to start on the mural again. That's very encouraging, don't you think?"

"Astonishing," I said. "I'm glad we won't have to whitewash what's there."

"Yes, I'm looking forward to seeing what he does," said Flora. "Perhaps he'll have more freedom now."

~

I was returning from a walk with Fox, and was about to go back into the house, when I heard hooves and wheels on the gravel. A pony trap came up the drive, and as it came close I saw Phyllis, at the reins, accompanied by another young woman whom I did not recognise. And yet there was something slightly familiar about her that I could not put my finger on. She had a most attractive profile, with a slender nose and full lips. Where had I seen it before?

The two women jumped down, and Phyllis said, "Good morning, Thomas! I hope you don't mind us dropping in on you like this. Thomas, this is my friend Mrs Beatrice Harkness. Her husband William works as a designer at your pottery company."

"Thomas Rufford," I said. "Very pleased to meet you, Mrs Harkness. Would you like coffee? Or tea?"

Shipley had come out to see who had arrived, and was despatched to deal with the pony trap and fetch coffee. I ushered them into the drawing room.

"You have such a beautiful house, Mr Rufford," said Beatrice. "How fortunate you were to be given it!"

"Thank you – I know," I said. "I'll never quite live it down. I'm not even sure I've seen all the rooms yet. I found a hidden one the other day."

"Oh – how exciting!" said Beatrice. "It's a child's paradise."

Phyllis smiled. "Indeed – I'm sure plenty of Hawksbridge young ladies would be quite willing to help populate this place for Thomas."

"Oh, Phyllis," said Beatrice. "How naughty of you. That's not what I meant. I'm sorry, Mr Rufford, I spoke without thinking."

"There is nothing to apologise for," I said. "You are

perfectly correct, and most of the time, I feel like a child myself in this castle. So, fortunately, the magic of the place is not wasted on me. Although, the magic is slightly spoiled when the gutters start to leak, such as the one outside my bedroom. But it's churlish of me to complain about that."

"Now, Thomas," Phyllis said, her voice becoming more serious. "We have come for a reason. You know I said you should find out who the other angel in the painting was?"

Light dawned: it was in the Town Hall that I had seen her profile. I nodded.

"Well, I have done your work for you. Beatrice is the second model."

"Congratulations," I said. "It's a delightful sketch. I hope Shaw is able to finish it – I gather he's commencing work again."

Phyllis and Beatrice looked at each other, rather grimly.

"I suspect not," said Phyllis. "You see, Beatrice has found herself in grave circumstances, and came to me for help. I thought that perhaps you might be able to suggest something. Would you like to continue, Beatrice?"

Beatrice cleared her throat, and looked nervously towards the door. "Can I speak in confidence, Mr Rufford?"

"Yes, of course," I said, and got up to close the door. "Please, Mrs Harkness, feel free to say anything you wish, and I promise it will not leave this room."

"Well – this is difficult. But I suspect my husband of murdering Mr Walker, and I fear he may be planning to kill me, too."

~

After she had spoken, the coffee was brought in, giving time for Beatrice's statement to sink in. When the door was closed again, there was a short silence, and then I said, "I see. What makes you say that?"

Beatrice continued: "William wasn't happy about me trying out for modelling for Mr Walker and Mr Shaw, but I had set my heart on it, and he gave in. So I went to their cottage to present myself, and when I was chosen, I could scarcely believe it."

"So did your husband then change his mind, after you were chosen? And get angry about it?"

"No," said Beatrice, "he wasn't angry, exactly, it was more that he went quiet, which is his usual way of coping with things he doesn't like. But he didn't stand in my way. Of course, I should have stopped it then and there. But I was a fool, and they are – were – very charismatic."

"So why did you think he would commit –"

"Please let me explain what happened first. This is very hard for me." Tears began to roll down Beatrice's face, and Phyllis put a soothing arm around her.

"I'm sorry," I said. "Do take your time."

"I – I fell a little in love with Edward Walker," said Beatrice. "I suppose it was his fame, and his good looks, and the way he talked – he seemed to cast a spell on me. The more I sat for him, the more I seemed to feel for him. He would talk as he worked, and it made him seem the most sophisticated and talented person. I thought myself so honoured to be painted by him. It made me light-headed. And then he told me –"

She dissolved into sobs, and it took a minute before she composed herself again.

"I'm sorry. He told me that he was dying, and he only had a few months to live, and that he would never know the embrace of a woman again. So of course, like the idiot I am, I told him I would give him what he wanted. He said that it would soothe his soul and help him accept the inevitable."

"I see," I said. "I think most women would have found it

hard to resist Walker. It's nothing to be ashamed of, because he will have honed his technique over many years. He is to blame, not you."

"Yes, well, this time his story was true – he was ill. But that does not excuse what he and I did."

"And if I may ask," I said as gently as possible, "when did this... meeting take place?"

"The night before Mr Walker died," said Beatrice. "We had the cottage to ourselves."

"Ah," I said. "And then..."

Beatrice closed her eyes. "We were intimate. As intimate as possible." Phyllis squeezed her arm.

"Oh dear," I said, uncomfortably recalling Bess Shannon's confession. I knew far too much about the private life of Hawksbridge. "What time did you leave the cottage?"

"I suppose some time before ten o'clock."

"And no one saw you?"

"I don't know," said Beatrice. "When I was a little way from the cottage, I turned around, and I saw someone go into the lane. But I couldn't make out who it was."

"Interesting. And you think this might have been your husband?"

"It's possible, yes, because when I got home, he wasn't there. He might have suspected me and followed me, and saw me go into the cottage, and then when I left, he went in and..."

She burst into tears again, and Phyllis said, "Try some coffee, my dear, it may help." Beatrice nodded, sipped her coffee, and dried her eyes.

"Where did your husband think you were, that evening?" I said.

"I said I was going to see Phyllis. Oh, I'm sorry, Phyllis, I should not have dragged you into this."

"It's quite all right, Bea," said Phyllis. "I don't mind about that."

"When did your husband get back?" I asked.

"Late – maybe twelve o'clock. He said he'd been drinking, but he seemed odd to me – more than just drunk. Or I could have been imagining it. But then when we found out that Mr Walker was dead, he laughed, and said that it was probably just as well, given his reputation with women, and he looked at me with a horrible stare. He said any husband whose wife had been mauled by another man had the right to kill both of them. I've never known him this vindictive, Mr Rufford. And now I'm afraid every time he looks at me that he's planning to kill me, and that he's just playing with me like a cat does with a mouse!"

"But is your husband apt to be violent at all, Mrs Harkness?" I said.

"No, not normally, but sometimes when he gets drunk I can see he might like to strike me. He never has, yet. Normally we are happy, and he treats me well – it's just since Mr Walker died, or even when I started modelling for him, that he became miserable. This stupid mural has ruined us!"

"So, Thomas," said Phyllis, "do you think there is anything we can do to assure ourselves that it wasn't William?"

"We can try to find out if he has an alibi," I said, "but of course we will have to do it very discreetly. If he finds out that someone has been poking into his business, it might not improve his mood. The fact that he works at the Pottery might be helpful."

"Thank you so much, Mr Rufford!" said Beatrice. "I know you probably can't solve this one for me – I only have myself to blame, after all – but even talking about it seems to help a little."

"I thought, Thomas, that since you were already helping Shaw, you might have some insight," Phyllis said, and she turned to Beatrice. "We'll all put our thinking caps on, my dear, and we'll sort it all out. Please don't worry."

"I assume you haven't talked to the police about this, Mrs Harkness?" I said.

"No," said Beatrice. "I know I should have, but revealing myself to be such an immoral woman is more than I can bear. More to the point, William would then know for sure – at least now there is a tiny chance that he has no inkling. At the very least, it would destroy our marriage."

Phyllis sighed. "Beatrice is right. It would put her in more danger to tell the police, even though it feels wrong."

"I agree; it's the lesser of two evils to be discreet," I said. "Do you know what inn he frequents? Does he have a favourite?"

"Yes, he always goes to The Golden Fleece," said Beatrice. "It's right opposite the factory."

"That could be useful," I said. "One more thing occurs to me. Do you or your husband drink port?"

~

Phyllis and Beatrice left, with the latter grateful and glad to have shared her burden. I was almost disappointed that the answer to my last question had been 'no'. It would have strengthened the possibility that Mr Harkness was indeed a murderer. And if Mrs Harkness were to be partial to port, then even she could be a suspect. Not that this would be conclusive, since the port may not necessarily have been consumed by the person responsible for Mr Walker's death, if indeed anyone but Walker were to blame. And if Mrs Harkness were involved in a crime of passion against her lover, then she would hardly have confessed to drinking the port, far less come to me for help.

But there was another, albeit outlandish, possibility – that Mrs Harkness was trying to assign the blame to her husband as a way to eliminate him from her life. I had read a newspaper article describing a crime that had been used by an entirely unconnected party for their own selfish ends, to perpetrate a second crime. But surely she would not wish to expose her own reputation in the process. And as a friend of Phyllis, who I thought a good judge of character, Beatrice seemed perfectly genuine in her distress.

At least, I thought, Mr Harkness had not contacted Phyllis to ask her whether Beatrice had been with her that night. This provided a glimmer of hope that Beatrice's fears were entirely unjustified. But that being so, who was the figure she saw turning into the lane towards the cottage? Did she see a murderer? Or someone about their legitimate business? It would surely be impossible to know.

I decided to walk into town and talk to Shaw again. I might be able to glean something about William Harkness, from Shaw or the proprietor of The Golden Fleece.

It was a pleasant walk, and the sunshine buoyed my spirits, which had taken a beating from Beatrice's story. When I arrived at the cottage door, I hesitated before knocking, surprised: I could hear a peal of laughter, and it sounded very much like Flora's voice. I had not heard her laugh with such abandonment before. Not wanting to eavesdrop, I quickly knocked.

"Come!" said Shaw in a mock-magisterial voice, provoking another giggle from Flora.

I entered, and found Shaw and Flora at the dining table playing cards. A port bottle and half-empty glasses helped to explain the jovial mood.

"My God, man!" I said, horrified. "You're drinking the evidence!"

"Hello, Thomas!" said Shaw. "Will you join us? I'll let you win, to compensate for that sore head I gave you."

"I know, I know," said Flora. "We probably shouldn't have. I did try to dissuade him, but..."

I threw my hands in the air with exasperation. "Henry, I thought you wanted –"

"Calm down, Thomas. Mr Simmons came along to ask me about it – did you tell him? – and looked at the bottle, then shrugged and changed the subject. So what was I to do? Give it to the British Museum?"

I sighed and leant against the wall. "I don't know. Well, at least we have your word that the bottle had been opened. Yes – I wrote to Simmons about it."

"I saw it myself," said Flora. "It was in the sideboard."

"Untouched since Ned's death, I assure you," said Walker. "Anyway, as you can see, I am much better, thanks to this ministering angel. Ah! There's an idea."

"Oh no, thank you, Henry. I won't be one of your models. Not when I see how cold Mrs Campbell must have been in the Town Hall."

"One of Ned's best figures," said Shaw in a more subdued tone. "At least he was inspired before he was – cut short."

"I need to ask you another question, Henry, please. It's rather personal – Flora, I'm sorry, but would you mind awfully...?"

"Of course," she said, and she put on her shawl and stepped outside, closing the door behind her.

"Well?" said Shaw. "I hope we won't need to keep Flora waiting too long."

"No, I'll be quick," I said, and then noticed on the dresser shelf, tucked between a jug and a candlestick, a copy of 'Malamor'. I took it from the shelf and turned to the fly-leaf. The inscription read, 'Ned – Some nonsense to pass the time. Yours, Francesca.' "Interesting you should have this. I just read it myself – a strange book. Have you read it?"

"No, that was Ned's. Mrs Campbell gave it to him. I heard him laugh over it a few times."

"Curious." I placed it back on the shelf. "Sorry – that wasn't what I wanted to ask you. Do you know a Mr William Harkness, and if so, do you know if he spoke to Ned?"

Shaw thought for a moment. "No – but I suppose you mean Beatrice's husband. She and Ned got quite cosy. So I see what you mean. But no, I saw nothing of Mr Harkness. And of course I've not said anything to anyone about Beatrice."

"Thank you," I said, a little relieved. "I would be grateful if you could keep it that way."

"Do you suspect Mr Harkness?" said Shaw.

"No – I just needed to reassure Mrs Harkness that her warmth towards Ned was kept private," I said, stretching the truth somewhat in order not to alarm Shaw.

Shaw grunted. "Anything else?"

"No, that's it," I said. "I hope you're not leading Flora too far astray – and it's not good for you to keep drinking. Anyway, I thought you didn't drink port?"

"Don't worry yourself – she's quite capable of handling me. And we've only had one glass. I ran out of beer, and reckoned I'd keep a lady company. It's only polite!"

I felt I could interfere no further.

"Thank you, Henry," I said. "I'm glad you're feeling better. I'll come and see you in a day or two."

Shaw saluted in lieu of a goodbye, and showed me out. "It's safe to come back now, Flora."

Flora and I exchanged smiles and nods as she entered, and I exited.

I felt decidedly strange about this new association between Shaw and Flora: it showed her in a very different light. But who she chose as her friends was none of my business.

I was lost in thought, and very nearly walked past Francesca coming down the path to the cottage.

"Thomas!" she said, lightly touching my arm. "What a dream you're in. Hello! How are you?"

"Goodness – Francesca, you gave me a shock. What a nice surprise. I've just been making sure Shaw has recovered, which he emphatically has. He's playing cards with my neighbour, Miss Davison. He'll probably ask you to join them."

"Oh! I'll invite her too. What fun!"

"Invite her to what?" I asked.

"I'm giving a party! You are invited, naturally, and I was just going to ask Henry. It will save a letter, and gives me an excuse to go calling. I'm sorry we haven't got together again yet – but I'll show you around the house when you come. I do so want your opinion. You will come, won't you?"

"Of course," I said. "When is it?"

"Next Saturday. I know I said we would have tea then, but I promise we'll do that another time. Are you free?"

To her amusement, I kissed her hand ostentatiously. "For you, Francesca, I will always be free."

# CHAPTER EIGHTEEN

As I walked over to The Golden Fleece, I felt a little embarrassed by my unguarded behaviour towards Francesca, which was only half in jest. Then I remembered the copy of 'Malamor' in the cottage – Francesca must have taken a liking to it after she started reading it to me, and found another copy for Walker. Did that indicate a closer relationship with Walker than she had admitted to, or was she in the habit of giving books to people she had recently met? She was an impulsive woman, that was plain. Impulsive enough to...? No, that was not to be countenanced.

The Golden Fleece was one of the few thatched buildings in the county, whose roofs were generally tiled in terracotta or slate. It was pretty on the outside, but airy and rather stark on the inside, with its single floor open to the roof timbers and furnished with simple trestle tables that presumably could be cleared away easily for dancing.

I ordered lamb and beer for my lunch, and wondered how I could raise the subject of William Harkness without it getting back to him. When the landlord came over with a tray, I thanked him, and said, "I wonder if you know one of my employees – Mr William Harkness? I heard he was looking unwell – I haven't been in the office lately to ask after him. I hope he is feeling better."

"Oh aye, I know of him. You're his employer? Well! He's usually better for a jug of something bitter!" said Mr Tanner. "You're right, though – he's been out of sorts lately. Looks mighty tired – sunken eyes, a little underfed. Have you been working the poor fellow too hard, sir?"

"I hope not," I said. "But I will check with his immediate

superiors. There's no point in wearing out our workers! It's not good for business. So he's been in here regularly, has he?"

"Oh yes, he's certainly good for *our* business. Last few weeks, he's been coming in around ten, or shortly after."

"I see – I suppose also before that artist chap died. A Monday night, I think. Do you remember when he came in that night?"

"Yes – we also had a nasty brawl here that night, and the police came. Mr Harkness almost fell over the lot of them on the way in. A policeman asked me the time so he could write it in his notebook, so I remember it being half-past ten. Mr Harkness was needled by the commotion – huffing and puffing about it, he was – and then he went into the corner and drank until about midnight. One of my lads had to see him home, he was that legless. Well, enjoy your lamb, sir. Let me know if you need anything else."

I was not reassured by this information. Not only had Harkness seemed out of sorts with something, he had arrived at The Golden Fleece having had ample time to visit Walker's cottage, just after his wife left. It was frustrating not to be able to eliminate him as a suspect – I had imagined myself bringing good news to Mrs Harkness, and being rewarded by a delightful smile, a little agreeable praise, and further approval from Phyllis. Instead, I would now have to enquire more closely into Harkness' movements, which risked arousing his suspicion. That could be disastrous for Mrs Harkness – perhaps even fatal.

As I finished my beer and got up from the table, a dark mood came over me. I realised I felt lonely, a state exacerbated by the revelation that Francesca was still friends with Shaw, and had perhaps been even more to Walker: and I was not pleased that the intimate tea party she had promised me had been replaced by something much less exclusive.

Flora had revealed an expectedly frivolous side, which strangely bothered me; and Phyllis was occupied with her friend's woes. I felt the weight of my responsibilities regarding the Walker case, and regretted agreeing to any of it. But while I could bluster to Shaw, I was now far more obliged to Mrs Harkness, and indirectly, to Phyllis.

I craved a distraction from all this – some abandoned gratification. Indeed, did I not deserve it for all the selfless attention I had recently bestowed on others? And so, with feelings of dread and excitement, I left The Golden Fleece and chose the road to Bess Shannon's house.

~

Mrs Shannon opened the door and smiled at me. "What a lovely surprise!" she said, and flattened herself against the hallway to let me pass. It was not sufficient to prevent my arm from gently brushing past her ample chest.

"Thank you – I'm sorry I didn't let you know I was coming," I said, removing my coat and placing it on a chair. "I just... thought I'd see if you were home."

"I'm very glad you did. I wasn't doing anything much, just a bit of mending. Come in and have a cup of tea."

I was relieved that my presence didn't seem completely inappropriate, as I feared it might.

"That would be wonderful, thank you. I'm feeling jaded and I need some interesting company."

"I will do my best," she said, putting the kettle on the range. "But don't expect miracles! You're the one with the fancy education."

"I think that can be overrated, Mrs Shannon. I've had my fill of it."

"You can call me Bess, if you want to – Thomas!" she said. "Or am I being too forward?"

"No, I would like that. Bess – it's a fine name. Why does

it sound so sensual? Oh – perhaps because it reminds one of 'kiss'."

"Does it now?" said Bess, turning around and folding her arms. She looked at me with amusement. I could see her reading me, and I was sure her appraisal was correct.

"Perhaps I need reminding," she said.

I leaned forward slowly, giving her a chance to escape if she wanted. But she stayed where she was, closing her eyes as I drew closer.

When our lips met, my own daring, and her assent, amplified the physical pleasure of it. She wrapped me in her arms and pulled me closer, and I mirrored the movement. Her breasts, so crudely described by Shaw, pressed against me, and I longed to remove the cloth that separated our bodies.

Before I had had my fill of her lips, she gently pushed me away and said, "Now I remember. Let's make the tea first, shall we? No need to rush."

My desires did not agree, but I nodded, and watched her as she put out the cups and brewed the tea. Her cheeks had turned a pleasing pink and she wore a faint smile.

"You are a remarkable woman," I said, aware that a slight husk had affected my voice. "And very beautiful."

"Passable, perhaps!" she said. "Thank you." She poured the tea, and took the tray into the sitting room. I followed, and stood a little nervously waiting for her to sit down. I did not know quite what to do – I was out of practice as a lover.

She sat on the sofa, and patted the velvet fabric next to her. "Come on, then! Let's have our tea, and if you're very lucky, you can remind me some more."

I sat next to her, feeling that the bump on my lap must be very noticeable.

"So, what's it like living in your castle?" Bess said. "Do you feel very grand? Do you have hundreds of servants, and a special maid to wash you?" She laughed and took a sip of tea. "That would be a fine sight! Perhaps I should apply for such a job."

"I wash myself, unfortunately," I said. "I make do with very few servants. But if you would like to be employed in that role..."

"I think I would get soaked in the process, wouldn't I?" Bess put her hand on my knee and pretended to soap it, her fingers tracing little circles. "Do you think I would need to undress too, so I wouldn't get my clothes wet?"

"I would advise it," I said. I could feel my face flushing and my heart racing.

"I would be very good at it. I would wash every little part of you. And every big part of you." She giggled and squeezed my leg, before continuing: "I suppose we would need to keep the water for me. It would be a shame to waste it. And then I might ask my master to wash me. What do you think of that, Thomas?"

"I admire your sense of economy," I said, taking a sip of tea and trying to ignore the discomfort caused by my constrained erection. "And I would wash you just as conscientiously, perhaps with lavender soap."

"Good," she said, adding with a smile. "You'll need a large flannel! As you can see" – she looked down at her bosom – "God has favoured me generously." She undid a couple of buttons at the top of her dress to give me a better view.

I could wait no more, and, whispering "Then, praise be to God," twisted round to kiss her on the lips, before losing myself in the scent and soft skin of her breasts.

~

When I got back to Ramsburgh, I was afraid that the eagle-eyed Mrs Felton would somehow perceive what I had done, by my flushed cheeks, my guilty look, or even the scent of Bess.

But she gave no sign of it, and I retired to my room at the top of the house with Fox at my heels to try to make some sense of the day.

I veered between shame and defiance: had I used Bess? Perhaps, but she had encouraged me. She had not let me enjoy all the pleasures of the bedroom, but she had deftly released me from the torment of my frustration, and she had obviously derived enjoyment from it, judging from her excited, irregular breathing. As I had got back my own breath, she had turned her back on me and said, "Here's a little more of Bess for you to think about, 'til next time!" before pulling up her dress and petticoats for just a moment to let me savour the view.

The memory of those beguiling curves was indeed sharp in my mind, and my blood began to course again in anticipation of feeling Bess' willing rump under my hands. If any sense of the obligations to Bess that my affair might reap vexed my conscience, I confess it was swamped in an instant by carnal thoughts.

I fussed over Fox for a while, trying to wrest my thoughts back to more serious matters. I remembered with a sinking heart that I had not eliminated William Harkness as a potential killer. I would need to make enquiries at the Pottery – McPhee would be the man to talk to. It seemed a little hopeless. Perhaps the matter would be taken out of my hands – the police might have found another lead, or the Harknesses might be reconciled and Beatrice's fears melt away, so that line of investigation would become pointless.

My mind wandered again, and idly I took up 'Malamor' and leafed through its pages, hoping that I might alight on a passage that would illuminate its link with Ramsburgh (if link there were). My hand stopped at a page containing a passage of invective that I had noted previously.

> The Reverend Malamor moved easily amongst the most powerful of society. Amongst these were the stumpy, greasy

> factory owners who sat astride the belching monsters of industry, spreading a plague of factories that laid waste to traditional life and consumed men, women, children and self-respect.
>
> At their leisure, they ogled the salacious 'art' of the era. This was chiefly the class of paintings that aspired to classical and religious eminence but were in reality mere tawdry erotica: white slave women shamed in their nakedness before salivating men; sofa-draped Venuses with no coverings worth mentioning; attractive Magdalenes repenting to God while bearing their breasts in a sensuous frenzy; dubious gatherings with lascivious goat-men and eager naked nymphs.
>
> At church, the same worthies feigned piety, led by robed charlatans, who themselves had more interest in the choirboys than their flock and who to a man across the nation employed the same wheedling tones to delude the hordes into their cloying grasp. At home, our heroic moguls applied the same tyrannical principles as for their workers, with ill-paid staff and womenfolk whose principal permitted roles were to sew platitude-ridden samplers, reflect the glory of their men and submit to their beastly desires.
>
> And what of the governance of the nation? Behold a tyranny dominated by rulers who attained power with simple bribes and menaces; whose laws were self-seeking and unjust; who spent much of their time in a stupor in the drinking-halls of Westminster; and who were more concerned with their carnal conquests than the tedious needs of the lowly masses.
>
> At the apex sat an ungifted Queen whose bodily cravings were so notorious and excessive that the finest and most virile young males of British aristocracy could not satisfy her, and her plenipotentiaries had therefore been sent abroad to fetch her a Teutonic lover with little charm but energetic loins.
>
> In short, it was a society so reeking with corruption that it was fertile ground for one with the talents of Mr Malamor.

This might have been one of the passages to raise a snigger from Walker. Its observations, although I could not agree with all of them, had sufficient truth to stir a vague guilt in me that I was over-satisfied with the status quo and the easy life that my inheritance had conferred on me. Which reminded me of my obligations, and I sat down to write to Phyllis to inform her of my discoveries so far. Although I wrote with a positive tone, my optimism did not match my words. And yet with the act of addressing my new friend came a pleasant warmth of feeling that surprised me.

> Ramsburgh, 8th September
>
> Dear Phyllis,
>
> I wanted to let you know how I am getting on. I made discreet enquiries, and Mr Shaw professes to know of nothing that would incriminate Mr Harkness. So that is a mark on the credit side of the ledger. I then went to The Golden Fleece, and ascertained that Mr Harkness came in at half-past ten, before leaving around midnight. This timing leaves the matter a little open, but I will persist in my enquiries and try to find out what Harkness was doing between ten and half-past.
>
> It was a pleasure seeing you at Ramsburgh this morning, although I know the errand was a sorrowful one. I look forward to returning the kindness that you and your father showed me on Thursday and entertaining you both here.
>
> On another topic entirely – I am afraid I ignored your advice, and purchased the copy of 'Malamor' that you were holding when we met. I read it, and found it as you said: scandalous – but diverting nonetheless.
>
> However, something about the book troubles me, and I feel that you knew that it would. Am I being foolish, or are there certain correspondences between aspects of the book, and Ramsburgh's recent history? How could this be? I am sure it must be coincidence. Perhaps you have some insight about this reprobate Bland, that only a fellow novelist could have. Not that your philosophies and talents are in anyway comparable, of course! 'Lady Harlington's Estate' is a more enjoyable read in all aspects.
>
> Your respectful friend,
>
> Thomas Rufford

# CHAPTER NINETEEN

AFTER lunch on Monday, I set forth for the Pottery to find McPhee and see if he could help with the Harkness question. I was restless and keen to accomplish something, after a lazy Sunday walking Fox, re-reading my battered old copy of 'Gulliver's Travels', and chatting pleasantly about nothing in particular with Mrs Felton. I had not been in the mood for the Rector's brand of piety and hectoring, and had therefore not attended the Sunday service even though it meant forgoing a possible encounter with Phyllis.

Unfortunately, when I got to the Pottery, I was told that McPhee was visiting a relative and was not expected back for a week. I did not think it prudent to trust anyone else with my question about Harkness, so although the delay would be unpleasant for Mrs Harkness, I had to postpone that research for the moment. I decided instead to visit the Town Hall to check if Shaw had resumed his work.

As I approached, I could hear shouting – it was the characteristic tenor of Rector Neville. I hesitated. Did I want to be embroiled in whatever this was? But my curiosity overcame my reticence, and I climbed the flight of steps, wondering what I might find.

Mr Neville was energetically gesticulating to a grey-haired man I recognised as Mr Jeffries, the Town Clerk.

"I demand that this outrage be covered over immediately! It is a libel of the most despicable – not to say actionable – sort! I have never been so insulted in my life. I will not be made a fool of!"

"Of course, sir," said the Town Clerk, cowering a little. "I'm sure it's a misunderstanding, and I will ensure that the appropriate actions are –"

"What's appropriate, sir," thundered the enraged cleric, "is that we erase all evidence that these – scoundrels – were ever in Hawksbridge. Now will everyone understand what I have been saying for the past months? Or is everyone still blind and deaf? It is beyond my comprehension..."

He stamped his foot, and turned to go out. He cast a withering look at me, along with the utterance "Huh!", and marched down the steps with his black cassock billowing like a bat's wings as he muttered under his breath.

With an unimpeded view of the walls, I now saw what had outraged the Rector, and I broke out laughing despite the presence of the chastised and serious Town Clerk. In the lower portion of the mural, a man in black was orchestrating the flames of the disaster, emitting them from his bony fingers and looking up with derision at the angels. Clearly this was the Devil himself, and he wore the face of our Rector, with his unmistakeable cheekbones and hollow eyes. He was portrayed with a mad smirk, a parody of the insincere expression he used for greeting his congregation. It had only just been created, judging by the gleam of wet paint, and it was not yet finished.

"Oh dear," I said, trying to suppress my laughter. "Sorry. What a mischievous thing to do. But it is done rather cleverly, don't you think?"

Mr Jeffries grimaced and shrugged his shoulders. "Well, Mr Shaw may think it clever, but I doubt many others here will appreciate it. I will need to arrange for its removal. The question is, should all of it go?"

"Oh, surely some can be saved!" I said, alarmed to think of Francesca's magnificent portrait being abolished. "The angels and the landscapes – they could be completed, and I think we owe it to Mr Walker – it's his last painting. I'm sure we could persuade Mr Shaw to behave himself. It should be very little trouble to whitewash over just that part." I regretted even having to support that, since I admired Shaw's composition and the sheer affrontery of it. But certainly it was provocative.

"I think this project may be beyond recovery," said Mr Jeffries with a sigh. "We will convene the Committee again and see what's to be done."

As I descended the stone stairs, I thought with regret that few people would see this well-executed rendering of the Rector. Now that would have been a picture with which to entertain visitors to the town. But where was Shaw, and might I be able to persuade him to quickly wipe out the devil-Rector before opinion hardened against him? I set off briskly for the cottage.

When I got there, I knocked, and there was no reply, so I tried the latch. The door opened, and I entered, going over to the table where Shaw and Flora had been playing cards.

"Mr Shaw?" I said. "Are you in?" I was once again answered with silence, and on looking down, I saw a letter on the table. Although I was not in the habit of reading other people's correspondence, I thought the present situation warranted myself being in grasp of all possible facts. With a pang of shame, I read the following:

> Ramsburgh, 8th September
>
> Dear Mr Shaw,
>
> You gave me no choice in leaving so suddenly this morning. I have enjoyed your company, perhaps too much for my own reputation, but there is no excuse for the brutishness you displayed – no doubt due to drink, but that does not absolve you. You say you have feelings for me, which you probably believe, but which I cannot believe are compatible with such coarse lunges and grabs.
>
> I know you have been visited with misfortune lately, and I am sorry, but for your own sake, and that of any others you care for, if there truly be any: you must forgo liquor and rein in your animal passions.

In sorrow and memory of our fleeting friendship,

Miss Flora Davison

So – as suddenly as it had began, Shaw and Flora's association had dissolved. I was not surprised. Shaw was unstable, with the stereotypical artistic temperament that was made far worse by his friend's death and the hostility shown to him by the town. It was probably for the best – at least Flora had not been hurt as much as she might have been on longer acquaintance with Shaw.

Perhaps it was this letter that had set Shaw off in anger to the Town Hall to vent his feelings with his cynical portrayal of the Rector. The likely follow-up to this would be getting steaming drunk. Reluctantly, I left the cottage and made my way to the bar of The Duke's Head. I had to try to calm him down and attempt to salvage the bedevilled mural, just one more time.

A ruddy-faced Shaw was holding forth, a mug of beer in one hand and a cheroot in the other.

"Here's what I think, gentlemen. Your precious smarmy Rector and that little runt who pretends to be an artist, Johnny Falkirk – they both did it. Mr Neville wouldn't have the guts to do it himself, so he somehow got Falkirk to do it. They've both pulled the damned wool over your eyes, gentlemen, and the police's eyes" – he annunciated the last phrase with some difficulty and had to repeat it – "the police's eyes. The Inspector's just looked the other way. Corrupt little fucker, he is."

He dragged on his cheroot and blew the smoke back into the eyes of the nearest customers. I was about to plead for his return to the cottage, but at that moment the door slammed loudly. Everyone turned – the Rector stood there, clearly burning with rage.

"Shaw!" he roared. "You've had your fun. Now go and wipe that... abomination off the wall this instant! Or I will sue you for every penny you have, or will have; and if you think you have it bad now, by God you will be in the gutter soon enough and sorry for your very existence! You hear me, man?"

The customers turned their gaze back to Shaw, awaiting his response as if they were at the theatre.

"Oh, I hear you, Neville. But do you sound like a man of God? Or merely a trumped-up, small-minded dullard who can't take a joke? I'm not going to destroy my art for you, or anyone. It's the truest thing I ever did!"

All eyes returned to the Rector, but he disappointed them by standing silent for a moment glaring at Shaw, then opening the door and walking out without another word. The door slammed behind him.

Shaw fell into a laughing fit, partly prompted, perhaps, by the tension in the silence left by the Rector's departure. When he could speak again, he said, "What a fucking coward! Anyway, most people would be overjoyed to have their portrait painted by Mr Henry Fucking Genius Shaw. The man's immortalised, which is more than his damned lie of a religion will do for him."

I found my voice. "Henry," I said, "can I have a private word with you, in the cottage? You can bring your drink." I was careful to keep a little distance this time: enough to avoid the swing of an arm.

He grunted, and followed me into the cottage, staggering and singing a bawdy song.

I've had them young, I've had them old
I've had the timid, had the bold
But none so sweet as Fanny Brock
Who loved me and my preening...

"HENRY!" I said, severely. "Do you mind?"

"Prig," he said, and slumped into a chair at the table. He was in danger of slipping onto the floor, so I managed to get him up again and into bed. He lay there conducting himself as he repeated the dirty song.

I fetched him some water, and said, "I know you're angry, but you can rescue the situation by erasing that picture. You can paint me as the Devil if you like, I don't care: but then you'll be paid, and you can get back to what you enjoy doing. If you keep playing up, no one will employ you."

It was probably hopeless to try to reason with this man, but it was surely worth the attempt, even though this project was probably as the Town Clerk had said: beyond saving.

Shaw stopped conducting, his arm falling to his side. Tears suddenly welled up in his reddened eyes.

"You're right," he said. "You're right, Thomas. Tom. Tomty-tom, Tom. What a strange, lonely little word that is. Thomas is right, Henry is wrong. Thomas is always right, because he's the lord of the fucking manor, and I'm just a fucking painter. Only I'm not even that any more. I'm a nobody. This town hates me. Women are disgusted by me. I'll just drink and drink until nothing matters any more, nothing hurts any more."

He turned and looked at me with a trembling lip. "You don't like me any more, do you, Tom?"

"I liked you when you were sober, Henry," I said, "and creating great works, as you are still capable of doing. And I will like you again when you are sober once more."

# CHAPTER TWENTY

I WAS out of sorts when I returned to Ramsburgh. I left Shaw sleeping, without much hope for either his mental state or the mural. It was too bad that he no longer had Flora as an impromptu nurse and champion of his better nature. I headed up to my eyrie for some much-needed solitude. I did not want to think of any present troubles, so decided to distract myself by investigating the contents of Mr Kington's desk. I had put it off for too long.

I pulled the top drawer of the bureau open and found it to be stuffed with correspondence from banks, tailors, builders, and directors at the Pottery. I would need to sort out what could be disposed of – probably all of it.

The next drawer was filled with stationery, but the bottom and deepest drawer proved to be locked. I looked in the recesses of the other drawers for a key, but none could be found. Knowing that bureaux often have secret compartments, I discovered that there was a loose panel to the right of the green baize writing surface. This slid open to reveal a small space that could have hidden keys or love-letters, but it was empty, save a dead beetle and the dust from many decades. Next I tried the numerous little pigeon-holes and little drawers at the back of the bureau, to no avail.

I remembered a distinguished and well-patinated bureau in college, housed in a beautifully panelled study, examples of which Oxford was so well endowed. The room was the domain of a gangling, nervous old theologian prone to little rushes of enthusiastic, high-pitched speech that required some concentration to interpret. On more than one occasion he had treated myself and my colleagues to the intricacies of his old bureau, of which he was very proud – to a rather charming extent – and which induced his excitable mode of articulation. His bureau had several secret compartments, and also a plethora of drawers and divided spaces of varying sizes behind the desk. But the cleverest portions were the two columns that decorated and divided parts of this nest of drawers and pigeon-holes: these pulled out and revealed themselves to be hollow, for the secretion of small items.

I looked at my bureau: there were no columns, as such, but there were a couple of flat dividers that looked to be solid parts of the desk's construction. To make sure, I tugged at one, and my hand met with resistance. Yet there was a little give in it, which encouraged me to pull harder, and I was surprised to find it finally slide out. On turning it upside down, I also noticed a flexible tongue of metal on the underside that together with a recess in the bureau, had meant that a little force was required to extract it, offering another – if minor – obstacle for the inquisitive stranger.

I was disappointed that no key had fallen out, but I took it to the window to examine the article in a better light. To my delight, I saw that a key had been wedged inside with several folded papers, and it was quick work to extract the key with Mr Kington's letter-opener. If this was the key to the drawer, what could Mr Kington have wanted to conceal? A cache of love-letters from a mistress, perhaps? A journal, that would catalogue my father's sins and Mr Kington's sad physical and mental decline? I was not altogether ready for the latter, and it would have been impolite to peruse the former.

With a little apprehension, I fitted the key in the lock – and it turned. What I found in the drawer, heavy with papers and books, I had not at all expected, and it elicited a mixture of rcactions.

(You will, I hope, forgive me for taking some five hundred words to open a drawer: but it is necessary to give you a sense of the tension I felt during this search, followed, as it was, by a disconcerting discovery.)

For Mr Kington had placed in this drawer an extensive collection of erotica, of the most blunt kind.

A few items I had seen before. In my research, I had occasion to view reproductions of those wall-paintings of Pompeii that had made their excavators blush, sufficient to compel them to brutally chisel these portraits out from their walls and lock them away in a museum in Naples. Seemingly the Romans – or at least these Romans – thought nothing of decorating private and public rooms with cheerful acts of lust. Their purpose surely could not have been only to inflame, as we would think in our own times; but to signal something – who knows what? Perhaps status, or perhaps it was simply part of the elaborate aesthetic sensibility we can see in other exuberant Pompeiian art. But whatever the motivations and phlegmaticism of the ancient Romans, such images have a definite aphrodisiac effect in the nineteenth century.

Some of the Pompeiian lithographs and drawings had been attractively coloured, and I supposed that the artists had reconstructed some of the damaged elements of the frescoes – a missing leg here, a crumbled breast or phallus there. My eye was caught by a pale woman with her hair up and naked save for a little red band of cloth around her chest, squatting over a dark-skinned male who was reclining with his arm casually behind his head. His lover's head was bent as if in concentration, and her right hand was out of sight behind her leg, seemingly facilitating the start of coitus. The naturalness and intimacy of this portrait of love startled me with its beauty, and – yes, I admit – aroused me a little. I pulled out another drawing: the woman had her left leg over the shoulder of her lover who knelt between her legs, and her expression seemed to be one of serene enjoyment. An abundance of coital positions were represented in further drawings and prints, and I began to imagine how Bess and I might very agreeably pass the time by attempting some of them.

The usual prints from the last century and this were to be found in Kington's collection, from preposterous – especially those involving nuns, monks or more than two participants – to sweet and almost innocent, where young and seemingly married couples are seen enjoying their bedchamber and each other. Works by Boucher and Fragonard were particularly plentiful. There were also books of a saucy nature, from the seventeenth century onwards, and in a variety of languages.

But the majority of Kington's erotica collection consisted, regrettably, of a never-ending variety of depictions of that strange Greek myth, Leda and the Swan. As you will doubtless know, the core of the myth – many permutations of which exist – is that the god Zeus turned himself into a swan and seduced Leda, who bore Helen and Polydeuces as a result. Art that depicts this peculiar union has been produced from ancient times to this day: in more modern times, it has perhaps been a means of evading the censure from religious or civic authorities that the portrayal of two intimate humans would prompt. (My belief is that it is also an attractive subject for artists because it provides a bold aesthetic – strong, raised wings against a nude – and a visceral shock, in no more elevated a fashion than a penny dreadful.)

That Mr Kington had an obsession with this topic was in no doubt. Looking through these pictures, I had to admire the imagination of artists in devising new ways in which Zeus could seduce Leda. In most of them, Leda does not seem as horrified as one would expect a woman to be in receipt of such fluttery, feathery advances. Indeed, in many of the pictures, an expression of rapture is present. That is, in Leda, since the expression of a swan is notoriously hard to read. To me, they always seem to have a beetling, angry brow.

Every person who has laid eyes on a portrait of Leda and the Swan must, if only for a moment, have thought of the mechanical implications and then felt a little nauseous. This was certainly the case with me. However, attempting to overcome my initial revulsion at such a theme, I began to think only of Leda's pleasure, which I believe is what the artists generally wish us to concentrate on, once the shock of the subject subsides. Treated as a mere allegory of female desire, it is easier not to glance away in mortification. And what fiery lusts these females express – welcoming her downy lover with upturned head and parted hips and lips, or pressing the beast to her loins, or – as a drawing of a classical tablet showed – one hidden hand guiding her Cygnus sweetheart as in the Pompeiian portrait alluded to above. As this pointed occlusion of the hand is a recurring theme, I suspect it of having been discovered as a potent erotic motif by the ancients, and copied by artists ever since.

One of the most striking of these representations has Leda in a glade, bent forward slightly and hanging onto a bough. The artist's view is from the front, and behind her, Zeus folds his wings around her and bends his neck around to grasp Leda's right nipple in his beak. Leda has a beatific expression, giving herself up to the moment and her own sensuality. The glade, and the countryside in the background, is portrayed in pleasing detail. If you can think only in allegorical terms for a moment, with the swan merely standing in for the pleasures that a human husband might provide, this is a beautiful portrait of feminine enjoyment – and a notable demonstration of artistic skill – for both sexes to appreciate. But of course, viewed literally, it is a scandalous piece of pornography drawn for and by degenerates, and worthy only of burning.

Whether or not Mr Kington took an allegorical or literal view of his collection, I could not say. But the scope of this assemblage did cast an interesting light on his character – obsessional, and apt to wallow in a fantasy where human men present no sexual challenge.

I finally began to tire of looking through this trove, and wondered what to do with it. I could chuck the lot on the little grate in this room and soon be rid of it. But it was certainly worth a lot of money, and I was not in the habit of transforming cash into ash. Besides, when bored, or in need of inspiration in the bedroom, I could refer to this archive and learn from the Romans this method or that. Because Kington had amassed it, it was not 'my' erotica collection. It was simply something that was already here, a quirk of the house, a piece of history that should be preserved. That was an excellent excuse, with which I was well pleased, and I locked up the drawer in a somewhat hot state that required a cooling walk with Fox.

But just before I got to the door of my closet, it suddenly occurred to me that Mrs Kington must have realised a little of her husband's fixation, perhaps chancing on a bunch of receipts for what must be expensive items. There, with a turn of a key, the mystery of the swan massacre was solved.

# CHAPTER TWENTY-ONE

HALFPENNY House, the new seat of Mrs Francesca Campbell, was quite as pleasant as I had imagined. Its tidy brick façade was divided vertically into three sections by virtue of a protruding centre portion and brick pilasters at either side. The architect had sliced it horizontally with two decorative stone courses, and the windows were also of stone, with arched mullions. In short, it was a delight to behold, and I could see why Francesca had fallen in love with it.

As I drove the pony trap up to the door, I felt sorry that Flora had decided against going to the party. But since Shaw would be present (assuming he was sober enough to attend) it would certainly have been awkward for her. I felt a little nervous about it myself. I fervently hoped Shaw would not make a scene; but on the other hand, it would be worth that discomfort to see Francesca's ebullient personality given free rein in her new domain.

Having entrusted Jenny to the care of the groom, I was ushered into the drawing room, where several of the guests were already in attendance: I spotted the Cravens, the Harrises and another couple I did not recognise. Was that a monkey on the man's shoulder? I had to stop myself from staring.

Francesca gave me one of her radiant smiles. "Oh, Thomas! I'm so pleased you could come. You look so dashing! Some of you know Mr Thomas Rufford – the man who is responsible for recommending this great town to me."

"I didn't entirely do that, Francesca," I said, "since I didn't know anything about Hawksbridge. I merely mentioned the place – and your charming recklessness did the rest."

"Well put, sir," said Mr Harris. "Charmingly reckless. I do

believe you have caught Mrs Campbell's essence." I saw Mrs Harris dig her elbow into her husband's side while maintaining a polite smile.

Francesca curtsied. "I would be quite happy with that description on my headstone," she said.

I was surprised to then see Phyllis and her father arrive with Beatrice Harkness and her husband, whose innocence I had yet to confirm. I thought it prudent to pretend that I was not acquainted with Beatrice.

"Very pleased to meet you," I said as I shook hands with the Harknesses. "Mr McPhee is full of praise for your diligence, Mr Harkness. I'm looking forward to seeing the fruits of your labours." He acknowledged the compliment with a smile and a nod.

"Good evening, Dr Drummond, Miss Drummond," I said. "Tell me, Mrs Campbell, how did you all meet?"

"I confess I was my usual bumptious self. I was in Hunter's when I heard Mrs Harkness refer to Phyllis, so I asked if she was Thomas' Phyllis, the novelist. You" – she said, looking at Phyllis and Beatrice – "were good enough to humour me. And so naturally, I wanted you for my party! You are so very welcome."

"Thank you – we are honoured," said Mr Harkness, who seemed much less drawn than before. The couple's demeanour suggested that their relationship had taken a turn for the better.

"I confess I heard that Mr Craven was going to be here," he continued, "so I had an additional motive for coming. He's my old art master – and I want his advice for a pattern I'm working on."

"Oh, splendid!" said Francesca. "I'm so glad you'll have plenty to talk about."

I caught Phyllis' eye, and she smiled back at me. If she – and Beatrice – had known that Shaw was due at the party, surely they would not be so composed? I decided to be on my guard to interject, should Shaw appear and engage Beatrice or Mr Harkness in any inappropriate conversation. But even his presence might be dangerous, given Mr Harkness' objection to his wife's stint as a model.

After some small talk, Mr Harkness excused himself and went to talk to Mr Craven, while Beatrice spoke to Mrs Craven.

"My dear Miss Drummond," Francesca said, having found a chair for Dr Drummond, "I am hoping you will tell me which of your novels to read first. It's so exciting to talk to a real, live novelist! You must be incredibly proud of your daughter, Dr Drummond."

Dr Drummond nodded. "I'm afraid I have yet to finish one, Mrs Campbell. I'm always so busy."

"That is a little shocking!" said Francesca. "But then it might be odd to see your daughter in a different light."

"Aye, that's probably it," said the doctor. "I suppose I want to keep thinking of Phyllis as my little girl – not a writer, having to consider all the disagreeable things that go on in the world."

Phyllis snorted. "Surely not as disagreeable as some of the things you have to do as a doctor?"

"Perhaps, my dear," Dr Drummond said, patting Phyllis' leg, "but that's quite different. I'm a man."

Phyllis shrugged and looked at the others as if to say, "You see what I have to put up with?"

"But I must say, as a Scot," added Dr Drummond, "I'm not so unhappy with her choice of profession when I remember she earns more than I do!"

"Please, Father!" whispered Phyllis, looking mortified.

"Now," said Francesca, tactfully changing the subject, "I've been itching to ask – would you like a little tour of the house? I won't ask anyone else – it would be too ridiculous to have everyone tramp through the place at once."

Phyllis said, "Yes, please!" and I nodded, while Dr

Drummond held up his hand. "Not me, thank you – I have a twinge of arthritis and I'll be quite happy here. If someone could get me a little something to drink."

A brandy was fetched, and Francesca led us out of the drawing room.

"This is the rear sitting room," she said, ushering us into a smaller room, "which I want to make into a cosy parlour. I will be getting rid of this awful wallpaper, of course," she added, waving at the red striped walls.

There were two large folding screens across one end of the room, each painted with floral patterns. "We're going to have a tableau before dinner," she said. "I have a box of costumes all ready – I'm rather hoping you, Phyllis, will be Minerva – Goddess of the Arts!"

"I'm not sure..." murmured Phyllis, frowning.

"Oh, please!" said Francesca. "It will be such fun, and you will be perfect for it."

"You'll be wonderful," I said, encouragingly.

"Oh, all right," said Phyllis. "I don't want to spoil anyone's fun."

"And Thomas," said Francesca, with a hint of mischief in her voice, "how would you like to carry me off and ravish me?"

"I beg your – oh, I see," I said. "You're doing 'The Rape of Proserpina,' I take it?"

"Precisely! Your Shaw and Walker 'Proserpina,' no less! Naturally, I'm taking the title role."

"I shall attempt to be Pluto, then," I said. I had been in some amateur productions at school, so I was not entirely unused to the concept of striking attitudes. "In which case, who shall play Venus?"

"I have earmarked the beautiful Mrs Harkness for that," said Francesca. "After all, she has already been an angel in the Town Hall, has she not?"

"I'm not sure her husband will be entirely –" Phyllis

began.

"I will find out!" said Francesca. "Please bear with me for two minutes."

She hurried off in search of Mrs Harkness, and Phyllis and I looked at each other with amusement.

"She's rather a collector of people, is she not?" whispered Phyllis. "Did you see the man with the monkey?"

"Yes – it's too bizarre! I hope it won't cause any trouble. And you're right, she is a collector. But having met her, can you imagine the world without her?"

"True, I would find that hard now," said Phyllis. "I just slightly worry I'm insufficiently eccentric for this party."

Francesca returned with a triumphant gleam in her eyes. "She was modest, but she will do it. Mr Harkness seemed eager for her to be Venus – perhaps he was worried he was neglecting her for Mr Craven."

"Yes," said Phyllis, "he may not wish to seem over-protective. Besides, what man would not want Venus as his wife?"

"Exactly!" beamed Francesca. "Now, let me show you upstairs. I would like your opinions about decorating the best guest room."

~

Pluto changed into his costume on one side of the screens, and Proserpina, Venus and Minerva into theirs on the other. Our robes showed a fair amount of skin, and as Francesca looked at a mirror and a print of the work, borrowed from Henry Shaw, she pulled at the material to reveal further curves, as befitted a mythological abductee.

"Now, Pluto, you need to put your arms around me, so – half holding me up. Excellent. Now, if you can put me down –

thank you, Pluto – let me direct you, ladies. Venus, you stretch out to me and hold my arm, while Minerva, you kneel on one knee and grab my leg. Oh! I think we're nearly there."

Finally, we had perfected our pose, and Yates, Francesca's butler, ushered in the audience.

"Ladies and gentlemen, Mrs Campbell and friends present 'The Rape of Proserpina'," Yates said, solemnly, and he and another servant pulled back the screens.

Behind us, Francesca had hung a large, bucolic tapestry for a backdrop, adding a couple of large branches in pots to give depth. The early evening light streamed through two large windows, which could not have been bettered to illuminate our scene in a painterly glow. For Pluto, putting on a lustful expression was not difficult for one who held in his arms warm, soft, female flesh. Francesca was perspiring a little from her directorial efforts, and her scent was quite heady.

We held our positions while the audience applauded and smiled at our efforts. And then, the door opened, and a man with a glass in his hand strode in to examine the scene.

"By Jupiter!" he said, raising his glass. "Not a bad effort. Who'd have thought Ned's angel would turn into a goddess!"

In the mirror, I could see Venus' cheeks flushing crimson, and then she collapsed in a dead faint on the floor.

"Oh, Henry!" said Proserpina, making her escape from the grasp of Pluto. "Look what you've done!"

~

With water, smelling salts and reassuring words from Phyllis, Francesca, and Mr Harkness, Mrs Harkness recovered enough to join us at the dinner table, and I was placed between Phyllis – which pleased me – and the monkey man, Mr Harold McMadden – which did not. The monkey had been placed under a console table against a wall with a supply of nuts and apple pieces, which he was greedily munching his way through while making furtive glances towards us, presumably in case we tired of waiting for our own dinner and came for his.

On the other side of the table, Shaw was knocking back the wine and raised his glass to me. "Tom! Good to see you. Any – 'news' for me?" he said, winking. I shook my head, and he shrugged and gave his attention once more to the wine. I could not, of course, say that I was currently contemplating Harkness as a suspect. Mrs Harkness was putting on a good front, but occasionally her eyes darted to Shaw, no doubt fearful of any indiscretion from him. Phyllis was clearly uncomfortable with the situation, but hid it with cheery conversation.

She leaned forward and turned to the monkey man. "So, Mr McMadden – please tell me all about your animal! Where did you find him? Or her?"

"With pleasure, Miss Drummond," said Mr McMadden. "Sir Percy is a 'he', and I acquired him from an zoologist acquaintance who died. He was going to be destroyed, and having the greatest admiration for our fellow creatures, I couldn't let that happen."

"Ah! Sir Percy!" said Phyllis. "A noble name for a noble animal."

I thought the name quite as silly as a grown man walking about with a monkey on his shoulder, but said nothing.

"I gather you are a novelist, Miss Drummond," Mr McMadden said. "In fact my wife has been enjoying one of yours. Haven't you, dear?"

"Very much, Miss Drummond," said Mrs McMadden. "I do you admire your talents. So much better than the author of that awful 'Malamor' that I caught my husband reading the other day." Mr McMadden grunted and smiled. "Have you ever come across it? The most disgusting thing – I had it thrown out of the house! Our poor Queen. He manages to insult everyone and everything in the country." She shuddered.

"I heard he was a foreign spy, this Mr Bland," Mr Harris interjected. "An operation by the French to demoralise us. Quite clever, in that case."

"Funniest thing I ever read," said Shaw, and Mrs McMadden turned a steely gaze on him. "Ned was given it – by someone I shall not name" – he looked at Francesca in an exaggerated way – "and I have been reading it."

"Oh?" Mrs McMadden said. "Do you not think some things – and especially our religion and our esteemed personages – should remain sacred and respected?"

"Only if they deserve it," Shaw said, "and perhaps not even then. We are a free people, and we should be able to make fun of whoever we like."

"Well," said Mrs McMadden, "I have to say, Mr Shaw, much as I enjoy your art, I have to disagree on this. You can't just go around hurting people like that."

"However – if we legislate against all offence, we are in murky waters," I put in. "Who decides what is offensive?" Mrs McFadden seemed to be struggling to come up with a suitable riposte, and gave up with an exasperated sigh.

"On which topic," said Francesca, "I hope you have been a good boy, Mr Shaw, and apologised to Mr Neville?"

Shaw grimaced. "Yes, yes, I've apologised to the old fool. And painted out my little portrait in the Town Hall. Now that needed a brandy or two, I can tell you."

"Excellent – good for you," I said, smiling at Shaw.

"Yes, thank heavens for that," said Francesca, raising her glass to Shaw.

"Don't read anything into it," said Shaw. "I've done what was asked of me, but as far as I'm concerned, the slimy bastard – pardon my language – is still as guilty as hell for what happened."

"But coming back to 'Malamor,'" I said, turning to Phyllis, "is there not something familiar about it, to

Hawksbridge residents? Are there not some correspondences with Ramsburgh? I have an odd feeling that some people know this, and do not wish to discuss it. The bookseller, Hunter, for instance. He really didn't want me to buy it, as if he thought it would outrage me."

Phyllis just shrugged, and Mr Harris took on my challenge. "Perhaps he thought you were too refined for what is quite a crude book. But yes, there has been some speculation. However, whatever may have happened at Ramsburgh before your time there bears no comparison with the viciousness of the book. So I think in reality, it is all coincidence: the kind that leads men to see patterns that have no meaning, and then write whole books espousing outlandish and entirely erroneous theories. Would you not say, Miss Drummond?"

"That is the most likely explanation," Phyllis said.

Shaw said, "Well, Ned thought Malamor was Mr Neville, both being pompous asses! Makes sense to me."

"No!" said Phyllis emphatically. "Malamor couldn't be Mr Neville."

All eyes were on Phyllis.

"And why, pray, is that?" said Shaw.

"Because Mr Neville only came to Hawksbridge five, maybe six years ago, and the book was published over ten years ago."

"Of course," said Mr Harris. "That settles it."

"All I think about that book is" – Phyllis paused – "Mr Bland must be ashamed of it now. It is a stupid, unworthy book, and best consigned to history as an idiotic fad. Ah! Soup. That looks delicious."

The beef soup was indeed welcome after the considerable wait, and silence fell for a while. Mr Craven was the first to break it.

"Speaking of Mr Neville," he said, "did you know that he had artistic pretensions?"

"That dried-up husk of a man?" snorted Shaw. "There's not an artistic bone in his body."

"Well," continued Mr Craven, "he was good enough to invite myself and Mrs Craven to dinner a couple of years ago, and he took me aside to view some paintings he had done when he was younger. He asked me whether there was still hope for him – apparently he originally wanted to make a career of it, before he decided on the church."

"What did you tell him?" I asked.

"I lied, of course!" he said, to much laughter. "I immediately saw that there was little prospect of him improving, but I said something about the worthiness of creative ambition. I felt sad for him. To yearn for what we cannot have is always a melancholy state, especially when the cause is a limitation in ourselves."

"That is a shame," said Mrs McMadden. "I sympathise with the poor man – I try and I try to play Chopin, and my fingers just won't obey me!"

"I recommend strong coffee to energise the nerves, Mrs McMadden," said Mr Craven. "At least it helps me when I feel dull about things."

"Oh! That reminds me," said Mrs Harris. "I gather a new coffee shop is opening in Hawksbridge in a few weeks. I suppose it won't be a respectable place for ladies," she added with a sigh. "Perhaps we need a ladies-only coffee shop."

"I heartily agree," said Mr Craven. "There should be places where a woman can easily go to meet friends and have some relief from her husband and her house. I'm sure Mrs Craven would agree with me."

"Oh – I wouldn't have put it quite that way," said Mrs Craven, "but it would be nice, yes."

"Aha! Mr Rufford!" said Mr Harris. "If you wish to make your mark on our town, there's an idea for a business, is it not?"

"Good Lord," I said, rather struck by this thought. "I

have to admit that that is rather appealing. I don't have the least bit of experience, though."

"I'm sure lots of people would be willing to help you," said Francesca. "What fun that would be! I would invest in such an enterprise. Oh, Thomas, it's a wonderful idea. Mrs Harris, you're a genius."

"Watch out you don't get mistaken for one of those temperance fanatics," said Shaw. "Out to get the honest drinker, they are. After a hard day's work, we who earn a living by the sweat of our brow need some reward! A proper drink, not that ditch-water that passes for one."

"Well, you may still have your inns," said Phyllis, "and we ladies will go to our coffee houses. The point is surely to have a choice."

"Did you know," said Mr McMadden, who looked as though he had had too much wine already, "that Isaac Newton once dissected a dolphin in a coffee house?"

"A myth, I fear, Mr McMadden, but a pleasing one," said Dr Drummond.

"Goodness!" said Francesca. "That would put me right off my coffee. I sincerely hope that in your shops, Thomas, dolphins and dissections will be banned."

"I assure you that a notice to that effect will be prominently placed," I replied.

The lamb arrived, and conversation turned to the weather and recent attempts to stop the ancient remains of Hawksbridge Castle from further disintegration.

At that point, I noticed something strange about Sir Percy. He appeared to be shaking. "I say," I said to Mr McMadden, "is your monkey..."

He turned, and said, "Oh Lord, not again. Sir Percy, no!" He made a grab for him, but Sir Percy fled with a shriek and jumped onto the dinner table, to the consternation of all of us.

He was crouching in front of a horrified Mrs Craven. He continued his strange vibrations with a bare-toothed grimace, and it became only too apparent what he was doing. Before any of us could react, Sir Percy let fly a stream of pale grey liquid that landed on Mrs Craven's décolletage and her half-eaten lamb.

"Oh!" she screamed. "I – you horrible beast!"

Mr Craven came to her aid with his napkin, but his wife got up from the table and ran, crying, out of the room. Mr Craven followed her, muttering "Please excuse us" as he went.

Most of us were open-mouthed and frozen to the spot, but as I might have expected, Shaw was bellowing with laughter, so much so that he struggled to breathe and had to get up and lean against a wall. Francesca looked furious with him.

By now, Mr McMadden had secured the monkey. "I am so, so, sorry, Mrs Campbell. We should leave now. Come, my dear," he added to his mortified wife. "We have had a wonderful time and I very much regret causing this scene. Please convey my sincere apologies to Mrs Craven."

"Thank you, Mr McMadden," said Francesca. "You have given us a memorable evening, to be sure!" The McMaddens and their pet left with as much dignity as they could muster, which was precious little.

Mr Shaw slowly gained control of himself, tears still running down his cheeks, and he took his seat.

"Oh my God," he said, catching his breath. "I don't know who spent more on the food – Mrs Campbell, or Sir Percy!"

# CHAPTER TWENTY-TWO

MRS Craven had been fussed over by the servants and cleaned up, and then she and Mr Craven had taken their leave. The reduced party had eaten their syllabub desserts in a subdued manner; Francesca did not have the heart to press on us the syllabub-tongue competition that she had planned. One disgusting event was quite enough for the evening.

Phyllis and her father left as soon as they could, taking the Harknesses with them, as Dr Drummond's arthritis was making him uncomfortable; Shaw fell asleep and had to be escorted home in a cab. Finally, after some cards and music, the remainder left, leaving just me and my hostess.

"I had better go too," I said, though I was reluctant, especially when I had Francesca more or less to myself.

"Please stay a little longer, Thomas!" said Francesca. "The end of a party is such a melancholy thing. Will you have some coffee?"

"But your servants..."

"Nonsense – ignore them!" she said. "They are paid to keep their opinions to themselves."

"Very well – I'll stay for a little while," I said. "I don't want to keep your people up too long, or mine."

"Thank you!" Francesca said. "Yates, please fetch us some coffee."

Yates thus despatched, Francesca lightly touched my knee and said, "Thank you for being my Pluto. That was fun, wasn't it? I hope you didn't get cramp."

"None, I'm glad to say, and holding Proserpina was no chore. I would quite happily have torn her from her goddess friends and carried her away."

This elicited such a beautiful smile that I was sorely tempted to kiss her. That would not do, but another form of intimacy was available. I could tell her about the scenes from my history that were haunting my dreams and waking thoughts.

"Francesca," I said, "do you think it's right for a person to burden a friend with troubles from his past? Things that might reflect badly on him?"

"How fascinating!" she said. "I suppose that depends on what those things are. And of course, how reliable the friend is! Do you wish to confide, Thomas?"

Yates brought in the coffee, and I was silent until he left.

"I think so... I don't know. It's maddening and frightening me, and I have no one to talk to about it. I don't know anyone who would understand, except you."

"Goodness," said Francesca. "You poor thing. I think you should tell me all about it. I'm sure it will help to talk about it, if you can bear to."

"Very well – thank you." I took a sip of coffee for fortification.

"When I was seventeen or eighteen," I began, "I had a friend, Bertram Mercer. His parents were well off and had a large house, with a number of servants. I used to regularly go to see Bertram, and I got to know a maid there – Hazel Sharpe."

"Aha!" said Francesca.

"Yes – I fell madly in love with her. I used to write silly letters to her, and eventually she agreed to some trysts, mainly in an abandoned farm building on the Mercer estate. I couldn't believe my luck – she was very pretty, with a lovely laugh. When I said I loved her, she said she liked me very much, but nothing could come of it – we were too different. Like the fool I was, I said it didn't matter, so long as we wanted to be together. Love overcomes all! That sort of thing."

"You romantic man," said Francesca. "That is so sweet.

And – I fear – so doomed."

"Indeed," I said. "At the same time, my friend Bertram was having a much more sophisticated affair – with a friend of his mother's, Mrs Fanny Richmond. Happy as I was with Hazel, I was pretty envious about that. Mrs Richmond was nearly forty!"

"Imagine!" said Francesca. "But on the subject of Hazel again – let me guess. You impregnated her and abandoned her. Is that it? I do hope not."

"No," I said. "It's far worse than that."

"Worse? But what did you get up to in that outbuilding, then?"

"Oh, that was fairly innocent. It was the first time I had touched a woman's – chest. It was heaven, and I couldn't believe that she would enjoy me doing that."

Francesca smiled and said, "The depths of men's ignorance about feminine pleasure are boundless. So you simply touched her?"

"Well," I said, hesitating, "I confess I kissed her. She said I was like a cat licking her. Forgive my frankness – that's just an odd detail that has stayed with me. She was my first love, and everything was new."

"Goodness," said Francesca. "And that was all?"

"Yes, although of course I wanted more. But she was sensible."

"Sorry, I interrupted you about Mrs Richmond. That was very daring of your friend."

"Yes – Mr Richmond was often away on business, and was not very attentive of his wife. So Bertram had his opportunity, and he could be very charming. I showed him the outbuilding, and so they sometimes met there. Once I went to the building, and they were there – I heard them before I saw them. I was left in no doubt about what they were doing. I'm ashamed to say I lingered. She was urging him for more, and he said he was exhausted, and should he get his friend

Thomas? She laughed, but I nearly sprang from the bushes and offered my services. Instead I crawled away, and had some very interesting dreams for a while."

"Good for Mrs Richmond," Francesca said. "I think I would have got on with her."

"I think so too," I said. "She was full of life and wit – she made a mistake marrying her oaf of a husband, wealthy though he was. Anyway, to return to Hazel: she was being bullied by the butler, John Oliphant, and also – touched."

Francesca grimaced.

"Hazel put up with it, though I begged her to tell the housekeeper and Mrs Mercer. She said that she would simply be let go without a reference, and that she would suffer much less where she was. That she could handle Mr Oliphant. But sometimes she would cry and tell me that he had cornered her and put his hands where he shouldn't. He would threaten awful things if she should tell."

"That must have been hard – impossible – for you to hear and do nothing," Francesca said.

"That is the crux of the whole thing," I said. "I told Bertram to tell his parents to get Oliphant sacked – and he managed to do it. Perhaps he didn't even have to mention Hazel, I don't know, but in any event, Hazel stayed, and Oliphant left. But instead of being grateful, as I had assumed, Hazel was furious with me. She said that because of me, she had made an enemy of Oliphant, and marked herself as being difficult. She hated me for interfering, and she would not see me any more. I was heartbroken."

"Poor Thomas," said Francesca, patting my arm. "I wish I had been on hand to comfort you."

"I wish so too," I said with feeling. "Anyway, soon after Oliphant had left, he tried to get revenge on Bertram by blackmailing him – Oliphant had managed to get hold of some of Mrs Richmond's love letters to Bertram, and was threatening to show them to Mr Richmond. Of course, that would have caused a colossal scandal and the end of the Richmonds' marriage. Bertram might also have been disinherited, so a great deal was at stake." I paused to take another sip of my – by now, tepid – coffee.

Francesca's eyes were wide and her lips were parted. "Go on!" she said. "What on earth did Bertram do about it?"

"He didn't have access to the kind of money Oliphant was asking for, so we came up with a plan. A very stupid plan, but Bertram was in a hole and I wanted to help. We decided to recruit a friend, Peter McNulty, and go to Mr Oliphant's house – which he had inherited from his late mother – to find the letters."

"Ah," said Francesca. "Oh dear. Risky, but quite understandable."

"Yes, and this, of course, is where things go really wrong. First we thought of raiding the house at night, while he slept, but we couldn't bring ourselves to be that reckless. So we went to his house first thing and when we knocked, there was no answer. On opening the door, we found him groaning at the bottom of his staircase, in a dazed state, with cuts and bruises. He had evidently fallen down the stairs in the night – he was lucky he didn't burn the house down, but his candle had gone out when it fell.

"We got him on the sofa, and I used my handkerchief to clean up his cuts, and gave him some brandy – fine, hard-bitten vigilantes we were! – while Peter and Bertram went to search the house for the letters. They found nothing. By now, Mr Oliphant was feeling a little better, and Bertram asked him as politely as he could for the letters back. Oliphant demurred for a while, and then said it was all too much trouble and told us where he had hidden them. Bertram found them under a loose floorboard under Oliphant's bed. We thanked him, and asked if he wanted us to fetch a doctor, but he said he didn't need one and he couldn't afford one anyway. So we left, rather awkwardly, but nevertheless with some elation that we had accomplished our mission."

"So far, so good," said Francesca.

"So we thought," I said. "But that evening, I overheard a servant saying that Mr Oliphant had been found dead on the sofa in suspicious circumstances. I was terrified. The following morning, Hazel was arrested – I realised why when I tried to find my handkerchief. It was one of hers that she had given me – initialled, and one of my most prized possessions – and in the excitement, I had left it in Oliphant's house with his blood on it."

"Oh Lord," said Francesca.

"Quite," I said. "Others at the Mercers' house confirmed it was one of hers, and one that was newly initialled since Oliphant had left, since she had started using a different colour of thread. And she had motivation to wish him harm because of his bullying and harassment."

Francesca leant forward and squeezed my leg in sympathy, her eyes urging me to continue the story.

"Unfortunately, Oliphant's brother was a warder at the jail. He had an incontinent temper, and soon after Hazel arrived – and before I could present myself as the true owner of the handkerchief – he beat her, and kicked her, and split her head wide open." My eyes were brimming and my voice was breaking.

"She died?"

I nodded. "Oliphant's brother was eventually hung as a result."

"Oh, no, Thomas!" Francesca said. "That is too awful." I saw her eyes fill with tears too. "What a terrible, terrible story. You must not blame yourself. You were trying to do the right thing, for everyone."

"Yes – imagine if I had tried to do the wrong thing! It could not have gone any worse. Oliphant was not a well man when he left service – perhaps one of the reasons he was let go, along with his behaviour – and the fall must have triggered an internal injury, whose effects were delayed. I assume it was a stroke of some kind."

"Surely his doctor – if he had one – could confirm he was unwell?" Francesca said.

"Perhaps," I said, "but it's still impossible to prove that we didn't assault him. We were there that day, and that might be all a jury can see."

"But," said Francesca, "this was a long time ago – if they thought Hazel was guilty, then presumably there is no reason why they should investigate it again?"

"Ah. There is one more thing I haven't mentioned."

"Yes?"

"Hazel Sharpe's brother has found another trove of letters – the wily old reprobate must have divided them and hidden them in two places. The letters constitute a motivation for Oliphant's apparent murder, and Sharpe is blackmailing me for a considerable sum. Although I have the money ready, I have no certainty that he won't nevertheless tell the police, potentially sending me to the gallows for Oliphant's death."

# CHAPTER TWENTY-THREE

I FELT some relief that I had told my sorry tale to someone, in particular to one I could rely on for sympathy rather than condemnation. Before I left Halfpenny House, Francesca had embraced me and soothed me – I confess I shed some tears that I had been holding back for too long.

But at the same time as I gained solace from sharing my woes, the details of the story once again brought back memories – of heartbreak, of terror, of my part in this cascade of events that had destroyed several lives. And the reminder that it was not yet over – Alan Sharpe would appear and would most likely tear up my contentedness at Ramsburgh as easily as a sheet of paper. Now I wanted him to come and get it over with, one way or another.

I had strange dreams – as well I might – ranging from the erotic to the macabre, and I spent a listless Sunday recovering from my excessive drinking and generally feeling sorry for myself. This was not helped by the realisation that in my self-absorption, I had entirely forgotten to quiz Francesca further on her relationship with Walker when I had the ideal opportunity to do so.

The following day, I resolved to resume my Harkness enquiries, and talk to McPhee who would now be back from his travels. At the Pottery, I greeted McPhee with my excuse: an enquiry into the progress of our Marbleware business.

"Dandy, Mr Rufford, dandy – only a few more tests, and I think we have our formula. We have high hopes for this venture. We have been selecting from the classical myths and gods, so if you have any suggestions, please let me know!"

"I will have a think," I said. "I suppose Leda and the

Swan would be a step too far."

"Ha!" said McPhee, roaring with laughter. "Leda, the poor old girl – we might have trouble getting that one past one or two of our directors. I assume you're not serious?"

"By no means," I said hastily. "I just came across the image recently. Its popularity is... puzzling."

"Yes, equally offensive to swans and humans," said McPhee. "But there's no accounting for taste, and should we find there's a market for it, who knows?"

"While I'm here," I said, "there's something I've been meaning to ask you. I was a little concerned with an employee – Mr William Harkness. He has not been looking well – although a little better recently – and I was wondering if he is perhaps working too hard."

"Ah – good of you to think of it. Yes, he's a very conscientious chap, is William. He's been working flat out on a new design – Northumberland Flowers – and it's possible we've made unreasonable demands on him. Let's look at the register, shall we?"

I followed McPhee to another office, where he opened a large book recording the employees' comings and goings. Each worker signed it on entering and leaving the building, and recent entries showed Harkness working late. I turned back to Monday, the twenty-eighth of August.

"Look at that!" said McPhee. "He puts me to shame."

The entry for Monday had Harkness' signature next to seven-thirty in the morning, and ten twenty-seven at night. He could have forged the time, but the presence of timed entries above and below his suggested otherwise.

"I agree, Mr Rufford, we should speak to him. He will wear himself ragged. That was the night of Mr Walker's murder, was it not? Yes – I was in The Golden Fleece that night. There was a bit of a commotion that the police were sorting out. I watched Mr Harkness come across the road from his office, and thought at the time how fortunate we were to have such dedicated people. Now I think I was being a little naive. Yes, I will certainly talk to him. Thank you!"

"Thank you, Mr McPhee," I said. "Could you please avoid mentioning my name? It would be a great service to me."

McPhee slapped me on the back. "How modest you are. Of course, if you wish it. Now, all this talk of The Golden Fleece is making me peckish. How does an early lunch sound?"

~

McPhee's energetic talk of the Pottery's manufacturing processes was interesting but quite exhausting, and I was glad to finally say goodbye and collect my thoughts. My next port of call had to be Phyllis, so that she could assure Mrs Harkness of her husband's innocence. At last, I could bring good news.

Dr Drummond's maid went to check if Phyllis was prepared to have a visitor, while I stood at the door trying to shake off the fuzziness of mind that two mugs of beer had induced.

Phyllis appeared at the door. "Thomas!" she said, holding up an inky hand in greeting. "How nice to see you. Do come in."

"Thank you," I said. "I hope I'm not interrupting your work, but I have some interesting news for you."

She led me into the sitting room. "My father has gone to see a patient, so we may speak freely. I'm glad to be interrupted."

I sat down in an armchair and said, "I have been examining Mr Harkness' movements on the night of Walker's death, the twenty-eighth of August. He went to The Golden Fleece at half-past ten, so from that information – as I mentioned in my letter – he still had time to go the cottage and see Mr Walker."

"I know. That is very worrying," said Phyllis.

"But don't worry," I said hastily, "because I ascertained from Mr McPhee at the Pottery that he definitely came straight from work to the inn. In fact he has been working late for a while, which rendered him rather pale and out of sorts. So there was no time for him to go to the cottage. Mrs Harkness can rest assured."

"Oh, thank goodness!" said Phyllis. "How clever of you. She will be so relieved. As you probably saw on Saturday, she and Mr Harkness have been getting on quite well in the last few days. I was petrified that Shaw was going to undo that progress, but fortunately poor Beatrice fainting did not arouse her husband's suspicions. If Mr Harkness had been brooding about it, at least that awful monkey business was a distraction."

"Yes, that was... unexpected. Poor Mrs Craven, but it was a little funny. Anyway, I am very glad I could help," I said. "I was rather dreading being the bearer of bad news about Mr Harkness."

"I suppose Shaw still thinks it was murder?" Phyllis said.

"Yes, and there are two things that still make it possible," I said. "First, the mysteriously opened bottle of port on the night of Walker's death, and second, Mrs Harkness' recollection of a figure approaching the cottage. They may mean nothing, or they may be vital clues. Unfortunately, while the police know about one, they cannot know about the other without compromising Mrs Harkness."

Phyllis nodded. "So," she said, "there may still be a murderer walking about in Hawksbridge – we may pass them by without knowing, or even talk to them!"

"Well, at least you and I can talk to each other with no fear from the other," I said.

"I'm glad you think so," said Phyllis, giving me an attempt at a sinister stare.

"Sorry, you still have too much charm to be frightening," I said. "By the way, are you working on a new book?" I said. "I saw your hands..."

"Oh! yes," she said, examining the stains. "Often I write in pencil, but I wanted a change, as it looks so much more real and definite on the page in ink."

"May I ask the subject of your new novel?"

"Of course," she said. "It's about a restless young woman in the seventeen-fifties who runs away to sea, to explore the world."

"Ah – disguised as a boy?"

"Precisely. She becomes a sea captain, and falls in love with a Spanish aristocrat and has a host of adventures in Europe, before fighting her own English relatives in the Seven Years' War. Eventually she has to choose between killing her lover, or her relatives."

"Goodness!" I said. "And which does she kill?"

"I haven't decided yet," Phyllis said.

"Perhaps herself, instead?"

"More than likely!" Phyllis replied.

"It sounds exciting," I said. "Do you want to run away to sea? Or maybe, just run away?"

"Do I look the restless type?"

"Maybe not," I said, "but your books are full of discontent and adventures."

"How do you think I'm so content here in Hawksbridge?" she smiled. "I have plenty of adventures, but they're all in my head. At least until your arrival, and then this dreadful Walker business."

I was amused that my arrival had been a landmark for her. Had she let something slip that she had not meant to?

"My arrival?" I said.

"I mean, it coincided with Walker's death," she said, a little flustered. "That's all I meant."

She fiddled with a button on the sleeve of her dress. "Oh,

all right, I'll say it. Something seemed to change when you arrived. I don't know what it was. I don't even know what I mean. Please ignore my ravings!"

"I shall do no such thing," I said. "Your ravings are always interesting. And I think I know what you mean, because I was very glad to find you as a friend. And we have barely begun to get to know one another, which means that most of the enjoyment lies ahead of us. Or am I being overly sentimental?"

Phyllis had flushed red. "Oh, what nonsense we are talking! Enough. How is Flora? I miss her. Are there any suitors?"

"She is well, as is her cat. No, no suitors that I am aware of. She briefly befriended Mr Shaw when he was ill, rather oddly, but they are estranged because... well, you know how Shaw is. He may be a genius with oil, but he is unrefined in his manners, and an unreliable friend."

"Yes – poor Flora," Phyllis said. "She has been unlucky with men."

"I suppose there is no chance that you and she –?"

"No, I'm afraid not," she said. "I know you mean well, but please don't ask it again."

"I'm sorry," I said. "I won't. On another note, what do you think of Mrs Harris' idea of a female-only coffee shop? Would you patronize such a place?"

"I think it's very promising – and yes, I might well. If it has stalls, I could imagine going there and writing a few chapters, for a change of scene. I might even be inspired by the characters coming and going."

"Ah!" I said. "I could have you there as a mascot, scribbling away at your distinguished novels and attracting customers. And you could sell your books there at the same time. Everyone is satisfied."

"I am not a performing seal, Thomas," Phyllis said. "But do you realise you are talking like an entrepreneur?"

"Oh dear!" I said. "This enthusiasm could prove very expensive. I don't know if I would be brave enough, but it's an enjoyable pastime to speculate about it."

"I think you should do it," said Phyllis. "I'm sure you would make a very good coffee-shop proprietor. And who knows, if 'Rufford's' were successful in Hawksbridge, why not open more in other towns? And you have a ready source of inexpensive table-ware."

"Don't encourage me," I said. "I will get delusions of grandeur. But thank you, I appreciate your confidence in me."

Phyllis smiled. "Well, my father will be back soon," she said, "and I think I had better get back to my writing before I forget what I was doing. Thank you for coming to see me – I hope we can talk again soon."

"I hope so too," I said. "May I?"

"If you wish," she said, and I kissed her inky hand.

~

After visiting Phyllis, I went to Hunter's bookshop, and to Mr Hunter's surprise, bought the complete works of Iona Tavistock – six novels, including the one I had already read. It was time I got to know her better. On my return to Ramsburgh, a letter awaited me.

Hawksbridge, 14th September

Dear Thomas,

It seems a long time since you visited me and we had such a lovely afternoon together! The last few days have been so dreary and with so little company that I long for a diversion. My beloved cat, Fossil, died two months ago and I do not even have him for comfort.

My maid Lizzie is back after looking after her sick mother for a while, but I can easily send her away again.

Have you seen Henry Shaw lately? I wonder how he is coping with his grief. Oh, but I should not talk of Henry. You are, I assure you, worth ten Henrys, however talented he may be. That is, I do not mean to say you are not talented – in any event, if you wish to demonstrate any facility to me, I will, as you know, welcome you warmly.

I am trying to imagine you strutting around your castle, master of everything. But you seem too modest a man and I cannot conjure up this image. Instead I only see you in a way that my own modesty forbids me to describe.

I do not mean to impose myself on you, my dear Thomas, but only to say that if you have a little time that you do not know what to do with, then it might be pleasant for both of us to spend it together.

Your affectionate friend,

Bess Shannon

Bess – I had not forgotten about her; she resided in a corner of my mind, a warm presence, breaking through to my conscious thoughts now and again. But having befriended her, I had neglected her, and so I determined to see her again this week.

As I lounged on the sofa in my eyrie, caressing Fox and dreaming of pleasant interludes with Bess, I heard hasty feet on the stair. The wicked Malamor flashed through my mind, and then I heard Shipley knock and say, "Begging your pardon, sir, but there's a lady downstairs to see you – it's very urgent, she says. Miss Drummond."

I leapt up, alarmed, and said, "Thank you, Shipley, I'm coming down." The daylight was starting to go, and Phyllis would not have visited me so soon after we had spoken together without it being some kind of emergency.

Phyllis was in the hall, pacing up and down. "Oh, Thomas!" she said. "Please help – it's Beatrice. Mr Harkness was sent a dreadful letter and became so angry that he threatened her, and she had to flee. I don't know what to do."

"Good Lord," I said. "Where is she? Is she safe?"

"She's in the pony trap outside. She didn't want to come in before knowing if she would be welcome, but I thought she would be safest here. Do you think you could help her, and take her in?"

"Of course!" I said, and strode out to the trap, where Beatrice was wrapped in a blanket and clearly in a state of shock. "Mrs Harkness – I'm sorry to hear about this latest development. You are most welcome to stay here as long as you like."

Beatrice nodded and managed a brief smile, and we bundled her into the house, making her comfortable in the sitting room. Mrs Felton rose to the occasion, delivering sympathy, brandy and more blankets.

"Everything will be fine, Bea," whispered Phyllis to her friend. "You are safe now, and I'm sure it's all a misunderstanding that we can correct."

Beatrice sniffed. "William gave me the letter to read while he was shouting at me about it," she said to me. "I held on to it." She produced the letter from under her blankets, and I read the following.

> Dear Mr William Harkness,
>
> I have information from a reliable source – indeed, several sources – that may interest you.
>
> It has been unfortunate that you have let your wife stray from the bounds of wifely duty and as far as the cottage in which Mr Henry Shaw and Mr Edward Walker have been residing. It is my sad duty to report that she has been not only an artistic model for Mr Walker, but his lover, as witnessed both directly (by sight) and indirectly (through belongings left by her, and overheard remarks). These witnesses I have promised not to name, but are upright people and are naturally shocked.
>
> But as if that were not enough, Mrs Harkness took up for a short while with Mr Shaw, who comforted her after the death of her lover. These same witnesses will swear on oath that they

have seen Mr Shaw and Mrs Harkness intimate together, in a manner that should be solely your preserve.

It is with no pleasure that I bring your attention to these unfortunate facts, Mr Harkness, but I can solemnly assure you of their veracity. After much deliberation, in which I considered the pain that this news would bring you, I concluded that on balance you would wish to know the truth.

With deepest regards and sympathies for your situation,

A well-wisher

I read the letter again and it was quite as horrible as I had gathered from my first reading.

"The terrible thing is," said Beatrice, hoarsely, "that it has some truth in it. I did succumb to Mr Walker, briefly. But someone has twisted it, and made up this story about Mr Shaw. How clever, because I could hardly reply to William that not all of it is true!"

"This is dark work, Mrs Harkness," I said. "Very dark work indeed. But we shall get to the bottom of it."

"How do we even make a start?" said Phyllis.

Mrs Felton came in with some biscuits, and I said, "Mrs Felton – do you mind just staying with Mrs Harkness for a few minutes? I would like to discuss something with Miss Drummond alone."

"Of course, my dear," she said, "it will be no trouble. Now, Mrs Harkness, I've brought some biscuits, and I can fetch another blanket if you need it."

I beckoned for Phyllis to follow me out of the drawing room and into my ground floor study. Then I said, "We can start by asking ourselves this question: who gains from this? If the author of the letter were genuinely concerned, he would stick to the truth, and talk about Mr Walker only. Unless the person has been misled, then we must conclude that he is trying to manipulate Shaw, Beatrice, or Mr Harkness, or all three. But to what end?"

"What is the obvious consequence of this?" said Phyllis. "To make William furious and do something he might regret."

"Agreed," I said. "Something involving either Beatrice or Henry Shaw."

"But who would want to harm Beatrice?" said Phyllis. "She surely has no enemies. She is the sweetest creature alive."

"Yes," I said, "I cannot see anyone wanting to punish her. I can only think there is perhaps an unknown, infatuated man whose obsession has turned sour, but that is quite a supposition."

"And Mr Harkness – I don't know him very well," said Phyllis, "but I think Beatrice would have said if she had known he had made enemies."

"So that leaves Shaw," I said. "I know he made himself unpopular with certain people in the town – in particular, the police, Falkirk, and the Rector – but I cannot imagine anyone going to such abominable lengths as these. Is the idea to have Mr Harkness attack Shaw?"

"Oh, heavens," said Phyllis. "That is truly devilish. Do you think William is capable of...?"

"It's possible. A man who has had his heart torn out like this – to be betrayed by the woman who is his lover and his best friend – he will not be in his right mind."

"Then we must go to Mr Shaw, immediately!" said Phyllis. "He is in terrible danger."

# CHAPTER TWENTY-FOUR

PHYLLIS drove the trap as fast as safety – and her pony – allowed.

"Poor Beatrice," said Phyllis, as we turned onto the road to Hawksbridge. "She worked so hard to make things better with William, and I haven't seen her so happy for months. And now everything is ruined, by some wicked person. It's awful to think there could be someone so wanton, so despicable in Hawksbridge."

"Yes, I'm afraid it's a reminder that humanity is a very strange mix of creatures," I said. "But if the police don't find who's responsible, I'm damned well going to myself."

"I hope so," said Phyllis. "It would be unbearable for Beatrice to never know who hated her so much."

"Thank goodness for Mrs Felton," I said. "She will be a great comfort to her."

"Yes, you are lucky to have her," Phyllis said.

I was worried about the light for our return journey, but although the daylight was nearly gone, there were few clouds, and it looked as though there would be sufficient moonlight.

"Will you stay at Ramsburgh tonight?" I asked.

"Yes, please – if you don't mind. I think Beatrice will need me, perhaps for a few days. I'll pick up some things from home when we have checked on Mr Shaw."

As we approached Shaw's cottage, we could see that the lights were on, and as we drew closer we could make out the noise of someone sobbing.

We looked at each other in consternation. Jumping down, I knocked on the cottage door. The sobbing continued. I gently opened the unlocked door and glanced inside. A horrific scene met my eyes, and I immediately closed the door.

"Phyllis, please stay back – in fact, fetch the police. Something is wrong here."

She nodded, and ran off down the lane.

I opened the door again, and slowly went in.

"Mr Harkness," I said, "it's Thomas Rufford. We met the other day. Are you all right?"

William Harkness was sitting on the floor, sobbing uncontrollably, blood smeared on his hands and body. In front of him, Henry Shaw lay stretched out with a large pool of blood by his head and a blood-soaked hammer nearby.

Above Harkness, someone had daubed the words 'LEVITICUS 20:10' in blood on the wall. Frustratingly, my Bible scholarship was not up to recalling the verse, but I supposed it would be something depressing.

William seemed not to have registered my presence; he was distraught and absent. I repeated my name again, and he finally looked up despairingly.

"Mr Harkness," I said, "did you have anything to do with this?"

He shook his head. "Beatrice," he groaned, "I loved you so much! Why did you have to do it? I loved you, for ever and ever."

"Mr Harkness," I said, "the police will be here soon. You have to tell me what happened. Please, if you can pull yourself together – it's important. Was Shaw dead when you arrived?"

William nodded.

"You came to speak to him after you got the letter?"

He nodded again. "To speak to him, yes. I deserved to know whether it was true. I would not have harmed him – I don't think I would. But he was like this" – he gestured at Shaw – "and I tried to pick him up, in case he was still alive. But it was no good."

"And the writing on the wall? Was that here already?"

He nodded, and burst into tears again.

"The letter was full of lies, Mr Harkness," I said. "Someone was trying to hurt you, or Shaw, or your wife. But Beatrice still loves you, and you love her, so please don't let this destroy your happiness."

"How can I love her now?" he wailed. "She has betrayed me. She has destroyed me."

"The letter is malicious, and if Beatrice has done anything wrong, you can forgive her," I said. "But she has not wronged you as the letter says. Do not fall victim to it, as the author intends you to!"

I could hear the clatter of hooves on the path. "Just remember, Mr Harkness, if you have done nothing wrong, do not confess to anything – the police may be very persuasive, and you are not yourself. Mr Harkness – do you understand?"

He nodded, and the door burst open. Inspector Simmons came in with three constables.

"Good God," he said. "What have we here? Mr Rufford! An explanation, if you please."

I realised I would have to mention the letter, reluctant though I was to expose the Harkness' private lives to public scrutiny.

"Good evening, Mr Simmons. In a nutshell, someone has sent a letter to Mr Harkness making mischief. Mr Harkness came to Mr Shaw to talk to him about it, and found Mr Shaw dead. Mr Harkness tells me that he was not responsible for this, or for the writing." I pointed at the Bible reference on the wall. "I believe him."

"Is that so? And you and Miss Drummond just happened to be passing?"

"No, Inspector – we deduced from the letter than Shaw could be in danger, so we came as quickly as we could."

"Interesting. I will ask you for more details later. Mr Harkness, can you give me your full name?"

"William Harkness," he muttered.

"Thank you, sir. Mr William Harkness, I am arresting you

on suspicion of murder. Constable Eaton, please guard the cottage. Constables Taylor and Gawley, please convey Mr Harkness to the police jail and clean him up."

I knew it was useless to plead for Mr Harkness to be allowed to go home. Covered in blood and in an emotional state at the scene of a crime, he was the obvious and, at present, only suspect.

The Inspector sighed. "What a mess. A lot of people will be missing out on sleep tonight. Mr Rufford, I would be grateful if you and Miss Drummond could give a short statement to the sergeant at the police office, and then you can go home. But please return first thing in the morning."

"Certainly, Mr Simmons. Good luck!"

The Inspector grimaced, and turned back to examine the scene while I gladly joined Phyllis outside, waiting in the pony cart.

"I'm sorry," I said. "The police were bound to take him in. But it will be straightened out, I'm sure." Phyllis nodded. "We are to go and make a statement at the police office, and then we can collect your things and return to Ramsburgh."

"Was it very awful in there?" Phyllis asked.

"I'm afraid so. There was a lot of blood. And a Bible reference on the wall – does Leviticus 20:10, mean anything to you?"

"No, I'm afraid I will have to look that up."

We drove in silence until we got to the police station, where we described our movements and observations as best we could. We were allowed a few minutes to speak to Harkness, in which we tried to reassure him and promised to get him his solicitor. We then headed for the Drummond home to collect some necessaries for Phyllis and Beatrice. Phyllis' father was not there, having already been employed by the police.

As we drove up the hill to Ramsburgh, our path and the surrounding fields illuminated by the moonlight, Phyllis turned to me and said, "Thank you, Thomas. I couldn't have done this on my own. I am so tired." She looked as though she were struggling not to cry, so I took the reins with one hand, and put my other arm around her shoulders.

"It will all work out," I said, as confidently as I could. "William will be vindicated, and somehow we will get him and Beatrice talking to each other again. I will make sure of it." But my words felt false, when all I could visualise was that grisly scene, and a broken William Harkness in the midst of it, covered in Shaw's blood.

~

In the hall at Ramsburgh, Flora was waiting anxiously. She and Phyllis acknowledged each other with curt nods, and Flora then said, "Is Henry all right? I heard that you were worried about him. Did you see him?"

My heart sank at what I had to tell her. "Flora, can you go to my study? I will talk to you there in a minute. Let me just have a word with Mrs Harkness."

Phyllis and I had the painful duty of telling Beatrice that her husband had been arrested for murder. Her subsequent paroxysms of misery must have been awful for Flora to hear, and I went to her as soon as was possible, leaving Phyllis and Mrs Felton to comfort Beatrice.

Flora was walking quickly up and down my study, and turned to me with an anxious face when I came in. I closed the door, and said, "Please sit down, Flora. I have some difficult news."

She did not sit, but said, "Please just tell me, now, Thomas! Is he –?"

"Yes, I'm afraid Mr Shaw is dead. I am so sorry. I know you were friends."

She put her hand over her mouth, tears filling her eyes. "How?" she managed to say.

I hesitated. "Someone has murdered him. The police have arrested Mr Harkness, but I don't think it was him."

"Then why should they think it was him?" said Flora.

"I... I don't know if it's helpful for me to..."

"Why do they think it was him?" Flora repeated.

"Because Harkness was covered in Shaw's blood."

"Oh...!" Flora said with a sob, and ran out of the study. I felt helpless. Should I follow her? I concluded she would need to be on her own to digest this unpleasant information.

I thought of the writing on the wall – a detail I was happy to spare Flora – and found a Bible on one of the shelves in my study. Turning to Leviticus 20:10, I read:

> *If a man commits adultery with the wife of his neighbour, both the adulterer and the adulteress shall surely be put to death.*

~

It was strange waking up and realising that Phyllis was in a bedroom just a few feet away. For a pleasant moment, I entertained a fantasy that she was visiting as a friend, with no dark clouds hanging over us, and that we would greet each other with smiles and eat breakfast together, before wandering through Ramsburgh's grounds talking of novels and coffee shops. There was so much I wanted to ask her – I knew a little of the preoccupations of distinguished author Iona Tavistock, from reading 'Lady Harlington's Estate.' But how much did I know about the woman, Phyllis Drummond? One thing was very clear – her loyalty to her friend, Mrs Harkness. I perceived a speck of jealousy in myself, and realised that I coveted that affection and familiarity. And besides, my nature forbade me from walking away from a puzzle.

The burdens of the day became too much to ignore, and after a hasty breakfast, the three of us were soon heading into town, Phyllis and Beatrice in the Drummonds' pony trap, and myself in charge of Jenny. I was a little relieved to be spared Beatrice's grief in close quarters.

We presented ourselves at the police office, and Beatrice, enquiring after her husband, discovered to her distress that he had been taken to St John's Asylum suffering from a mental and physical collapse. There was no possibility of her being allowed to see him.

After Phyllis was interviewed, I found myself in the familiar, bare interrogation room with Inspector Simmons and a constable.

"Mr Rufford – thank you for coming in," said the Inspector. "Our little chats are becoming quite a regular occurrence, aren't they?"

I nodded. "I like to help the police if I can," I said.

"Very commendable, sir, very commendable," he said, checking his notes. "Now, if you don't mind, please take me through the events leading to your being at Mr Shaw's cottage last night. From the first event that might have any bearing on this matter."

I considered how far back to go. "I was alerted by my servant Shipley, at around eight o'clock last night, that Miss Drummond had come to see me. She explained that an anonymous letter had been sent to Mr Harkness, and that Mrs Harkness was with her, in an emotional state. We settled Mrs Harkness in my house, and then Miss Drummond and I realised that the letter might persuade Mr Harkness to visit Mr Shaw."

"And you thought that Mr Harkness might harm Mr Shaw?" said Mr Simmons.

"It was a possibility that occurred to us, yes," I said, reluctantly. "Even if –"

"I see," the Inspector cut in, writing in his notebook. "Please continue."

"When we got to the cottage, we could hear sobbing. I looked in, and I saw... Shaw and Harkness." I stopped to gather my thoughts. I did not relish recalling and describing the scene.

"Mr Shaw was lying with his head in a pool of blood: there was a hammer next to him. Mr Harkness was sitting against a wall, with blood on his hands and torso. He was crying. Above his head, there was a Bible reference written in blood, presumably Mr Shaw's – Leviticus 20:10."

The Inspector nodded. "A nasty little message, to be sure," he said. "We looked it up, as I expect you did."

"Yes, Inspector. It puts Mrs Harkness' safety in some doubt, does it not?"

Simmons shrugged. "Well, that would only be the case if we don't have the culprit in custody, and I think we do."

"It's quite a risk, Inspector. There may still be a maniac at large."

"Well then," Simmons said, "I suggest that Mrs Harkness stay at your house for a while longer, while we establish the facts. You are able to keep a close eye on her, I take it?"

"Yes, I have very capable staff, and I think Miss Drummond will stay at Ramsburgh for a while too."

"Capital," said Inspector Simmons. "Now, sir, do you have anything to add to your account? Any wisdom" – he emphasised the word with just a touch of sarcasm – "for us that you can share?"

"There is one thing, Inspector," I said. "Before this happened, I took it upon myself to check whether Mr Harkness could have been responsible for Mr Walker's death."

The Inspector's eyebrows went up. "Oh, you did, did you?" he said, sitting back and folding his arms. "So you didn't have confidence in the police investigation? I am eager to hear your viewpoint, Mr Rufford. Eager, sir, and, I confess, a little excited."

I could have done with less of the Inspector's attitude, but I tried to ignore him and pressed on. I began with a false attribution of my motivation, to spare as many of Beatrice's blushes as possible, but the substitution made no material difference.

"I felt sorry for Mr Shaw," I said, "and to humour him – as he was not satisfied that his friend's death was an accident – I tried to think if anyone might have had a motive to kill Mr Walker. I considered Mr Harkness, as he was known to find his wife's artistic modelling unpalatable. But after enquiries at the Pottery and The Golden Fleece, I found that he was working late on the night in question, to which his colleagues will attest, and then went to The Golden Fleece, after which he was escorted home by family of the inn's proprietor. So it is not possible that he was responsible for Mr Walker's death."

The Inspector made a few notes, and then sat back again, regarding me with weary amusement.

"Well, well," he said. "Oxford has given us an amateur detective. Hawksbridge is truly blessed. I suppose you think that because Harkness is in the clear with Mr Walker – if, that is, what you say is true – then he could not have killed Mr Shaw? That does not at all follow, I'm afraid, sir."

He leaned towards me. "If I may give you some advice, sir – from the heart, sir, because I care about the people of Hawksbridge. It's my job to care. And so, with all the respect due to a distinguished gentleman like yourself, my advice to you is –"

He paused for dramatic effect, snapping shut his notebook and standing up. "Leave the bloody police work to us, won't you, sir? You're not cut out for it, and you'll only get yourself and others into trouble."

# CHAPTER TWENTY-FIVE

IF this latest emergency had taught me anything, it was that I could not continue to rely on the pony trap for transport. It was ungainly, slow and a little undignified. Having my own horse would give me more freedom, as well as the pleasant prospect of taking riding advice from Francesca. When Phyllis, Beatrice and I returned from Hawksbridge, a solicitor having been found for Mr Harkness, I ensured that my guests were settled and then I went to Shipley for advice.

"Of course, sir," he said. "Howard will be happy to have a new horse to look after. I happen to know that Mr Turnbull – he's a farmer in Highford, about six miles north – has a bay mare he's looking to sell. There's a saddle you can use here. We could go this afternoon in the trap, sir, if you wish? I don't think that mare will be with Turnbull for long."

"An excellent idea, Shipley, thank you." As much as I liked Phyllis and her friend, the atmosphere at Ramsburgh was becoming claustrophobic and I longed to escape for a few hours. "Oh, and Shipley – I've never ridden. Can you give me a few tips, just to get me started?"

Shipley chuckled. "Certainly, sir! I'd be glad to. You'll get used to it soon enough."

We took Jenny, a saddle and a purse of guineas to Highford, where we found Mr Turnbull investigating a broken gate.

"Rotten through, that," he said to himself as he turned to see who was approaching. "Mind you, must be twenty years old if it's a day. Ah, Mr Shipley! And would you be Mr Rufford, sir?"

"Yes indeed – I'm very pleased to meet you, Mr Turnbull," I said. "Especially as I believe you have a mare to sell – is that still the case?"

"Certainly is, Mr Rufford. You've come just in time, though, because a fellow in Hawksbridge was asking about her. Let's go and take a look at her, shall we?"

At the stable, Mr Turnbull led us to a handsome bay mare, who exhibited mild curiosity at our visit.

"I'll be sorry to see her go, Mr Rufford, but the missus is carrying again, and she'll be driving, not riding, so there's no need for her. But that's to your advantage, sir, because she's all broken in and ready for a kindly owner, as I'm sure you'll be. Lovely nature, has Celeste. Five years old. There's her teeth, sir, nothing wrong with those. Better than mine!" He smiled to make his point.

Mr Rufford brought her out of the stall and walked her around the courtyard while Shipley and I examined her further. She was truly a beautiful creature, and I patted her neck, marvelling that it was even possible to simply buy such an elegant creation of Nature.

"Tell you what, Mr Rufford," said Mr Turnbull, "ten guineas, and any trouble within a month, you bring her right back. You won't regret it! The missus will, but you won't."

I glanced at Shipley, and he nodded.

"I'll take her," I said, my heart beating faster. "Thank you, Mr Turnbull! Please assure your wife that Celeste will be in good hands."

~

Shipley rode Celeste back while I drove the trap. I wondered if I should have haggled, but it would only have been for appearances, since I had the money, and had expected to pay more. Indeed, it would have been an insult to the mare to pay less.

Shipley fetched old Howard, the groom, and his eyes lit up when he saw her. "Fine animal you got yourself, sir, damned fine animal, begging your pardon!" he said, patting Celeste's neck. "Will be a pleasure to have her in the stable, and Jenny will be glad for the company."

"Right, then, sir," said Shipley. "There's light enough for you to try her out."

Shipley and Howard helped me up, and I could tell without looking that they were exchanging wry smiles at my ungainly ascent. I was surprised how high up I felt on Celeste. A fall would be extremely painful.

"Best not to look down for a bit, sir," said Shipley.

I walked Celeste around the stable yard for some time, getting used to controlling her and keeping my balance. My confidence grew, and when the light started to go I was reluctant to dismount. I had formed a new relationship with an elegant, noble creature, and it was a welcome counterbalance to the sombre atmosphere that currently pervaded Ramsburgh.

~

I now felt confident enough with Celeste to ride into town and not make a total fool of myself. So in the morning, after a little more practice, I decided to visit Bess and impress her with my new steed.

She was gratifyingly surprised and pleased to see me.

"Oh! Thomas, how lovely!" she said. "And you have a horse! It's beautiful."

"She's called Celeste," I said, "and she has been more patient and good-natured than I have any right to expect. Which she has in common with you."

Bess smiled. "A gentleman will always win a lady's heart by comparing her with a horse. Celeste, let's get you into the yard and find you some water."

We tied Celeste up at the back of the cottage, and Bess fetched her a pail.

"There, she'll be fine. Now then, Thomas, a cup of tea for you? Or something stronger?"

"Tea, please," I said. "I don't trust myself to ride while tipsy."

In the kitchen, a maid of around twenty years was drying some dishes. I could not help admiring her red hair and fine features, and the cat-like elegance of her movements.

"This is Lizzie, Thomas," said Bess. "Lizzie, I'll do the rest – you can have a break."

"Thank you, ma'am," said Lizzie, and curtseyed for me as she left.

"Now then, Thomas," said Bess. "She's not for the likes of you, and she has a young man."

"Sorry – did I stare?" I said. "She's a handsome young woman. But I prefer a more mature specimen."

Bess rolled her eyes. "What a way with words you have today, Thomas."

I drew closer to her. "Then it's probably for the best that we occupy ourselves wordlessly," I said.

"All good things come to those who wait," said Bess, filling the teapot. "Would you like to hear me play?"

"Certainly," I said, "but play what?"

"The organ. No, the harp, silly! Did you not see it previously?"

"Oh, yes, I remember now. I would love to hear you. You make me sorry I never got on with my music master – I was always a dunce at the piano."

"However," said Bess, taking the tea tray, "a musician needs an audience, so you will be making yourself useful. Especially if you ignore my mistakes."

In the sitting room, Bess put down the tray and went to settle herself on the stool by her harp.

"Bess, before you start," I said, "I have some upsetting news, which perhaps we should discuss first."

"Ah," she said. "You mean Henry Shaw. I heard."

"I am very sorry, Bess, when you and he –"

She raised her hand. "It was the briefest of acquaintances. He was an interesting man, but alas, also a difficult one. I have shed my tears over him already. But it is a terrible thing – first one, then the other. Hawksbridge is not the quiet place it once was!"

I nodded, and decided not to tell her just how much I had witnessed.

"In case you're wondering," Bess said, "I was here all that day, and Lizzie was helping me make a dress."

"Ah, but I really didn't think –"

"I'm glad to hear it," she said. She suddenly straightened her back. "Now then, away with horrible thoughts. I've been keeping this piece ready – I thought you'd like it. I arranged it for harp myself, since it's written for piano."

"I'm already impressed," I said.

"It's called 'The Waves and the Wind,'" she said, and started to play the introduction. I was fascinated to see her fingers stroke the instrument, finding the strings with ease in a way that seemed miraculous to me. Then, to my surprise, she started singing, in a clear, confident voice with a touch of vibrato. Everything about the piece was wistful: the music, the words, and Bess' beguiling soprano tone, and it shot an arrow of sadness and beauty through me.

My love said he'd come back and wed me one day
Then the waves and the wind they sailed him away
But I've waited for him for five years or more
And the waves and the wind don't bring him to shore.

Now merchants and farmers, they knock on my door
They take off their hats and they cry and implore:
'Wed me, and have all a woman could crave'
But I've turned them away, be they rich, be they brave.

*So pity me, pity me, maiden am I*
*No lover to kiss me, nor with me to lie*
*A maiden I'll stay, unkissed will I be*
*Till the waves and the wind bring my true love to me.*

When she got to the first chorus, I realised I had heard it before: but where? To my annoyance, I found I was starting to quietly cry. Not noticing at first, Bess continued:

Now some say I'm mad, that I'll wither away
If I don't marry now, that a maiden I'll stay
Well, they may marry the first man they see
But only my William will lie next to me.

*So pity me, pity me, maiden am I*
*No lover to kiss me, nor with me to lie*
*A maiden I'll stay, unkissed will I be*
*Till the waves and the wind bring my true love to me.*

"Oh! Thomas, are you all right?" Bess said, and hurried

over to put her arm around me. "Whatever's the matter? I didn't mean to make you cry!"

"It was beautiful," I said, choking back the tears. "I don't know what's wrong with me. I liked it very much."

"Have you been holding something back from me?" said Bess. "You can tell me, and I won't mind."

I recovered myself with the help of a proffered handkerchief and tried to comprehend what was inducing this mortifying display. I realised that it was a combination of events and feelings, in addition to the guiles of the song: the Sharpe affair, the disturbing scene I had witnessed in the cottage, and also my guilt concerning Bess. The lava of my woes had been building up, and Bess had blown the mountain cap off.

"It's been difficult lately – Walker, now Shaw, and a friend in distress," I said. "But I also feel I have been – well, trifling with you. I don't think I can be a good man, and I do so wish you to think well of me!" My emotions once more overcame me, and she gently pulled me towards her, so my head lay on her shoulder.

"Oh, Thomas – you don't have to think that. I know exactly what you mean, and credit to you for saying it, but you are thinking as most people think – like the nagging women in the song. They assume everyone is the same. I loved my husband – but that doesn't mean I want to live the same life over again. I also love my house, and my freedom. I have most of the things that I need. But sometimes I just want a friend I can be close to, and have fun with."

I looked up at Bess, and said "Truly?"

"Truly," she said. "Now, have some tea, and you'll feel better in no time."

"Thank you," I said. "I do already." I sipped at my tea and then took some deep breaths.

"Good. Now, what did you think of my playing? You can be honest – but perhaps not too honest."

"You were wonderful," I said. "I didn't know you could play like that, or sing – it was just extraordinary."

Bess smiled. "I supplement my pension with some music tuition. I'm so glad you liked it!"

"I've heard the song before," I said. "I'm trying to think where." And then I remembered. "I know – the hotel in Newcastle where I spent a melancholy night on my way up here."

"Well, it's quite popular, and of course it's not sophisticated. But I find its simplicity helpful for my pupils. They can quickly get a sense of accomplishment, and that encourages them. Oh dear – I'm talking like a fussy old schoolmistress!"

Bess stood up and went to the door. "A moment, please!" she said, and then I heard her going up the stairs and saying, "Lizzie, you can visit your mother if you wish!"

"No, thank you, ma'am," came the reply. "We had words yesterday."

"Oh," said Bess. "Well, you can go into town if you wish."

"I'd rather stay in my room, if you don't mind, ma'am."

There was a pause. "Very well, Lizzie! But please don't disturb me."

"Of course, ma'am!"

Bess returned, frowning, and sat down on the sofa. "I tried – but don't worry, I don't think she'll come down for a couple of hours."

I responded with a kiss. "I don't mind if you don't," I said, and we locked our arms around one another.

~

I will not embarrass my publisher or my readers with a full

description of what happened on the sofa. Suffice it to say, I came away with a song in my heart and a better understanding of feminine pleasure than before; though, again, to avoid tempting fate, I did not pursue every avenue, so to speak. But we played and we caressed, and many indications of pleasure would have been heard by a maid listening at the door, which I fervently hoped had not been the case.

As I mounted Celeste with what I fancied was panache, I said, "I forgot to say: I'd like to buy a copy of that song, for guests to play. Can you let me know the composer and publisher?"

"Of course," said Bess. "It's called 'The Waves and the Wind,' and the composer is J. Bland. The publisher is – let me think – Dorner and Sons."

I was confused. "J. Bland," I repeated. "Are you sure?"

"Yes, but I can fetch it if you like," she said.

"No, no – thank you. I will be back to see you soon, Bess!"

She smiled at me and watched me go, and when in a moment I turned to glance at her, she was still leaning on the front door of her cottage, looking contently after Celeste and me. I could have been looking at a painting by the likes of Sir David Wilkie.

I headed for the bookshop to see if they had a copy of the song, and tied Celeste to a post in the lane adjoining the shop.

Mr Hunter received my request with amusement, went to find the music, and quietly hummed the tune as he wrapped it in brown paper. "My daughter plays it," he said. "Now I'll have it in my head for the rest of the day." He looked over the top of his spectacles at me. "Collecting all works by Mr Bland, are we, sir?"

"Well, it can't be the same fellow as the 'Malamor' Bland, can it, Mr Hunter?"

"I have no idea, I'm afraid, sir. But I don't suppose so.

That would be most odd. Here you are, sir. I'll put it on your account."

I thanked Mr Hunter and made my way back to Ramsburgh, savouring the bracing September air and the reverberations of the morning's pleasure that I could still feel in my body. I would have to face the grim realities of recent events soon enough.

# CHAPTER TWENTY-SIX

DESPITE Mrs Felton's endeavours to be cheerful when bringing us our lunch, the muted atmosphere at the table contrasted with my care-free morning, bringing back my old nemesis: guilt. It seemed that I could not enjoy myself without paying for it.

"Mrs Felton tells me you have a new horse," said Phyllis. "Are you now proficient?"

"Hardly that," I said, "but I am quite comfortable with her now. I took her into town this morning. It's a powerful sensation, being high up and in charge of all that muscle. When she's responding instinctively, it's a little like being a centaur. I suspect she's learning to read my mind."

Beatrice was subdued and pale, but she smiled and made an effort to join in. "What is her name, Mr Rufford?" she said.

"Celeste!" I said. "It suits her, I think."

"It's a beautiful name," Beatrice said. "I should like to see her some time, if you don't mind. It would be a welcome distraction."

"Of course," I said. "Perhaps we can all ride together – a picnic, maybe?"

"When I feel a little better, that would be delightful," said Beatrice. "But just now, I can't bear to think of going far. I don't suppose you heard any news when you were in town?"

"I'm afraid not," I said. "I only bought some music – a folk song – and I thought you or Phyllis might want to try playing it."

"That's very kind," said Phyllis. "Perhaps later."

After lunch, Beatrice retired for a rest, and Phyllis and I took coffee in the drawing room.

"What's to be done about poor Harkness?" I said. "I take it his solicitor is working to get him bailed?"

"Yes," said Phyllis, "but I fear there's little hope of it. The police are convinced it was him. It's simply dreadful. He might even end up being – no, I can't bear to think of it!"

"Then we will have to do Mr Simmons' work for him. He was not pleased with me for looking into William's movements on the night Walker died. I suppose I can see his point – he wouldn't want arbitrary members of the public interfering and potentially affecting the case. But if he's not going to do his job properly, what choice do we have?"

"Quite," said Phyllis. "Can we think of anyone who might have wanted to kill Shaw?"

"Let's eliminate William first," I said, taking a draught of fortifying coffee. "Could he have done it? He has motivation: a letter that horribly – and perhaps plausibly – destroys the reputation of his wife."

"But Beatrice was virtually mesmerised into one act of folly by that snake Walker. Everything else is a pack of lies."

"I know," I said, "but it's a well-known trick to seed a lie with a small truth. Even if William hadn't known everything about Walker and Beatrice, he probably had his suspicions: an instinct that his wife had too much admiration for him."

"Even so," said Phyllis, putting down her empty coffee cup, "I don't think William would have it in him to kill anyone."

"Before this," I said, "I would have agreed, from what I know of him. But the letter was so vicious, and the ramifications so painful, that I don't even know what I would do in such circumstances. However, the main thing that works against William's guilt is that the letter is clearly designed to goad him. This pushes at least some responsibility onto the sender, even if William did attack Shaw."

"But," said Phyllis, "could it not be the case that the sender was misled by someone else into believing Beatrice had been close with both men? In which case, the letter may have been written in good faith, although I hate to say it."

"It's possible, but it seems unlikely, because it's an obviously provocative and destructive thing to do. No remotely rational person would think sending that letter is a reasonable act. So I think the author of the letter is also the author of the lies. In which case, they want harm to come to one of the three people involved. And since one of them is dead, it points to antagonism towards Shaw."

I got up and rang the bell-pull by the fireplace for more coffee, before continuing: "But our saving grace is that we don't necessarily have to prove that Harkness didn't kill Shaw – that may be impossible to achieve. We merely – merely! – have to find out who did."

Phyllis nodded. "Do you have anyone in mind?"

"Shaw was still suspicious of Johnny Falkirk, though we eliminated him from Walker's murder. I think it highly unlikely Falkirk would have anything to do with Shaw after his interview with the police – he will be keeping a low profile. And besides, what would be his motivation? With Walker dead and Shaw pretty much incapacitated, there was little chance of the mural being finished. There was no need to kill Shaw."

"True," said Phyllis. "Shaw had an absolute hatred of the Rector, so I suppose we should consider him."

We paused as Mrs Felton appeared. "More coffee?" she said.

"You read my mind," I said. "Yes, please."

"Certainly, my dear. Do you think Mrs Harkness would like some tea or coffee in her room?"

"I'm sure she would," said Phyllis. "Tea, I think. Thank you!"

After Mrs Felton had left the room, I said, "Yes, Mr Neville – such a highly-respected man makes an unlikely villain, but he should not be overlooked. He has been against Shaw and Walker from the start."

"But to kill a man because you disapprove of him?" said Phyllis.

"Or men," I said.

"Oh, surely not. Mr Neville kill two men out of pious distaste? He would have to be mad, Thomas, and although he can be emphatic in the pulpit, I don't see signs of lunacy."

"It's hard to imagine, I know," I said. "But we don't have many suspects. We definitely need to consider him."

"Very well – anyone else? Who did Shaw know?"

"Not many – the innkeeper, Minto; Mrs Shannon; and – I'm obliged to say – Mrs Campbell."

"Ha!" said Phyllis. "I know Mrs Campbell likes to try many things, but I don't think even she would take up murder as a hobby."

"I'll ask her," I said. I was joking, but there was a flicker of misgiving in my mind. I had not quizzed her properly about her relationship with the two artists, and her original denial of friendship with them had not been credible.

"Mrs Shannon?" said Phyllis.

"She was Shaw's lover, and was with him on the night of Walker's death. I have spoken to her" – naturally, my incorrigible mind's eye immediately conjured up a fleshy, naked Bess – "and she is, in my opinion, utterly incapable of anything like this. Although she was abandoned by Shaw, she had quickly accepted that fact. I had no sense at all of any bitterness towards him – only a little concern for his health. As for an alibi – I bumped into her this morning, in fact, and she said she had been making a dress with her maid on the day Shaw died. I can quiz the maid, but I believe we can rule Mrs Shannon out."

"Good. Have you met Mr Minto?"

"I have spoken to him briefly," I said. "He was kind to Shaw after his friend's death, and he gains nothing from the horrible events at the cottage – no inn would want that kind of reputation, and he has much to gain from them leaving the cottage alive."

Fresh coffee arrived, and I smiled up at Mrs Felton. "You are wonderful," I said, unguardedly. "Thank you."

She went quite pink at my praise. "Oh, it's a pleasure, my dear! Just ring if you need anything else."

When we were alone, Phyllis said, "How sweet! Almost like mother and son. Mrs Felton is a gem, isn't she?"

"She certainly is – she's always so cheerful, and brings such a warmth to the place. I couldn't do without her. In fact, I should review her pay – and that of all my staff. I wonder when they last had an increase."

"There is something that is bothering me," said Phyllis, sipping her second coffee. "Who knew about Beatrice's assignation with Walker? Or was it just a good guess?"

"Good point," I said. "If we could find out who knew about it, we might trace the information to the killer. So Beatrice told only you about it, as far as you know?"

"Yes," said Phyllis, "and then she told you."

"And I have told no one," I said. "Shaw didn't seem fully aware of it himself, but I suppose there's a small possibility that he might have blabbed to someone if he had had suspicions."

"And for that matter, so might Walker himself, if he was the boastful sort," said Phyllis. "And servants at the inn might have seen or heard something, as the letter implies."

"Bother," I said. "That does muddy the waters. But we should still keep in mind how else the information might have travelled."

"What about your servants here? Might they have overheard us?"

I considered for a moment. "There was no one in the room, apart from the three of us, so I don't think so."

Phyllis sighed. "Oh, it's impossible!" she said, standing up and walking to the window. "I can't think what we can do. But we must do something."

"Don't despair," I said. "We haven't yet considered the evidence at the scene of the murder."

"If there was anything there, the police will have it," Phyllis said. "We can't even look at it."

"We don't necessarily need to examine it," I said. "Bear with me – I have an idea."

~

Celeste and I were both happy to be outdoors again. I used the opportunity to practise a spot of cantering, which was exhilarating – I wanted to be able to impress Francesca when I finally went riding with her.

The old ironmonger's, J. Cramlington and Sons, was a shop I had been intending to visit for some time. It was a delightful chaos of tools and devices, the walls hung with racks of rules, saws, files and other objects of whose use I was entirely ignorant.

I was examining a hammer when Mr Cramlington came out from the back room.

"Good morning, sir! Lovely day, isn't it? How can I help?"

"Ah, good morning," I said. "I'm looking for a hammer – about a foot long. Something like this one." I turned the hammer over in my hands – it looked a reasonable match for the one used to kill Shaw.

"Yes, that one is nicely finished," he said, "with a hickory handle. Comfortable to hold. Otherwise, to be honest, sir, there's not much more to be said about a hammer! Mainly depends on what size you want."

"Indeed!" I said. "Do you sell a lot of these?"

"The trouble is," said Mr Cramlington, "they're so solid they very rarely break – and most people like to use tools that have been in the family. You've probably got a few yourself, sir – smoothed down and stained from years of use, to the extent they're like old friends. So, no, we don't sell a lot. But now you mention it, we sold one of these only yesterday. First for several weeks!"

"How curious," I said. "I hope I'm not about to buy a duplicate – it might have been one of my staff coming in to buy one for me. What did this customer look like, if you don't mind saying?"

"Not a bit, sir. He was a young man, mid-twenties I would say, light hair, a little shorter than you. Perhaps a footman – that kind of thing. Didn't look like an artisan to me."

"Ah, not one of mine, I don't think. Well, Mr Cramlington, I'll take this one, please." I felt that having provided such interesting information, Mr Cramlington deserved the sale of a hammer. Anyway, it would surely find some use on the estate.

"Very good, sir." He took the hammer carefully from me, as if it were a newborn baby, and put it on the counter for wrapping. "It'll probably last a couple of generations, maybe more," he added with a slight hint of regret.

# CHAPTER TWENTY-SEVEN

When I got back to Ramsburgh, I found Phyllis taking some air in the garden. Having stabled Celeste, I returned to Phyllis, at the edge of the wood.

"What have you got there?" she said.

I unpacked the hammer and presented it to her triumphantly.

Phyllis looked alarmed, and glanced around her and up at the house windows. "Oh goodness, Thomas! Don't let Beatrice see that. It's not the actual...?"

I put it back in its wrapping. "No, don't worry. I just bought it."

"Why ever would you do such a thing?" said Phyllis. "Have you lost your mind?"

"Not yet," I said. "I went to the ironmonger's – Cramlington's – to see whether they had sold any hammers of this size recently." I took a deep breath of air, which was infused with a pleasant damp-leaf smell from the nearby trees.

"Well?" said Phyllis impatiently.

"Yes," I said. "Yesterday."

"But they probably sell any number of hammers. And yesterday – that was after the murder! So that's no use at all, is it?"

"On the contrary – they sell very few. So someone going in and buying a hammer not long after the death of someone who was murdered by a hammer... that is significant."

"But Thomas!" Phyllis said, the frustration palpable in her voice. "You have just done that very thing yourself!"

"Yes, but the difference is, I am not a murderer. I bought

it only to get information."

"But even so," said Phyllis, "why would the murderer buy a hammer *after* killing someone with a hammer?"

"Isn't it obvious?" I said with a smile.

"No!" she said, almost in a scream, and beat her fists on my shoulders with frustration. "No, it isn't. Oh! You are impossible!"

"I'm sorry," I said, a little gratified at the intimacy implied by the imminent bruises on my shoulders. "I will be clearer. The murderer may have been intending to remove the weapon, but for some reason didn't. Or he only realised afterwards that the hammer would be missed. So he purchased one to replace the one he used, so no one would be the wiser."

Phyllis stared at me for a moment with wide eyes. "Oh goodness," she eventually said. "You may be right. I'm sorry I hit you! You're cleverer than I thought."

"That," I said, "is a high compliment, coming from you."

~

The following day, Phyllis, Beatrice and I convened in the sitting room.

"Do you not think I might try to see William in the Asylum?" Beatrice said. "I can't bear the thought of him all alone, ill and frightened."

"I really don't think so, Bea," said Phyllis. "He's not himself and seeing you might make him worse. Besides, Mr Simmons said you shouldn't see him. I'm so sorry."

Beatrice's shoulders slumped. "I suppose you're right," she said.

I explained my theory about the hammer. The problem was making use of it, and trying to find a specific hammer in a town the size of Hawksbridge presented a considerable challenge. We had to narrow it down.

"What about the inn – The Duke's Head," said Phyllis, "since it was so close to the scene?"

"Yes, let's put it on the list," I said. "I'm not sure how we would go about searching it, though, without drawing attention to ourselves. Beatrice, would you mind if we checked your house? I know it's unlikely, but it's possible someone might have taken the hammer from your house to incriminate your husband."

"Of course, if you wish," said Beatrice.

"And then there's the Rector's house," I said.

"That won't be easy," said Phyllis. "But don't forget the church. They must have tools there."

"Ah, of course," I said. "We just need to avoid morning or evening prayer, when Mr Neville will be there."

"Shall we try the easiest two first?" said Phyllis. "Beatrice's house, and the church?"

"Good idea," I said. "Any idea how to get at the tools in the church?"

"If we take my pony trap," said Phyllis, "yes, as it happens!"

~

Phyllis and Beatrice once more took the Drummonds' pony trap, which was still at Ramsburgh, and I rode Celeste, who was much admired and fussed over by the two women. The Harkness' home was part of a recent development on the east side of town, on the site of a defunct tanning works. It was a tall town house whose surface was charmingly punctuated by patterns of coloured bricks, and it had some eccentric ecclesiastical touches such as leaded Gothic windows and an arched stone porch. It was a house clearly waiting to host a crowd of small Harknesses, and that was now sadly in doubt.

Beatrice was welcomed by the housekeeper, who was concerned about her mistress' health and state of mind. Reassured on that front, the housekeeper invited us to inspect the cellar where the tools were kept.

There were two hammers, and both of them had plenty of signs of age. The housekeeper could not recall anyone buying new tools in a while, and confirmed the tools had not been used for at least a month. We also searched a shed in the garden, but to no avail.

It was a relief not to find any possible incriminating evidence here, so I felt that in that small regard, we had been successful.

We set off for St Ninian's to put Phyllis' plan into action. I entered the church, and found no sign of the Rector. I went to find the vestry, and knocked on the door. The curate, Mr Garrard, opened the door and beamed at me.

"Mr Rufford! How nice to see you. How can I help?"

"Ah, Mr Garrard, thank you. I have a small practical problem concerning a couple of ladies."

"Indeed?"

"Yes, their dresses are catching on a nail in their trap. I wonder if you would be so good as to help knock the nail back?"

"Of course, sir! Let me find the church toolbox. It's in this cupboard."

I followed Mr Garrard into the vestry, and he unlocked the cupboard. I could immediately see that hanging amongst some venerable old wooden tools, a light-coloured hammer stood out.

"Huh!" the curate said. He retrieved the hammer and looked at it for a moment, turning it over in his hands.

"Not what you were expecting?" I said.

He looked at me, puzzled, and then back at the hammer. "No, sir. No. Funny you should say that."

"It looks new," I said. "Perhaps the old one broke."

"Yes," he said. "I'm sure that's it."

"I expect you had workmen in," I said, "and they opened the cupboard and –"

"Oh, no, sir," he said. "That's not possible. It's always locked, and only Mr Neville and I have keys."

"Ah," I said. "Well, this nail should only take a couple of taps."

The curate greeted Beatrice and Phyllis, with whom I exchanged significant glances, and quickly hammered in the nail that we had previously inserted in a suitably awkward spot inside the trap, with the head just proud of the wood.

"Thank you, Mr Garrard," I said as I went over to Celeste. "You don't know how helpful you've been."

"Don't mention it, sir," he said. "Good day to you all!"

We left him, trembling with excitement at our discovery, not daring to look back in case our ruse had been rumbled. We had only gone a short distance when a sudden, horrible realisation hit me, and I felt a hot prickle of fear. If the Rector was indeed the perpetrator, and should the curate mention this incident to him, we had surely just placed ourselves in grave danger.

# CHAPTER TWENTY-EIGHT

WHEN we returned, the builder was overseeing the construction of scaffolding on the front of the house to look at the leaky gutter I had spotted earlier. While Howard took the trap and Celeste into the stable yard, I spoke to the builder.

"Good morning, Mr Laughton!" I said. "Thank you for coming so soon."

"Good morning, Mr Rufford," he said. "No trouble at all. It's a pity we didn't spot it when we were doing the stonework, but that's always the way, isn't it, sir?"

"Unfortunately, yes," I said. It was not ideal for Beatrice's nerves to have men coming and going and generally making a din, but I had become protective about Ramsburgh.

Mrs Felton brought us a well-deserved pot of coffee in the drawing room, and also presented a seed cake she had made.

When we were alone, Beatrice said, "Surely, surely it could not be Mr Neville, could it? Someone else might have replaced the hammer. Mr Neville has always been so kind to me – how could he become such a monster?"

I dug my fork into my slice of cake. "Either the curate replaced the hammer – and he seemed genuinely surprised to see a new one – or Mr Neville did, unless someone else got hold of the keys, which is a stretch. As to his character, it's a puzzle, but all I can say is that he can be forceful in his sermons, and I have seen him angry in The Duke's Head when confronting Shaw. It's not impossible that his anger has boiled over, despite Shaw's apology, which I suspect was quite insincere."

Beatrice shook her head in disbelief. "Then surely we should go to the police now, so they can arrest him and free William?"

"Alas," I said, "it won't be as simple as that. For a start, the replaced hammer is only suggestive of Neville's guilt – not absolute proof. And we have to contend with the police's fixation on William, which blinds them to other possibilities, and then there is Mr Simmons' antipathy to me, and by extension, probably any of my acquaintances. If we go to the police too soon and with insufficient evidence, it may impede our case – and therefore endanger William. Do you not agree, Phyllis?"

"I'm not sure," said Phyllis after a moment. "Well, yes, I suppose we do need to think carefully, because, as you say, we don't know what the unintended consequences might be. We must not waste what we have. So – we need more evidence."

"The man who bought the new hammer is key, surely?" I said. "I assume he would be one of Mr Neville's servants, unless he used a more tortuous method to cover up the purchase."

"Yes," said Phyllis, "but we can't very well go to Mr Neville's house and ask all the young, male servants if they bought a hammer recently."

"That is a problem," I said. "But assuming we can get the police to investigate him at all, at least they are likely to gather more evidence that way, even if we can't. So we need to keep thinking abut how we can safely find more clues."

"If you don't mind," said Beatrice, "I will retire to my room – I have a headache coming on. Thank you so much for all you have done, Thomas, Phyllis – it gives me great hope!"

"It's a pleasure," I said. "Oh – I trust you won't find the workmen too noisy. They should only be working on the south side, but please let me know if you are disturbed."

Beatrice nodded, smiled, and left.

"More cake?" I said.

Phyllis accepted, and we ruminated for a minute or two, the silence broken only by the clatter of forks on plates.

"I didn't want to say anything before and alarm Beatrice," I said presently, "but if Mr Neville knows that we have evidence, we may all be at risk from him."

"I realised that too," said Phyllis. "I'm afraid we shall all need to stay here with you for a while longer, Thomas, if it's not too much trouble?"

"Please do, for as long as you and Beatrice like," I said. "I will have a word with Shipley – nothing specific, just to keep him alert."

"Could we smoke him out – Mr Neville, I mean?" said Phyllis. "That is, send an anonymous letter saying that his secret is out, and setting up a meeting somewhere – perhaps on pretence of blackmail. If he keeps the appointment, he's likely to be guilty."

"Too risky, unfortunately," I said. "It would have to be done in conjunction with the police, for our protection and so there are witnesses. Also, we could be accused of actual blackmail, since our intent might be questioned. We might be on shaky legal ground."

"Yes, I can see that – it could go badly wrong." Phyllis shuddered.

"Something may yet occur to us," I said. "If we really can't think of anything, then we'll just have to go to the police with what we have."

"I suppose so," said Phyllis. "Is that someone at the front door?"

I could hear male voices. "Yes, I'd better see who that is," I said, and went to the hall, where a police constable was talking to Shipley. I recognised him from when I was at Shaw's cottage.

"Ah, Mr Rufford, is it, sir? Constable Taylor, sir. I was just saying to this gentleman here that I need to speak to Mrs Harkness, on a pressing matter. I gather she's not seeing visitors – I can quite understand, and I'm sorry to intrude, sir, but I will only take a couple of minutes of her time."

"Yes, very well, Constable – Shipley, I'm afraid we need to disturb her. Can you fetch her, please?"

Beatrice appeared, looking tired and pale, and I ushered her and Constable Taylor into my study and left them, closing the door.

A minute later, I heard Beatrice's raised voice, followed by sobs. The door opened, and the constable emerged with an apologetic expression. "I'm sorry, sir," he said. "It's a very difficult time. I've never known anything like it before in Hawksbridge. Good day, sir."

After he had left, I went back to the study, where Phyllis was comforting a sobbing Beatrice. "What's happened?" I asked. "What did he say?"

Phyllis looked up with a grim expression. "William has been charged with Shaw's murder, and he's been transferred from St John's Asylum to the county prison."

~

Phyllis declined to accompany me on a walk, since she felt she needed to stay with Beatrice, so I took Fox up to the hills and found a measure of calm. I tried to imagine how we could corner the Rector – it was increasingly frustrating that the man had his freedom, while an innocent man languished, broken, in a sordid prison. But no ideas came to me.

I decided to return a different route from usual, cutting through some woods and then taking the road down to Ramsburgh instead of doubling back through the fields. A few minutes after reaching the road, I saw what I thought for a moment was the Rector coming up the hill towards me. But it was only his long, black coat that was familiar: on closer inspection, the wearer looked like a labourer, and he had a bottle of beer in his hand. His gait was a little unsteady, and he was singing tunelessly. As I approached, the man tried to straighten his shoulders, grinned at Fox, and said a cheery "Good evening, sir!"

I stopped, and said, "Good evening. That's a very fine coat you have there!"

"Yes, sir!" he said proudly, fingering its lapels. "No one has the like, that I know. Have to be careful," he said, winking. "There are folks who'd pinch it off me back!"

I peered at the coat, and noticed some brownish stains, realising with horror what they might be.

"Tell me, if you don't mind," I said, "where did you get the coat?"

He backed away. "It's mine, sir. I found it, so it's mine."

"I know, I know. It's just that I'm looking to purchase one like that myself. But if you'd like to sell yours..."

"Oh, I don't know, sir. I don't know as there's any money that will persuade me to part with it. Me and the coat, sir – we're like friends. Can't sell a friend."

"Not even for a guinea?"

He gawped at me. "A whole guinea, like?"

"Yes – a guinea, and the story about where you got it from."

He considered. "Well, I suppose," he said slowly, "before I found the coat, I had sixpence in my pocket, and now you're saying, I might have no coat, but I'd have a guinea and sixpence, and I'd be better off than if I'd never found the coat!"

"Exactly," I said, approving of his excellent logic.

His eyes narrowed. "Do you *have* this guinea?" he asked.

I had to admit that this part of my plan was wanting.

"I don't have a guinea now, but I could get it to you as soon as –"

"No guinea, no coat," he said, and started to walk back

up the road.

"Hold on," I said, catching him up. "How about we meet this time tomorrow, right here, and I'll bring you your guinea? You can give me the coat then."

He stopped. "All right, then. I usually come up this way about this time. Can't say as it'll be exact."

"Fair enough," I said. "I'll be waiting with your guinea!"

He grinned and trudged off, and I hurried back to Ramsburgh in an excited state to tell Phyllis of my encounter.

~

I found her in the drawing room, reading my old copy of 'Gulliver's Travels' that I had left on a table.

"Sunbeams from cucumbers, indeed!" she said. "Dr Swift was a genius."

I agreed, and then told her about the man in the coat.

"My goodness!" said Phyllis. "So there's a man walking around the countryside right now with the evidence that could hang one man and save another?"

"Yes," I said. "I wish I could have got hold of the coat, but I could hardly wrest it off him."

"Couldn't you have swapped it for your coat? Or Fox? Well, obviously not Fox, but..."

"Definitely not Fox," I said. "Perhaps I should have offered my own coat. Sorry, I didn't think of it. Of course, he might not have liked it so much."

"Well, let's hope he turns up tomorrow. I take it you took his name, just in case?"

"Oh, blast," I said. "That didn't occur to me either. What a dunderhead I am."

"Never mind," Phyllis said. "You won't be threatening Mr Simmons' job just yet. I wonder where he got the coat?"

"I expect Neville hid it somewhere, perhaps hoping to find it later and dispose of it properly. Obviously he chose a poor hiding place. I shall find out more tomorrow," I said. "Should we tell Beatrice?"

"Not just yet, I think," she said. "If we feel nervous about this, imagine how she will feel! If we fail to retrieve the coat, it will be devastating for her."

"If he doesn't turn up," I said, "we will have to go to the police, and hope that they believe us."

"Yes," she said. "Oh, what a tangle this whole thing is. Worse than one of my novels!"

~

I was dreaming that I was running up the hill with Bess, and we were both completely naked. Mr Neville was standing at the edge of the wood, holding out his coat. Somehow we both fitted into it, and then Mr Neville pushed us down the hill, at the bottom of which we fell into a pool of blood. A tree overhanging the pool was breaking, making an awful cracking noise, and it was starting to topple towards us. I was powerless to move out of its way.

I woke with a start in the darkness of my bedroom to find that the cracking noise was real: someone was prising my south-facing window open. The lock broke with a final crack, and the sash slid open. I sat up, petrified. Mr Neville had found me, and was about to dispatch me, and perhaps everyone else in the house. I cursed myself for not having gone to the police already.

The intruder pushed the shutters open, snapping the latch, and climbed in. Moonlight poured into the room, illuminating him: it was not Mr Neville, but someone I remembered from my past, with features that contained the ghost of Hazel. It was Alan Sharpe, brandishing a jemmy.

"Well, if it isn't Mr Thomas Rufford!" he said with a leer. "It's my lucky day. I thought castles were supposed to keep people safe! But you kindly provided a ladder up to your room. Not very bright, are you?"

I tried to keep my composure, which was hard when the man in front of my bed held an iron implement that could brain me with a single swipe.

"Good evening, Mr Sharpe," I said. "This is an unusual way to rekindle an old acquaintance. Do you have the letters?"

"Not so fast, Mr Rufford," he said, but he instinctively touched his breast pocket. "Now I've come all this way, we should have a little chat." He pulled up a chair next to my bed, and I felt incongruously like a patient receiving a visitor.

He pushed his straggly black hair from his face, and said, "I suppose you thought you'd got away with what you did to my sister? Did you?"

"I have never forgotten Hazel, or what happened," I said. "But I did nothing deliberately to hurt her. The police were wrong to arrest her."

"But why did they arrest her? Because they found her handkerchief. No, *your* handkerchief, wasn't it, Mr Rufford? I helped clear out Mr Oliphant's house, and guess what I found in the loft? Some letters. Very particular letters with hot-blooded words, from a married woman to a young man. So I says to myself, who might want to kill old Oliphant over these? Why, young Mr Mercer, of course, the subject of these letters, and perhaps a friend or two. Meaning you, Mr Rufford, with my sister's handkerchief, and maybe Peter McNulty, who I know you were tight with. I put it all together, which makes me cleverer than the police! Tell me if I'm wrong, won't you?"

I had no choice but to attempt to explain the truth, unlikely as it was that he would believe me. "Mr Sharpe, we did not kill Mr Oliphant. When we came to his house, he had fallen down the stairs and injured himself. We helped him onto the sofa and made sure he was feeling better, before we left. His fall is what killed him."

Mr Sharpe stood up angrily and started to pace the room. "You expect me to believe that?" Despite his mood, he maintained a hoarse whisper in order not to disturb the other residents of the house. "What a stupid story that is. You admit you went to Oliphant's house – that says it all. The rest is just flim-flam. The end result is that my sister is dead, cheated out of her life by a scoundrel."

My initial surprise and terror having subsided, I regained a little presence of mind. I remembered that there was a bell-pull by my bed, by a miracle of engineering that involved a complex system of copper wires and pulleys within the walls. The second time that Sharpe turned his back on me to traverse the bedroom, I pulled it.

I tried to speak in a voice loud enough to alert anyone coming to my assistance, but not so loud that Phyllis and Beatrice would wake and put themselves in danger.

"Oliphant and his brother are the real scoundrels in this story, Mr Sharpe," I said. "The police made a mistake – and I made a mistake by stepping over Oliphant's threshold – but those two are the origins of all this. Blackmail followed by assault. I blame myself for a lot, but I do not take responsibility for what those brothers did."

Sharpe returned from his outward journey across the room, and drew closer to me. "Someone has to pay, Mr Rufford. Someone always has to pay. Talking of payment – have you got what I asked for? Because if not –"

"Yes, yes," I said. "I have the money. New guineas, as you said. But I need to know you have the letters."

Sharpe moved back into the middle of the room, reached into his breast pocket, and retrieved a packet of letters. He had opened his mouth to say something, when the door burst open, and in came Shipley, brandishing his truncheon. He quickly closed the door behind him, and said, "Who in God's name are you, sir?"

Sharpe was so surprised that he dropped the letters and raised the jemmy, hitting it against the end of the bed, whereupon it fell out of his hands onto the floor. For a split second he looked as though he was deciding whether to pick it up and defend himself, and then seeing Shipley advancing quickly towards him, he ran to the window and hurled himself out. He must have put too much energy into it to stop himself again on the scaffolding, and there was a grunt, a short silence, and then an awful crunch. I knew that he was probably dead.

# CHAPTER TWENTY-NINE

A MAN falling to his death in the middle of the night is not, unfortunately, an event that can easily be concealed from members of the household. Shipley had the wit to tear a sheet from my bed, and we hurried downstairs. Sharpe's body was twisted horribly, with his neck clearly broken and no signs of life. We quickly arranged the sheet over the body, and used gravel to weigh down the edges, before Mrs Felton and Phyllis appeared. I could see Flora peering down from her tower.

"Oh Lord!" said Mrs Felton. "Who is it? Not Mrs Harkness...?" Evidently her mind had jumped to self-murder.

"No, Mrs Felton," I said, "it's none of us – he's a stranger. He got in through my window. I thought the window catches would be enough, but he had a jemmy."

"Not... Mr Neville?" said Phyllis.

"Now why on earth would it be the Rector?" asked Mrs Felton. "Heavens!"

"No," I said. "Not him."

"So, a burglar, then?" said Phyllis.

"Perhaps," I said, not wanting to go into any details at that moment. That could wait. Now, we had to decide what to do about the body.

I sighed. "Someone will have to go and fetch the police," I said.

"I'll do it, sir," Shipley said. "There's just enough light."

I thanked him, and said to Phyllis, "Can you just go and make sure Beatrice doesn't come out here, or – if possible – even look out of a window? It's the last thing she needs to see. Fortunately, her bedroom is west-facing."

"Yes, of course," Phyllis said, and went to check on her

friend.

I went back to my bedroom, picked the letters up from the floor where Sharpe had dropped them, and took them upstairs to my closet. I put them in the lockable bottom drawer for safekeeping; I could decide exactly what to do with them in due course. They were potential evidence, so I could not act on my immediate instinct to burn them.

Coming out of my closet, I could hear Phyllis and Beatrice talking in Beatrice's bedroom, which was on the same floor. I knocked gently on the door.

"Come in," said Beatrice, and I entered. Beatrice was in bed, and Phyllis was sitting on the edge of the bed in her dressing gown. I tried not to be distracted by how charming a picture this made.

"Excuse me – I just wanted to let you know that the police will probably be here before too long," I said. "So you might want to get dressed – I expect they will want to interview all of us, however briefly."

"Thank you," said Beatrice. "Whatever can this mean? Do you think this man was employed by Mr Neville? Perhaps he's the man who bought the hammer."

I sighed, knowing I would have to give a little explanation. Lies would be too hard to row back from, and this counted double where the police were concerned. "He's the brother of someone I used to know, over ten years ago," I said.

"You knew him?" said Phyllis, looking shocked.

"Very slightly," I said. "He has been harbouring a grudge because his sister died, and he blamed it partly on me. I wasn't responsible, but in his grief he thought I was."

"So he came to take revenge, after all these years?" said Phyllis.

"Yes – and he thought he might get a little money out of me."

"And you think he might have intended to kill you?"

"Well, he was standing over me with his jemmy, so if he hadn't got what he wanted, who knows?"

"Oh Lord!" said Beatrice. "Thank goodness it wasn't Mr Neville."

"Although if it had been the Rector that had died, it would have solved a problem," said Phyllis.

"Except then there would be no chance of a confession that could exonerate William," I said. "We would have to rely on scant evidence, although coming to murder us in our beds would be telling. Anyway, I shall leave you to get dressed."

~

Mr Simmons interviewed each of us in the dining room so that he could easily take notes, and, I supposed, intimidate us across the table in emulation of his police interrogation room. Fortunately, Phyllis, Beatrice and Flora were first in line and could retire after a short time.

By the time I was summoned by Constable Taylor, I had taken a small whisky to calm my nerves. Mr Simmons was sitting with his hands under his chin, staring at me as I came in. His expression was chilly, and I imagined that this stance was reserved solely for me.

He looked at me for a short time after I had sat down opposite him, sighed, and opened his notebook.

"Mr Rufford," he said, perusing his notes. "I hardly know where to begin. Can you tell me, sir, why it is that I keep finding myself speaking to you? Are you to me as a hypochondriac is to a doctor? And yet the situation in each case is very serious. If I were to judge merely on appearances, I might conclude that you have an unhealthy affinity with criminal activity. What would you say to that, sir?"

"I would say, Mr Simmons, that I quite understand that

impression; but it is incorrect. This matter is entirely unconnected with the Shaw and Walker cases, and in fact Shaw and Walker should in my opinion be considered as belonging to a single case. That means that there have really only been two cases in which I have become involved."

"Two cases, but three deaths. Any way you slice it, it's not good."

"I couldn't agree more, Inspector. Not good at all, and I'm heartily sick of it. It's not been the happiest introduction to Hawksbridge."

Mr Simmons stared at me suspiciously for a moment and then said, "Very well. Let's get to the facts pertaining to tonight's adventure. Please give me your account of it."

"Certainly. I noticed nothing out of the ordinary in the evening, and went to bed as usual, at around ten o'clock. I was awoken at about one o'clock this morning, or shortly thereafter, by the noise of breaking wood at my bedroom window on the south side of the house. The shutters opened, and I realised that an intruder had climbed the scaffolding and got in through my window, using a jemmy."

"Most unlucky," said the Inspector. "Please continue."

"I recognised the man as Alan Sharpe, the brother of a maid I had been friends with when I was eighteen. This was in London."

"Yes, your friends mentioned that you knew him, which I find very interesting."

"I barely knew him, Inspector – I met him only once. He had got the idea into his head that I had had something to do with the death of his sister, Hazel."

"Oh, here we go," said the Inspector, looking up at Constable Taylor. "Another death. I trust there are those of your acquaintance who survive meeting you, Mr Rufford? Should I be worried for myself?"

"I suppose I have been unlucky," I said, at a loss for how to counter his sarcasm.

"I'll say," remarked Constable Taylor.

"Shall I continue?" I asked.

"It's like a bloody Greek tragedy," said the Inspector. "But be my guest."

"I'm afraid I have to introduce two more deaths, Inspector. Actually, three."

"Lord Almighty," said Mr Simmons.

"John Oliphant was a butler, again in London, who worked with Hazel and treated her very badly. He was in poor health, and was found dead in his home. Hazel was arrested, since she and he had been on bad terms, and she was killed in jail by Oliphant's brother – he himself was hanged as a result."

"And somehow this Alan Sharpe blamed you? Any reason why?"

"I don't know," I said. "I assume the grief twisted his reason. I was friendly with Hazel, and I was a convenient target."

"Friendly, sir?" said the Inspector.

"We had a short affair," I said.

"Which ended because?"

"She was angry with me because I helped to get Oliphant removed from his post after hearing about his behaviour."

"I see. I think." Mr Simmons scribbled some notes for a minute or two, before sitting back and sighing.

"And you don't know why Sharpe left it this long to come and find you?"

"No," I said. "But I assume he was hard up and his grief had grown over the years. He asked for money."

"Speaking of which, let us go back to the moment he opened the shutters. That's when you recognised him?"

"Yes, Inspector. He then proceeded to blame me for Hazel's death. He was still holding his jemmy, and implied violence if I didn't give him money. When he wasn't looking, I rang the bell to alert the servants."

"You were still in bed at this point?"

"Yes. Shipley turned up about a minute later, and advanced towards Sharpe holding his truncheon. Before he got close, Sharpe dropped his jemmy and fled through the window. He must have overbalanced, because we heard a grunt, and a second or two later, the thud when he hit the ground."

"I see. So neither of you actually touched him at all?"

"No, Inspector."

"I certainly hope that's the truth, Mr Rufford."

"You may be assured that it is, Inspector. I can lay my hands on a Bible if..."

"No need at this point, sir. So you laid a sheet on him, and came for us. Can you think of any other details?" He yawned; his powers of concentration had obviously reached their limit.

"No, Inspector, but if I do, I will come and tell you, or write to you."

"Thank you, sir. We'll get the body laid out in your wash-house as I arranged with Mr Shipley, and we will return tomorrow – that is, later this morning. Do you think Mr Sharpe's family are likely to want him back? Otherwise a subscription will have to be raised for his burial."

"I'm afraid I don't know, Inspector," I said. "I didn't know any of his relatives in London apart from Hazel, and I rather suspect no one will claim him."

"Very well. That's all for now – thank you, sir."

With some relief, I left the dining room, half expecting to be called back for more questioning. But I was able to leave, and as I did not wish to return to my bedroom yet, Mrs Felton turned the sofa in my closet into something resembling a bed. I was pleased to be near Phyllis and Beatrice up at the top of the house, but whether out of consideration for their protection, or for my own reassurance, I was not entirely sure.

# CHAPTER THIRTY

When I awoke at around nine o'clock, the Inspector's men were already interviewing the staff and examining the scaffolding and my bedroom.

I got dressed as quickly as I could, and knocked on Flora's door.

"Good morning," I said. "I wanted to see that you were all right, and also have a word, if I could come in for a moment?"

"Of course," she said, and led me to her sitting room. "I'm a little shaken by what has happened, but I'm all right."

I went over to the window. "This looks as good as new," I said. "But it'll take a few years for some of the trees to recover properly from the storm."

"I know the feeling," said Flora.

I sat down. "Flora, I owe you a great apology," I began.

"Whatever for?" said Flora.

"You may have heard – the man who died was someone I knew in London."

"Ah!" said Flora. "That would explain why the Inspector was so insistent to know whether he had been seen around here before. But I didn't see his face, so I couldn't be much help. So, who was he?"

I explained what I had told the Inspector, omitting, as before, the fact that I had been in Oliphant's house and had – fatally – left a handkerchief. These were details that could yet harm me, although I knew I was innocent.

Flora was surprisingly calm throughout my account, perhaps because lately she had become habituated to death, and afterwards said, "I am so sorry about your friend, Thomas.

That must have been hard to bear."

"Thank you – it was," I said. "I had not had someone close to me die before, and the manner of it was cruel."

"So why are you apologising?" said Flora. "You weren't responsible for this man's behaviour."

"Perhaps, but I feel I have brought mischief here – no, danger – and coming on top of everything else –"

"Then answer me this," Flora interrupted. "Why is it, do you think, that I have felt safer here since you arrived? I know that may sound absurd in the circumstances, given all that's come to pass in Hawksbridge in the last few months, but it's true. I resented you when you arrived, to be sure. But I understand you a little better now. And my instincts may have served me badly with Henry Shaw, but I know – don't ask me how – that you are a good man. So there's no need for this."

"Thank you," I said, hoarsely, wiping tears of relief and gratitude from my eyes.

She smiled at me. "Oh, I do so hate an emotional scene," she said. "I'm no good at this kind of thing. Let's change the subject."

"Very well," I said. "You said – it seems a long time ago now – that you would show me your work. May I see it? I confess I was a little put out when Mr Shaw got to see it before me."

"Certainly," said Flora. "If you're sure? Don't you have to go and attend to the Inspector?"

"I'm hiding from him," I said. "He doesn't like me, and I'm not very keen on him. Besides, Shipley can manage, and I don't particularly wish to see the body taken away."

"An ulterior motive for visiting me, Thomas?" Flora said. "I'm disappointed."

My face fell for a moment, before she smiled and said, "I'm teasing you. Let me get my embroidery."

She returned shortly with a box and laid the pieces out on the tea-table in front of me. I looked through them, lost for words: each one seemed more beautiful than the one before. Flora had drawn from nature and mythology, and the vivid colours of exotic birds and writhing plants gave way to leaping centaurs, dragons poised to incinerate knights, and a host of animals I was unable to name. Flowers were so delicately rendered in thread that I had to resist an urge to pick them up. In some pieces, intricate borders were drawn like the edges of an illuminated manuscript. It was quite impossible for me to conceive how pictures of this complexity could be made with needle and thread.

When I had seen them all, I stared at Flora. "Good God!" I said. "These are simply incredible. Should you not have an exhibition?"

"You like them?"

"I love them," I said. "They are exquisite."

Flora smiled, and started to pack them away. "I don't really like people to see them. Perhaps it would spoil the pleasure if I was suddenly obliged to make them. And each one takes a very long time."

"But you are depriving the world of beauty!" I insisted. "These pieces belong in the light –"

"Where they will fade," Flora said.

"Oh, surely not that quickly," I said. "I think it's the light on you that you are afraid of."

"Very perceptive," she said. "You may be right." She hesitated. "There's something else..."

"Yes?" I said.

"I don't know. It's foolish. I made some sketches when the Town Hall mural was first put forward. I must have been insane, but I did some drawings. Of course, I never submitted them. After all, with such famous artists in the running, I would only have embarrassed myself. Sorry, please forget that I mentioned it – your praise must have gone to my head!"

"Flora," I said, "I'm not budging from this room until you bring me your sketches. You're obviously dying to show them to someone, and I'm dying to look at them."

"Oh, very well," she said. "I will regret this." She went to a cupboard and fetched a large portfolio. She brought out a large painting depicting the redeeming angels diving into the fire-ravaged factory to retrieve lost souls, portrayed in a less bombastic style than Shaw's and Walker's mural, but just as engaging, and skilfully composed. There were further variations, some just drawings, others vibrantly coloured.

I shook my head incredulously. "These are wonderful. Perfect, in fact." Flora smiled. "You must take these to the Mural Committee," I continued. "The mural could yet be saved."

"Oh, I don't know," she said. "I don't have any experience in large-scale works, and the materials and techniques that would be needed."

"But I believe Mr Falkirk does," I said. "Could you not team up?"

Her expression brightened. "What an interesting idea, Thomas. It's a thought."

"I'll talk to Mr McPhee at the Pottery," I said, "since he's on the committee, and we can arrange a meeting to show him your sketches."

"Thank you," said Flora. "I'm sure nothing will come of it, but you're right – I should make more effort. I just get so embarrassed showing my work. I only want to do it, not hawk it around."

"I'm sure a balance can be found," I said, and then the shadow of the Rector passed over my mind. "Oh – there is something else I need to talk you about. A topic not as pleasant as your art, I'm afraid."

"Yes?" she said.

"It's about Shaw. Do you know if he will be buried in Hawksbridge?"

"He won't be," said Flora. "His brother has arranged to take him back to his family in Dorset, now that the inquest has been held."

"Ah," I said. "Phyllis, Mrs Harkness and I think we may know who his killer is – and it's not Mr Harkness."

"Oh gracious," said Flora. "Who on earth is it, then?"

"Alas, I can't say, because it might put you in danger. But I wanted you to know that it may be coming to a head soon, and then we will take our information to the police."

"Really?" said Flora. "But surely you should go to the police now, if you know something?"

"That would be counter-productive, I'm afraid, because the police won't believe me on such slight evidence, and then the opportunity to change their minds may be lost. We need confirmation – and that's what we hope to have in the next couple of days. I just thought you should know that we won't let Shaw's killer go unpunished."

"Thank you, Thomas," said Flora. "Please, please be careful!"

~

By noon, Sharpe's body had been carried off and the police had finished their work. I went to talk to the staff to ensure they were not anxious, but – probably because they had something to gossip about – they seemed in surprisingly good spirits, apart from some grumbling from one of the maids, Alice, the start of whose day off had been delayed by the police. As Alice left, I noticed that there seemed something different about her – had she put on weight? At least that implied that the staff were getting decent nourishment.

An uneasy quiet returned to Ramsburgh, with Phyllis and myself full of apprehension for what lay ahead. I waited nervously for the appointed time to meet my new acquaintance about a stained coat.

I did not want to transmit my nerves to anyone else, so I retired to my little room at the top of the house and tried to read an Iona Tavistock novel. But engaging though it was, I could not settle to it. Finally, the sun started to sink and I went downstairs to find Fox and a guinea.

Just as I was walking out of the front door, I heard the noise of a carriage on the drive, and a four-wheeler bearing a police insignia pulled up. My heart sank. What did they want now?

"Hello, Inspector," I said, as cheerily as I could. "Did you forget something?"

Mr Simmons did not reply at first, and climbed down with his constables, Taylor and Gawley.

"Mr Thomas Rufford," he said, "I am arresting you on suspicion of the murder of Alan Sharpe." The constables came up to me, and Taylor took Fox's lead and handed it to Gawley before putting me in handcuffs.

"I'll just pop the dog in the house, sir," said Gawley, opening the front door and pushing Fox through it.

"Arresting me? On what possible grounds?" I said, incredulous.

The Inspector simply pursed his lips, and in a moment, I was in the carriage and heading down the road to Hawksbridge. Before the house disappeared from view, I could see Phyllis on the gravel holding Fox's lead, and gazing after me in horror. When I found my voice, I said again, "On what grounds, Inspector?"

"We will talk in the police station, Mr Rufford," said the Inspector. "For the moment, sir, it's best for everyone if you say nothing."

"But this must be a misunderstanding, Inspector," I protested. "You had a witness statement from Mr Shipley that he and I –"

"If it's a misunderstanding, sir," he said with forced calmness, "then I'm sure we will sort it out. At the station."

I gave up, knowing it was pointless saying more in the carriage. I felt sick when I remembered that I would not be able to retrieve the coat. Vital evidence would in all probability be lost, an innocent man would be hanged, and a guilty man would be left free to kill again.

# CHAPTER THIRTY-ONE

"WE have a witness," said Inspector Simmons, "who swears that when Mr Sharpe was exiting your bedroom via the south window, you rushed forward and pushed him with some force. This caused him to fall off the scaffolding, whereupon he died of a broken neck and other injuries. Is this an accurate statement?"

"No, it most certainly is not, Inspector," I said, trying to keep my temper. "I stayed in bed throughout, only getting up after Mr Sharpe had fallen. He was threatening me, so I had no opportunity to get up, and when he ran to the window, it all happened so quickly that I didn't have the chance to even get out of bed, let alone run to the window and push him."

"I see," said the Inspector. "Well, it's a case of your word – and Mr Shipley's – against that of the witness."

"What witness?" I said. "There was no witness. There was only me, Mr Shipley and Mr Sharpe in the room. Mr Shipley shut the door behind him when he came in, to block Mr Sharpe's way. No one was else there, unless they were hiding in my wardrobe."

Simmons looked up coldly from his note-scribbling as if to warn me against sarcasm. That was his sole prerogative in the interview room.

"Someone might have seen what happened from the ground, of course," said the Inspector, "but as it happens, our witness says they were in your bedroom."

"That's impossible," I said. "Who else would come into my bedroom?"

"A servant, sir. I am reliably informed that servants can sometimes move around a house unexpectedly. Especially if something unusual is going on. It would be a natural reaction to run towards a place where a commotion could be heard, would you not say, Mr Rufford? A diligent servant might do such a thing."

"Perhaps they might, Inspector," I said. "But they didn't in this case – only Mr Shipley. Which I'm glad about, since he can take care of himself, and my other staff would be more vulnerable."

The Inspector sighed. "So how do you account for the difference between your story, and that of the witness? And you must admit that you have a motive for wanting to be rid of this man, to silence his demands for money."

"Since I didn't do what he accused me of, I had no motive to kill him," I said, although I had to admit to myself that his death was convenient for me. "I can only think that someone has a grudge against me – that someone has paid a servant to say this, in order to discredit me. Someone has very quickly understood that an advantage could be had from the misfortune of Sharpe's death. What a cynical piece of opportunism that is!"

"And do you have an idea who this opportunist might be, sir?"

"I do, Inspector, but you're not going to like it."

"Try me," he said.

"The Rector – Mr Horace Neville."

The Inspector laughed, and had trouble stopping, since a lack of sleep had apparently taken its toll on his nerves.

"The Rector," he said after a moment, wiping his eyes. "Oh Lord, Mr Rufford, you are a humorist, you are indeed."

I attempted to justify myself, although I knew it was probably futile. "Mr Neville has not been happy with me since I failed to stop Shaw and Walker from being contracted to paint the Town Hall mural. He publicly denounced them from the pulpit. From what I've seen, he has a filthy temper. He and Shaw got into a fierce argument in The Duke's Head: it was disturbing. I have taken an interest in both men's deaths, and this is the consequence."

I did not dare add the evidence of the hammer: it would have to be deployed at a more favourable time, when my credibility was not at such a low ebb.

"You'll have to do better than that, sir. I don't see any reason for him to kill one, possibly two people, and then play a prank on you."

"What is clear, Inspector," I said, "is that a malevolent person has used you to get at me. Your witness is a liar. I kindly ask that you let me go."

"You may be as kind as you like, sir," said the Inspector, "but I decide who goes and who stays. And I'm afraid you're staying, for the time being, while we consider what's to be done."

"I cannot believe this!" I said. "I have always been cooperative, Inspector. Do you simply not like me? Is that it?"

The Inspector waved his hand dismissively, made a signal to Constable Gawley, and left the room. The constable then took me to a cell, and the door clanged shut. I was alone with four bare walls, a chamber pot, and my own raging thoughts.

~

Phyllis had followed me in her pony trap, but she had not been allowed to see me – only to give a message of support. Presumably she had prioritised me over the coat, had she even been able to identify the meeting spot, and so the evidence was lost. This fact hit my morale hard. Not only had I been deprived of my freedom and dignity, but also any hope that William Harkness might be saved and Horace Neville brought to justice.

It had been a clever move of Neville's to damage my

credibility – perhaps even see me tried for murder – to ensure I was no longer a threat. He must have known from my interest in the hammer that I was on his trail. I did not have any guarantee that he would not also pursue Phyllis and Beatrice, but I thought that there was a chance that he would underestimate them and leave them alone.

I pondered how he had managed to engineer this. News of a dramatic death was likely to travel quickly, so he must have contacted one of the servants and offered a handsome reward for making up a story. The obvious person suddenly occurred to me – Alice! She liked to meet a young man at another establishment on her day off. That establishment must be Neville's. Could this also be the conduit that allowed the Rector to plan the letter smearing Mrs Harkness? If Alice had been listening at the door, she would have had a very tasty morsel of gossip to bring to the Rector's servants' hall. And if the Rector liked to avail himself of this gossip, perhaps via his housekeeper, then he would have had all the material he needed.

Alice would have known that she would be ejected from Ramsburgh without a reference, so it must have been a sum that would allow her to live independently, at least for a while. Perhaps she had not put on weight, but was with child, which would give her a strong motive to earn a large amount in exchange for a simple untruth, as her employment at Ramsburgh would have ended anyway. I would have liked to have spoken to this girl, but it was improbable that she would be returning to the house.

~

Constable Gawley was good enough to give me a blanket, and I spent an uncomfortable night. At ten o'clock in the morning,

I was marched to the interview room to await the Inspector.

When he eventually arrived, he was stiffly polite.

"Good morning, Mr Rufford – I hope you have not been too badly inconvenienced. You are free to leave, but please do not stray from the environs of Hawksbridge and your home. We do not have sufficient evidence at present to charge you. We have spoken to Mr Shipley again, and his account of Sharpe's death is convincing. He has also revealed some flaws in the witness' character which undermine her – or his – credibility."

"Good God, man!" I said. "I've been treated like a common criminal. I think I deserve an apology! And shouldn't you arrest the witness?"

"As I say, sir, it's been a pity to inconvenience you. We have reprimanded the witness, but we do not believe it to be in the public interest to make any more of it. Now, I'm afraid I must attend to other affairs. Good day, Mr Rufford!"

Gawley looked a little embarrassed, and escorted me from the building. "I'm sorry about all this, sir," he said in a whisper, looking about him in case the Inspector was listening. "I didn't think it was right in the first place. It's shameful, in fact!"

"Thank you, Constable," I said. "I appreciate that. I don't suppose someone can take me back home?"

"I'm afraid not, sir," he said. "But you can pick up a cab at The Duke's Head."

I was strongly tempted to go straight to Bess' house, bathe myself while telling her my latest troubles, then blissfully sleep in her bedroom to wake, perhaps, with her soft body against mine. But I knew that Phyllis would be worried about me, so I did as the constable suggested.

~

"Oh, Thomas, thank goodness!" said Phyllis when I walked into the drawing room. She got up and embraced me. "I have been so worried. They wouldn't tell me anything – why did they arrest you?"

"The Rector found a way to get to me," I said, "but fortunately, the maid he bribed to say I pushed Sharpe wasn't altogether convincing. I don't think they'll charge me."

"And they believed her enough to put you in jail overnight?" said Phyllis. "What a complete imbecile Simmons is!"

"I must have rubbed him up the wrong way," I said. "Anyway, we're a maid down. I'll have to ask Shipley to find me another."

"I suppose we've lost the coat now," Phyllis said.

"I'll try again this evening," I said. "But now I must have a bath, and sleep."

"Of course," said Phyllis. "I'm so glad you're back."

"Thank you!" I said, pleased that she had been concerned about me. "I must say, so am I. I was beginning to have visions of being tried for Sharpe's murder."

"Since Simmons is so obtuse about William and Mr Neville, I fear it would not have been entirely impossible," said Phyllis. "It doesn't bear thinking about."

I looked in on Flora to tell her I was back, and she too was glad for my return. I had to admit to her that it had resulted in some evidence being lost, but she did not blame me. I left her to her embroidery, and finally had the hot bath I had been fantasising about all day.

I got a little sleep, and went out to see if the coat-wearer was in evidence, but there was no sign of him. Why had I not at least asked his name? It might still be possible to track him down, although going around mentioning a coat was dangerous since it might alert the Rector to the fact that the evidence was at large, and also that I was still determined to bring him to justice.

~

The following day, I waited for the man without result. Beatrice and Phyllis continued to stay at Ramsburgh, since Beatrice's nerves were still in a bad way, and we all felt that she was safer here.

Then on Tuesday morning, I received an unexpected letter: from Mr Neville himself. It read as follows:

> St Ninian's Rectory, Hawksbridge
>
> Dear Mr Rufford,
>
> I am sorry to hear that you have recently been the subject of police attention. It must be difficult when one's reputation is besmirched, for no good reason.
>
> I feel I may have been a little hasty and rude when we discussed artistic matters in previous weeks. As an incomer with no power, it was not for you to influence the outcome of the Mural Committee's deliberations. So by way of apology I wish to offer you a handshake of reconciliation, and refreshments, at the Rectory on Wednesday evening at eight o'clock, if this is agreeable to you. My groom will be happy to look after your horse, which I hear is a delightful bay mare.
>
> Yours cordially,
>
> Horace Neville

"Well!" said Phyllis when I showed it to her in the drawing room. "Can you credit the cheek of the man? I take it you aren't taken in by his smarmy tone? What an absolute devil."

"Don't worry – he doesn't convince me," I said. "He evidently enjoyed reminding me about my tarnished reputation – thereby putting me in my place – and I think he may also be referring to Shaw's verbal attacks on him."

"And perhaps to your own investigations into him," said Phyllis. "And by mentioning Celeste, I suppose he is telling you that he is keeping his eye on you."

"Good point," I said. "So – should I go?"

"Seriously?" said Phyllis. "You would even consider for a second walking into the lion's den? I cannot possibly allow you to take such a chance!"

"It would certainly be a risk," I said, "but by doing nothing, there is also a risk to William, and in the future, if Neville remains free, to us all. By going to his house, I might learn something important – perhaps a weakness that allows us to make some progress."

"Such as?"

"I have no idea," I admitted. "Perhaps something unguarded he says."

"That is equally true of you," Phyllis said. "You might let something slip too. He's clever, and he must have a reason for inviting you."

"It's possible, and I would have to be vigilant about engaging in nothing but the most neutral conversation."

"Easier said than done," said Phyllis.

"I know," I said. "But consider this – what if I refuse to go? Then he knows I am his enemy. That might be dangerous. At least if I go, I am not immediately admitting any such thing."

Phyllis sighed. "Perhaps. But what do you think he wants to talk about, Thomas? To warn you off? To persuade you he is as white as the driven snow?"

"Who knows?" I said. "Who knows the mind of an ordained murderer?"

~

St Ninian's Rectory made a show of pious austerity, with its blocky, unadorned stone façade, but it did not fool me. It was large and well-appointed: Mr Neville lived a luxurious life and it was not impossible to see how a man, after making a bad misstep, could be motivated to compound it in order to retain such a living. Especially, I reflected, when the alternative might be a short time spent inside a noose. It was not lost on me that I was up against all the wiles that came from the survival instinct, a motivation I would be well advised to adopt myself.

I was shown through a hall – hung with dour portraits of former rectors – by a shortish, young butler with light hair, who might easily have been the man described by the ironmonger. He led me into a panelled drawing room, and Mr Neville rose from a comfortably-upholstered armchair to greet me.

"Mr Rufford!" he said, holding out his hand. "I'm so glad you could come. I regret the fact that we have never really had a proper conversation, at least one that doesn't involve contentious art."

"Thank you for inviting me, Mr Neville," I said, shaking his hand and searching for a compliment that would be expected from a guest. "I feel inspired by your home. It must be calming for the soul to have one's physical and aesthetic needs met so well."

"You are entirely right," said Mr Neville. "Some may call it indulgence, but it does allow for a purer contemplation of the divine than a more meagre home could provide. Of course, it cannot compare with your own. A castle, no less!"

I smiled, and the Rector continued: "I am reminded of the phrase, 'an Englishman's home is his castle,' which is meant to convey legal invulnerability. And yet a stranger did manage to penetrate your defences – how distressing that must have been!"

"It was a shock," I said. "But it's a rare enough event, I believe."

"And to be accused of murder! Even more shocking," said Mr Neville, handing me a glass of port that had already been poured for me. "Perhaps it was some kind of – warning?"

I was not going to let myself be intimidated. "Yes, a warning from God to keep me from the sin of complacency!" I said with a laugh. "I will take a much more serious view of security in future."

He frowned, obviously annoyed that his arrow had bounced straight off its target.

"I quite agree," he said. "The security of oneself and one's loved ones is of the utmost importance. One cannot be too careful."

"Indeed so," I said, evenly, and sipped my port.

"You are not yet married," he said. "Perhaps some of the young women of Hawksbridge have caught your eye?"

"Not really," I said. "I have some good friends who are female, but I do not have designs on any of them at present."

"What a pity," said Mr Neville. "It might allow you to settle down and see what is important in life. You might be grateful for a future that includes a loving wife and children. Miss Drummond might make a gratifying partner, perhaps?"

"I'm sure she's far too busy writing her novels to give marriage a passing thought," I said, finding Mr Neville's probing distinctly uncomfortable.

"Or perhaps Miss Davison, since she is already in close proximity? You must know her very well by now."

"Likewise, too devoted to her work, Mr Neville, charming person though she is."

"Ah, all these delightful friends," he continued. "You are a lucky man. I do so hope they live long and fruitful lives."

At this point, I was getting fed up with his insinuations, and this last remark was direct to the point of ineptitude. Against my better judgement, I replied, "Any reason why they should not?"

"Oh, I'm sure not," Mr Neville said, "with sufficient care and wisdom."

I decided to put to the test the motto, 'attack is the best form of defence'.

"And what of you, Mr Neville? I assume you are a widower, in which case, you have my heartfelt condolences."

"Thank you, Mr Rufford," he replied. "Yes, my wife died eight years ago, God rest her beautiful soul. A canker of the brain, I regret to say."

"How awful," I said, draining my port glass. "But at least one might be glad that she did not have to suffer these trying – perhaps frightening – times in Hawksbridge." I could do my own insinuating, if I pleased.

He nodded. "Yes," he said, "even death can have its comforts."

He put his glass down and turned to face me squarely. "Now then, Mr Rufford," he said in a less placid tone than before, "are we to be friends? It would be agreeable to know that we can count on each other. Cooperation is such a powerful and important notion in a civilised society. Without it, we have only chaos and pain. I'm sure you hate these things as much as I do, eh, Mr Rufford?"

At that moment, when I should have reined in my feelings and let him hear what he wanted to hear, I let my utter contempt with this vile man get the better of me.

"But the trick, Mr Neville, is knowing with whom to cooperate in the interests of progress, truth and justice, would you not agree?" I said.

He considered this, gave a bitter, short-lived smile, and started to walk towards the door. "I will have your horse brought around, Mr Rufford," he said. "Thank you for honouring me with your time."

~

On the north road to Ramsburgh, the evening light was nearly gone, and the moon was struggling to make an appearance. The world was painted grey, and in addition, an alarming haze filled my eyes. I struggled to balance on Celeste and my head pounded. I had only consumed one glass of port: why should it have had such an effect on me? Too late, I realised that the glass – already sitting, full, on its silver tray – must have been drugged. I tried desperately to focus on the road ahead and keep upright, but the haze was getting worse. I knew I had to get off my horse before I fell off, and so with difficulty I slipped from Celeste onto the ground, and lay there, powerless to get up.

I heard the sound of another horse: vague shadows filled my eyes, and I felt blows rain down on me. Then came excruciating pain, and all went dark.

# CHAPTER THIRTY-TWO

BEFORE I opened my eyes, I heard faint scratching sounds. Had a mouse got inside my head? It certainly felt like something was in my skull and beating a tattoo. My limbs were filled with pain, too, and my face felt swollen.

I tried moving my eyelids, and reluctantly they opened to reveal a world that was far too bright. At least it was my world – my familiar, comforting bedroom. Gradually I became accustomed to the light, and turned my head – painfully – to find the source of the scratching. Sitting next to my bed, Phyllis was busy with a notebook and pencil. For a minute, I watched her; unaware that I was awake, she converted inspiration into grey marks with the energy of a squirrel hunting nuts. Every now and again, the pencil would stop, and her eyes would dart to the window, to the walls, to the ceiling, as the ideas filled her head before once more spilling over onto the page.

Despite my swollen face, I smiled, waiting for her gaze to come to rest on me.

"Oh!" she said, jumping a little in surprise. "You're awake!"

"Yes," I said, hoarsely. "I'm sorry to disturb your thoughts. I was enjoying watching you write."

Phyllis closed her notebook and placed it under her chair.

"Don't worry," I said. "I'm in no shape to take a peek. What time is it?"

"About four in the afternoon," she said. "We found you around one in the morning. You scared us all – they gave you quite a beating. How are you feeling?"

"Groggy, to be honest," I said. "Could I have some

water?"

"Of course," she said, and went to pour some water from a jug on the chest of drawers.

"I can't believe everyone has to look after me again," I said after I had taken some painful sips of water. "I'm sorry to be so much trouble."

"Don't be silly," said Phyllis. "You didn't ask to be beaten black and blue. Whoever it was, took your coat. Did you have any money in it?"

"Oh, damn, yes," I said. "I had a few guineas. But – what about Celeste? Did they take her?"

"Thankfully, no. We found her wandering not far away from you. She's safe."

"Good, good," I said and sank back on the pillow. "When did you start looking for me?"

"I waited until midnight, and then Mr Shipley and I came in my pony-trap, and Flora followed in hers. There was a little moonlight, but it was heavy going."

"Thank you," I said. "That's the second time you've had to rescue me. It was stupid going to see Mr Neville. The bastard drugged me – please excuse my language."

"Drugged you? Oh! We thought you were drowsy because of the beating. How awful."

"His lackey probably meant to kill me, and make it look like a burglary," I said.

"Or a warning?"

"I think Neville may have got beyond warnings," I said. "He dropped some heavy hints not to make trouble, and I'm afraid I lost my cool."

"Oh, Thomas! Whatever did you say?"

"He said we should cooperate, and I said something about needing to choose who to cooperate with. It was meant to rile him, and it obviously did. I'm sorry."

"You silly thing! That's the trouble with men – they always have to feel they've had the last word. No wonder the world has so many wars."

"I know, I know. I couldn't help it. He was being so obnoxious."

"Do you think we should tell the police?" Phyllis said.

"Ha!" I said. "I can't imagine that would do me any good. The Inspector will just say it was a robber who will be miles away by now. And I will get an even worse reputation for crying wolf."

"I suppose so. Anyway, I don't understand why Neville would try to win you round, if he was going to drug you and then beat you up anyway."

"I suspect the drugging was to confirm he meant business and show his power," I said, "but then he decided I wasn't going to cooperate, so when he went to tell his man to get Celeste for me, he ordered him to follow and assault me."

"I do wish you hadn't provoked him," said Phyllis. "Well, what's done is done. Now you just need to rest."

"How can I?" I said. "That damned coat of his is out there. We need to find it."

"Don't worry about that now," said Phyllis. "I think that's my father coming."

Dr Drummond's characteristic, slow plod up the stairs, accompanied by heavy sighs, gave him away.

"Good afternoon, Mr Rufford," he said as he put his bag on the end of the bed and drew a chair up to the bed. "Now then. What did I warn you to do, on more than one occasion?"

"To stay out of trouble?" I said.

"And what have you done?" he said, taking my pulse.

"Dived right back into it, Dr Drummond. Head first, it seems. Sorry – I'm incorrigible."

"But it was all in a good cause," said Phyllis.

"Oh?" said her father. "And what cause can be good enough for a man to end up looking like a punch-bag?"

"I'm afraid I can't say," I said. "Not just yet."

"Ah – a man of mystery," said Dr Drummond, drily.

"How exciting. Still playing detective? Or perhaps you are now a spy, saving us all from the French. Now then, let's have a look at these bruises."

The doctor examined me thoroughly, and thought that aside from a cracked rib or two, I had not come to serious harm.

"They'll heal, Mr Rufford, if you're very careful. And that means no more spying! Rest, rest, and more rest is what you need."

He shook his head. "I don't know what you've been up to, Mr Rufford, but you really need to stop it. If you rush about like this, how will you find yourself a wife? A father-in-law needs to feel the lad has his feet on the ground." And he looked at Phyllis, and then at me. The poor man evidently had hopes in this direction, and I was immensely flattered and touched.

"I take your point," I said, "and I will do my utmost to reform. Thank you."

Shaking his head again, he got up. "When are you coming back home, my dear?" he said. "The house feels strange without you."

"Not long now, I promise, Father. Perhaps a couple of weeks."

Dr Drummond sighed and said, "Goodbye, Mr Rufford. Remember: no spying! Goodbye, my dear."

~

Shipley found me a cane that belonged to Mr Kington, and the next day, Friday, I was able to hobble around the grounds, Fox impatiently circling my feet. I knew how he felt. I was desperate to advance the Neville case, with William Harkness' trial growing nearer. But I was aware that I had to consolidate my strength first, so I spent some time in my closet, enjoying my supply of Iona Tavistock novels and – I blush to mention it – refreshing my memory of certain Roman frescoes. To my mind, possessing energy for this small pleasure was a hopeful sign for my recovery.

When I awoke on Saturday, I felt sufficiently improved to plot a search for the coat. I asked Shipley for a likely starting place, given the man's direction and occupation, and he suggested a hamlet a few miles north of Ramsburgh, by the name of Sallingham. I found Phyllis in the library, scribbling some notes from a history of Spain.

"But," she said when I had told her my plan, "you heard what my father said!"

"I know, but I have rested," I said. "Anyway, I'm too anxious to relax properly. I have to find this evidence. If – and when – I find it, then I'll take your father's advice, I promise."

"You mean, when *we* find it!" said Phyllis, closing her notebook.

"Phyllis, I can't let you put yourself in danger –"

"Fiddlesticks!" said Phyllis. "I'm coming with you, or you're not going at all."

I smiled. "Well, at present I dare say you have the power to restrain me. If you insist. Shall we make a start in, say, half an hour? We can take your pony trap, as I don't think I'm up to riding just yet."

I put on an old coat and collected a handful of guineas from the safe, in case bribes were necessary, and we were soon on the road to Sallingham, with a few supplies that Mrs Felton had kindly packed for us. It was not quite the picnic excursion I had previously imagined, but it was companionable nevertheless.

"I expect he'll be at work," I said, "but at least we might find out where he is, and when he might be back."

"I suppose Mr Neville's lackey might have it by now," said Phyllis.

"Possibly, but we cannot assume that," I said. "But even the absence of the coat would be evidence, would it not? A man who matches the description of Neville's servant comes and snatches or buys a stained coat – highly suspicious behaviour."

"I hadn't thought of that," said Phyllis. "Whether stupid Inspector Simmons would take it into account is another matter."

After half an hour we turned onto a road that was little more than a dirt track, as Shipley had instructed, and then after another quarter of an hour, a worn milestone told us that we were entering Sallingham, a string of small cottages. Outside the second cottage, children were playing, and their mother was sitting on the doorstep mending a pinafore. I struggled out of the pony trap and raised my hat to the young mother. She looked at me and Phyllis with puzzlement.

"Good day, ma'am!" I said. "I wonder if you can help me. My friend and I are looking for someone who offered to sell me his coat. I don't suppose you would know where he lives? It's a black, rather clerical-looking coat with some stains."

Her brow furrowed. "I know the one you mean," she said after a moment. "It's trouble. Are you here to make trouble?"

"Not at all, ma'am, I assure you," I said. "In fact, I believe I have been at the receiving end of the trouble you speak of, as you can see." I waved the cane. "I simply want to buy the coat and leave. I am here with some money, as I missed the chance to buy it previously."

"Well, you both look all right," she said. "Yes, Beadie will want to speak to you, I expect. He's at number twelve."

"Thank you very much, ma'am," I said. "I am very grateful to you." Phyllis smiled at her and her children, who had stopped their play to stare at them.

I walked with the trap as Phyllis drove it to number twelve, and she got down and tied the pony to the house's gate post.

With trepidation, we knocked on the door. A middle-aged woman answered the door, and she had a frightened look on her face.

"Yes?" she said, folding her arms.

"I'm sorry to disturb you, ma'am, but I believe a man named Beadie lives here – your husband? – who was going to sell me his coat."

She did not confirm this, but said, "What do you want?"

"I would like to complete the bargain," I said, "if it's still for sale."

"Let me check," she said, and closed the door. A moment later, the door opened again and she ushered us inside.

In the dingy front room, a familiar figure lay in a makeshift bed, cuts and bruises on his face.

"Ah!" he said, sitting up with a groan. "You found me." He peered at my cane and swollen face. "Oh Lord," he chuckled, "we've both drunk from the same cup, haven't we, sir?"

"I think we have!" I said. "Was it a fair-haired young man?"

"That's he. Make yourself comfortable, sir – ma'am – and I'll tell you all about it."

Beadie's wife brought two chairs over, and we sat down.

"This fellow came a couple of days ago, nasty looking man – that sour, his mam's teat must have gone dry when he were a nipper – and said he'd been told that someone had found a coat that didn't belong to them. I should have said I didn't know anything about it, but I says to him, 'Oh no, sir, I found a coat that *does* belong to me, seeing as I found it.' And he says, no, it's stolen property, and for me to hand it over at once. And I says, 'I can't do that, because I don't have it any more.' Which is true, sir, because I lent it to old Joseph, who feels the cold terrible."

He stopped to cough, and then took a few seconds to recover from the pain of doing so.

"Lord. That divvie can punch. So, I lent it to Joseph, and I thought to myself, I'm not going to tell him where Joseph is, for one thing, because this fellow doesn't look the friendly type, and for another, if so many people are after this coat, it has to be worth summat!"

I nodded. "So what did you tell him?" I asked.

"Said I'd burned it when I couldn't get the stains out!" He chortled, and continued, "I were pleased with that. But he weren't. Went into a right radge, yarked me in the face in front of Kathy – but I still didn't tell. Then he went over the place trying to find it. Which he didn't, of course. Then he beat me, more thorough, like, and swore like a sailor in a swarm of bees, and walked out."

"I'm very sorry, Mr –"

"Beadnell. Folk call me Beadie."

"Mr Beadnell. So can I ask – where is the coat now?"

Mr Beadnell grinned. "Where indeed, sir, where indeed. Now, like I say, this coat has to be worth more than a guinea. I mean, look at me! I've earned a pretty wage for a busted snek, wouldn't you say, sir?"

"Would two guineas suffice, Mr Beadnell?"

"Well..." Mr Beadnell screwed up his face in thought. "That's better'n one, granted."

There was a pause, presumably for me to increase my offer.

"Three guineas, Mr Beadnell, and also a description of where you originally found it."

"Very fair, sir, very fair. Three guineas'll do it. I'll tell you where I found it. It were behind a hedge just by the milestone, on the north road on the edge of town. Found it on Tuesday morning previous, I think it were. Around dawn – no, an hour or so after."

"Thank you, Mr Beadnell! And the coat...?" I held the guineas ostentatiously in my hand, to encourage him.

"Kathy – can you get it? I would, sir, only I can't climb a

ladder at present! I stuffed it under the rafters, you see."

I looked at Phyllis – neither of us could believe our luck. But we weren't counting our chickens yet. Something was surely bound to go wrong – it would be the wrong coat, or it would have mysteriously vanished, or maybe Mr Beadnell's mind had been affected by his injuries and the truth was entirely different.

But sure enough, his wife emerged from the loft a short while later, holding Mr Neville's coat.

"There you are, sir," said Mrs Beadnell. "I must say, what a lot of fuss about a coat!"

"Thank you, Mrs Beadnell, and Mr Beadnell," I said. "I'm very grateful, and I'm sorry you had to go through this." I placed the guineas in Mr Beadnell's hands, and he was entranced by them. He had probably never seen this amount of money before in his life.

"Na, thank *you*, sir, I'm sure," Mr Beadnell said. "I just wish I had another coat, for your lass!" And he winked at me.

~

Mrs Beadnell offered us a bite to eat, but we declined politely as we were anxious to get the coat – and ourselves – to safety.

As we made our way back, the coat hidden in a sack that Mrs Beadnell had provided, our nerves and the length of time we had been on the road meant that we were visited by calls of nature. We stopped at a suitable hedge, and one at a time, we aroused the curiosity of a herd of cows. I could not speak for Phyllis, but I found this intimate task increased my sense of fellowship with my friend. It was not possible to stand on ceremony in this situation, when knowledge of what the other was doing could not be hidden. In addition, there was something sublimely primordial about performing this duty in the open air, next to the beasts of the field and under blue skies.

We finally arrived back at Ramsburgh, still prickling with the dread of being intercepted, and thankfully stuffed the coat into the Ramsburgh safe. By now, it was sufficiently late in the afternoon to justify a glass of wine, which I desperately needed, and Phyllis went to fetch Beatrice so that we could give her our news.

I had hoped that in the last few days, following Sharpe's intrusion, she might have rested and mended her nerves a little. But when she came in, that notion was dismissed, as she had been crying, and looked thin and wan.

She settled herself on the sofa and dabbed her face with a handkerchief. "William's trial starts next week," she said, quietly, trying to suppress further tears. "Constable Taylor kindly came to tell me."

"Oh, Bea!" Phyllis said, and went to sit next to her, and put her arm around her. "I'm so sorry. But it will be all right."

"That is vexing news, Mrs Harkness," I said. "I'm very sorry to hear it. But we have something that might cheer you up."

"Oh yes?" said Beatrice, looking up at me, her eyes widening.

"We have Mr Neville's coat, complete with blood stains, and an account of when and where it was found that incriminates the owner."

"No!" she said, looking at Phyllis and then back at me again. "This is some kind of joke, isn't it? Please don't tease me, Mr Rufford. I can't bear it." And the tears began to flow once more.

"It's no joke, Mrs Harkness – the coat is in the safe, right here in Ramsburgh. Now, proving that Mr Neville was wearing it at the time of the murder is not straightforward. But it is very strong circumstantial evidence nevertheless."

"That, and the hammer evidence," said Phyllis, "could be

enough for us to finally go to the police and make our case."

Beatrice dried her eyes and said, "Oh, thank you! Thank you, thank you, thank you!"

"However," I said, taking a draught of wine, "there is a small but not insignificant chance that Simmons will be blinded both by his conviction that William is the killer, and by his antipathy to me and by extension, my friends."

"Oh," said Beatrice, her shoulders slumping. "I do hope not – after everything!"

"So," I said, "I have another proposal to make to you both. It's not without risk, but if it works, it might seal the Rector's fate, once and for all."

# CHAPTER THIRTY-THREE

SINCE she was estranged from Phyllis and avoided contact with her whenever possible, Flora did not usually attend church. But I persuaded her to overcome her scruples this time. And so the four of us found ourselves in the Ramsburgh pew near the front of the church: Flora, Phyllis, Beatrice and myself. I had my cane, and a carpet bag borrowed from Mrs Felton that I had placed at my feet. For once, I was pleased to see Inspector Simmons, several pews away, and we nodded formally at each other.

When Mr Neville climbed the pulpit to give his sermon, he followed his usual habit of scanning the congregation, as if searching for the most sinful of us on which to target his two principal weapons: reproach and platitude. I met his gaze unflinchingly, and to my satisfaction I detected a small indication of discomfort on his face.

His theme today was forgiveness. As he started his pious observations, I opened my bag, and put on a coat.

"Luke taught us," he boomed, "to love your enemies, do good to those who hate you, bless those who curse you, and pray for those who abuse you."

When he paused to let these words sink in, I stood up.

"Malamor!" I said loudly, and Phyllis hissed at me, "What are you doing?" and the assembled congregation turned sternly towards me as if I had lost my mind.

The Rector started, and looked at me. I could see the fear in his eyes, as he recognised his own coat.

"That is outrageous, sir! Why are you wearing my – that coat? Please do not interrupt my sacred duties. Kindly leave this church."

"Malamor!" I repeated.

"How dare you!" he said. "Why are you saying that?"

"Is that what you showed to Mr Walker and Mr Shaw?" I said. "Love for your enemies, Mr Malamor?"

The Rector gripped the pulpit, the veins standing out on his temples. "May I remind you, Mr Rufford, that the last man to call me Malamor is no longer alive!"

Then he realised what he had said. "That's not what I meant, of course."

"It's the truth, though, isn't it?" I said, leaning on my cane. "Mr Walker called you Malamor, even when you had offered the hand of friendship, as a fellow artist. Is that what happened? Your hidden admiration for – and jealousy of – the talents of Walker and Shaw led you to their cottage. Walker poured you a glass of port, which neither Shaw nor Walker drank, but which had clearly been drunk by someone that night, and you tried to ingratiate yourself with Walker, perhaps talking about your own efforts as an artist, many years ago."

"Rubbish!" scoffed the Rector.

"But Walker offered you nothing but contempt and humiliation. Your campaign against the pair of them had exasperated him, and he finally got to speak his mind. He compared you with the hated figure of Malamor, a caricature of an evil cleric from a popular novel he had just read, and you could not stand it. You pushed him, and he hit his head. He might have been saved, but you left him to die."

The Inspector got up and tried to reach me in our pew, but Flora and Beatrice blocked his path.

"This is nonsense! Leave this instant!" the Rector raged.

"And then, because you thought Shaw would expose the real cause of Walker's death, you decided to kill him. He could not be left to rant and rail against you. So, under cover of a scurrilous letter to provoke Mr Harkness and make him look guilty, you attacked Shaw with a hammer rather like this one."

I drew the new hammer from my bag and brandished it.

The Rector went from puce to pale.

"This is a new hammer. The second of its kind to be purchased at Cramlington's for several weeks. The previous purchase was to replace the old hammer you used to brutally murder Mr Shaw."

The curate was now looking intently at the Rector.

"You showed me the replacement hammer, did you not, Mr Garrard?" I said.

"I did, Mr Rufford," he said. "You asked me to hammer down a loose nail on your pony trap."

The Rector laughed. "This gets more absurd by the minute. Why would I be so stupid as to leave the weapon at the scene of the crime?"

"Because you still had a small scrap of humanity left in you, and you could not bring yourself to retrieve a hammer that still had traces of Mr Shaw's brains on it. So you abandoned it and ran."

"There is absolutely no evidence –"

"And then there's this coat, Mr Neville," I continued. "The one you were wearing when you killed Shaw. You can still see the bloodstains. You hid it under a hedge, but before you could retrieve and destroy it, someone found it. And now I have it, Mr Malamor, despite your attempts to discredit and kill me."

"Stop calling me that!" the Rector bellowed. "I will not have it, not from you, not from Walker, not from anyone! I will be respected, as I deserve! If you had all simply listened to me, none of this would have been necessary!"

The Inspector had stopped trying to get into my pew, and was now staring at the Rector. He started to walk towards the pulpit.

"Mr Neville," he said, "I need to ask you a few questions, so we can ascertain the truth of what Mr Rufford is alleging."

The Rector's eyes were wild, and he was evidently

deciding what to do. He suddenly bolted down the pulpit stairs and rushed for the door near the vestry. The Inspector ran after him, and McPhee followed along with a few other brave members of the congregation. The Rector fell in his haste, and was soon restrained, and to my immense relief, I could hear Mr Simmons saying, "Mr Horace Neville, I am arresting you on suspicion of the murders of Mr Edward Walker and Mr Henry Shaw."

~

Neville had been hustled out of the door by the vestry. As the bewildered congregation sat in silence trying to comprehend what had just happened, Francesca was the first to start the applause. It quickly spread through the church. Still standing and leaning on my cane, I was exhausted by the effort of making my speech, and shocked by what I had done. I recovered my composure enough to smile an acknowledgement to the crowd, and then I noticed that Phyllis was looking pale and miserable, so I sat down and put my arm around her.

Francesca came up to us. "Thomas! You were wonderful!" she said. "I had no idea about the Rector. What a ghastly wretch he is! I didn't like him, but I didn't imagine he was a murderer. Are you all right, all of you? Do you need anything?"

"Thank you, Francesca!" I said. "You are very kind. I think we will just need to catch our breath here."

"Of course – I will leave you, but you must all come and be my guests soon. I promise there will be no monkeys."

She left, and gradually, the worshippers filed out of the church, whispering to each other, and the four of us were left in silence to consider our accomplishment.

Phyllis eventually managed to smile at me and say, "Well done, Thomas. Thank goodness it worked. You certainly know how to rile a man up."

"Thank you so much, Mr Rufford," said Beatrice. "I imagine this means that William can be released?"

"Well, it should," I said, "but the processes of law may take a few days. We should head over to the police office. They will no doubt be coming to fetch us shortly anyway."

"Henry will get justice," Flora said, touching my arm. "Thank you, Thomas!"

"You're very welcome," I said. "Now, please help me take this awful coat off. It reeks."

~

It was a rather different Mr Simmons who came in bearing a cup of coffee for me in the interview room.

"Well, well, Mr Rufford," he said. "It's not often that I'm lost for words, but I'm damned if I can even start to think what to say."

"It's been an unusual day, Inspector, so it's entirely forgiveable."

"Yes, well," said Mr Simmons, "the Rector was going on about forgiveness, before you interrupted him, so I had better get that part over with. I'm sorry I didn't take you a bit more seriously, sir. Mr Neville put on a pretty good show, what with –"

"It's fine, Inspector," I said. "The important thing is, he's now in custody. I take it you've charged him?"

"Yes, Mr Rufford. On top of your evidence, he condemned himself out of his own mouth, so it was an easy decision to make."

"And Mr Harkness will be released?"

"Very soon, yes. I'm sorry about Mr Harkness. This must have been very difficult for him."

"In so many ways, yes," I said. "But now he can start to recover from it, and perhaps in time he'll be reconciled with Mrs Harkness."

"One can but hope, sir, one can but hope," said Mr Simmons. "Now the paperwork, I'm afraid, sir. You brought Mr Neville's coat?"

"Yes, Inspector, I handed it to Mr Taylor when I came in."

I answered many more questions to Mr Simmons' satisfaction. I had to admit that when recapitulating all that had happened, my efforts seemed not unimpressive. Of course, I was careful to acknowledge the help I had had from my friends.

When the interview ended, we shook hands.

"Thank you, sir. I wouldn't recommend you get yourself involved with the pursuit of justice all the time, Mr Rufford – not unless you want to join us in an official capacity! – but in this particular case, you have been very helpful, no question."

"I'm glad, Inspector. No, I have no plans to join the police, or to become embroiled in anything else. I just want to go home to my bed."

"An excellent plan, sir. Good day!"

~

I went with Flora back to Ramsburgh, and Phyllis and Beatrice went to the Harkness home, where Mrs Harkness could start to rebuild her life.

"Do you think Mr Harkness could ever forgive his wife?" asked Flora as Jenny stoically pulled us up the hill. "Once trust has been betrayed like that..."

"I think William will have to remember that Mr Walker was a very persuasive man. Using his imminent demise from tuberculosis as a seduction technique was unusual, to say the least. In my opinion, that kind of emotional blackmail absolves Beatrice."

"And there was no truth in Mrs Harkness having an affair with Mr Shaw as well?"

"None whatsoever," I said.

"Good," she said. "Now *that*, I think, would have been too hard for even a saint to forgive."

We travelled in silence for a few minutes, and then I said, "I have to confess, I enjoyed being treated in a civilised way by Mr Simmons, for a change. I actually detected a modicum of respect when I went over the business with the hammer."

"He must feel mortified that he didn't think of it himself," said Flora.

"Yes, I hope he doesn't feel too badly about it," I said. "No one's perfect."

Flora smiled. "That's very generous of you," she said, "considering how he treated you."

"Not really," I replied. "It just comes from self-knowledge. There's always room for redemption and forgiveness – or I am a condemned man, for my many sins."

"Goodness! Do you mean to try for the position of Rector? You might look good in a surplice. And you made quite a speech this morning."

"Wild horses wouldn't drag me to a seminary," I said. "I have no right telling other people what to do, when I have enough doubts about myself."

"Perhaps, Thomas," said Flora, "for one day at least, you might allow yourself a little pride in your achievements!"

"I will," I said. "I suppose I've earned it – that, and sleeping like a rock for the rest of the day."

# CHAPTER THIRTY-FOUR

NOT long after, I was strong enough to take Celeste up to Sallingham and thank Beadie and his wife for the role they had played in the Rector's arrest. I took him a new coat, of quite a different style to the Rector's, and he was so pleased that he gave me an item that was a perfect gift for Bess. On the way to her cottage, this warm, living offering nearly escaped the voluminous pocket in my coat.

"Oh, Thomas!" she said when I pressed the wriggling, jet-black ball of fur into her hands. "How wonderful – I have been missing Fossil so! Is it a he, or a she?"

"A she," I said. "I hope she's not too much trouble."

"I'm sure not. And anyway, she can't be any more trouble than you, can she?"

She kissed me on the lips, and then went to find something for the cat to eat and turn a basket and a blanket into a nest for her. I stood in the kitchen doorway as she fussed over the animal, and they made a delightful pair. It was touching to see her lavish her affection on the kitten, which was more curious about, than agitated by, its new surroundings.

Finally the kitten exhausted itself and curled up to sleep in the basket. Bess carefully brought the basket into the sitting room, and we sat on the sofa.

"So!" she said, running her hands through my hair and caressing my cheek. "How is my hero? The Hawksbridge Herald was full of your praises. Is it all going to your head?"

"I don't think so," I said. "I'm just glad that this strange initiation rite into Hawksbridge society is over."

"I am too," she said. "I was so worried – though had I

known the truth, I would have been much more so!"

"I'm sorry I couldn't tell you everything. It might have put you in danger too."

"I gather the Rector confessed," Bess said. "I suppose that will put less burden on your evidence."

"Yes – the evidence has had its greatest use already, in provoking him. In the end, his temper proved greater than his wits."

"I don't want to think about that dreadful man any more, Thomas. Kiss me, please."

I obliged, and kissed her lingeringly on the lips. "Like this?"

"It's a start," she said.

~

Francesca invited me to ride with her on the following Saturday. She had some useful advice to give me about controlling Celeste, whom she admired tremendously.

"I have you to myself at last," she said, as we skirted woodland near Halfpenny House. "How things have changed since I first came to visit you!"

"Yes, and not all for the worse," I said. "I have made good friends, and my mettle has been tested. In a strange way, it's what needed to happen. I found myself questioning my purpose, and I have at least some answer to that."

"And only three people needed to die to accomplish it!" she said.

"What a ghoul you are," I said, and I leaned over and tapped her lightly on the back with my whip in rebuke. "But it's four, if you count Mr Neville," I said. "I fear he's headed for the gallows."

"Good riddance," said Francesca. "Let's hope the Bishop

vets the next incumbent more carefully."

"Sometimes, it's impossible to tell what people are capable of – good or bad. People like Mr Neville will always slip through the net, I'm afraid."

"You are beginning to sound like a policeman, Thomas! Don't tell me you're tempted by that life?"

"I'm more tempted to open up a string of coffee shops for ladies!" I said. "On the other hand, I'm happy to lie fallow for a while and read my Swifts and my Tavistocks."

"Interesting – very different kinds of book," said Francesca.

"Different is good. That's why I like you," I said. "You are quite unlike anyone else I know."

"So I've been told," she said, wielding her whip and breaking into a gallop.

She stopped, and when I caught up with her, she was watching me with an amused expression. "Very good, Thomas! You'll be galloping soon. When we're flank to flank and all out of breath, it will be glorious, just you wait and see!"

"I look forward to it, ma'am," I said, examining her face to see whether the double meaning was deliberate. She was either being entirely sincere, or she was a good poker player, and I strongly suspected the latter.

"Shall we go back for tea?" she said.

"Yes, please," I said. "You have quite worn me out."

"It's something I excel at," she said, and she deftly turned her horse around.

~

"You never told me about the incident with Mr Sharpe," Francesca said as she poured the tea. "I read about it in the paper, of course."

"There's not much more to tell," I said. "I had the money to give him – which I didn't mention to the police – but first he wanted to give a little speech about how Hazel's death was my fault. If he hadn't been so aggressive, maybe I wouldn't have rung the bell, and simply fetched the money, and he might have lived."

"But of course, he might still have come back and threatened you again."

"Yes," I said, "which is why his death makes me so uncomfortable – it's convenient for me. Mr Neville knew exactly how to get to me, by having me arrested for Sharpe's murder. I almost felt responsible."

"Don't be silly, Thomas. You're not."

"But now the police here know about Hazel," I said. "I suppose there's a faint chance that their correspondence with the police in London will open things up again."

"No, Thomas, you've suffered enough. Let's put those fears to bed. On which subject," she said, taking a long sip of tea to mischievously give me time to wonder just what she was going to say, "would you like to see what I've done with my bedroom?"

"I'd love to," I said, and drained my cup.

~

I stood furtively at the threshold of Francesca's bedroom, wondering if any servants were about.

"Come, Thomas!" said Francesca. "It's just a room."

But when I entered, I found it was hardly just that. The strange image that immediately formed in my mind was that it was the wheel-house of the magnificent ship *Francesca Campbell*, ploughing through life's ocean flying a flag of passion, beauty and defiance.

Its walls were adorned with red and gold wallpaper, patterned with vases and flowers. Several large ornate mirrors made it possible to view parts of the room from several angles at once. A couch, and a group of chairs and a small table, gave it the aspect of a luxurious sitting room, as did the richly-coloured Persian carpets on the polished floor. On a cabinet in one corner, Cupid and Psyche were frozen in a fervent marble embrace. The star in the room's firmament, though, was undoubtedly the ancient four-poster, draped with fleur-de-lis curtains recalling medieval French aristocracy.

I stood for a moment, taking all this in, and then my eye was drawn to a secretaire with a glass bookcase above. I had always liked the ingenuity of these pieces: the fold-down front made to look like two drawers, the sliding brass fittings that held the open front level, and the way the drawer – complete with pigeon holes and fretwork frills – slid out to form a desk. I opened it up and ran my fingers over the polished surfaces, and then turned back to Francesca, who was waiting expectantly.

"Well? What do you think?" she said.

"Incredible," I said. "It's exquisite. I suppose," I added, turning back to the secretaire, "this is where you write all your love letters."

"Oh yes," Francesca said, throwing herself onto the couch and adopting the pose of a love-lorn maiden. "To my many, many lovers."

"Did they include Walker, or Shaw?" I asked. "I think you were a little... disingenuous about how friendly you became with them."

"Goodness!" she said. "Surely we can forget all about them now?"

"I'm just curious," I said. "It was a piece of the jigsaw I never could fit. There you were, in the middle of it all. Posing for Walker, friendly with Shaw... what went on in that cottage?"

"Oh, gracious, Thomas. Do I detect annoyance that I had a little amusement with them? Well, you can hardly expect a woman to spill the beans on such private matters. But perhaps I had too much to drink once or twice, and perhaps in that state, we were... convivial. But that, my fine friend, is all you will get from me on the subject."

She got up and walked to the window. "Wouldn't it be wonderful to be in love again – really in love? What fun. A fluttering heart, and indescribable yearnings. But, alas, I'm not an eighteen-year-old virgin any more. I have a rather more measured view of relations between the sexes."

"You, measured?" I said. "I can't see it. I think you will always favour the heart over the head – certainly from what you have just told me. And why else all this?" I gestured at the room.

She smiled. "I think it would be wonderful to fall in love with you. Shall I? Then I would have all the head massages I could desire."

"You might have those for the asking," I said. "I will absolve you of the need for romantic attachment. I know you better than to think I could possess you."

"Am I so transparent? And so flighty? Perhaps I am."

The room's wilful magic was difficult to fight against. "I admire you, of course," I said, moving to stand next to her. "You probably guessed."

"You are so sweet!" she said. "Yes, I guessed. But I can't stop you admiring me, even if I wanted to, which I don't. Who doesn't want to be admired?"

"Indeed," I said. "Anyway, I expect I should be going, since I'm in danger of becoming mawkish."

"Oh, I suppose so," she sighed. "Might you have time to pay just a little attention to my poor head?"

# EPILOGUE

AUTUMN had decisively banished the summer, and my female guests were clutching their shawls about them in the garden as we mingled before dinner. I had decided that I was ready to throw a party to entertain my new-found friends, as well as the more interesting acquaintances, and we had hired temporary staff for the occasion.

In the garden, I found myself in a little knot of people that included Flora. I had assured Flora that she would be at the opposite end of the table from Phyllis, and when I had pointed out the absurdity of her sitting in her tower while the rest of us enjoyed ourselves below, happily she had agreed to attend.

The ever-cheerful Mr McPhee had downed several glasses of wine and was a little flushed. He turned to Flora and said, "Miss Davison – let me offer you my congratulations on your recent commission. It will be wonderful, of that I have no doubt, having seen the quality of your work."

"Commission?" Mrs Harris asked. "May I ask the nature of it?"

Flora looked slightly embarrassed to be the focus of attention. "I have had the good fortune to be allowed to complete the Town Hall mural, with Mr Falkirk. Obviously we will be in the shadow of great artists, but we will do our best!"

"Oh, what marvellous news!" said Mrs Harris. "Will you be incorporating the angelic Mrs Campbell? I do hope so." She looked over at Francesca, deep in conversation under a tree with Mr Harris, who was clearly basking in the glow of her attention.

"Yes," Flora said, "we want to pay homage to Mr Shaw

and Mr Walker. So although the tone and technique of our work is quite different, we will make it work."

"Thank goodness! And poor Mrs Harkness?" said Mrs Harris.

"Unfortunately, not enough of her was completed, so she will be painted over," Flora said.

"What a pity!" said Mr McPhee. "She has such a lovely profile. But it may be just as well, in the circumstances. Does anyone know how Mr Harkness is? I must go and see him, when he's well enough."

"Phyllis told me that his nerves are recovering satisfactorily at home," said Mrs Harris. "And there is every prospect that he will be reconciled with Mrs Harkness."

"That is a relief," said Mr McPhee. "We miss his talents in the design department. Oh, speaking of which, Miss Davison," he added, taking another glass of wine from a passing tray, "thank you for your advice at the Pottery. Everyone is very pleased at how it's working out."

"You intrigue me," I said. "What has Flora done at the Pottery?"

McPhee tapped his nose with his finger. "I have said too much! Just wait and see, wait and see. I am excited to find out what everyone thinks!"

I wondered what it must be like to be such an optimistic person. He must have had his dark moments, but I had seen none. And today's enthusiasm was beyond the norm, so my curiosity was piqued.

I cast a querulous look at Flora, but she just smiled. It was good to see her fulfilled in her work – a new confidence was visible in her demeanour.

I was just about to go and see if I could rescue Francesca from Mr Harris, when Shipley came to announce that dinner was ready.

~

I was gratified by the bonhomie and ready flow of conversation. This was by far the largest social occasion I had ever presided over, and I had been nervous.

The first person to finish his duck breast was Mr Harris, a notably speedy eater, to his wife's chagrin. Arranging his knife and fork carefully on his plate, he turned to Phyllis and said, "Miss Drummond, I'm fascinated to know what it's like to be a distinguished author. Have you any insight for one who aspires to that life?"

"Thank you, Mr Harris," Phyllis said, "but I wouldn't call myself distinguished! I'm still relatively young, so it feels wrong to give advice. What works for me, may not work for others. And of course there is an infinite variety of authors, and kinds of book."

"But if you had just one piece of advice," Mr Harris persisted.

"Very well, Mr Harris, since you press me. If you speak of fiction, I would arrogantly quote from one of my own books: 'Where the heart leads, the head surely follows.'"

"Yes, yes!" cried Mrs Harris. "It's from 'The Author of Kingshorne Priory' – it's my favourite book of yours. In fact, if I may be so bold, it's my favourite book of any author! David, you simply must read it. It will inspire you."

"Gracious," said Phyllis. "I am truly flattered."

"Now, I must find that passage," said Mrs Harris, "or I'll be trying to remember it all evening. Does anyone have a copy?"

I nodded and got up from the table, and returned in a minute with the as-yet unread volume.

"Oh, bother," Mrs Harris said, "I don't have my spectacles. Miss Drummond, do you think you could possibly...?"

Phyllis duly found the passage, and then handed the book over to me. "Thomas – could you read it? I'm afraid I can't bear reading my own work aloud."

I nodded, and started reading from where her finger pointed.

> Georgina climbed the hill as she had so many times before, and sat on a broken tree trunk to survey the valley. The tall chimneys of Kingshorne Priory peeked out of its shroud of elm trees, reminding her that a hundred expenses were needed to keep it from falling into ruin.
>
> Her father's illness could no longer be dismissed as a passing ailment, and without swift action, the family would soon need to sell their beloved home and move to insalubrious accommodation in town. Her sister's interest in fossils, intense as it was, could never bear financial fruit, and her brother's melancholia and love of wine meant that the only person who was capable of redeeming this predicament was Georgina herself.
>
> Writing was almost her sole interest. A score of first chapters lay piled in a drawer; her journals were filled with observation and ideas. But she never felt that she could dare to pit herself against the authors of the day. She surely did not possess the intelligence and knowledge that were required to complete a full work and offer it to a publisher – let alone the public – for their meticulous and potentially damning scrutiny.
>
> But as she sat on her lightning-struck bench, watching the magpies and the spindly harvest spiders in the tall grass, and listening to the swish of the breeze, a phrase came into her head, and with it came a rush of realisation and hope.
>
> 'Where the heart leads, the head surely follows.'
>
> Who said these words? She looked about her, and saw no one. Did she imagine it, from the noise of the wind? Was there a wood sprite whispering in her ear? Was it the God with whom she had recently failed to commune, but perhaps watched over her nevertheless? Whatever the source, it was suddenly clear to Georgina that she possessed more ability than she had yet perceived. After all, did she not see and pity the human species

> with as much sorrow and joy as anyone? Did she not observe and record the characters of the people she encountered, as well as any of her favourite authors? Had she not constructed her own phantom population, her own stories, her own imagined tragedies and triumphs?
>
> She knew then that her heart would indeed lead her into this profession, and her head would know how to set down – eventually with eloquence – what her heart told her. She knew also, with an intense sadness, that this was the last day of her childhood: one that she would look back on with the distant curiosity of a butterfly remembering its caterpillar self.

"Enough?" I said.

"Quite enough," said Phyllis.

"Oh, goodness, Mr Rufford," said Mrs Harris, dabbing her eyes with her handkerchief, "how well you read! You and Miss Drummond have made me cry."

I nodded my gratitude for the compliment.

"It's so sad," continued Mrs Harris. "When they finally have money, they move house, and then Georgina loses her muse. And she can only get it back by reclaiming Kingshorne Priory, and to do that, she must marry the –"

Mr Harris put up his hand. "Stop, Olivia, stop! I don't wish to know the whole plot before I read it."

Phyllis' phrase reverberated in my head: 'Where the heart leads, the head surely follows.' It seemed familiar, although I had not yet read the book in question. Then I remembered, imperfectly, a passage from 'Malamor:'

> There was no need for Malamor to worry that the seeds of persuasion would fall on stony ground. Logical thought could easily be usurped by the power of the emotions: he was careful to plough that furrow. And where the heart leads, the head surely follows.

With a mixture of shock and elation, I realised that my suspicions had been confirmed. Phyllis' talents were deeper than most people knew. I decided to test my hypothesis.

"Your epigram is clever, Phyllis," I said, "but I suppose

the ignorant would think it to be..."

I paused to take a sip of wine and locked my eyes with Phyllis'. "Bland," I said with emphasis.

"Oh, surely not," said Mrs Harris. Phyllis looked down, her cheeks flushing pink, a look of consternation briefly crossing her face. She looked up again at me, searchingly, and I nodded almost imperceptibly in answer. She raised her finger to her lips, as if absent-mindedly, but I understood her message.

"I would like to propose a toast," I said, raising my glass. "To my friend Miss Phyllis Drummond: an author whose talent is startling and boundless, and without whom, Mr Neville might never have been caught."

~

After dinner, I waited for a lull in Phyllis' conversation with Mr Craven, and then said, "Miss Drummond, can I borrow you for a moment, please?"

She excused herself, and I steered her into my study and closed the door.

"What did you want to say to me, Thomas?" she said, innocently perusing the bookshelves.

"You know very well, Phyllis," I said. "I don't wish to pry into your affairs, but I think I am owed an explanation if what I suspect is true – which I can scarcely believe."

"And what is that?" she said.

"That you are the author of 'Malamor'!"

"How absurd," Phyllis said, pulling a copy of 'Keats' Collected Poems' off a shelf and feigning interest. "How could that be?"

"I know it's absurd, but there is so much evidence. Your epigram appearing in both a Bland book and a Tavistock book.

Your reluctance to let me buy the book. The similarities between Malamor's house and Ramsburgh. How you become defensive whenever anyone discusses the book. And how upset you were when I called Mr Neville that name. This cannot be coincidence!"

Phyllis sighed, and snapped the poetry book shut, placing it back on the shelf slowly to delay the moment when she would have to explain herself.

"I'm sorry," she said, sitting down. "Yes, you're due an explanation. But I'm so ashamed of it – I don't want anyone in Hawksbridge to find out. They will hate me. Someone already does."

"Ah – Flora," I said. "So this is what you fell out over?"

"Yes. Stupidly, I used her for a character – although they are totally unalike, and I could have used any name, rather than Rose. I was being too clever for my own good."

"And somehow she found out about you being the author?"

"Yes, we were in my bedroom at home, as we were best friends. We were both eighteen years old. She caught sight of a statement of royalties I had carelessly left on a table. She was so mortified that she demanded to be taken home immediately, and we have barely spoken since. It's entirely my fault, and I don't think I can ever say anything to put it right."

"There must be some hope," I said. "I assume you didn't mean to imply Flora had been attacked in that horrible way."

"No, I didn't. It was so stupid of me. But she has kept my secret nevertheless."

"And you wrote it at such a tender age," I said. "It reads like the work of a far older person."

"I wanted to see if I could mimic the style of older satirists – and I had plenty of help from my editor. We became fond of each other. He was excited about the book, and he suggested many things, and tidied up my prose, and goaded me into ever more outrageous writing. It became more coarse than

I had intended."

"Extraordinary," I said, shaking my head. "Were you in love with your editor?"

"I believed I was," Phyllis said. "Or perhaps I was giddy with the prospect of notoriety. In any event, I thought he might propose, and then – just a month before publication – he was killed by a carriage in Fleet Street."

"Oh, Lord," I said. "I'm so sorry."

"Yes, the book has been rather cursed. I wish to heavens I had never written it."

"But why did you?" I said.

"Because I was angry at the stupid restrictions imposed on women. I felt that the whole of society was corrupt, from top to bottom, and I wanted to get my revenge on it. And I wanted to show that I was as good as any man."

"Well, you certainly did that," I said.

"I'm so sorry I used your father's affair with Mrs Kington," Phyllis said. "Can you forgive me?"

"Of course I can," I said. "All novelists take inspiration from real life and real people. Otherwise there would be no novels."

"Thank you. But the truly awful thing," she said, her eyes filling with tears, "is that it was my book that –"

She stopped for a moment to gain control of herself. "That caused the death of Mr Shaw and Mr Walker, and nearly caused your death too. My stupid, stupid arrogance. I feel that I have got away with a crime, and should hand myself in to Mr Simmons immediately." And she broke down, the tears flowing freely.

I knelt by her chair and took her hand. "My dear Phyllis, none of it is your fault. You should not blame yourself for anything. Sometimes little things have unexpected consequences. A novel is not a weapon, it's simply a novel. If Mr Walker had not called Neville 'Malamor,' he might have done something else equally provoking."

I let the flood of tears exhaust itself, and eventually Phyllis started to breathe normally. "I suppose you're right," she said. "If I could only see it – feel it – properly."

"You will, in time," I said. "At present, these unpleasant events are raw. But I promise the clouds will blow away."

She nodded and attempted a smile.

"Oh – speaking of wind," I said. "Now that absurdity has changed places with normality, I suppose I should believe that 'The Waves and the Wind' is yours as well, being attributed to a Mr J. Bland? Or am I now being ridiculous?"

Phyllis laughed. "That was another of my youthful adventures, yes. I thought if I could write 'Malamor' and get away with it, then a pastiche of a folk song would be easy. And it was. I wrote the words in two hours, and the tune in three. I drove my poor parents mad pecking away on the piano! I had help with the arrangement, though."

"Astonishing. Did you know Bess Shannon has arranged it for harp?"

"She has? How funny!" she said. "I should like to hear that."

I squeezed her hand once more, and went to sit in my customary chair.

"How do you manage it?" I said. "You are a celebrity three times over. Are you extremely rich?"

"I am only a celebrity – and a small one at that – as Iona Tavistock. The only people in the world who know about my other work are my publishers, Flora, and now you. And I am embarrassed to say, yes, I have done quite well from my scribbles."

"And yet you live so modestly!" I said.

"Well, you heard what happened to Georgina," Phyllis said. "I'm terrified of losing my muse, and my comfortable, simple way of life. I wouldn't want the nuisance of owning a mansion – so many servants, so much formality! No, thank you. I have given a little to charity. As for the rest – I will be comfortable when the muse finally deserts me."

"I am sure it never will," I said. "You will be writing when you are a hundred and three."

"I hope so," said Phyllis. "Thank you – you have made me feel much better. I so wanted to tell you, but I thought you would think worse of me."

"Nothing could be further from the truth," I said. "I still think you are wonderful. Perhaps even more so than before."

"Good," she said, tidying a loose wisp of hair. "Shall we rejoin the party?"

~

When Mr McPhee had arrived, he had brought two wooden boxes from his carriage. He now placed their contents, each concealed under a cloth, on a table in the window of the drawing room, and waited for everyone to convene. Flora stood by his side as his assistant.

He then said, "Ladies and gentlemen! Mr Rufford has kindly allowed me to make a little presentation, by way of testing the waters for two new products of the Hawksbridge Pottery Company. These are the final prototypes for a new line in our proprietary 'Marbleware', which we are very proud of. Without further ado, I present the first. If you would be so kind, Miss Davison," said Mr McPhee.

Flora gingerly took away the cloth, to reveal a white statue of a familiar scene: 'The Rape of Proserpina.' It had been slightly modified from the Shaw and Walker design, to restrict its width, but otherwise was a commendable reproduction of it, with the same sense of drama and movement.

My guests crowded around the statue, marvelling at the beauty of the figures and the intricacy of their garments, and lavishing compliments on McPhee.

"Well, that was the reaction I was hoping for," beamed McPhee. "Now, something that is, in my opinion, even more special. When we first cast around for subjects for our statues, we trawled through ancient mythology – hence our choice of 'Proserpina'. But then it occurred to me that we have our own mythology, right here in Hawksbridge. So, Miss Davison has been collaborating with our designers to create this. I am proud to present..."

Flora removed its cover, and McPhee triumphantly finished, "'The Hawksbridge Angels'!"

I could see instantly that Francesca was still the model for the major element of the piece: the mature, gentle angel orchestrating the rescue of souls. She was higher than the other two angels, her wings spread majestically, her arms outstretched, one bosom exposed. Inside a model of the burning building, a body was being lifted to the heavens, and white flames licked at white brickwork.

The response to this statue was much greater than for the first. Spontaneous applause broke out, and my guests were fascinated and at first, dumb-struck. At that moment, the question of whether it was art or ornament was neither here nor there: it was beautiful, and it was part of Hawksbridge's mythology, both for the history of the fiery tragedy, and for all the pain and drama that had surrounded the creation of the mural.

~

With Fox at my feet, I watched the last carriage crunch down the drive, and savoured the evening breeze on my wine-flushed cheeks. McPhee's Marbleware spectacle had reminded me that humans can find the good in almost anything: from the factory disaster came beauty, and from my troubled beginnings at Ramsburgh came a resourcefulness in me, of whose existence I was quite unaware.

How nervous I was, earlier in the year, to make this change in my life – how I worried that though I might desire a country seat and a new existence, my mind would atrophy with little to do but oversee my property and give orders to servants. And yet here I was, after my leap in the dark, with new friends and something of a local reputation for solving deadly puzzles. As I led Fox inside and pulled shut Ramsburgh's great oak door, I reflected that I could not put it better than Miss Iona Tavistock, or Mr John Bland, or indeed Miss Phyllis Drummond: *Where the heart leads, the head surely follows.*

~ THE END ~

# DRAMATIS PERSONAE

## *Ramsburgh*

Mr Thomas Rufford: owner of Ramsburgh

Miss Flora Davison: niece of the previous owners, the Kingtons

Mrs Margaret Northcutt: Flora's housekeeper

Mr Matthew Shipley: Thomas' butler

Mrs Norah Felton: Thomas' housekeeper

Alice, Pearl: maids

Old Howard: the groom and dogsbody

Jenny: a pony

Celeste: Thomas' horse

Titian: Flora's cat

Fox: Thomas' dog

## *Hawksbridge*

Reverend Horace Neville: a Church of England rector

Phyllis Drummond: a novelist

Dr Anthony Drummond: a doctor and Phyllis' father

Mrs Francesca Campbell: a friend of Thomas

Mrs Beatrice Harkness: a friend of Phyllis'

Mr William Harkness: Beatrice's husband and designer at the Pottery

Mr Johnny Falkirk: a local artist

Miss Mary Barker: Falkirk's girlfriend

Mr Edward Walker: an artist

Mr Henry Shaw: an artist

Mr David Harris: a former banker

Mrs Olivia Harris: Mr Harris' wife

Inspector Ralph Simmons: a detective

Constable Taylor: a policeman

Constable Gawley: a policeman

Mrs Bess Shannon: a widow

Mr Garrard: a curate

Mr Frederick McPhee: a director at the Pottery

## *Elsewhere*

Mr Beadnell: a labourer

Mrs Beadnell: Mr Beadnell's wife

Mr Fenwick: Thomas Rufford's family solicitor in London

# ABOUT THE AUTHOR

Julian Smart was born in Nottingham, England, and studied Computer Science at the University of St Andrews. He has a doctorate from the University of Dundee. Julian has worked for the University of Edinburgh, the Artificial Intelligence Applications Institute, the Scottish Crop Research Institute, and Red Hat UK.

Julian started the wxWidgets open-source GUI toolkit project which is used by many organisations and individuals worldwide, and by Julian for his own projects, including the e-book editing software Jutoh. Jutoh was used for creating all books by Julian and Harriet Smart.

Julian collaborated with Harriet Smart to write *Emma Vernon's Northminster Ghost Stories*, a spin-off from Harriet's Northminster Mysteries which he has edited since 2010.

Julian is currently working on *The Thomas Rufford Mysteries*, a series set in nineteenth-century Hawksbridge, a fictional town in the north east of England.

Made in the USA
Las Vegas, NV
03 April 2024

88136998R00204